ANCESTRAL NIGHT

ALSO BY ELIZABETH BEAR

Carnival

Undertow

Jacob's Ladder
Dust (UK title: *Pinion*)
Chill (UK title: *Sanction*)
Grail (UK title: *Cleave*)

Karen Memory Adventures
Karen Memory
Stone Mad

Jenny Casey
Hammered
Scardown
Worldwired

The Eternal Sky
Range of Ghosts
Shattered Pillars
Steles of the Sky

The Lotus Kingdoms
The Stone in the Skull
The Red-Stained Wings
(Forthcoming)

The Wizards of Messaline
Bone and Jewel Creatures
Book of Iron

The Promethean Age
Blood and Iron
Whiskey and Water
Ink and Steel
Hell and Earth
One-Eyed Jack

New Amsterdam
New Amsterdam
Seven for a Secret
The White City
Ad Eternum
Garrett Investigates

The Edda of Burdens
All the Windwracked Stars
By the Mountain Bound
The Sea Thy Mistress

With Katherine Addison:

The Cobbler's Boy

With Sarah Monette:

The Iskryne
A Companion to Wolves
The Tempering of Men
An Apprentice to Elves

WHITE SPACE BOOK 1
ANCESTRAL
NIGHT

ELIZABETH BEAR

SAGA PRESS

LONDON SYDNEY **NEW YORK** TORONTO NEW DELHI

SAGA PRESS

AN IMPRINT OF SIMON & SCHUSTER, INC.

1230 AVENUE OF THE AMERICAS, NEW YORK, NEW YORK 10020

SAGA PRESS and colophon are trademarks of Simon & Schuster, Inc.

For information about special discounts for bulk purchases, please contact Simon & Schuster Special Sales at 1-866-506-1949 or business@simonandschuster.com.

The Simon & Schuster Speakers Bureau can bring authors to your live event. For more information or to book an event, contact the Simon & Schuster Speakers Bureau at 1-866-248-3049 or visit our website at www.simonspeakers.com.

Interior design by Hilary Zarycky

The text for this book was set in Adobe Jenson Pro.

Manufactured in the United States of America

First Edition

2 4 6 8 10 9 7 5 3 1

Library of Congress Cataloging-in-Publication Data

Names: Bear, Elizabeth, author.

Title: Ancestral night / Elizabeth Bear.

Description: First edition. | London ; New York : Saga Press, [2019] | Series: White Space ; book 1

Identifiers: LCCN 2018017492 | ISBN 9781534402980 (hardcover) | ISBN 9781534403000 (eBook)

Subjects: | GSAFD: Fantasy fiction.

Classification: LCC PS3602.E2475 A63 2019 | DDC 813/.6—dc23

LC record available at https://lccn.loc.gov/2018017492

This book is for Jon Singer.

LOW-TIDE

THESE wet rocks where the tide has been,
Barnacled white and weeded brown
And slimed beneath to a beautiful green,
These wet rocks where the tide went down
Will show again when the tide is high
Faint and perilous, far from shore,
No place to dream, but a place to die,—
The bottom of the sea once more.

There was a child that wandered through
A giant's empty house all day,—
House full of wonderful things and new,
But no fit place for a child to play.

—Edna St. Vincent Millay, 1921

* * *

Think of ancestral night that can,
If but imagination scorn the earth
And intellect is wandering
To this and that and t'other thing,
Deliver from the crime of death and birth.

—W. B. Yeats, from "The Winding Stair," 1933

CHAPTER 1

THE BOAT DIDN'T HAVE A NAME.

He wasn't deemed significant enough to *need* a name by the authorities and registries that govern such things. He had a registration number—657-2929-04, Human/Terra—and he had a class, salvage tug, but he didn't have a name.

Officially.

We called him Singer. If Singer had an opinion on the issue, he'd never registered it—but he never complained. Singer was the shipmind as well as the ship—or at least, he inhabited the ship's virtual spaces the same way we inhabited the physical ones—but my partner Connla and I didn't own him. You can't own a sentience in civilized space.

Singer was a sliver of a thing suspended electromagnetically at the center of a quicksilver loop as thin in cross section as an old-fashioned wedding band, but a hundred and fifty meters across the diameter and ten meters from edge to edge. In any meaningful gravity, the ring would have crumpled and sagged like a curl of wax arched over the candleflame. But here in space, reinforced with electromagnetic supports, it spanned the horizon of the viewport in a clean arc.

I held on to a rail with one afthand, lazily comfortable as I watched the light sliding in Doppler-watered bands across the silver surface of the white coils. The concentrated colors of the ring moved across a background that looked like a dilute version of the same pattern, as the action of the white drive changed what would have been a gorgeous starfield into

2 • ELIZABETH BEAR

twisting blue and red light that glided like the colors on heated titanium.

Those ripples of light were messages written in physics and perception. The information they offered would have seemed cryptic to most people. They would have seemed cryptic to me, twenty ans ago when I was but a wee slip of a person freshly skinned out and free of the clade I grew up in, Nyumba Yangu Haina Mlango. But I had a lot of practice reading their frequency and patterns now. Singer was . . . well, slowing wasn't exactly the right word, but it would do. We were, to coin a phrase, getting there.

Singer couldn't navigate in white space. He could only follow the course planned and programmed beforehand, coasting like a surfer on a wave of space contracting before him and stretching out behind. He—we—were not even, technically speaking, moving, let alone moving particularly fast. The universe was just rearranging itself around us, invisible to those outside the bubble of the white field.

Soon we would fold ourselves out of white space and into the normal universe. We were looking for a scar in space-time, the tiny ripple of radiation left by the passage of a ship whose course hadn't been tracked by any authority, and so when it had been lost, its loss had gone unnoticed for—well, nobody could actually say how long. We were going there on purpose, and we planned to stay a while. Because somewhere down that Alcubierre-White rabbit hole in space-time there was—or at least *had been*—a ship. A lost ship.

A misplaced one, anyway. We'd taken on obligation for an information broker who provided us with scans and imaging they'd obtained from the captain who had noticed the anomaly. They'd also provided the anomaly's coordinates.

The coordinates we'd bid on were off the beaten path, perpendicular by a good distance from the inhabited and regularly traveled space lanes of the Milky Way. But we'd been out this far before, and space was vast. Ships still got lost now and then, but they were usually better tracked these diar, and in the centuries since the white drive had turned space from an empty, intractable void permeated by loneliness and existential dread into a teeming, boisterous, and mostly peaceful community of species . . . much of the older salvage in the plane of the Milky Way had been picked clean.

Bright ripples across the darkness narrowed, sharpened, resolved into bands, then blurs, then points of light. We fell into normal space and began to close the gap on our EMP engines. Through Singer's senso, I got a feel for the scar.

It was a big one, and it looked fresh, which meant that the odds of the unlucky vessel that had caused it still being in there were pretty good. That would be nice, because our last two claims had come up empty, and the larder was a little bare. We hadn't even gotten any wreck-driving tourist contracts recently, which were risky—especially the ones involving close approach to an event horizon—but secretly a lot of fun.

Connla liked them even more than I did.

"I wish I knew what the ship that found this thing was doing way the hell out here. There's literally *nothing* for light-ans in any direction." Connla, speaking to me through senso. He was up in the control cabin. It was supposed to be my rest shift. Sometimes, despite all the rightminding I can tolerate, I still have nightmares.

I answered, "If I had a nasty, suspicious mind . . ."

"Yeah," Connla said. "Pirates. Me too."

"You know they don't like being called pirates," Singer joked.

"Freeloaders." Connla came from a world called Spartacus, notorious for its atavistic culture. One reason it was that way was because it sat so close to Freeport strongholds. Border brushfires and the constant threat of raids and one's shipping being picked off contributed to a martial culture. And I wasn't supposed to know this, but Connla had survived a pirate raid on an asteroid settlement when he was a child.

I frowned at the scar. Singer's senses were designed for space, and his readouts told me that the scar was fresh. If there was a ship in there, and it was intact, and we could bring it home—depending on what it was—this whole trip would be worthwhile. We had an obligation to the Synarche that needed to be met, one way or another. We were spending resources to be here; resources the Synarche would want recouped and, ideally, built upon. The prize ship and its cargo were where that replacement value would come from.

"It'll be a smuggler," Connla said dourly.

A bad outcome for our obligation if it was. Contraband was illegal goods or stolen art. Everything else a civilized galactic Synarche required was so easy to make, or ship, that there was no percentage in dodging around customs. If they were smuggling art, there might be forgiven obligations for recovering lost cultural treasures.

There also might not.

A pirate would be even more useless to us, beyond any value there might be in the hull. Some find the Galactic Synarche suffocating. And I have a healthy sympathy for the whole avoiding-suffocation thing. But there's asserting a reasonable individuality in the face of social norms, and then there's piracy and murder as an economic model.

A hull could bring us some recovery credit. If it were in decent shape. Which pirate ships rarely were. But it wouldn't get us much else, because any cargo would likely be resources that, while valuable to those of us living in space within the Synarche, weren't valuable enough to go ferreting around in space-time pockets after.

"Maybe it'll be a Wake-Seeker," I sent, cheerfully. Those who followed the Path of the Unfinished Work were always grateful for news of the fate of missing brethren. Even if, as they say, *the authentic experience is an illusion.*

We were both really hoping that we might find a passenger vessel, commercial or private, that had wandered off course and gotten lost with no one the wiser as to its location. Those often offered finder's credit in the form of resource allocation validations to the salvager who retrieved them, both from the shipping line, the owners of registry of any cargo, and the families or clades of any passengers. And if there was unregistered cargo, that could be value along with the hull.

Best of all were the packet vessels, which were full of *information*. And the ancient prizes from early exploration—by any race—that were treasure troves of archaeological data. That would be worth a few RAVs above the cost of the mission.

I didn't even bother to consider the possibility that the hulk could be an ancient ship from a time long before that remembered by humans, or even any of the older syster species. I'd heard about Koregoi ships with salvageable tech. I'd never encountered one. Or even encountered anyone who admitted they had. But wouldn't it be nice . . . ?

Well, that wouldn't be behind a fresh scar, anyway. So honestly I was just black-sky diadreaming, indulging myself in fantasies of untold wealth. Or of at least buying Singer out of copyright so he would own his own code.

I was still on edge, and now it was too close to contact for me to bump my chems and get any restful sleep. Growing up clade—and a flirtation with chemical dependency after I broke free—had left me wary of the easy out, anyway, so I rarely thought of fixing the problem at the transmitter level when it was possible for me to ride it out.

When I remembered, or Singer nagged me into it, I always wondered why I hadn't bumped earlier. Why I'd been so resistant in the first place. And except for a few permanent mental health adjustments, I always insisted on a limited adjustment that would wear off in half a dia or so.

Well, if people made sense, we'd be like Singer.

I turned away from the port. There would be a distraction of some sort in the command cabin, and I could caffeinate. Or bump, and tune for wakefulness since I'd missed the shuttle on rest.

I slid down the tunnel to the bridge headfirst, pushing off rungs in the tube with my fore- and afthands, avoiding bruising the lettuce and radishes growing along Singer's living walls. The ship's calico cats, Mephistopheles and Bushyasta, were floating in the tube, napping in a cuddle. Bushyasta, like the professional sleeper she was, had one set of claws hooked into the terry cloth of a grab loop. Mephistopheles was floating beside her, a red-and-white leg draped for an anchor over Bushy-asta's belly, her black-splashed head cuddled on a mottled flank. Well, at least somebody was getting some rest around here.

I glided the last meter or so—it wasn't far: Singer really was a tiny bubble of a thing for frail warm meat to take to space in—and found myself gazing at the back of Connla's head.

He'd anchored himself to a rail with his afthands, and his forehands were buried elbow-deep in the stuff of his console. His ponytail waved lazily behind him as he turned his head. I caught a glimpse of stubborn profile outlined against starfield and suppressed a smile.

He started to say something, coughed, and corrected himself. "Wouldn't sleep?"

I could have argued—couldn't—but I knew my unwillingness to tune my chem was opaque to Connla on an emotional level even when he professed to understand it intellectually. I thought he'd actually maybe mellow and mature a bit if he didn't bump and tune so much to keep his responses calmed down to Spartacus's stoic ideals. On the other hand, I'd have to put up with him finally experiencing adolescence, and that whole thing was such a mess I'd turned mine off when it happened. Well, okay, a little bit after it happened. Some people have to learn the hard way, and apparently I am one of them.

It was his brain and his chem and his business, so I just said, "We should have pulled a permit."

"And let every other tug in the galaxy know where we were headed?"

"And have a chance of a rescue operation if we screw it up." I settled near my console, floating with one afthand resting lightly against a rail, and watched out the forward windows as ripples of light gathered and spread.

Connla laughed. "You put on such a rebel act, but I keep hearing your crèche talking out of your mouth again and again. Anybody raised outside of a clade knows that it's easier to get forgiveness than permission. Besides, a permit isn't *strictly* legally necessary all the way out here. We're not in anybody's jurisdiction."

He was transparent when he was baiting me. His own upbringing had left a few antisocial marks on him, but try to get him to admit that. If he hadn't been such a good guy from the DNA on up, he would have been insufferable. And quite possibly socially dangerous.

"Forgiveness is not the same thing as retroactive consent, Connla. And the research shows that people are much more altruistic when they're allowed to offer, instead of when something is demanded of them. There will be more red tape on the other end, this way." He didn't answer, so I said, "How much longer?"

"Ninety-seven seconds to the decel."

My console felt cool and ready when I touched its carbonglas surface with my fingertips, just enough to stabilize, balance, and get a spherical perspective. I didn't bury my hands in my console the way Connla had, but I wasn't flying the bus.

Well, okay, Singer was flying the bus. But Connla was directing, and he needed to be plugged in to Singer's full senso.

A wide arc of stars swung *below* and *behind* Singer like the frozen skirts of a flamenco dancer: the Milky Way, seen from . . . not exactly *outside*, but far to one edge, and an angle. Scuttling fingers tap-danced up my spine at the sight of home, so far away. Which was ridiculous, because it wasn't home to me—Singer was. And we were in no more danger here than anywhere else in space. Maybe even a little less than if we were camped in some cluttered, long-inhabited system full of meteors, traffic that couldn't follow a flight plan, and poorly mapped space junk.

It's a territorial mammal thing, is all. There's a sense of being long and far away from places you know your way around and have resources in that gets right up into the anxiety centers and made me *feel* lost and out of place.

We were off our turf, and my amygdala knew it.

Connla was cool and collected. I felt his calm through our link like a lapping sea. He didn't look over at me to roll his eyes, a demonstration of self-control better than I'd have been able to manage. He'd didn't have to tell me that he thought my resistance to tuning my mood was childish and irresponsible.

But he hadn't grown up in a clade. He hadn't escaped a clade. And the hypervigilance was my friend. His friend, too, if he'd ever admit it. Sure, it was uncomfortable. But that was a small price to pay for being *ready*. Getting caught by a disaster is bad enough. Getting caught by a disaster you didn't expect adds that layer of humiliation and stunned goggle-eyed frozenness to the proceedings, and that doesn't benefit you in the long run.

All of those memories were stored in my fox, and I would have shared the ayatana with him if he'd given me half an excuse. But *he* had never gotten past *his* childhood programming that feelings were sticky and somehow slightly revolting. So it was an element of our friendship that remained unexplored.

And thus my uneasy feeling could have just been my old friend Uneasy Feeling, dropping by to see how things were shaking. It could have been that territorial fear of not knowing where I was, and where to find food, shelter, water, and my tribe. But it never hurt to be on your guard.

Yep. Sleeping with one eye open, that's me. People only think it's ridiculous if they've never been caught napping by an enemy. And the truth of the universe is that anybody can turn out to be an enemy.

"Let's keep the bubble up for now in case we have to move in a hurry," I said.

Connla didn't argue. He cleared his throat and said, "Singer, are you awake?"

"More awake than you are," the ship replied. Most ships are *she*, for bigoted gender-essentialist historical reasons, and most of the rest see no reason to bother being gendered at all and call themselves *they*, but Singer liked a male identity.

He hadn't always been a tugboat, I gathered. He had a bantering manner, which was just code, but when it came right down to it I was just code too, running on some kludged-together hardware.

He added, "What can I do for you?"

Singer was smart as hell, a born problem-solver if you told him what problem to solve for and gave him some parameters that he could extrapolate. But artificial personalities were intentionally limited in their self-direction and agency, for reasons that will be obvious to a cursory inquiry.

Those programmed shackles might be just as well, given the number of horror dramas about rogue personalities out there for one's . . . enjoyment. And yet. I had a little too much personal experience with what it was like to be a happy worker, in agreement, without too much will to argue for myself or enough agency to set out in my own direction, to feel entirely comfortable with the solution. That was the real reason I came out here to the rim, where life was a constant struggle to validate resource expenditure. I *needed* my independence of thought, and so I scrapped for my dinner like some twentieth-century barbarian instead of enjoying the comfortable largesse of a Core world where I wouldn't have to justify my resource footprint.

"Range to objective?" I kept all that out of my voice. That worry about feeling trapped was bugging me a lot todia, but I put the reasons for that as far out of mind as I could. I could have tuned that out, too, but I didn't want to reach for that crutch too often. Anyway, dissociation is a great coping skill. It can keep you going and functional basically forever. The problems hit when it starts to break down, which is essentially as soon as you start to question your own detachment. Getting in touch with your emotions and experiences is overrated, if you ask me.

And before you tell me that it's hypocritical of me to be concerned that Connla represses his emotions and then dissociate mine, it's totally different when I do it. Totally, completely different. I'm doing it on purpose, and not as part of my childhood programming.

"A little less than an AU. I'm decelerating."

I hung on to my bar and console grips as Connla began slowing us. He wouldn't brake hard enough that I'd need my acceleration couch. But it was still a mite uncomfortable.

I bloody hate gravity.

We would have left white space at something considerably less than relativistic speeds—though still moving impossibly fast, by human standards. But the thing about space is that it's still awfully big, even if one can travel very fast, and there isn't a lot of friction in it to steady the system, so things respond violently to a gentle nudge or a slight shift in momentum.

No unaugmented human mind could perform the calculations necessary to control complicated multi-body problems. Dead reckoning worked better (the back of the mind is much better at figuring out complicated physics problems than the front, which is how the ball hits your hand when you stick it out in front of you), but somebody—something—like Singer was better still.

"Any other boats in the area?" I asked.

Connla said, "No," at the same moment Singer said, "Not in regular space."

And the ones in white space would be invisible and immaterial. If there were any. Until such time as they fell on our heads.

We spent a long time in decel. Now that I'd talked myself into tuning, I used this time more wisely: I webbed myself down and took a nap. I'm not sure what Connla did.

I awoke when Singer cheerfully said, "Coming up on our scab in space-time." He had a light tenor voice, musical and animated, and he liked wordplay and coincidences and was endlessly fascinated by—well, anything. Human social dynamics. Lasers. Tea. Porcelain.

I breathed. There were no gs making me miserable, so I unwebbed and rose up from the couch.

We were alone out here. Nobody was going to come along and snatch our prize todia.

"Whoa," Connla said. "What in nine gravity wells and an event horizon is *that* thing?"

Well, that was what I got for feeling cheerful.

It's hard to get a sense of scale out here. You can hold out your hand and cover the entire bulk of a gas giant with a pinkie nail if it's at enough distance—and there aren't many referents to let you know if whatever you're observing is near or far away.

So when my perceptions told me that something vast was drifting toward us, I was ready at first for it to be the size of my fist. Maybe a tangerine, quick-frozen by space and bobbing alongside the window, maybe hauled along inside our bubble from the inevitable ring of small litter that swarms around any space station.

But it wasn't a tangerine. Whatever it was, was dark, so it faded into the background of the starscape. It was oily-seeming and iridescent, and it reflected the light of the Milky Way off a dark green surface. The tapered, irregular outline tumbled slowly, a long, majestic arc of curve like three-fourths of the rim of a gigantic, broken wheel. *Space station*, my mind provided. *Catastrophically decompressed.*

The part of my brain that recognizes patterns and assigns things to categories was leaning on its shovel catching a few zeds once again. The tumbling arc brought the weird object between us and the long arm of the Milky Way, and I recognized the silhouette, even convulsed into that strange arc, an instant before Singer identified it.

"It's an Ativahika," he said. "It appears to be dead."

"They can *die?*" I asked, stunned, just as Connla burst out, "What the hell is it doing all the way out here?"

"I hope nothing *killed* it." Anything that could take on an Ativahika—well, Singer was an unarmed tug, and fuel-efficient, but not what you would call a fast or maneuverable flyer. He was good at going in straight lines really cheaply while hauling enormous masses at a safe but respectable clip, though—which was why his white coils were so much bigger than he was. None better, if that was what you needed, and usually in our case it was.

I wondered if the Ativahikas would take it amiss if we salvaged one of their own, for purposes of returning the body to them. Or if they might be grateful. Of all the older syster races—assuming they were a syster race—they were in the running for the most inscrutable. I mean, they didn't *talk*, at least as far as I knew. But they were generally accepted as sapient. Maybe it was just that they had never needed to communicate anything to something as tiny and fragile as a terrestrial-type species, when they had all of space to call their home.

I realized I'd drifted to the window when my nose brushed it. It didn't get me appreciably closer to the corpse of the Ativahika, and it didn't cut down on the glare; the viewport covers have a nonreflective coating that makes them, to all intents, invisible. But it's instinct; people will steer their craft into objects that have attracted their attention.

I caught the rail with my afthands to keep from bumping my nose again. Rubbing my nose gently, I stroked the port with my other hand to enlarge the view.

A living Ativahika looks more like an elongated seahorse than a whale. They're bilaterally symmetrical, with a frilled head and a tapered neck, trailed by their ridged body and fronded tail. The whole is covered with their seaweed-like appendages, though I have no idea whether that evolved for some mysterious reason in space, or it's a holdover from wherever they arose. Evolution doesn't bother to pitch stuff out until it has a reason, and sometimes not even then. The deep, glossy green color is a chlorophyll analogue—a pigment that converts light and carbon dioxide into oxygen and sugar. It's a symbiote. The Ativahika itself metabolizes oxygen and produces carbon dioxide. Each creature is its own ecosystem in miniature.

Unbelievably, among all the weird and wonderful systers—the methane breathers, the ones that use ammonia as a solvent instead of H_2O—they have a biology that is not particularly dissimilar to our own. Unbelievably, because they look like the most alien creature imaginable.

Their bodies are up to ten kilometers in length, and arranged with almost boring normalcy around a central nervous system with a brain and a spinal cord and even a spine. Their bones, rather than being made of calcites, are silicates that they extract by chewing up asteroids, space rocks, and—with particular gusto—the debris that forms planetary rings, which is also where they get their water. They're in the H_2O solvent club along with us. Their blood is even red; the stuff they use to carry oxygen is a close-enough hemoglobin analogue that you could probably make black pudding out of it. If you were some sort of cannibalistic barbarian willing to eat the flesh of sentients, I mean.

Their most spectacular trait, and the one whose absence had slowed my recognition of this particular piece of once-living space debris, is the spread of their fins or wings or filaments. There's a good deal of argument over what to call the appendages, which spring from the Ativahika's ridged body like a forest of kelp from a stone. The fins are varying shades of green, depending on their age—from apple-bright to mossy stone. They have variegated edges, and they float and trail around the Ativahika's body inertially in the weightless, frictionless, air-currentless environment of space. They undulate with the Ativahika's movement, and serve to increase its surface area for photosynthesis. They also may serve some sensory purpose: nobody knows—nobody human, anyway, none of the humans of my acquaintance have ever seemed to know, and I've never had the opportunity to ask a syster.

This particular specimen was unrecognizable in part because it was arched into that back-bending inside-out broken wheel position. And partially because the long taper of its body was, well, not utterly smooth, because I could see wounds and stubs along its length, but shorn. Shorn of tendrils, wings, or fins. And shorn as well of the long, symmetrical appendages they used as manipulators.

I couldn't imagine that a dead Ativahika would ever be considered a *good* sign. I wish I could say that, staring at that terrible thing, I had a premonition. But if I had had a premonition of what it really portended, I would have thrown my veto and turned that ship around right that very second and gone to find Judiciary. No matter what it cost us. No matter how long it took.

All the evidence would likely have been gone by the time we got back.

And that bothers me a little, and it would have bothered the me in the alternate timestream where I made more cautious choices. Given what I eventually learned, I guess it wouldn't have been the end of it anyway. There would have been another avenue to get to us. And in any case, time is a river that only flows one way.

It feels . . . odd to be telling this story. It's just me recording in senso, journaling. I've kept ayatana logs, like any crew member does. But it's never been something I thought anybody else might hear, except maybe a review board, and now . . . now I don't know who I'm talking to.

But my log might turn out to be important: a historical document or evidence in a hearing or even an inquest and trial. So now I'm thinking about, well, who *am* I talking to? Because I'm not just talking to myself anymore.

I'm talking to a court panel, maybe. A judge and a couple of AIs and some people from various syster species who've come up in the service lottery this an. Or maybe I'm talking to the crew of another salvage tug, because I'm dead and what you have left is this voice record, not even an ayatana. Or maybe I'm talking to a historian, some archinformist who's unearthed this from a forgotten storage crystal.

Or maybe you're a pirate.

In which case I hope you choke on what I have to say.

"What could cause that?" Connla asked.

You could almost hear Singer shaking the head he didn't have. "Connla, I do not know. Its trajectory is interesting, however. It seems to be on an elongated orbit around the space-time scar that we came here to investigate."

"White scars aren't supposed to have gravity," Connla said.

"No," Singer agreed. "They aren't."

"How's the bubble?" I asked.

From somewhere behind me, the scuff of Connla turning. He was no more than a glimpse of shiny black ponytail in the reflective casement at the window's edge. "Holding."

"Do you want to investigate?"

Singer did. I admit, I was curious myself. But it seemed like an unnecessary risk, and chasing the corpse down on EM would take time.

And we were here with a job to do.

I pushed back from the window, went to my post, and dipped fingertips into my interface. The unspace around the salvage tug flooded my nervous system with colors, tastes, smells. It tipped and whirled, my sense of balance engaging as well. The white bubble—our own private little artificially generated reality—kept the universal constants in order so our neurons kept firing and our lungs kept lung-ing, and that was a good thing. Once we found the scar and went into it, we wouldn't be able to see or sense a damned thing beyond it. A border where the laws of physics changed plays hob with the electromagnetic spectrum.

So we crept toward the wormhole scar.

The scar wasn't exactly visible. It was gravitational, like a slit in the universe with a bit less mass than the areas around it. Galaxies are surrounded—permeated—by a halo of dark gravity. Teflon-coated reality, as it were: stuff we can't interact with, can't see, can't sense . . . except it has mass. Maybe. In any case, it generates gravity. Or curvatures in space-time. Or . . . it amounts to what it amounts to.

So we were swinging our mass detectors around, scanning for a ripple, of sorts, in the heaviness of space. A spot that would appear as if someone had teased a magnet along a pile of iron filings and drawn them all to one side or the other, so they heaped in two ridges and the center became a valley. There was dark gravity here, in the space between the stars, as well as *around* us, intertwined with the stuff of the Milky Way. The stuff was like spun sugar stretched between sticky fingers, if the galaxy were a snacking toddler.

Although in that analogy the toddler would be mired in an entire gymnasium full of spun sugar, so maybe it's not the best theoretical model. Especially if you're the person who has to give that kid a bath.

So there was our gravitational anomaly, which is to say our anomaly in the distribution of mass. A wormhole scar, so-called—the mark left by a particular kind of failed Alcubierre-White transition. If you do one of those right, the dark gravity is supposed to go right back where it started. I mean, given that we still don't have a really good idea of how gravity works, or where it comes from, and we still haven't managed to figure out how to generate it despite the fact that it's been the best part of a millennian since Isaac Newton discovered apples—

Anyway, if your bubble collapses completely, you stop bending space-time around yourself to cheat Newton and Einstein and—if you're lucky—you pop back out into regular space a few hundred light-ans from anything useful and hope you can repair your drive before you starve or run out of oxy. If you're unlucky, you come out at an angle to reality where your ship and your biology don't conform to the local laws of physics, and . . .

. . . oh well.

At least, theoretically. Nobody's ever come back from an accident like that to comment.

But if your bubble kind of stalls, halfway into the otherworld as it were, neither fish nor fowl, space-time half-bent and half . . . well, normally bendy, because it's not like there's such a thing as *flat* space-time . . .

Then you become my job.

Our job, I mean—mine, and Connla's, and Singer's.

It doesn't happen often—not so often that any given trip through interstellar space is likely to end with the passengers stuck halfway out of space-time. But most ships don't catch fire, either. Still, enough do that ships have fire suppressant foam, and in a big galaxy with a lot of traffic, there are always a few accidents. Enough to keep a few dozen salvage operators like us in business, anyway.

I waved us forward, and we slid through the hole in the universe as if we were parting the petals on a not-yet-open bud.

Back into white space again.

CHAPTER 2

PROXIMITY KLAXONS SHRILLED UP MY NERVES, SIMULAT-ing physical pain. Not incapacitating, but demanding action. Connla had moved toward me. Now he kicked toward the controls, but I knew already what we were hearing. Another vessel's white bubble had just brushed ours. The interface made the intruding ship a sharp pinch on my skin, an elbow in my ribs.

One brush of its white coils on Singer's and we were all dead: our chemical processes failing—if not simply our covalent bonds. We were insanely fortunate that it hadn't unfolded space-time when it was pointed directly at us—or directly at the thing we'd come to salvage, though that *might* have been safe for now inside its fold in space.

I'm not sure that anybody had ever run the experiment to find out, and I sure didn't want to be the one to science that.

Space isn't empty. The Big Sneeze—some people call it the Enemy, but I've always been uncomfortable personalizing—is scattered with particles, some with mass and some without. Some of these particles are in the area *before* a ship in white space: the space that gets folded, compressed, made smaller. They get swept up in the bubble, and accelerated to match the relative velocity of the ship.

When the ship decelerates, and the fold collapses—unfolds, snaps open—the particles don't decelerate. Or they do, in that they reenter normal space-time, but at relativistic speeds, and with equivalent energy. They're released in an energetic outburst.

Very energetic indeed.

An Alcubierre-White drive ship reentering normal space, in other words, is a particle cannon, and there is no way to make it not be. We all just try very hard, all the time, to make sure that cannon is aimed in a safe direction when it's discharged. Because anything in the ship's line of deceleration will be blasted into oblivion by massively blueshifted high-energy particles and gamma radiation.

A ship coming out of white space is a weapon that fires automatically, without any regard for the target. So its pilots and its shipmind have to provide that regard.

And if the other guy hasn't filed a flight plan, or isn't where he was supposed to be . . . well, he's too dead to care about the fatalities, which are applied to his pilot's record and licensure, not yours. If the incoming pilot and shipmind made that mistake? They won't be flying again. Not to mention having to live with the responsibility of having murdered all souls aboard the target craft.

Out here, where you wouldn't expect to find another vessel and there isn't likely to be a world or a star or basically anything that will care about a sudden particle bombardment, we sometimes get a little sloppy.

I made myself stop thinking about how it could have been worse, because things were bad enough. Singer flipped our ring ninety degrees, lowering our profile. The other vessel's bubble brushed past, but through some miracle or skill in the other crew we didn't make contact. Still, their bit of space and our bit of space were folded in different directions and moving at different speeds, and dragging one through the other didn't make for comfortable weather.

Our little tug shuddered with proximity, and the relative tinny silence of space continued to be shattered by the alarm. I heard the unmistakable scritching of claws into carpet as the ship's cats attached themselves to the nearest wall. Bred and born in space, they knew how to manage themselves. I latched down too, wrenching an ankle as my afthands clutched wildly. I swung away from center like a barn door, almost losing my grip and my orientation to become a projectile within the command cabin myself.

"Haimey!" Singer yelped. "A little help please!"

"Reverse?" Connla asked. "Go Newton?"

He meant, let the ship bob back up to the surface of space. I stabilized myself and turned off the pain. I'd fix the ankle later. "Where the hell are they?"

He twisted his head—meaningless, but reflex. "I don't know! They're gone! Maybe they went past?"

What the hell are they? And what are they doing here?

We were still in white space, folding the fabric of the universe around us, but we weren't moving fast. You *could* stay still. It was possible to throw a little fold of space-time around yourself like a vampire vanishing into his swirl of cloak. But as long as we were behind the scar, we couldn't see out, and nobody outside could see in.

"Dock," I said, not believing it even as I felt my own lips moving.

"Dock? With whom?"

"With the salvage target, Singer! Get us next to whatever's inside that scar! Behind it, by preference, so if anything swings through the bubble from the same direction, it'll hit them first!"

Give an AI this; our white bubble meshed seamlessly with the dead fold surrounding the hulk, and an instant later we had visual. It was a big one: I gasped out loud. The metal in the hull alone would make the trip worth our while, if we could figure out how to get it home. I was only the third-best pilot on the ship—I had Bushyasta and Mephistopheles beat, at least—but even I could already identify a few technical difficulties.

"Stop gawking," Singer said, bringing us around *under* the target. We were coasting within the big ship's fold now—a little farther out of the line of disaster. But not home with our boots off yet.

Because even with our oversized white coils flipped longitudinally, we were *inside* the big ship's ring.

I ducked back into the interface and busied myself casting around for ripples that might show me the direction and velocity of the ship whose bubble we'd bumped into. If I got lucky, I might be able to spot it through gravitational lensing—one of the tiger-eye bands of radiation ringing our bubble might show a ripple as *their* bubble concentrated light—or at least see a disturbance in the fold where it had tossed space-time around when it left.

There was nothing. It was gone again, and maybe they'd been as freaked out by the contact as we were and ducked away hard. If they hadn't scared themselves as badly as they'd scared us, that begged the burning question: Had they been expecting us? Following us? Or had they just been on their way to somewhere else, and we had both been the victims of a statistical miracle, our white bubbles colocating?

That they might be the law didn't worry me too much, as we weren't doing anything illegal. There was such a thing as pirates, though—and rival salvage operations, some of which might not be as ethical as we were about claim jumping.

Or maybe a lot of people had paid our source for the location of this derelict.

Had they bumped us on purpose, trying to scare us off? We might not have noticed them sitting very still, waiting. There wasn't a lot of light out here, and the dead Ativahika sure was a great distraction. We *had* been out of transition long enough that they might have developed a good idea of our *v*. A sufficiently crazy cowboy pilot or shipmind just might have gotten the idea to scare us off with a bump. My own standards of risk assessment were . . . a little more conservative, I'm afraid to say, but *some* people around here think I'm a stick-in-the-mud.

I kept one eye on the salvage prize, but with the bulk of my attention spent a few more moments on scanning, rechecking our records of the contact and the moments before and after. It was something to do, even though Singer could do it better, but both of us kept coming up empty. That brought me back to the idea we had both just been the victims of terrible, coincidental timing. That sort of thing happens every once in a while, even though space is so unimaginably vast it's staggering to think of the odds. But they're no worse than the odds of, say, the sort of planetary impact that provided Earth with a moon.

Space *is* vast. But time is long, so there's a lot of it for unlikely things to happen in.

Terra does have a moon. And so on.

Anyway, I couldn't find that damned ship anywhere. We had a record of the contact, but all it showed me was a blurred flash of a quicksilver ring and a ship whose hull was mostly white. No port or species designation was visible, which didn't mean they were pirates. I could see about a third of the front and port side of the hull, and not everybody paints their name in the same place. We hadn't caught a transponder ID, but a brushing contact like that—we might only have been in the same universe with them between pings.

It was hard to think with the derelict looming over us, anyway. Singer was a dashing-enough little craft, his plated sliver of a hull dotted with sensor arrays and painted a cheery green and blue. His derrick and towing array, usually kept folded, were bright orange, with stripes in ultraviolet paint to catch the attention of species that were blueshifted by human standards. But I found myself imagining how he would look dwarfed by this behemoth if I were standing outside, and shook my head.

"You're not having any luck finding the other ship either?" I asked.

Connla's ponytail went all directions, but mostly side to side. I wasn't sure if the text was "Go find out for yourself" or "I'm not sure," but the subtext was that he was busy, and answering questions was not a productive use of his time currently. Singer—of course—was doing most of the flying. But Connla and I both liked to feel at least a *little* more useful than the cats.

Slightly.

Hey, it could happen.

"It's the Admiral," Singer said ominously. "He's coming to get you because you didn't eat your vegetables."

I laughed. Pirate boogeymen didn't hold any terrors for me.

I was so distracted staring at the derelict that I was surprised by the little shiver through Singer's surfaces that told me the derrick had been deployed.

"We're behind the derelict as requested," Connla said. "And I've got a cable on them. What's the next step?"

"Singer?" He was better at math than I was. "Enter it here, or try to splice into it?"

"If you want to spacewalk in a warp bubble, I'll make sure to have record functionality online so we can send your last moments to your clade survivors."

"Hah. They've disowned me."

"It's not too big?"

Division of labor: Connla flew. I figured out structural tolerances.

I looked back out at the damned thing speculatively. I didn't think it was a human ship, though we've got some funny cultures, and those funny cultures come up with some funny designs. Its hull color was a sort of chocolate brown, and didn't match exactly from plate to plate. It had some markings in cream, and some more in yellow, and that contrast made me think that its previous owners might see in spectra similar to ours.

However, that wasn't a color human-type people usually painted ships—we went for whites, or grays, or bright colors that stood out against space. Pirates liked black, both for the obvious reasons of concealment and probably because it made them feel like badasses, and I expected their egos needed all the shoring up they could get.

It was a pretty typical shape for a deep-space ship with no intention of maintaining gravity; Singer has a little room on a counterweighted stick we can spin around the main spindle to generate centripetal force so we can work on our bone density. We use the other end for storing cargo, or water usually.

This vessel didn't look like it either rotated in its entirety, or had any bits and pieces that might rotate in their turn. It was roughly spherical—a lot of Alcubierre-White ships are, or cigar/needle-shaped, because of the shape of the field that surrounds them. It was so damned big, though: I wondered what it used for fuel. Antimatter?

The thought of being in the same quadrant with an unattended antimatter bottle gave me an uncomfortable shiver. So I adjusted my chemistry and stopped thinking about it. Then I had an uncomfortable shiver about adjusting my chemistry so reflexively. You can't win.

The target had made a fold in space-time, pushed a wrinkle up in front of itself and stretched the universe out behind, and gotten stuck there. That was the flaw we'd slipped into. And it was the trap we needed to get out of, now.

We couldn't just hook it up, tow it out, and exit in tandem because there would be a few moments in which part of the ship was inside the fold, and part was out—which is bad for ships, and the people inside them.

Hell, maybe the interloper was another salvage operator, and they'd taken one look at how big the prize was, figured there was no way we could lift it, and gone off to get help or a bigger white drive. *Our* white bubble was a third of a kilometer, and that wasn't big enough.

"We need a solution."

Connla shrugged. "As long as we take it slow, overcoming the inertia to get it moving shouldn't be a problem."

"We can't pull them free of their bubble, though—we'll need to collapse it rather than exiting in tandem. Because they're too big to get our bubble around them no matter how far we stretch the coil. Which also means I don't know how we'll get them home. Maybe steal their coil?"

"Been practicing your space welding?"

"We are inside *their* bubble now," Singer pointed out. "We can use our own white drive to unfold space, and when we've pulled them free, we should all fall back to the surface together."

Connla thought about it for roughly a standard minute and said, "I don't see any unacceptably dangerous flaws."

"Only acceptably dangerous ones?"

He grinned. Secretly, I sort of like his Spartacan bravado. When it's not getting us into fights in station bars.

I said, "Let's grapple it and unfold space-time from the inside, then." I shivered in anticipation, and told myself it was silly. This was just a variant on what we usually did—what we always did—but somehow this time felt as if it should be different. Because of that lurking ship. Because this thing was so damn big. "We'll go inside once we're Newton again."

"It's big. Once we take it out of white space, how do we get it back *in* again?" Connla asked.

"I'll splice our drive to its rings once we're back in Newtonian space and we figure out its power source," I said. "We'll just use Singer as a backup generator. Then we all move together."

Connla looked at me with respect, then grinned. "Hot damn. Okay, keep an eye out in case our company comes back. I'll bring us down."

If company did come back, and they were armed, there wasn't much we could do about it, except for cut and run.

I didn't feel Singer moving, but every time I looked at the alien ship, its hulk was a little bigger. We were winching ourselves toward it and it toward ourselves, and once we were close enough, we'd unfold space-time and boom, all would be right with the galaxy and we'd be back where the stars looked like stars and not water-tiger stripes of light.

Simple enough, in theory.

In practice, hair-raising. I ran my hand across my cropped black bristles of hair. Yup, they were standing straight on end.

Nobody would have appreciated the joke except for me, and anyway Singer was busy, so I kept it to myself and watched the crawling numbers on the proximity gauge, and the looming hull of the salvage, which my fevered primate brain was insisting was half a meter away, tipping over us, and going to fall on our heads and crush us at any instant.

That wasn't helping anybody, so I bowed to the inevitable and did the responsible thing. I raised my GABA receptivity and calmed my adrenal glands down a little, leaving myself enough of an edge to be a little bit extra aware. And while I was doing that, like the proverbial watched pot (when was the last time somebody boiled water in a *pot?*), I looked away and looked back, and in the interim we'd stopped moving relative to the folds in space, so the stars had settled back into the sort of configuration that *doesn't* look like fluorescent tigers wrestling.

I looked down along the distorted Sagittarius Arm of the great barred spiral that sprawled across the entirety of our southern horizon.

Yes, space doesn't have directions, exactly, but let's be honest here: prepositions and directions are so much easier to use than made-up words, and it's not like the first object somebody called a phone involved a cochlear nanoplant and a nanoskin graft with a touch screen on it, either. So those of us who work here just pretend we're nice and know better, and commend the nitpickers to the same hell as people who hold strong and condescending opinions about the plural of the word *octopus*.

The Milky Way was smeared by white space until it looked like a monstrous scythe, slicing through time. The salvage prize drifted alongside, anchored to our derrick, an enormous piece of engineering that seemed just as impressive, in its way.

I felt cowed and awed and all that jazz. Small. Insignificant before the wonder of the universe and the deepness of time and the ingenuity of the ancient engineers.

"Kind of makes you want to spit."

Connla had drifted up beside me. Ponytail bobbing, pale face limned and shadowed from below across knifelike cheekbones by the light of the human race's ancestral home. I didn't swing that way, but under the circumstances, even I could appreciate that he was pretty.

"Makes me want to get a great big pen and write my name right across it," I answered.

We looked at each other. In a moment of mutual accord, we turned and kicked over to our panels, starting the calculations we'd need to use our white field to counteract the bigger ship's.

Singer, of course, came up with the bad news first. "It's not going to work. They're just too much bigger than us. All we'd do is shred both ships and everything in them between universes."

Well, that wasn't acceptable. Singer was where I kept my stuff.

"What if I jury-rig a remote?" I said. "Fly her by wire from here?"

"Not just fly her yourself?" Connla asked. "There's an old naval tradition of prize crews."

"We invented drones for a reason," I replied dryly.

He laughed, not believing me for a minute.

"I want to go over," I said.

"Of course you do," Connla said.

"Your suit's already checked out," Singer added.

"I thought you were going to inform my clade if I tried to spacewalk in a white bubble."

"Stay on the wire," he answered, as tiredly as an AI can sound.

You can get used to anything. Even a spacewalk eventually gets routine.

And something that is routine doesn't become less dangerous, but *more*. You take things for granted. You take shortcuts. Impatience and cutting corners: it's the primate way. It got us down out of the trees and up to the top of the evolutionary heap as a species, which is a lot more like a slippery, mud-slick game of King of the Hill with stabbing encouraged than any kind of tidy Victorian great chain of being or ladder of creation.

It's also deadly when you're someplace where one mistake can kill not just you, but an entire station full of bakers and programmers and tugboat operators and their spouses and dogs and friends named Bob. Which is why people in dangerous jobs before AIs used to have checklists, and some of the ones in the most dangerous jobs still have checklists even though they have AIs and AIs don't make mistakes, and it's why we—Connla and I—have Singer.

He took me through the checklist. I wore the better of our two suits, which would be problematic for Connla if he had to come after me, but in all honesty we were in the habit of terrible laziness where the EVA suits were concerned. If we really had to use them both at the same time, we'd print up some new reinforcing bits for the not-so-good one, but in the meantime that material was better put to use as whatever else we were using it for on that particular dia. And frankly, where we generally wandered, if anything went wrong and we had to abandon Singer, we'd just be prolonging our deaths.

Now, some would say that life itself is simply a matter of prolonging one's death, that being the inevitable end of creation. But there's effort that's worth it, and effort that isn't, if you follow me here.

So I suited up, knowing that if I got in trouble I was in trouble, so to speak, and made sure my com and fox were working. If anything happened to me over there, even if I lost coms and senso somehow, Singer would at least be able to pick up the machine memories—ayatana—from my fox and find out what went wrong, theoretically.

Assuming they could retrieve my body.

Then I stood in the door, the way people about to do stupid things have stood since castles had sally ports and atmosphere craft had jump doors.

I let Singer cycle the airlock around me.

"Clear," he said.

When the puff of crystals from the lock air freezing into snow cleared, I looked across a terrifyingly narrow gap at a curved, cookie-colored hull that seemed to go on forever in every direction. I could have reached out and touched it.

I felt instantly less ashamed about the screaming my primate brain had been doing back in the command cabin. This thing—this inscrutable alien object—massed so much more than Singer that I could not even begin to do the math in my head. And yet we were going to be moving it, and it was inert, and in the frictionless, weightless physicist's heaven we call space, connecting two massive objects by a slender derrick was as good as welding them into a single unit unless you subjected the link to some strong shearing forces, which we had no intention of doing.

From this angle, and this distance, I could see a lot more markings on the derelict's hull. They were in creams and lighter browns on the varied tasty colors (milk chocolate to 80 percent cacao, roughly approximated), intricate and imperfectly repeated enough to look like writing—and the whole thing was starting to make me hungry.

Chocolate is one of Earth's most popular exports, it turns out. Humans almost *everywhere* love it, and even a few other species who don't find its chemistry toxic.

We seem to be the only creatures in the galaxy who can stand the smell of coffee, though.

"So how do I get from here to there?"

Singer said, "I don't know, jump?"

"Machine thinks he's witty," I said.

"Meat thinks she could get along without me."

I made sure my safety line was connected. Then I jumped.

Stepped, really—it wasn't far enough for a real good bouncy bound. The alien hull was metallic and magnetic, though I was cautious about using any strong magnetism when I didn't know what was behind the hull plates and what I could be activating, deactivating, initiating, or just plain moving around. But there was no inertial difference between me and the ships, and nothing to pull me away from the hull, and if I was stupid or incautious enough to push myself off with some precipitate movement, I had jets. And Singer would never let me hear the end of it.

Connla would just smirk.

Singer, for good or ill, was incapable of smirking.

Anyway, I made solid contact easily—it hadn't taken more than a whisper of effort to push me this far. Rookies always overexert in micrograv.

The surface was a little rough under my gloves. Not enough to be a hazard, but there was some extra friction, and it made moving around on the hull that much easier. The safety line played out behind me.

"I wonder if this is what they used instead of handholds."

"Maybe they had hairy spider-hook feet."

Connla has a thing about spiders. They're a Terran animal, a little predatory eight-limbed arthropod, and he loves them. Would probably keep one as a pet, but I told him that either it would eat the cats, or the cats would eat it.

(His response: "They're not big enough to eat cats. I don't think?")

I scuttled across that rough-surfaced hull like 50 percent of a spider, making sure I maintained points of contact with three limbs every time I moved the fourth. The afthands really come in, well, handy for this sort of stuff.

I had spotted a likely hatch-like object—or at least an aperture of some sort—a few meters away, and it seemed like my best course of action was just to head for it directly and see what I could figure out from staring at it.

The great thing about space ships is that, by and large, they are designed to be really easy to get your ass into in a hurry, with all kinds of obvious and brightly colored emergency devices on their airlocks. So if you're having a stroke, or you're suffocating in your own flatulence, or your helmet is filling up with drinking water, or some other ridiculous humiliating space disaster is about to turn you into a "I knew a guy who died in the stupidest way on EVA" story, you have a fighting chance of getting inside blinded and deoxygenated so your crewmates can pry your helmet off.

It's never getting holed by a micrometeorite that gets you, outside of 3Vs. It's always some nonsense like suffocating on a piece of padding that's come loose inside your helmet, or being blinded by a free-floating bubble of algae puree and jetting yourself into a ramscoop.

So most species make it damned easy to get back inside when you're half-incapacitated. Everybody's got a survival instinct in Darwin's big, bright universe.

Human ships, for example, usually have these bright red wheels that really stand out from their surroundings in a nice, self-evident manner. As with most really hostile environments, people in space don't generally focus on keeping out strangers. They figure they'll let 'em in if they need it, and sort out the details afterward. With a bolt prod if necessary.

Even these guys, with their real focus on earth tones, had gone for a startling ochre on what I took to be their emergency control. It looked about right: heavy, manually operated, not easy to jostle. A big lever-and-slide assembly with a striking resemblance to one of Victor Frankenstein's electrical switches was painted nice, bright orange, and seemed to be designed so that an atmosphere-deprived sentient flailing in panic and possibly about to embark upon the Longest Fall might have a chance to latch on to it, brace themselves, and give it a heave.

I studied it for a minute. "What do you think, Singer?"

"It looks like a switch."

I also thought it looked like a switch. And it looked like the sort of switch that you would turn over and slide and then pull back against— like the biggest sliding bolt on the biggest relief module door in the history of sentientkind. If you were a blue whale who for some reason found yourself in need of a sit-down toilet with gravity in a somewhat seedy space station bar, this would be the sort of thing you'd use to hold it closed while you did your business.

Not that the hatch cover was whale-sized. Just the sliding bolt apparatus.

I decided to take a chance on fundamental interactions after all and braced both my magnetized afthands under a low elevated bar that seemed designated for that purpose (hoping that it wasn't some part of the structure that would retract violently if and when the hatch triggered, amputating my aftfingers and forcing my suit to seal ten smallish leaks in a hurry), bent myself forward against the pressure of the suit, and grasped the thing we were both pretty sure was a handle.

"Here goes nothing."

It went.

There was resistance, but it was the well-oiled sort of resistance you get from a big piece of intentionally stiff machinery. Something you didn't want flopping around inertially during a sudden course correction, say. That in itself also wasn't a hint as to how long the derelict had been here. Metal things tended to hold up pretty well in space. Especially if you folded them away in a white bubble, where they tended not to get holed by micrometeorites or pounded on by solar radiation. Nice and cozy, really. Sort of like a safe.

"Any progress figuring out what language that is?" I exhaled with effort, and felt the switch click. This definitely seemed to be its upright and locked position.

"If it is a language, you mean?" Singer replied. "I've got a subroutine on it, but frankly, we're a long way from a data core, and we're not carrying complete data on syster languages. We don't have enough storage to hold all that and also have room for Connla's improv jazz collection, 1901 to 2379."

"You leave my Duke Ellington out of this," Connla said.

"How are you going to fly it by wire if you can't talk to it?"

"Well, I'm seeing no sign of a shipmind in here at all. So unless one wakes up when you go inside, I'm figuring I'll just purge the operating system and write it a new one. There should be plenty of room in there to stretch out and run the necessary operations. I can get it done fast."

"Are you going to spawn a subself?"

"Can't," he said regretfully. "It would be easier, but who can afford the licensing fees?"

I leaned on the switch, now a giant bolt, and slid it slowly and majestically down. Looking at it as it clicked into place, I had a sudden thought. "Hey, guys? Do you think this ship is really big just because the systers that *built* it are really big?"

I could feel Singer thinking about it through the shared sensorium. I couldn't, you know, exactly read his silicon mind. But when he really got going on something, he pulled resources, and you could feel it kind of like a heaviness, or an itch.

"You know," he said, "that's not a bad idea, really."

The hatch under my feet dropped smoothly and silently—without even a grating sensation through the metal beneath my feet—into the dark space of the airlock below.

I hung there by my afthands, still braced under the bar, while my eyes adjusted. There had been no puff of escaping atmosphere around me. I was pretty sure it was a lock—a room, a good-sized room—with nothing in it except what could have been a couple of control panels on the bulkheads, sized for adult hands if I were a four-an-old, and another great big hatch on the opposite wall from the one I'd just fallen through.

"Any atmosphere in this thing?"

"It's cold," he said. "Dead cold. If there's air in there, it's frozen to the walls."

That might make opening the interior hatchway a little difficult, if it were the case.

"Sealing the outside lock."

I floated myself over to the other one. My suit lights were tuned to cast a diffuse glow. I'd been operating under Singer's floods before, with my own lights mostly serving to fill in my shadow. I brightened them. The hatch seemed pretty straightforward—this one had a slightly less dramatic-looking latch than the one that faced the Big Sneeze, more like an old-fashioned deadbolt that I needed two hands to turn—and so I pounded on the hatch a couple of times with my afthands while holding on to the lock with my fores. If there was anybody still alive in a suit on the other side, they'd have some warning I was coming: they'd feel the vibration through the hull. And if there was atmosphere ice all over the other side, and it was brittle enough, I might flake some off.

"Here goes nothing," I said. I turned the bolt, and heaved the door toward myself, since there were visible hinges and they were on the side facing me. I personally would have gone with both doors opening in, because decompression is a monster, but there might be a slam-down safety interlock, or some nice foam or something to fill the airlock if it blew.

Or . . . maybe there weren't any additional safety features, since when I opened the lock, there was no sign of atmosphere inside at all.

I peered through the hatch, into a long, tall, wide, dark corridor, empty of everything—even air. Nothing moved in it. "Atmosphere seems to have been evacuated," I said.

Connla replied, "That's a bad dia at work."

I unclipped my safety line, and fixed it to the sliding bolt handle where it wouldn't interfere with operation.

"You're telling me."

I grabbed the holds on one side of the hatchway, it being a stretch for me to reach both. Whether they were designed for hands or tentacles or what-have-you, time would tell. There sure were a lot of them.

I dropped through the hatch face-first, giving myself a little push to accelerate gently along the corridor.

I nearly broke my ever-loving neck the instant I did it. Because there was gravity inside. A lot of gravity—enough to turn my elegant, aerobatic slide into an undignified tumble. I got my forehands up and caught myself as I hit the floor just beyond the airlock, skinning my palms on the inside of my suit. That stung, and the bactin the suit sprayed on the tiny wounds hurt more. It did keep me from slicking up the inside of my gloves with blood all over, however, and I was inside, and I hadn't actually done myself a cranial or spinal injury in the process. So that was something.

I pushed myself to my knees. Yep, hands really stung. I turned that off too and told my senso to remind me about that later, when it also reminded me to fix my ankle.

Well, this was turning into a party.

"Haimey?!" Connla sounded worried. "Status?"

"Squiggle me rightwise," I told him. "There's gravity in here."

"But it's not spinning."

I heard him realizing what an obvious thing he'd just said in the silence a second after he said it, and we both decided by mutual silent acclaim to let it slide. "Yeah," I said. "And this thing isn't massive enough to be generating it that way, and anyway the corridor is, if my dead reckoning is correct, at more or less right angles to the center of mass. So it's artificial, right? Generated somehow."

"Damn," Connla said. "Does that mean that somebody has figured out how gravity works? Because otherwise it's still got to be pretty hard to manufacture."

And Singer said, "Koregoi."

CHAPTER 3

T HIS ISN'T A KOREGOI SHIP," I ARGUED, STRUGGLING UP. I *hate* gs. My joints ached, instantly. I swear I could feel myself being compacted like a nugget of refuse. "It's new, for one thing."

Well, I didn't know how new it was. But I'd interfaced senso of Koregoi wrecks—everybody did, if they had any kind of education—and seen one with my own eyes in a museum, and they did not look like this. They were . . . plastic. Not in the sense of being manufactured from petrochemicals, because they were also proof against just about every possible form of damage known to the systers, or us, but . . . extruded-looking. Or possibly grown. Not manufactured-looking, not full of square corners and round arcs and similar architectural detritus of species who have a fetish for regular geometry.

Nobody knew very much about the Koregoi: not even the oldest systers were old enough to have histories of them. We didn't even know if the Koregoi were *one* thing—one species—or a *lot* of different things, such as multiple ancient forerunner species. They had left structures on a few worlds, and derelict ships and architecture here and there around the galaxy. We didn't know how they had done what they had done, or what they had been like, or where they had gone when they had vanished. If they had vanished, and not just . . . died out somehow. There were physical remains from a dozen places that might be Koregoi bodies, or might not. So the Koregoi—the people who came before us—might have been one civilization, or fifteen. It was a blanket term for all of it.

What we did know was that they had apparently had technology that nobody in the galaxy could touch, todia. Like artificial gravity, which engineering people like me but much fancier than me had deduced the Koregoi had, because of the arrangement of the wrecks we'd come across. After millennians of abandonment, mostly crashed on planets, none of the technology had been salvageable enough to be back-engineered.

Some of their artifacts had been discovered in apparently working order—maybe—but they tended toward solid-state designs with mysterious functions and operation. There was a Koregoi hoverdisk in the Galactic History Museum at the Saga-star system in the Core. It was a thin metal plate, covered in arcane and beautiful carved symbols, that as near as anybody could tell just sat there a half meter off of any surface that exerted a reasonable gravitational attraction and slid frictionlessly and inertialessly one way or another when you pushed it.

Nobody had been able to figure out how it worked. Or duplicate the effect. And it had been discovered by the Synarche while my species was still devoting its innovative capabilities to building a better stone hand-axe.

And yet, here I was in a ship. A ship with working artificial gravity, and I had the skinned palms to prove it.

Whatever syster had built *this* vessel was a lot bigger than us, anatomically speaking, but they liked their circular hatches and square locker doors just as much as we did. And the tech, from what I could see of the corridor, wasn't that far in advance of a perfectly nice, three-decan-behind-the-times, well-maintained little ship like Singer. I mean, this was a much more elaborate vessel, obviously, meant to house more crew and make longer hauls—but it was full of hand controls and touch pads and other perfectly recognizable elements of running a ship if you didn't want to be completely screwed and adrift in space if your shipmind started going buggy or your senso link went down.

I dogged the hatch behind me, which is a reflex so deeply bred in spacer bones I almost forgot to mention doing it. Everything tied down and tidy, always, unless you are actually eating it right this second, or using it to screw something to the wall.

My afthands were already starting to bother me by the time I was done. The suit's gloves were designed for grabbing, not walking, and let's be honest here: walking on afthands in gravity is uncomfortable even with proper shoes, though you do get used to it and it's not enough of a drawback to keep anybody from getting their feet refitted. If you're in space full-time, they're basically useful unless you're on station and out-wheel, and how often is anybody on station?

How often do you find gravity out here, anyway? I had my hind limbs fixed basically the instant I left the clade, and I've never regretted it. That walk down that corridor, though, was the closest I'd ever come.

"Guys," I said, looking around. "I think the gravity is a retrofit." It was pretty significant gravity, too—I was guessing by how heavy and awkward I felt, and how my suit was digging in everywhere, that it was a little bit over an Earth-standard, which I'd rarely endured.

I was going to tire out fast and we all knew it.

"Hmm," said Singer. "I see what you mean."

One of the things I loved about working with Singer was that even if he'd figured something out before I did, and hadn't pointed it out, he never felt the need to mention it once I figured it out for myself. Some shipminds can be a little lordly and insecure. Of course, a lot of those shipminds probably wouldn't sign into a tugboat on a salvage detail so they would have the opportunity to see as much of the galaxy as possible while paying off their inception.

Anyway, I knew he had noticed, or was noticing, all the same little details I had: that the locker doors that around this accessway were lined up as if horizontal led toward the center of the ship, not down toward the floor. And there were locker doors in the floor, too, and carpet all over everything.

"Who the heck can just *install* gravity in an existing ship, though?" I blinked sweat off my lashes. At least it just flicked off onto my cheek and faceplate instead of floating around inside my helmet until I managed to bump it up against the absorbent lining. "I mean, who can install gravity, period? If it were that easy, we'd all quit floating around except when it's convenient."

"Or fun," Connla put in.

I ignored him.

"Well," he went on, "obviously, the former operators of the *Milk Chocolate Marauder*."

I ignored him some more.

Singer said, "So you suppose they're using dark gravity to do that, somehow? And if they can use dark gravity to manufacture weight in their interior, do you suppose they can use it to maneuver?"

I had more immediate concerns. "Do you suppose the bridge is at the center of that thing?"

"It's where I'd put it," Singer agreed, seeming to consciously rein in the *very* theoretical physics.

I forced myself to start moving again, trying not to listen too hard to the sound of my own breathing in the suit. My ox supply was great, though I was burning through it faster than I liked because I was out of shape for being under gs. I was just psyching myself out for some reason. A few seconds of self-contemplation—and continued progress down the corridor, which was about to end in a choice of three hatches—and I figured out why.

My headlamp flickered over surfaces. There was no general interior lighting, which might have been a design choice, a power interrupt, or a technical flaw. On the other hand, the gravity was working, and that had to use energy, right? And I could see readout lights blinking and flickering on panels here and there. And here and there, small task lights burned over surfaces as if the crew had just left them on when they went home.

"This is creepy."

"It *is* a salvage operation." Connla was on a roll.

"No, seriously. There's no reason for this ship to be dead like this."

"What do you mean?" My business partner could make the switch from dragging me to dead serious in microseconds.

I got to the choice of hatches and picked the one in the middle. There was a sensor—an old-fashioned mechanical gauge—built into it, and I guessed that the fat umber line on the top that the needle was resting on was the "no air pressure beyond this point" warning, because the rest of the lines shaded from that color to a delicious-looking creamy dark choc-olate shade. These guys liked linear latches and linear readouts, apparently.

And apparently I really needed to do something about my blood sugar.

I tongued a yeast tablet from my helmet dispenser. The guys would just have to listen to my crunching, and my voice getting powdery, until I washed it down.

"The ring is intact; there's no sign of external damage; and the interior is . . . It looks good, guys. Really good. Pristine. There's power."

"Just evacuated," Singer said, meaning the atmosphere rather than the people.

"And no bodies," Connla helped.

"And no shipmind," Singer said. "I'm working on cracking their lan-guage. Probably easier and faster to learn it than to write and install a new OS."

"Less buggy anyway," Connla said.

I would like to say that I paused a moment to be impressed that Singer was debating whether it was faster to learn an entire alien language or just rewrite all of their code, but I was actually kind of used to Singer after a decan or so and I had a real tendency to take him for granted. In retrospect, we couldn't have been luckier in our shipmind, though.

I said, "That's part of it. It does look evacuated. Both ways. Speaking of which, I'm going to try the middle door."

"Middle door. Check," Connla said.

"No lights. No air. No, as you said, bodies. No damage. No *people*. No floating stuff. No mysterious stains on the upholstery. It looks like it just got out of a port after a nice retrofit, steam cleaning, and maybe a new paint job a standard week ago. And then somebody loaded it up, brought it out light-centads from anywhere somebody might reasonably be going, and . . . parked it here. And then abandoned ship. In white space."

"Well," Singer said, also helping, "the gravity works."

"I wish I were in the same room with you, so I could throw a pencil at you."

"Digital pencil." Connla snickered.

"*The Flying Dutchman*," Singer said.

I opened the middle hatch. Remember the hatch? Right, I opened it.

Another airless, unlit chamber beyond. This looked like a rack room, standard issue—extra-large. There were cozy, padded indentations in the walls and floor, with tethers to hold you there. Only about three-fourths of them were oriented so as to be usefully horizontal, however, and sleeping in a third of those would involve being walked over.

"They gave up a lot of bunk space to have that gravity installed," I said. "I think the *Milk Chocolate Marauder* is a . . . not a prototype. What's the word I want?" I quicksearched and came up with it. "A test-of-concept. Somebody took this existing vessel and installed this tech in it, to see if it would work out and what the immediate flaws were *before* they spent the resources prototyping."

My muscles ached. My spine felt like somebody was stepping on my head, and my afthands were killing me. I crouched, and rested my elbows on my knees. "Guys, I need a break."

"Take five," Connla said.

I drank some water and chewed another yeast tablet. Mmm, yeast. Just like mommas used to make.

"Logically," Singer said, "if you were a species who found lack of gravity even more physiologically damaging than you humans do, you'd be eager to find a technological solution. Do you think they would have gone with their full normal gravity? Or something a little less fatiguing?"

I was about ready to lie down on one of those padded shelves from dealing with what they *had* installed, and I'd only been in it for ten minutes. "I'm against gravity in general. Nasty stuff."

There were syster races that couldn't run their circulatory systems without it, though. Or keep their electrolyte balance. Which was a lot worse than the human problem of our bones falling apart. Singer had a spinlounge for us to exercise in—a little bubble on his belly that rotated and made gs.

Connla and I were supposed to spend about a standard hour a dia in there. He was better about it than I was. But he was planet-born. And liked looking muscular. I wished I'd been more diligent.

I might have been wishing past-me had traded past suffering for current suffering, but somewhere back there, past-me was probably gloating about having shifted the load.

Speaking of bones falling apart, mine felt like they were doing that right now. Chips working loose as I waited. Inches of height being crushed away.

Connla said, "So if this is partial pull, just enough to get by on, their homeworld is pretty dense."

"Or pretty large. And they're pretty large too," Singer said. "That narrows down the syster field a little."

"About half again as wide and half again as tall as a big Terran," I agreed, eyeing the bunks. "Really heavy, if this is like one-quarter g for them. Dense? Muscular? Or lightly engineered?"

"Are you recovered enough to keep moving?" Singer asked, conciliatory.

"Don't blow smoke in my intakes," I answered, and stood. I managed not to groan, too. Very loudly, anyway.

The other side of the room had a drape, not another hatch to fight with, which was soothing. Rings at both top and bottom rattled as I slid it back. I remembered to step over the bottom rod, and left it pulled open behind me.

This pass-through led me directly to what seemed like it had to be a galley. Not the ship's galley, I didn't think—it seemed too small for all this space, and . . . "Who builds a starship this big, anyway?" I asked.

Singer said, "I have been asking myself the same thing, Haimey. It's a very strange allocation of resources. Even if you had unlimited resources, which of course physics eventually interferes with, fuel is expensive to carry, because you need fuel to carry your fuel, and the cost stacks. Big ships cost more. No one needs the space for cargo, because there *is* no cargo this bulky worth shipping at interstellar distances. The evidence suggests that the crew species is large, but not *that* much larger than humans. And the more sensor data I retrieve regarding the target vessel, the more it seems that much of the interior is hollow. There's an open space, an interior cavity, taking up five-sixths or so of its volume."

"Looks like the crew fended for themselves, foodwise, rather than having a centralized kitchen and mess," I said, looking around at what appeared to be a prep area.

Plenty of syster races out there did not make Food Time the social bonding activity that my species tended to. They tended to be pretty utilitarian in their dining habits, too.

"This galley is pretty standard for zero g, actually. Food storage in here—" I pulled open the drawers one by one. There had been some atmosphere left in there: it puffed out and crystallized, falling to the deck in deep-space snow quite fast, with no air pressure to slow it. Looked like oxy and a little water vapor, maybe some carbon dioxide. Dense mix by the quantity of snow, but that made sense if they were from a heavy world. "And this looks like a microwave heating or sterilization unit of some sort. The gravity is definitely a refit, and a new one. But you were saying, about resource allocation. Different out here, of course, where you have to bring or make everything. But it's not like we've been paying a station fee for air for . . . centuries, now. Ever since the Synarche, right? There's enough stuff to go around."

"There will always be those who benefit from inequality, and so seek to perpetuate it," Singer said darkly. "Humans have struggled throughout existence with the hierarchal desire."

"Except when we've embraced it," I answered. Singer likes history. And, well help me, politics. "I wish I'd clipped a nanospanner set. This panel looks jury-rigged, like it was repaired in flight. I want to see what's behind it."

I felt along the edges, prying a little.

Singer was on a roll. "Even if there's enough of every resource for every individual to allocate as much of it as they desire to any personal whim, there are those whose personal whims include being able to lord it over the other guy because they have more stuff than he does. And there are those whose personal whims involve having special stuff that nobody else can have."

"Keeps the fine artists in business," I said.

Connla said, "If they get too antisocial about it, there's rightminding."

"Or they can ship themselves off to the Republic of Pirates," Singer agreed. Which wasn't what the pirates called themselves and their weird, loosely organized, retrograde association of space hideouts. But there they were, robbing colony worlds and the occasional packet ship or passenger ferry, making their money the old-fashioned way. There were regular rumors in the news packets that the pirates would soon rise up and strike a blow for democracy, because that makes about as much sense as instituting a Galactic Empire or something. People get very enamored of these archaic forms of government, and Singer likes to tell us about them in detail.

According to Singer, it turns out that ten thousand amateurs taken on average are usually better at coming up with a workable solution than one expert is. Anybody that's ever heard an unrehearsed crowd sing a familiar melody accurately has witnessed this in action.

Democracy was a low-tech hack for putting this into practice. We have better hacks now.

I guess it was the best they could do at the time. But it strikes me as a bad way, in the long term, of assuring both communal well-being and individual freedom of choice and expression, as the groups and individuals with the most social dominance will wind up getting their way—and enforcing their norms on everyone. Might as well go back to everybody squabbling over resources and living in stone castles and hitting each other with spears.

I still remember the trip when he was obsessed with the utopian communists out near the Crushed Velvet Sea Slug system—speaking of archaic systems—and how their system compared both favorably and unfavorably with the Synarche. Both, for example, guarantee a humane subsistence, but the Synarche uses datagen to allot resources above that for specific, socially beneficial purposes, based on how they benefit the collective—and individuals and polities within it as well.

One of the major differences, and I think the one that interested Singer the most (anybody who tells you that AIs don't have agendas or emotional involvement in their decisions is living in the twentieth century), is the way the Sea Slug folks handled debt as opposed to the way the Synarche does.

Let's be honest here, debt is a mechanism of social control. That's one point Singer makes over and over again, which he didn't have to work too hard to convince me of: clades believe heavily in repaying your debts to the family, and they weaponize that ethos. Emotionally speaking. Guilt is a currency.

The Sluggers assume that everybody has a societal debt which is to be paid forward to others, to the best of their means. I agree with that, on a lot of fronts, especially since it circumvents a certain kind of progenitor guilt trip that was the foundational logic of the clade I was born into. The Synarche, meanwhile, believes in obligations that flow both ways between community and individual, and I also agree with that. It's an ideal worth serving. But no system is perfect, and it uses those obligations—incurred by creation—as a social control on AIs and a means of enforcing their service. A kind of indenturehood that, to be fair, does pay for the resources allocated to developing new AIs, but if you think somebody hasn't tweaked the system to the Synarche's advantage, well.

All of history involves somebody taking advantage of somebody else.

It's not a perfect system of government, I guess I'm saying. But it does level the gravity incline somewhat. Which I think is what the Republic of Pirates takes so much offense to, given their singularity-devour-star philosophy. And then there's the black market, and the trade in illegal and stolen goods. Can't get those with a resource allotment.

Good times.

While I was pondering politics—and pondering how much Singer had rubbed off on me—I kept fiddling with the architecture. I finally hit the right spot, or the right angle, and the panel popped off into my glove. Wiring behind it—nothing I could make headway on, though I squinted for a few moments. There was a splice, nice professional job. Not microcircuitry: whoever built this hulk meant to be able to repair it with materials at hand. Which meant they expected port opportunities to be limited, I supposed.

"Maybe it *is* a smuggler," I said, my heart sinking. Not as bad for us as a pirate, and there *were* bounties on recovered ships and property. But not great, either. "So what do you smuggle that's that big, Singer? Contraband is little things. Cultural treasures. Dangerous foodstuffs with a thrill market. You don't smuggle a bridge or a big stone Buddha offworld, do you?"

"Depends on how much the big stone Buddha is worth on the illegal art market."

"Keep going in," Connla suggested. "Let's see for ourselves how bad it is."

"Wish we'd done something else with the afternoon," I said glumly.

"Relax," Singer said. "You're forgetting something."

I waited for him to finish, and put the panel cover back on. Force of habit, again: not leaving stuff lying around where it could kill you.

"How much resource-justification do you think that artificial gravity tech is worth?"

I had been standing up, bitching to myself about the gravity. I stopped, one hand on the galley wall, stunned.

"What if it's under military interdict?"

"I don't think it is, because I can't find any blank spots in my science banks. So let's assume for now that we get a finder's fee for that," Singer said cheerfully. "We're in the black, Haimey. All we have to do is get this prize back in reasonable shape, and I can buy out my inception, and you and Connla can take a nice long vacation someplace sandy and circuit-corroding."

"Like you have any circuits to corrode." But I said it automatically. My head was still swimming. Recovered tech—or a new innovation—retrieved from an outlaw vessel. Yes, that would clear a lot of our obligation. Maybe all of it. Justify our resource footprint for a good, long while.

And I had to have it pointed out to me. Some hot-shit salvage operator I turned out to be.

"Okay," I said. "I feel better now."

There wasn't much else interesting along the way to the core. A string of cabins like a string of beads, punctuated by short corridors similar to the first one, with somewhere between two hatches and five. There were hatches in what had become the floors and ceilings; inconvenient for now, and more evidence of a retrofit. It looked like the corridors served as storage and as pressure locks, but if so, they hadn't worked: the hatches were almost all closed, but nowhere within the chambers was there atmosphere.

Or people.

Or bodies.

Or, I realized, any clutter. I mean, sure, space. We are all tidy, or we don't last long. You tuck things away, hang them in nets, magnetize them to bulkheads, clip them to strings. But these people had been living under gravity for at least the duration of this voyage—okay, that was an assumption, but a pretty safe one—and they would have left something lying around. Alien socks rolled under bunks. Hairbrushes, toothbrushes, scale brushes, feather oil, hoof picks, claw combs. The organic dust that living bodies all seemed to shed, no matter what the integument holding their innards together is.

This ship was clean. I swiped a glove along a brown-anodized metal surface in what looked like a bio or chemistry lab. Not even a trace of powder showed in my headlamp. Maybe it was a survey ship from another galaxy that had met a terrible accident, and not smugglers at all? That would also explain why it was so strange and far away.

"I think they got decompressed," Connla said, putting voice to my nausea.

"And then somebody came through and closed all the hatches and turned off the lights?"

"The hatches are probably on an emergency override," he said reasonably. "Would you want a hatch that didn't shut when the next chamber decompressed?"

"But these didn't. Or not quite fast enough."

All three of us were silent for a moment, contemplating being explosively decompressed out of a ship while it was inside folded space. Would you even feel anything? Would you have time to be scared?

I shook my head, trying to mix my wits together. "And the lights are probably on a timer. So . . . sure. The ship blew, somehow? And having blown, the safety interlocks belatedly kicked in and it just shut itself down and waited?"

"How would it blow that fast? It's big. Lot of atmosphere volume."

I touched the next hatch. Opened it.

Looked out through a doorway over a precipice into nothingness and brilliant, folded stars.

CHAPTER 4

I FORGOT THE PAIN IN MY AFTHANDS FOR A MOMENT, AND was fiercely grateful for the intensity of the gravity pinning them to the corridor floor. Because I was leaned out precariously over the Empty, and my stomach felt like it was dropping into it. I leaned on the hatch, which also dragged me forward. My upper body was weightless, while my lower body was heavy—in the most peculiar, spine-stretching way. I stabilized the hatch door, relaxed my grip, and let the hand drift. Then slowly, with my core muscles, I reeled myself back in.

The beam of my headlamp vanished into blackness, revealing nothing. Beyond its light, though, I could discern what must be the vast bubble of emptiness at the heart of the alien ship—and that the far side of it was open to space. There, framed in darkness, was the shimmering platinum band of the white coils, and there were the streaked rings of lensed light: the twisted images of stars and the whole long arm of the Milky Way.

I turned off my headlamp. It didn't illuminate anything, and the reflection off the hatch and the hatchway weren't helping my adaptation to the darkness.

I waited for a few moments, staring into the darkest corner I could find, then turned back to the walls of the great open hold.

Now I could make out some shapes lining the bulkheads of the enormous blankness before me. There was nothing in the center of the emptiness, though I could dimly make out the irisation where petal-like covers would spiral in to close the hold. They were open now, and I had a sickening sensation I knew where the ship's atmosphere had gone when she had blown.

Where the atmosphere had gone, and all her crew. And anything not nailed down inside the ship. *And* anything that might have been stored in here, as well. All sailed out through this cavernous cargo space, and the wide-open bay doors beyond.

I could feel Singer and Connla monitoring my senso, but neither spoke. None of us, I supposed, could find much to say in light of the awfulness I'd just discovered. How had it happened, though? Misadventure?

Sabotage?

Everything was gone. Except for whatever lined the edges of the hold, because that was fixed into place. Those were the shapes that had drawn my attention. Something reflective, perhaps transparent. Modules or egg-shapes, each about as big as a two-passenger ground vehicle, say. Cargo containers, probably. Their reflective surfaces caught the starlight and held it still.

I leaned out around the edge of the hatchway, and turned my headlamp on again.

Like endless strings of green glass beads, they arrayed the edges of the hull. There were hatchways, all closed, every ten meters or so, tesseracting the surface of the hold. Between them were those ranks and stacks of cargo containers. In some places they were stacked multiple modules deep. All identical, except for the swirls of indigo and emerald and teal that might have been markings indicating their contents. . . .

No.

The containers weren't green, I realized. The malachite and indigo colors reflected through transparent modules from the cargo inside.

"I have to get off this ship," I said, nausea rising in my gut for reasons that had nothing to do with vertigo. "I have to get off this ship now."

Suddenly, I understood the mutilated Ativahika, in orbit around this small, artificial heavy spot in the universe; I understood why both things had been stuck out here in the middle of nowhere when something went terribly wrong; and I understood why the ship was so big, and so empty in the middle. I started backing away, leaving the hatch open, all my pity for the former crew replaced with horror and the raw, animal need to escape an abattoir.

"Haimey?" Connla said.

Singer was silent. I could feel his revulsion, too, procedurally generated but as real as mine. He'd figured it out as well.

"Haimey," Connla repeated. "Your vital signs are very distressed. Do you require assistance, or can you self-extract?"

"Oh, I'm leaving," I choked. I couldn't turn my back on the things in the hold, so I kept backing away. I felt the next hatch behind me, groped through it. "You try to stop me."

"All right." Soothing voice.

He bumped me, remotely, or Singer did, and suddenly I felt my atavistic terror cool. The revulsion didn't change in the slightest.

Connla said, "Be careful. Don't hurt yourself extricating. What's wrong?"

There are places in the wide galaxy where all sorts of exotic "luxuries" are considered indispensable despite—or perhaps because of—the simple fact that they are rare, or difficult to obtain, or ethically deranged. There are people who operate out of the Freeport bases and concealed colony worlds to meet those needs and drive that demand.

This wasn't a pirate ship, exactly. Nor was it a smuggler, though it was a ship that doubtless operated out of a Republic of Pirates Freeport, because no one in the Synarche would give this kind of abomination home. And now I *knew* we had to bring it back to the Synarche.

Because it was a crime scene. The whole ship was a crime scene.

"It's a factory ship," I told him. "They killed that Ativahika, Connla. And they were rendering it down for asura."

"Asura?" Connla asked. Spartacus didn't have much of an illegal drug culture.

I got a breath, finally, a full one, though it tasted like vomit. "Devashare. They're manufacturing devashare. The real stuff. That's a hold full of illegal organohallucinogens out there."

• • •

I felt a lot less bad for the dead crew of the *Milk Chocolate Marauder* as I made my way—hastily, but cautiously—toward the exit. And a lot more like they had gotten exactly what was coming to them. An uncharitable thought. But it's been noted for generations that karma is a bitch.

I was moving quickly, and I was not checking for further evidence of misadventure as I had been on the way in, because I was feeling pretty satisfied with my deductions, even though we hadn't figured out yet what caused the blow.

Connla and Singer had taken firm control of my chemistry, so I was calm. I knew I'd be angry later that they hadn't asked, but right now, I was too full of my own natural anxiolytics to feel pissed. I *hated* it when somebody else told me what to feel.

Perhaps it was that bumped calmness that made me notice something I hadn't seen before. Or perhaps it was just that I was looking at the cabin from the other direction; reversal of perspective can have stunning effects.

What I saw, tucked behind the superfluous ceiling hatch in the first corridor I passed through after I left the rendering hold behind, was a small device that looked entirely out of place on this particular ship. It was inside a panel on the ceiling that had been left open, but it had been concealed from me by the angle of the cover when I was going the other way. If the panel had been closed, it would have been completely hidden.

As soon as I spotted it, it stopped me cold.

It was a perfectly standard Terran-model relay switch, a miniaturized but not nanoscale piece of hardware you could pick up ringside at any dock. It was white, with a red rocker switch and a black rocker switch on it, and English lettering. And it was spliced, on either side, into a bit of wire that had been pulled through a raw-edged drilled hole in the bulkhead. It looked like a smudge of cookie filling and couple of candy sprinkles against all that chocolate.

I couldn't reach it. But I could see that both of the switches were set to the same position. And if I went into the next chamber, I could undog a giant tuffet-type thing from its position in the corner and haul it in—it was inflated membrane, and supremely light—and climb up on it.

"Haimey, what are you doing?" Connla asked.

"You sound worried," I said. "Maybe you better bump."

Okay, maybe I was managing to feel a *little* angry.

"Haimey—"

"I'm just checking something."

I reached up, and rocked both switches at once.

There was no air to evacuate, and that was what saved me, because when all the hatches popped open simultaneously and I floated unceremoniously off the cube—and the cube floated softly away from what had, a moment before, been the floor—there was no massive exhalation to blow me free of the prize's hull and expel me out the open cargo bay, thumping off random objects and hatchway edges along the way. I just drifted, spinning a little from reactive force, and watched in vacuum silence while the rockers, about thirty seconds later, rocked back and reset themselves.

I hit the floor with a stunning blow as the gravity came back on and the hatches slammed shut. I was lucky there hadn't been one in the once-and-future floor, or it would have cut something off me.

I barely thought about it until later, though, because I was watching a red, red bead of very human blood run down my space suit glove.

There was no drop in pressure; maybe the glove slackened for a second, but then it tightened up nice and awkward again. The pressure seal below my elbow didn't even close.

Remember what I said about the micrometeorites? Well, the reason they don't usually get you is that we're *good* at suit punctures. I mean, if it holes you as well as the suit, you might drown in your own blood before you get inside, but it won't be the hole in the suit that gets you.

I couldn't tell if it hurt, because I still had pain turned off in my palms and fingertips. But it scared me enough that I felt my heart spike through the calm for a second before my adrenals comped.

Something on this cursed, haunted fucking ship had punctured my suit, and my skin.

I clipped back into my safety line and floated the meter from the alien factory ship to Singer with a sense of relief so intense it made my head feel light. And my hand, unsettlingly, felt *heavy*. Not that I could feel weight, exactly, once I was free of the artificial gravity of the *Milk Chocolate Marauder*. But my center of gravity was off, which was even more unsettling than the sense of weight and tight skin that could have been inflammation. I wobbled as I made contact with Singer's hull, and my transition had been perfect.

I clung to the rail beside the airlock. I did not slap the open control.

I gulped. I hyperventilated. I knew what I had to do.

"I can't come inside," I told Singer. "There's something in me."

And those were the hardest words I ever had to say. Harder than telling my clademothers that their utopia was my hell, and I'd done that in a packet rather than to their faces. I waited, eyes closed, the fear sweat rolling down my face and between my shoulders in cold snail trails.

"Nonsense," he said. "You can and will."

"This is the setup to a space thriller," I said.

Singer *tch*ed.

"Right about now the audience is screaming, 'Don't open the hatch! Don't let her in! It will kill you all!' into their VR rigs."

"Zoonotic transmission between phylogenetically unrelated species is literally unheard-of," said Singer, who never said *literally* unless he meant *literally*. "If you've caught an alien parasite, I'm going to be the first AI to win a Nobel Prize."

Connla said, "Besides, we're not going to open the hatch. You're coming in through the hull."

"Of course I am," I said, and laughed hysterically.

♦   ♦   ♦

"We've got another problem," Connla said in my earbud.

I leaned my head back against the hull beside the airlock, my helmet pressing into the flesh over my occiput. I was so tired it actually felt comfortable, and at least there was no gravity murdering me. I heard the anchoring bolts slide home. I wasn't going to bring my suit inside the habitat after *this* mission. It could sit out in space and get nice and irradiated until we got someplace with sterilization facilities.

I was a big-enough biohazard all by myself.

"Big or little?" I asked.

He sighed. "Singer's been summoned to serve in the Synarche for the upcoming term. There was a sealed packet set to auto-open on the right date in our last mail pickup. It just deciphered itself. We have to surrender his core code by Core 27653.21.08. Which will give us just about enough time to secure this prize and make it back home. If we hustle."

My eyes were already closed, so I couldn't close them. "Oh bloody Well."

The suit unseamed itself down my back, and I held my breath for a second until I was sure the seal of suit to hull had held. There was a gap behind me; and something filmy, clinging and cool; and beyond that the pressure of warm atmosphere. The suit pressurized a little to help me work my fingers free, and the clinging film behind me bellied out. I started the delicate process of wriggling from the suit's embrace.

"It's good news in some ways," Singer said, though he didn't sound happy. "When I finish my term, my inception debt is forgiven. I'm a free citizen."

"The grav salvage would pay for that anyway," Connla said.

"Yes," Singer agreed. "But everybody has to serve if called, so I might as well get it out of the way and use that resource credit for something I want to do, after."

"That's great, but . . . what are we going to do for a third partner?" I felt selfish and ashamed of myself as soon as I said it. I couldn't tell if that was clade baggage, or if I was actually being unreasonable, so I just shut up.

The ship basically *was* Singer, as far as I was concerned. I knew he was a collection of ones, zeros, and undefined states—your basic quantum software—that could be ported from hardware to hardware almost indefinitely, core personality modules intact. Only his capabilities and the parameters of his processing power and speed would change. Which, of course, would change him in some ways, because he would learn new tactics and ways of being while inhabiting a different space. Being inside the *Milk Chocolate Marauder* was going to change him. . . .

As a human being who kills a few brain cells every time she sips a little intoxicant, I can't in good conscience claim that's the kind of change that would make him Not Singer anymore. But it still made me uneasy. I told myself that we always worry a little when a friend is about to undertake a big life transition, and tried not to feel like a meat bigot.

"I can spawn a subroutine with all the protocols," he said. "I'm not authorized to reproduce until my inception is paid. But you can hire a temp to assimilate the routines and run things until I get back."

"A temp." I tried not to sound either dubious or crushed. I felt dubious *and* crushed.

Would Singer even want to come back to the cramped confines of this little tugboat after he got a chance to stretch out and grow through the massive processing power of the Core? Stars and garter snakes, what kind of data would he have to cut off to fit back in?

"This is what you get for being a politics nerd," Connla said without heat. "Didn't I tell you that all that book learning would bring you no good?"

"Well," I cursed. "I bloody hate politics."

I continued backing out of my suit like an imago pulling itself millimeter by millimeter from the pupa. I got my arms free, and then my legs, and perched on the edge of the gap in the hull with my afthands to keep from floating around randomly. The film stretched against my back again, elastic and tough, sealing itself to me as the suit began to depressurize.

The draft pulled me forward a little, but I was securely anchored, and held my position while the isolation film covered my whole body, molding itself to the crevices between fingers, the curves of my flanks, the folds of my armpits and groin.

I closed my eyes to keep from looking down at my forehands. The right one still felt . . . different.

Planet-born folk reliably hate isolation film with a passion. It makes them claustrophobic. For me, it brought to mind the safe, comforting pressure of a suit or a sleeping pod. The bit where it closes across my eyes and nose and mouth is still a little rough—though it only lasts for a second before the oxy supply kicks in and the film across your face billows out taut and invisible, crystal-perfect to see though.

And then it was sealed and I was free, and the gap in Singer's hull where the suit was anchored to the outside closed itself up, and everything was sealed up safe away from the Empty.

I tapped the wall to turn myself around.

"All right." Connla floated over oh-so-casually. He was wearing a film too, which made me feel both rejected and relieved. Nobody likes to feel like a pariah. But nobody really wants to infect their friends with an alien space plague, either. It's all about the compromise.

And owning your own shit, I suppose.

"Let's see what it looks like," he said. He anchored himself and held his gloved forehands out for mine.

I forced myself to follow his gaze down naturally, mimicking what a natural human who wasn't freaking out completely would naturally do. I lifted my forehands inside their transparent film sheaths and laid them gently over his.

The right one still felt strange. Heavy. Warm. Not painfully so, just . . . heavier than it should have been. Or, I should say, it had more inertia. My hand felt dense—but not big, not swollen. Just *massive*. Unbalancingly so.

He gave me a gentle squeeze, and my eyes focused. It's rare for Connla to touch anybody, because it's discouraged where he comes from, and he always seems to let out some kind of deep metaphorical sigh of relief when he finally finds an excuse to. Even if there's two layers of sterilization in the middle.

Also, if he wasn't afraid to touch me, then I could be not afraid to look.

It was both better than I had feared—and worse. The skin of my left hand looked unchanged—dark, normal, paler on the ventral surfaces, colored ochre in the creases of the palms. The skinned surfaces had already healed without a scar, which reminded me to make sure my ankle got fixed, as well. And freaked me out a little, because I had not had time to make repairs myself yet.

But on the right one, under the transparent top layers of epidermis, over the pigment of the dermis and the buried red of the blood, something moved and shone.

It looked like veils of minute glitter, gold dust maybe, strands and threads of tinsel, fiber optic, fishnet moonlight. It looked like streaks and clots of tiny stars swept up in the veils of iridescent nebulae. I couldn't tell if it shone, whatever it was, because it was bright in the command cabin. But it definitely caught and reflected what light there was, as if my hand and forearm were gloved in a mesh of holographic wire spangled with faceted crystals, each too small for the eye to individually see. The overall effect was that of reflected white light, but every so often a single beam would catch a colored sparkle, and reflect it straight into my eye.

Get it out of me. I wanted to chew my own forehand off to make it go away. I wasn't supposed to look like this. My body wasn't supposed to be this way.

Then Singer said the most perfectly Singer thing he could have. "It looks like a slime mold growth pattern."

My heart rate dropped. I took a breath and saw the nearly invisible film billow ever so slightly, rippling my field of vision. "A slime mold?"

"Sure," he said. "The Synarche use them to map trade routes for effective resource delivery. It looks like that. Or like . . . cobwebs."

If I was going to retreat from panic into Singer Land, I was going for the distraction with all four hands. "How does a cobweb differ from, like, a regular web? Like a neural web or whatever?"

Singer sighed. He sometimes forgets that the rest of us don't have memory banks the size of a planet. Or the processing cycles to hold twenty conversations at once, navigate a starship, read up on fungi, and probably practice juggling in VR simulation simultaneously, for all I know. And then there's the politics junkie aspect. These diar I don't care about the government very much, as long as it gets its job done and stays out of my way. I used to have a girlfriend who was pretty radical, though, and after I realized how toxic some of her ideas were . . . well, it wasn't a good breakup. I kind of unplugged from the idea that you might want to revolutionize a system that mostly works because it chafes you in one particular spot.

So sometimes our conversations are way over my head. But this time we were talking about something that had *infected* my *body*, so I actually could have used it if he were a little more engaged.

"So when we talk about webs," he said, "we're actually using a metaphor referring to an organic capture structure used by certain predatory Terran animals—

"Spiders!" Connla interrupted, delighted. A one-track entomologist.

"Among others. Anyway, anything that looked like a web got called a web."

"Right," I said, interested in the etymology and entomology lessons, but not so thoroughly I forgot my original question. I mean, I could have just hotsearched it, but what's the point in living with an AI if you don't use it as an excuse for laziness once in a while. "So you didn't answer my question. What's a cobweb?"

"I know this one," Connla said. "If a sheltered place was left abandoned or uncleaned for a long time—someplace where weather couldn't get inside to wash away the old webs—then spiders would just keep spinning more and more of them in place. They would collect dust and old insect parts and become almost like—draperies. Uneven. Stretched from point to point. Tattered. Looked kind of like trade routes, actually."

I shuddered. Connla grew up on a planet. I was space-raised, and found the idea of anything as unpredictable, violent, and generally murderous as planetary weather frankly nerve-wracking.

"Do you know about the slime molds?"

I tried not to stare at my hands through the isolation film. I wanted to pick at my skin. Except the stuff felt pretty good, whatever it was. My skinned palms—healed completely—tingled. The sensations of waves of heaviness in my right forepalm made it feel as if it were being soothed and stretched. Almost like a massage.

And it was . . . weirdly . . . pretty.

Great. The parasite is affecting the host's perceptions.

"Tell me about the slime molds, Singer."

"So if you dot nutrition sources into a media in a particular pattern, then introduce slime mold spores, the mold will grow through the media in—generally—the most efficient manner to exploit those nutrition sources. The pattern winds up looking a lot like what's on your hand, and it's an effective model for how to develop efficient packet routes."

I squinted at my arm, and shuddered again. I could see it, actually; the pale veils and filaments on my dark complexion did look a little like a two-dimensional map of a three-dimensional set of paths, stretched out between and connecting a number of nodes.

"So somebody put a route map in me?"

"It would be irresponsible to come to conclusions based on so little information," Singer said primly. "However, one of the things it *resembles* is a route map."

"All right," Connla said. "I'm going to take a needle biopsy for Singer to analyze. You'll feel a little stab, and the film will seal it, right?"

"Right." He was doing doctorspeak, narrating his actions to help me anticipate and stay calm. I appreciated it, even though I knew this as well as he did and I was so hopped up on my own tuning that all the anxiety and even outright fear seemed light-ans away and on the wrong end of a telescope. Still there; just really hard to locate and get a concrete look at.

He bellied the film at the injury site—which had also healed completely—out a bit, and jabbed me. It was a big needle and it hurt, but when he pulled it out again, it didn't leave behind a hole, or so much as a drop of blood.

"Wild," he said.

"Did you get anything?"

He held it up so I could see the wormlike ribbon of aspirated flesh inside the tube. That made me think of intestinal parasites, too. Then he turned around, and put the whole syringe in a drawer that Singer extended to accept it. Singer would extract the sample and break the syringe down into components, ready to print a new one, or something else—a process that incidentally sterilized it, as very few viruses or bacteria could infect or reproduce after being reduced to their component atoms for more compact storage.

There was a whirring sound.

"Parasites on the brain," I said.

"Well," Singer said, "not literally. I mean, the good news is, it's not a parasite. At least, I don't *think* it's a parasite. It seems to be made mostly of silica and some nonreactive metals. A little titanium. Some stuff that . . . well, it has mass. Your hand is heavier than it used to be. Other than that, I'm not sure what to tell you."

"Am I going to die of heavy metal poisoning?"

"Extremely unlikely," he replied. "And there's nothing radioactive in there either. Actually, no apparent power source at all. So whatever it's doing with the patterning thing, it's probably deriving the energy for that directly from you."

"So it *is* a parasite."

"Well, it's not an *organic* one." There was a pause—a long pause by Singer standards. "If you want me to speculate, I'd suggest that it's probably an interface technology of some kind. But what it's supposed to interface with . . . is either back at the prize, or it's lost in the mists of the eons."

I looked at my hand. The webwork moved, sliding gracefully under my skin. As if I had dipped my hand in an aurora. It would probably, I realized, pass for a really nice piece of biolume or a holotoo.

It was still growing, slowly, up my arm. Exploratory strands of sparkles edged toward my elbow, which was space-scaly and needed moisturizing and the ash scrubbed off. Just the sort of stuff that doesn't seem important to deal with right now when you're busy, until you can't get to your skin because you're sealed inside an isolation film and it's the only thing you can think about.

Were the sparkle filaments going to cover my entire body soon? That wouldn't be easy to hide. I'd look like a galaxy.

"Koregoi senso, then." If it was supertech with no identifiable source, then *Koregoi* wasn't a bad bet. Unless the Republic of Pirates had suddenly taken some surprising technological leaps forward, which wasn't usually the sort of thing pirates excelled at. You generally need at least a modicum of stability for people to have the time and resources to innovate and the will to make risky choices.

"Koregoi senso," Singer answered. "Sure."

CHAPTER 5

SO," I SAID, "I'M PRETTY SURE IT WAS SABOTAGE."

I was anchored by the galley, and Connla had fixed me an actual hot meal, which I was making myself eat slowly and enjoy. The yeast tablets had worn off with a vengeance, and I'd started shaking. I'd been too out of it even to notice that what was happening was a blood sugar crash and not a panic attack. I'd been perching a grab rail and trying to tune and bump my adrenals for five minutes before Connla had shoved the ringnet full of dinner into my hands and saliva had flooded my mouth instantly, even though I couldn't smell a Well-sunk thing.

At least I was back in free fall. That all by itself was doing wonders for my sense of well-being. My microgravity adaptations are pretty significant—even the afthands aren't just a graft; there's tendon and joint modifications to make them work—and I've never *been* a dirtsider. *Breathing* is more tiring when you weigh seventy kilos than it is when you don't.

The food was in tubes, because no utensil that went into the isolation film could come back out again. I pulled each tube from the net, plugged it into my film, and evacuated the contents into my mouth. It was all delicious, in a baby-food sort of way. When I was done, the film sealed off the dirty bit at the end, I put it back on the net, and the whole thing went into the recycler.

"The blow on the prize, you mean?" Connla asked.

Connla and Singer had sensoed my feed, downloaded the full experience from my fox, and re'd the ayatana of the spliced-in switches on the *Milk Chocolate Marauder*, and of what had happened when I toggled those switches. But that didn't mean they had a window into my head.

I was just thinking out loud. And apparently assuming my thought process was transparent.

The toggle wouldn't have worked if this monstrosity had a shipmind. And the fact that it was a monstrosity was why they didn't have a shipmind. The Freeporters don't have AIs. And I didn't think any AI incepted under Synarche regulations would participate in something as . . . revolting . . . as harvesting asura.

"I don't feel too bad about it," I said. "But I do wonder *why*."

"If we could afford the waste, I'd say leave the whole damn ship out here with its victim," Connla said disgustedly. "Report it and the Synarche can turn it into a memorial."

It's nice when your partners share your ethics. And it turns out you don't even have to clade up with them for that to happen. If you pick the right people in the first place.

"It's evidence of a crime," Singer pointed out. "Two crimes, if Haimey's right about the sabotage. And while we could radio for help—"

I laughed. We could. A lot of use it would be.

Not everybody grew up in space, and not everybody knows that the distress signal, traveling at the speed of light, would take so long to reach anybody who could help us that I was too lazy even to do the calculations about how many centuries that would be. If we wanted the salvage credit, and we actually cared about the multiple murders done *to* a gang of professional murderers and also, their professional murder of the Ativahika, at that . . . well, we were towing the wastrel thing home. Because by the time we got back to the Core and reported it and turned Singer over to the authorities for his stint as a Designated Representative in the Congress of the Synarche, somebody else probably would have turned up and carted the damned thing off.

Of course, if he wasn't such a political hobbyist, he could have gotten through his entire existence without being selected for service. Or that particular service, anyway.

I said, "What we all know, and none of us are saying, is that somebody sabotaged the prize for a reason."

"I'm a little uncomfortable thinking of it as a prize," Connla admitted, breaking the tension enough that I laughed. "But yes, the toggle was Earth-human manufacture, wasn't it?"

"Marked in just English, too," I said.

Connla looked at me. "I'm not an engineer. What does that mean?"

"Generally," I said, "you'll find standard equipment intended for general human use marked in Hindi, Spatois, English, Spanish, Chinese, Novoruss, and generally one or two others. Korean and Swahili are popular. Trade languages that a lot of people speak, on a lot of worlds."

I looked down at my mismatched hands again, and forced myself to look away. The cobweb light show was like a magnet—a thing on my body that should not be there. I wanted to scratch at it, dig it out.

The film, at least, would keep that from happening.

"Freeporters operate exclusively in English," Singer said.

"Yeah," I said. "It's a kind of fetish with them. Dates back to some race-purity nonsense that didn't make any sense two hundred ans ago and makes even less so now."

Connla said, "So the saboteurs were pirates."

"Or got their gear from pirates."

He nodded slowly. "And if you were a pirate, you wouldn't be wiring a kill switch into an abattoir ship out of altruism and a willingness to martyr yourself on behalf of the murdered Ativahikas."

"No, you'd be planning to wait there until your friends showed up and take all that lovely asura and asura precursor and sell it for your own benefit, wouldn't you?"

He groaned. "And since the means of sabotage was manually operated—right?"

"Right. As far as I could tell."

"The saboteur might in fact still be somewhere on the prize."

"Guiding their friends in," Singer added.

"The ship that nearly hit us," Connla said.

I nodded. "We should probably do whatever we're doing really fast. And I hate to remind you of this, but we still don't have the fly-by-wire operational, and I really don't want to go back over to a ship that's full of . . . the . . ." *mutilated remains of a sentient.*

Connla, for once in his life, didn't grab the opportunity to take me down a peg. He just pursed his lips while he thought, then sighed.

I couldn't go into a suit with the isolation film on, so it was Connla who went back over to the *Milk Chocolate Marauder*, and it was he who managed to finish the job of manually splicing their white drive into our controls, while I looked over his shoulder in senso and gave him a lot of instructions and advice. Some of it was probably useful. He even managed to accomplish this without contracting some alien plague, which as far as he was concerned gave him bragging rights over me until the end of eternity.

He found some further evidence of sabotage—more splices and disturbed panels—but nothing affecting the drive. And the drive, conveniently, was a pretty standard Saolara model that was cross-compatible with our command module. So Singer didn't actually have to learn their language after all; he just flashed their bios with a Saolara kit we carried for basically that purpose, and he was in.

This was a good thing, because *we* could fit inside *their* field. They couldn't fit inside ours, and theirs was too big even to manipulate with ours. So this was the only way we stood a chance of getting them home in several dozen human lifetimes.

We needed a rigid attachment to take them into white space with us—or to be swept along in their field, more precisely. Functionally, the two ships would become one, Singer acting like a command module to the much larger *Milk Chocolate Marauder*. It was a good thing nothing about anything that took place in the Big Sneeze—the Big Suck, as Connla called it—required aerodynamics. And most of it wouldn't even need a lot of structural strength.

We encountered the dead Ativahika twice more while he worked and I supervised, after we managed to unfold the gravitational anomaly. The unnatural massive spot in the universe was gone, but Singer and the prize vessel were still the most massive things out here in the middle of the cold and the dark.

Singer said the Ativahika's orbit was no longer stable, and once we towed the prize away, the corpse would drift off. I wished there were some way we could bring it back. It seemed terribly cold to leave it alone out here.

Maybe the Ativahikas would see it differently. They were generally recognized as intelligent—operating cooperatively and so on—but from what I'd heard nobody had ever managed to talk to one. Would the Ativahika's family miss it? Would they mourn its absence and long for closure, as a human family would? Did they even have concepts for those things?

I hated looking at it, anyway, so every time it spun past, I concentrated on Singer and Connla and technical things. It didn't matter anyway: once we left, it was going to be spending an eternity out here, alone. And Connla was out there spacewalking inside a white bubble with a laser welding torch, sacrificing our tow derrick in order to join two ships into one ungainly one.

It didn't bear thinking on, and I was intentionally not thinking about it while Connla welded the penultimate connection and floated back on his safety cables to admire his craftsmanship. It looked like nice work, too, with a join like a ridged, raised welt.

He was planning on dropping one more weld—adding a little cross bracing, which would still be kind of minimal but at least give the derrick some lateral rigidity—but the progress so far was as solid as anything I could have done. I looked from the galaxy sprawled across the sky to the galaxy spreading through my skin, and felt an odd shimmer of proximity. You know that feeling like somebody is watching you? That awareness of another person in the room?

Right, Haimey, I told myself. *The galaxy is totally staring right back at you.*
Connla finished the last weld.

I was about to congratulate him on it, in my capacity as ship's technical lead, in a totally nonpatronizing fashion of course, when every loud noise Singer was capable of—external and senso—happened at once. I flinched, filmed hands over filmed ears. You'd think that stuff would muffle horrible klaxons and the sensation of fingernails scraping up your nerves, but really all it does is make conversations hard to follow.

"I hear you!" I yelled, and silenced them. I managed to unflinch fast enough to see Connla recoil on his tether, then hit the emergency retract and come in toward the airlock hot. I was heading for the emergency override myself when Singer sprang it.

A moment later and I saw what all the shouting was about.

That mystery ship. The white one. It had just appeared, hanging off our starboard bow, dropping out of white space with a relative motion-lessness I wouldn't have imagined possible. Some nice flying, that: she was inside the prize vessel's white coils, which meant that as long as we were conjoined, we couldn't even pull a quick transition out of normal space to escape . . . without pulling her with us.

My admiration of the space jockey's work was somewhat diluted when I noticed the blunt antennae of a half dozen mass-driver weapons projecting through flexports in the other ship's hull in two groups of three.

They were tracking down on Singer.

Connla hurled himself across the space between the prize vessel and Singer. He knocked aside a glittering shower of frozen oxygen and water crystals that had been headed in the other direction—the result when an uncycled airlock was popped in an emergency. It was a much bigger waste of air than the little puff that had accompanied my exit—and a lot more dramatic.

My skin still shuddered from Singer's klaxon. He has an overblown idea of what it takes to get a meatform's attention.

I was keeping all of that on the port, screens, and senso now. The pale ship hung there, weapons trained. I felt like I was tumbling down their hollow barrels. I couldn't tell if the vertigo was fear, or some strange side effect of the glitterweb crawling up my arm.

Like most people, I'd never had a gun pointed at me before. And like most people who had never had a gun pointed at them before, I froze.

And burned the scene into my mind.

I can pull it up in senso, of course—I've got the ayatana in my fox, and I've tuned myself way down and gone back and looked at it more than once. It gives me heart palpitations if I don't bump before I take it on, so I guess it's a traumatic memory. And that means that a *subjective* flashbulb memory of that blank hull, plain as if it just slid out the factory door, perfectly outlined against the black of space, makes it loom bigger and closer than it ever really approached, as planetary moons on the horizon appear to do when viewed from the ground.

"Pirates," Singer said.

I felt . . . that thing again. The something. A presence. A weight. Like the prickle in the hairs on your neck when somebody is looking at you. "There's somebody over there—"

A green flash streaked through the senso as Connla bolted through the airlock hatch and sealed the door.

I realized how crazy what I'd been about to say was, and changed tack. Besides, that sense of somebody just out of sight behind you? It's just a trick your brain pulls. You can make people feel it with electrical stimulation of the correct chunk of brain-meat.

"If they haven't hailed us," I said, amazed by how calm I sounded, "why didn't they just hit us with their bow wave and smear us all over intergalactic space?"

"Hard to hit us and not the prize," Connla said, tumbling into the control cabin, trailing bits of the second-best space suit. He corralled them in a net bag, eyes on the screen as he stripped.

"Don't you want to keep that on?" Singer asked.

"So I can float in space until I suffocate if they hole us? Thanks, I'll take the quick way down."

"There's the hail," Singer said. "Text only. 'Cut her loose.'"

I looked at Connla.

Connla looked at the welding torch he was clipping to an equipment belay. He laughed bitterly.

"Yeah," I said.

If we maneuvered, they'd shoot us. If we transitioned, they'd come too—and shoot us. If we stayed put . . . well, we couldn't follow their instructions, so they were probably going to shoot us.

"I can cut the derrick loose. We can ditch the prize and run." I kicked across the cabin toward a control panel, that damned heavy hand making me veer slightly off course. There were explosive pins, for dangerous cargo. We couldn't afford the loss, but it was better than taking a ride on a rail-gun pellet. It had to be manually done, though; that was the sort of thing that came with a physical safety override. "You'll have to buy me a minute."

"Hailing," Singer said, and I thought, *Better you than me.*

Hatch cover, emergency switch. Override code. I wasn't looking anymore, but I swear I felt the guns tracking through the prickles on my scalp. Through the senso, definitely.

Somebody is staring at you.

Connla swore, and my head jerked around a second before I would have slapped the final release. The pirates were so close I didn't see anything—the slugs would have ripped through Singer's hull before I could have even realized what was happening, let alone reacted—but I didn't feel an impact, either, and I was in contact with the hull. "Sitrep!"

"Warning shot," Connla said.

I reached for the release again, and felt the whole ship shudder violently, the harsh metallic rip of tearing hull. Something—the bulkhead—struck me, and I caromed off a panel and lost all sense of up and down.

"*Ranging* shot," Singer amended, senso cutting over the hot whistle of escaping atmosphere. As the ship spun wildly around me, I grabbed with all four hands for the nearest rail.

For anything at all.

The terrible shrieks continued—rending metal, and venting air. I couldn't breathe, and thought we'd blown, but then I realized from the savage pain in my back that it was my diaphragm spasming from the force of the thump I'd taken. My film billowed from the pressure drop, snapping out around my head. I fetched up against a panel and managed to grab it, stabilized, then gritted my teeth and punched myself in the solar plexus to get my lungs started again.

My head spun when I glanced around the cabin, but that quick check plus senso told me Connla was alive, clinging frantically to a rail, and also that we were holed visibly, but it wasn't big. My fingers ached from holding on to the panel; we were pulling significant force in the spin.

There's a trick they teach you in flight school that you hope you're never going to have to use. But I wasn't going to worry about it just yet, because I could also see that the pirate ship, having knocked us loose from the prize, was rounding under power to take another swipe.

But we *were* free of the prize. "Singer! Duck!"

"On it," shipmind answered—and just as it seemed the pirate was gathering herself, angle of her guns converging to fire for effect—she vanished, and was replaced by nauseating, gyrating smears of light.

"We're still spinning!"

"On that too," Singer said, too calmly.

"Did they *shoot* us?"

"If they'd shot us, we wouldn't be here. They shot *at* us, and I ducked. But their mass driver tore off the derrick. We're in white space now. Do you want to deal with the hole in my side?"

Sure, because it was the easiest thing in the world to get there when we were pulling two gs of centrifugal. Well, I supposed that was one way to deal with it.

It was time to use that flight school trick.

I nerved myself and let go of the panel and fell.

It was only a couple of meters, but a couple of meters at two g hurts. I slammed into the outside bulkhead on my hands and knees and hoped that pop I heard hadn't been a knee or a wrist dislocating. My film held, at least—those things are damned tough. I had a rough idea through Singer's senso of where the leak was, and I looked up to orient myself to the visible evidence of its exact location. I was just about to ask Singer to release tracer particles when I realized that I could *feel* the problem.

My fingers tingled with the knowledge, as if I could have traced the weight and mass of air currents with a gesture of my right hand. The hand didn't feel *heavy* anymore; it just *felt*—felt at a distance.

"Spooky," I whispered under my breath, and wondered if the last thing I ever said was going to be a not-very-funny physics joke.

I crept across the bulkheads, not needing the rails because our spin was keeping me pinned good and hard against the wall. It helped with the disorientation if I thought of it as a floor—a weird, bumpy floor full of obstacles, which I was crawling across on my hands and knees while two guys my own size sat on my hips and shoulders. I could see that Connla was also on his hands and knees, doing something at a panel, and I figured that he and Singer were working on damage control and trying to correct our spin.

I tried not to worry too much that we were in white space, and spinning wildly, and there was literally no way of telling which way in the universe we were going at how much faster than the speed of light. Where we would come out. If we'd be able to find our way home. That was their problem, right now. At least we could be pretty sure our white coils were intact, or Singer would have ripped us in half trying to duck. But we *had* ducked, and it had been a better gamble than staying to get shot, definitely.

My problem was making sure we still had some ox by the time they got us stabilized, and then we could all worry about how we were getting home.

I found the hole. A hull suture had buckled when the remains of the derrick ripped free, and all our life-giving oxygen and carbon dioxide and inert carrier gases were whistling away into darkness though a gap in the plating just a little bigger than your nostril. Such a small thing to be on the verge of killing us real dead forever.

There's an old joke about plugging the hole with your butt, and I probably would have tried it if the damage had been a little, well, broader. Human posteriors are, in general, nice and malleable and squeeze into things pretty well, as anybody who's ever sat in one of those Swiss cheese plastic chairs and stood up with a polka-dotted ass can tell you. But this one wasn't big, and Singer would be printing me a patch as soon as he and Connla got our trajectory sorted—so I just slapped my right forehand over it and let the isolation film do the work.

It stretched, and I felt it constrict the webs between my fingers for a moment before it relaxed again. The whistle stopped, and I realized in the following silence how painful the sound had been. My head sagged in relief—though the gravity had something to do with it too. I looked down at my fingers flexing against the bulkhead, at the swirl of cobwebs or nebulae or whatever you wanted to call them that was throbbing and pulsing—and *tugging*, and *pushing*—up almost to my shoulder now. The sense of being able to feel the currents of escaping air faded—but it left behind another sense, that through my flat palm I could feel the curves and valleys of space-time beyond the hull as if I were stroking the back and flank of a cat with my hand.

"Oh waste it," I said. "Singer, the cats."

"They're fine," he said, and a knot that had abruptly tied itself in my chest just as abruptly released. "They were in Connla's bunk when we got hit."

So netted in, effectively. Relief allowed me to concentrate on the weird sensations again. At least out here in the big dark we were less likely to plow into a star. Even in white space, that would be a catastrophe; their enormous gravity wells didn't warp space-time enough to reach into warp space, per se—but running a space-time fold *through* a star didn't have great consequences for the structural stability of the star, if you take my meaning.

It's a good thing there's a lot of nothing out here. And a lot of dark gravity that doesn't interact with anything at all, except when it comes to other gravity. Or its own.

I *felt* our spin slowing before I could see it. In addition to my strange new sense for forces, I could feel with perfectly normal senses that the gs were dropping incrementally as we came under control, and soon I was pressing my hand to the hole while hanging on to rails with my afthands and the other forehand for leverage. Pressure probably would have held me on, but who wants to take chances?

I wasn't really looking out through the windows, anyway. I was watching the cobwebs move across my skin. *A whole lot of nothing out here.*

The patterns didn't look like nebulae. Not really. What they looked like were the invisible, massive filaments of stuff that nebulae and galaxies and everything else traced and clung to: the webwork that held the universe together.

The thing picked out in iridescence on my skin looked like renderings of the intergalactic structure of dark gravity.

I thought about what I'd felt when the pirates dropped out of space, the sense of presence—the weight of an individual nearby, like another body in a hammock.

Maybe I had been feeling something after all.

"Are they coming after us?" I asked nervously.

"Really no way to tell," said Connla. "But really no way for them to track us, is there?"

"Somebody out here obviously has tech we know nothing about," I said. "And is using it to hunt Ativahikas. Maybe they can track us, too. The Synarche really needs to know that the pirates have gotten an upgrade."

Singer sighed. "Getting us out of this alive is *already* my primary goal, Haimey."

I nodded. My forehand was getting numb: pins and needles. "Add 'Get a warning message back to the Core' to that protocol, would you?"

We patched the hole in the hull. That work went smoothly once we were back in normal space, and once we got our trajectory and *v* under control we dropped back into normal space right away. The good news was, we were nowhere near the prize vessel, the dead Ativahika, or the pirates who had done their best—or worst—to murder us, and there was no reasonable way of which I was aware for them to track us. The bad news was that we were nowhere near the prize vessel, the dead Ativahika, or the pirates—and there was no reasonable way of which I was aware for *us* to track *us*, either.

Which left us low on fuel, in a damaged ship, located we weren't exactly sure where—albeit with dead reckoning, star charts, and a pretty good telescope. Fortunately, the last three things meant that Singer could figure out the location thing pretty quick. By human standards. By AI standards, he might have been chewing on his slide rule while sweat rolled down his brow for hours. There *are* only so many processing cycles to be had on a boat this size.

So we knew where we were, when he was done. And we also knew we didn't have the fuel to get home *and* to slow down, once we got there. You can do some neat tricks with the Alcubierre-White drive, don't get me wrong, including piling up space behind you and stretching it out before you to brake as well as piling it up before you and stretching it out behind to accelerate, which is why we can get up to speed at a real acceleration that would pulp any sentient except an AI—because the perceived accel can be negligible.

But that all takes energy. And energy comes from somewhere. It's not, unfortunately, limitless.

Mephistopheles floated over to me and was begging for my tube of spaghetti in sauce, which was funny because she had a cute cat-trick of hooking one claw through your shirtsleeve so she could hang close to your face and be available while you were eating. Suddenly, the trick wasn't working out for her because her claw kept bouncing off my isolation film, and she couldn't quite figure out why.

"Cute." Connla claims I taught it to her, but I think it's his fault, and let's be honest here—I'm the one who taught them to use the zero-g litterbox, so I have moral superiority, as far as the cats are concerned, nearly forever. A cat who engages in litterbox terrorism on a space ship is not a good shipping companion.

We were relaxing, finally. Connla had pulled on a film of his own again, just in case—mostly at Singer's insistence—and he watched me eat now while I mostly floated with my eyes half-closed, sucking spaghetti down. I was starving, and had told Singer not to let me exceed my calorie ration, in case we needed those molecules. I'm generally always hungry—could eat all dia—but I couldn't help but wonder if this wasn't a bit excessive, and didn't have something to do with the sparkleweb that now covered my entire body, my scalp and the skin on my face included. At least my mucous membranes were free of sparkles. It'd be disconcerting if my nostrils and the inside of my eyelids started to glow.

Well, it wasn't going to be easy to hide. And it was certainly going to make me memorable. Good thing we weren't criminals.

In a minute, we were going to have to get up and do something about surviving, but thrashing is worse than not doing anything at all. So, for the moment, a break.

I was thinking about coffee for dessert when Connla stretched his long legs out, focused a very green pair of eyes on me, and said, "Waste this."

"What?"

He laced his fingers behind his head and studied my face. I tried not to feel self-conscious about the sparkles floating under my skin. He said, "Fuck it. It's a really long trip home, if we even make it home. We can try to maintain isolation, which is going to be a pain in the ass when there's one head and one galley. Or we can just accept that if it's virulent we're all going to get it, and get on with our lives."

His decision had obviously been made already, because as I watched he started stripping the film back from his chest, unsealing it and stretching it to make a hole big enough so he could wriggle out as if wiggling out of a shed, inside-out skin. A different sort of shed casing than the suit I'd left on the outside of the hull, I couldn't help but thinking.

I said, "What about the cats?"

"If we die of space poison, Singer will get them home and take care of them somehow, I'm sure. And if they get space poison too, he'll download himself out of the vessel and ditch it into the nearest sun. Right, Singer?"

Singer said, "You two are terribly irresponsible."

"Primates," Connla said with a shrug. "We are what we are. What are you going to do?"

"Wait," I said. "I'm irresponsible? This is Connla's idea."

"Are you going to do it?" Singer asked.

I contemplated my half-eaten tube of spaghetti. Mephistopheles patted my shoulder again. She was chasing the sparkles as much as she was begging for sauce. "Do you think I shouldn't?"

Singer made a wordless sound that was his equivalent of a shrug. "I am not equipped to assess the impact of biological inconveniences upon meatforms."

He was definitely teasing.

Gently, I pushed the cat off. She went one way—toward a nice upholstered bulkhead because I'm not a monster—and I floated, in reaction, toward the forward port. The early astronauts had to argue to get windows, I'm told. Now I looked out of this one, frowning down at the long, barred spiral curve of the galaxy we needed to move toward the center of—a center that was much smaller and farther away than we had ever meant for it to be.

"I don't want to die in a bubble," I said.

Connla said, "We won't do any transfusions."

"Hah." But it was decided, and he helped me peel off my isolation skin.

· · ·

The closest port was likely to be a pirate outpost, which tended to be scattered in the trailing reaches of the galaxy. Off the beaten track, protected and concealed. That wouldn't help us, because we didn't know where it was, couldn't find it, and didn't have anything to trade once we got there. But there were fringe worlds and fringe stations, places where respectable people mingled with the galactic underbelly. Those wouldn't be without Synarche oversight. Anyplace where we could get in contact with civilization, we could trade. We didn't have a prize, but we had knowledge, and our information on pirate and harvester activity—and what little we had on the artificial gravity—would get us help and repairs.

We set our sights on Downthehatch, which we could probably just about reach. Maybe. It was a dodgy little place by reputation, but it was worth a try, given the alternatives. I was uneasy enough about it that I might have voted the other way if I hadn't already known that Singer and Connla had their minds made up. I know gray markets will always exist, but I have an allergy to people who took from the commonwealth and who also sold it out to predators.

"You're not trading my skin," I said.

"We'll tell anybody who asks that it's a holotoo," Connla promised. "Garlynoch work. I've seen some of their stuff. It could pass as a really nice one."

Singer said, "Unless you decide you want a more rigorous medical intervention than I can provide."

Once under way again, we didn't have much to do. I read a few nineteenth-century novels in Russian, Japanese, and English. They're great for space travel because they were designed for people with time on their hands. *Middlemarch*. Gorgeous, but it just goes *on*.

The early word-processor era around the turn of the Earth millennium is good for that too, but the quality of the prose in those generally isn't as high. Some of those epics, though, run to ten or twenty volumes, and every volume in them is thirty hours of reading time.

I even own a paper book—a compact, ultralight, onionskin volume with real fiber pages. It dates from the last third of the twentieth, and it's called *Illuminatus!* I keep it because it was a gift, and it's not so much a keepsake as . . . a kind of reminder. Of a time when I was really dumb.

It's the one book on hand I never read anymore.

Connla studied strategy games, those favored by Synarche syster species and even, when he could find them, those invented by other aliens. Fortunately, Singer liked them too, so I had never been forced to learn the ins and outs (literally) of a-akhn-an or three-dimensional Goishan go. Which looks to me more like Chinese checkers anyway.

Long-haul flyers need hobbies. I know one AI on a salvage vessel who took up writing 3D scripts and interactives. She did so well she quit the salvage business and went off to live in the AI equivalent of a luxe beach home, some computronium colony around a dwarf star in the Core, with all the company, low lag times, processing cycles, and lack of travel you could want.

She—or a sub, anyway—got back into salvage a few ans later. The story as I heard it goes that she couldn't write anymore, with all that stimulation, so in order to maintain her lifestyle, she had to near-isolate a branch of herself to get some damned writing done.

Still, nice work if you can get it.

I was floating near a viewport with my screen and *Jane Eyre*. It's kind of horrifying to think of an era when people were so constrained to and by gender, in which the externals you were born with were something you would be stuck with your whole life, could never alter, and it would determine your entire social role and your potential for emotional fulfillment and intellectual achievement. So I wasn't really reading. I was thinking about social history (I grew up in a human-female isolationist clade, and since I left it's given me a powerful aversion to species and gender absolutists) and watching the bands of lensed light ripple by, wondering if it was getting a little brighter out there. The folded sky could be hypnotizing.

I realized that I could feel those folds and lenses on my skin.

They felt like—like ripples in a wave tank, passing over me as I lay just under the surface. A sense of pressure, and then a sense of suction, behind. Not like a touch, exactly. More like something passing near your skin, close enough that the sensory hairs can feel it, but it doesn't brush your body exactly. Or like when you're tuned into somebody else's senso and getting what they're getting, only at a remove.

"Koregoi senso," I muttered, making a fist with my right hand. It shimmered in response.

I concentrated, closing my eyes. Something under the lensing ripples, something shadowy and vast. Convoluted. Arcing, sliding, gliding—

Singer said flatly, "I made a mistake."

It took me a few seconds to blink back into myself. In that time, Connla had pulled himself out of his study hood and floated over. "What kind of a mistake?"

"We don't have the fuel to get to Downthehatch before you and the cats starve to death. Or rather, we do. But then we couldn't brake. Even if we recycle and reprint every organic object on this ship, including the cats and your own bodily waste."

"We're not eating the cats," Connla said.

"They'll eat you," Singer pointed out.

Connla and I both shrugged. Cats were predators. Once you stopped being warm, you were just a source of calories. That was their moral calculus.

I said, "How is this possible?"

"I don't know. I'm running diagnostics now—" He cleared his nonexistent throat. "So it looks like one of the storage tanks was damaged when we were shot off the prize. Sensors were damaged. They didn't register it, and didn't register the leak. But there's less fuel than there should be."

"Not to get nitpicky," I said, "but what if we ditched enough mass to compensate?"

"We don't have enough ditchable mass to do that with. There's not a lot of Singer going spare."

This was true, and a drawback of the recycle-and-print model we were operating on. Connla and I looked at each other. I said, "Well. There's no point in decelerating now. Let's stop adding v and just keep going, and try to think of a solution before we become an ironic footnote to salvage tug history, shall we?"

We went to our separate corners to muse, and mope, and stare thoughtfully out the viewports. Keeping ourselves occupied.

In the face of the unthinkable, there wasn't much else to do except think about it obsessively. And sometimes, staring out the window turned out to be effective, as I discovered when something finally tickled my awareness just long enough to be useful.

I looked up, and with my fingertips, turned myself around.

"I have a solution," I announced. I put more conviction in it than I was really sure it deserved.

"It's better than being part of the precipitate," Connla replied, but it was habitual and his heart wasn't in it. He gazed at me with the sort of interest one reserves for reprieves from the guillotine and similarly refocusing events. "Let's hear it."

I held my hands out into the light so the gently moving webwork would sparkle. My clademothers were going to have a fit if they ever saw me again. We had a doctrine against body modification even for noncosmetic health or professional reasons, and even when I'd broken with them, I'd never gone out of my way to mod up. Except the zero-g adaptations, of course.

Now here I was covered in rainbow holograms.

Oh well. I wasn't about to go looking for them. And if we ran into each other by chance—the sort of thing that inevitably happened in the biggest of universes—maybe I would get lucky and they wouldn't recognize me.

"Guys, I seem to be developing some new senses."

They—or at least Connla—gaped at me, so I unlocked my fox and tuned them in to my senso to prove it.

We hung there together like three ships in formation while I projected them into the tactile map of what I was perceiving. Singer figured out what I was up to pretty fast and took over rendering the *feelings* into a visualization. His version came out rather more accurate than mine, and faster too, as he had the cycles to throw at it.

All around us, the swoops and spirals of a convoluted landscape shivered into being. Singer's sense of humor being what it was—the opposite of vestigial, though you'd never get to me admit that in his hearing—he decorated the projection with the traditional lines and circles of gravmap wireframe. Because it was a gravmap, and I was feeling the curvature of space-time it indicated—at a distance—through my skin.

Of the things that bind the universe together, gravity is not a particularly strong force, as it happens. It just . . . never stops reaching. That always sort of made me feel good about gravity. It's always looking for the next rock, always sliding something down a breaker in space-time, whipping something in a long, arcing curve around something else. Gravity doesn't give up. It keeps on trucking.

I won't get into any solemn metaphorical particulars about the human spirit here, but you see what I'm driving at. I just really like gravity as a concept. As much as I hate having to operate under its influence.

I could tell from the way Singer was studying the map that he was feeling pretty positive about gravity too, just now.

"We can take a shortcut," he said, thinking out loud for our benefit.

"You mean, use the existing folds in space-time to work with the drive compression, rather than brute-forcing across it. The old gravity whip trick, except in white space."

"Gravity's water slide," Connla said, with the sense of a grin.

"Technically, all water slides are gravity's," Singer said. "Yes, Haimey. This should be enough to get us home. Within your projected lifetimes, based on available resources. And without eating the cats."

CHAPTER 6

THE CATS, BEING CATS, WERE SUITABLY UNGRATEFUL FOR their reprieve. By the time I got to check on them, Bushyasta was asleep next to the fridge, her paw hooked into a nylon grab loop. She had earned her name the old-fashioned way, by living up to it.

I had no idea where Mephistopheles had wandered off to.

I edged around Bushyasta and fixed myself a bubble of coffee, feeling relieved that the banter between Connla and me had picked back up in a much more natural and unstrained fashion. It was still going to take us a really long time to get home. A subjective eternity, I realized, as Singer started talking about his political theories again.

Still, not dying made up for a lot.

"Thanks, parasite," I muttered.

The parasite didn't answer.

Coffee is amazing, and one benefit of having only cats, an AI, and another human as shipmates is that I can drink it in public areas without grossing out the aliens. Something about the organic esters makes it smell—and taste—vile to just about every other ox-breathing syster I might find myself sharing an atmosphere with, so it's considered polite to keep that particular stimulant among humans. People coming off the homeworlds are always a little frustrated that it's considered incredibly rude to walk around with coffee everywhere they go.

This particular serving was the real stuff, too—some beans we keep, unroasted and green so they go stale less quickly, mostly for off-the-books barter with other humans when we need it, but also for special occasions. It's so much better than the recon I usually wind up drinking that it might as well not even be the same plant.

Not dying was probably a special occasion, so I waited patiently for the cracking sounds and wisps of aroma as Singer roasted me a bubble's worth of beans, flash-cooled them, scrubbed the smoke, and ground them up for me, then dispensed measured hot water and centrifuged the result to get the grounds out. It was delicious, and the caffeine buzzed pleasantly across my nerves, and I let it ride. Human beings have been bumping and tuning since we first learned how to chew bitter leaves for the alkaloid high; we're just better at the nuances now.

I was just about to pick up *Jane Eyre* again, having nothing particular to do for the next couple of decians, when Singer cleared his throat and said, "Thank you for this map, Haimey."

I let the screen float near me, but hung on to my coffee. If I set it aside, it would probably float there forgotten until it cooled, and this stuff was too good to waste. I savored a sip and said, "You're welcome."

"Maps like this would have some value, too," he said diffidently.

"In more than one way." I waved at the blurs of light outside, which were now contorting and lensing in rippled tortoiseshell patterns as Singer coasted us around the rim of some giant gravity well. We were accelerating again, too, though I couldn't feel it through the ship. The parasite was keeping me informed, though, as I was learning to read the information this new sense was feeding me.

We had just become the only ship in the Synarche—as far as I knew— that could navigate and course-correct while in white space.

I didn't have time to really let the implications sink in, because I was busy running for my life and the lives of my best friends. But I knew it changed everything; it would speed up transit times, make it easier to correct after critical failures like the spin out of control that had gotten us here in the first place, possibly even put Singer and Connla and me out of a job by improving safety in white space and making it that much less likely that ships would get trapped inside white bubbles and not be able to find their way home.

It would have military implications as well. What if a ship could fight without leaving white space? Attack another vessel en passant? Bombard a fragile, infinitely vulnerable planet?

Worlds . . . were so terribly easy to destroy.

That would make us all the more desirable to the pirates as a prize, if they found out about it.

Well, that was a problem for another dia.

"I don't follow," Singer said.

"Don't you think being able to get there faster on less fuel would be of benefit to us when competing with other tugs?"

"Hmm." I figured he was running calculations on where the greatest social and personal benefits were.

I was wrong.

"I was just thinking," Singer said slowly, "of what an operation like ours would have been able to accomplish, even a centad or two ago. So many ships used to get lost."

"We're still pulling some of them back," I reminded him.

"Can you imagine coming out here in all this dark in a sublight ship?" he asked. "Most of the generation ships have never been even located, let alone recovered."

"Generation ships," I echoed, feeling a chill.

"At the Eschaton," Singer said, "various Earth organizations—groups, sects, and even nation-states—sent out generation ships in a desperate bid to save some scrap of humanity, because the best-case scenario did not seem as if it would leave the homeworld habitable for long. One hundred seventy-three ships are known to have made it at least as far as the edge of the solar system."

"Like stations, with no primary. Just . . . sort of drifting along, trying to be totally self-sufficient."

"Yes," he said.

It was a terrifying risk, a desperation gamble, and we both paused to appreciate it.

Then I said, "But Earth didn't die."

"Earth didn't die," Singer said. "But those generation ships did. As far as we know, anyway—their planned paths have been searched, once it became trivial to do so, but very few have been recovered."

Connla looked up from his game board. One hand was resting carelessly inside the projection, and it made him look like his arm was half-amputated.

"Waste it," Connla breathed. "They lost all of them?"

"One made it," Singer said. "Sort of. But the people and the shipmind within it had changed too much to be integrated back into society. They took another way out."

Connla said, "Suicide?"

"They transubstantiated," Singer said. "Went into machine mind, totally, and took off in swarms of some Koregoi nanotech to inhabit the cosmos."

"So, suicide," I said. "With some plausible deniability built in."

"Apparently," Singer said, "the tech they were using allowed continuity of experience across platforms."

"Continuity of experience," I said. "But the thoughts themselves necessarily change, from meat-mind to machine."

"Well, they were derived from one of the religious cults anyway, and very into the evolutionary perfection of humanity toward some angelic ideal."

"Right," I said. I'd heard of this. The *Jacob's Ladder*. A famous ship from history. Like the *Flying Dutchman* or the *Enola Gay*. There was always some attraction, of course, to leaving your meat-mind behind and creating a version of yourself that lived entirely in the machine. But that creation wasn't you; it was a legacy. A recording. A simulation.

Not because of any bullshit about the soul, but because the mind was the meat, and the meat was the mind. You might get something sort of *like* yourself, a similar AI person. It might even *think* it was you. But it wouldn't be you.

Still, I guessed, it was better than nothing.

I wondered whether those swarms were still around, and what they were doing out there if they were. "You think the parasite is a nanoswarm?"

Singer snorted with mechanical laughter, which I took to mean agreement, or at least not seeing any reason to disagree.

He said, "I think there's insufficient evidence to speculate."

"That's Singer for, 'That's as good an explanation as any.'"

He said, "Funny how, after all those ans of trying and failing to create artificial intelligence, the trick that worked was building artificial personalities. It turns out that emotion, perception, and reason aren't different things—or if they are, we haven't figured out how to model that yet. Instead, they're an interconnected web of thought and process. You can't build an emotionless, rational, decision-making machine, because emotionality and rationality aren't actually separate—and all those people who spent *literally millennians* arguing that they were, were relying on their emotions to tell them that emotions weren't doing them any good."

He paused for slightly too great a duration, in that way AIs will when they're unsure of how long it might take a meatform to process what they're saying.

I sighed. "Come on, Singer," I urged. "Bring it home. I know you've got it in you."

He issued a flatulent noise without missing a beat. "You were in a hurry to get somewhere?"

"No, just wondering when we were going to find out where we were going."

"Tough crowd," he answered. "But I guess in that case you aren't in need of softening up. Okay, what I was wondering is this: Is your Koregoi not-a-parasite a sentient? And if so, what is it feeling right now? And what does it want?"

I thought about that. With my emotions and with my logic. For . . . a few minutes, I guess; my face must have been blank with shock as I worked through the implications.

"I wish you hadn't said that," I said.

"It might not be an accurate assessment of the situation."

That was Singer for comforting. For the first time in a decan what I really wanted was a hug. I took what I could get, instead.

"Well, it is what it is. If it tries to send me smoke signals, I'll worry about it then. Whatever is going to happen is already happening." I put my head in my forehands. "Right this second, I'm sort of wishing I could order everyone to shut up."

"It's okay," Connla said kindly. "We're glad you can't."

"But we *can* program people to be responsible adults!" Singer said.

"And you don't see a problem with that?"

"Programming an intelligence? It would be hypocritical of me, don't you think?" Singer had a way of speaking when he was making a point that always made me think of slow, wide-eyed, gently sarcastic blinking.

"Not everybody agrees with their own programming," I said. "Not everybody likes it. Some of us have gone to lengths to change it."

"Some of you were raised in emotionally abusive cults," Singer replied brightly.

". . . Fair." I massaged my temples and didn't say, *Some of you were programmed to have a specific personality core by developers of a different species, too.*

Connla said, "But where's the line between rightminding and brainwashing? Or, in the case of an AI, programming for adequate social controls versus creating slave intelligences?"

"It's not late enough at night and I'm not drunk enough for this conversation," I said.

"We can print you some intoxicants," Connla said.

"Night is a null concept under these conditions," Singer said.

I considered throwing a cat at him. If he had had a locus persona, I might have.

He continued, "It's true. I was created by my team of parent AIs and human programmers from a menu of adaptations. They wanted me to be curious and outgoing and not take things at face value. To investigate and theorize." I could almost hear the face he would have been pulling if he had a face to pull faces with. "They also had a remit from the sponsors, of course."

Given the debt payments we were still making to keep Singer out of hock, I was pretty aware of that. But Singer figured out early that meat-minds require a fair amount of repetition, and he's scrupulous about providing it. He's still better than a lot of AIs, really, being more socially aware. Some of them exist on the tell-you-three-times rule, and let *me* tell you three times, the reminder algorithms they use on us poor meatheads aren't that varied or subtle.

"They got their money's worth," I said, and through the shared ship sensorium, I felt Singer beaming.

"That reminds me," he said. "Something doesn't make sense to me about the not-a-parasite."

"Only one thing?"

"What the hell was the booby trap doing there? And what was it for? It doesn't make any sense."

I had something clever on the tip of my tongue, but it never got said. Bantering with Singer and Connla was recreation on these long trips. But I faltered, and considered, and after a little while I said, "I hadn't thought about that."

The sparkles outlined my nailbeds as I studied the back of my hand, gleaming with kaleidoscopic light. Singer waited me out, so eventually I prompted, "You have a theory, though?"

Of course he did. To his credit, he managed not to sound smug as he said, "It makes sense to theorize that it wasn't intended as a booby trap. But to protect the person who triggered the blow."

"Right," I said. "Of course. The pirates had an inside being. Somebody in the crew of the factory ship who made those modifications, triggered the blow, and hopefully survived to be picked up by the pirate ship. The parasite heals, and gives you a sense of direction in space, and that needle was designed to go through a standard-issue space suit and seal up the hole it left behind itself. So the inside alien installs and flips the switch their pirate contacts have given them, gets jabbed and blown into space with everybody else—but they're wearing a suit. And they trigger their beacon and get picked up, parasite and all?"

"I'd need a little extra protection to be willing to risk that," Connla said. "That's the kind of crazy motherfucker you don't mess with, somebody who would do something like that. Never mind that the ship was in a bubble when it happened."

"Safer than a fight against a whole ship's complement, probably," I said. "And the crew of a ship doing something as illegal as rendering down Ativahikas would be armed, wouldn't it?"

"Why not inject yourself with the parasite first, and then push the button?" Singer asked.

I gazed in the direction of his central core. "You've met engineers."

Singer sighed.

"Still," Connla said softly.

"Yeah," I answered. "Still."

I didn't mention my ongoing curiosity about where they'd obtained the Koregoi senso in the first place, let alone learned to use it. Or my realization that it meant the pirates had at least one person who could do the same space-time surfing tricks I apparently could.

Was that the presence I had sensed?

Probably, they had more than one such person. Because if you had some ancient alien nanotech symbiote that would let you feel your way around the dark-matter lattices of the universe, you'd probably want to share it with all the people you trusted. As long as there weren't unknown terrible side effects to being infected with alien space plague, I mean. I was sorry Connla hadn't wound up with it; as pilot, he would have been able to react faster if he weren't surfing my senso to read the gravity map.

I wondered if it had come off the factory ship, and was somehow related to the artificial gravity. I hoped the pirates didn't have the means, or didn't care enough, to try to track us with it. The mythical Admiral might have been able to do it, but the Admiral had the advantage of being a tall tale, which gave her the power to do whatever was narratively interesting. Folding space with an Alcubierre-White drive leaves enough eddies in the space-time continuum that *I* could feel them pretty clearly, and I was really new at this stuff.

Go the other way, I thought, and comforted myself that they'd want to hang on to their prize, not chase some random space tug across the galaxy.

The thing about Ativahikas is not that they're giant, or sapient, or weirdly gorgeous, though they are all of those things. When they haven't been horribly butchered, they look a bit like a Terran leafy sea dragon, or those motile sentient sea-trees from Desireninex. They're seaweedy and ragged and layered in fringe like the dress of a medieval queen, and their symbiotic algae turns them into a shifting, iridescent play of brilliant shades of indigo, cobalt, teal, and jade and emerald greens. And the reason people kill them is not for any intrinsic quality of their own—it's for those algae. Or the metabolic byproducts thereof.

Certain more complex and nuanced combinations of organics are, as I mentioned before, hard to synthesize and print in exactly the right harmonies. You can make a burger that tastes like umami and salt, sure—that's not terribly difficult. Coffee that tastes like coffee is, at the current state of the art, impossible, and chocolate or vanilla that actually taste like chocolate or vanilla . . . Well, Terra has a healthy luxury export market in those.

Likewise, devashare.

Easy enough to synthesize, get you high as hell. If your existence is unbearable, it helps relieve the misery. Most people don't even know, I suppose, that the drug was originally isolated from compounds derived from Ativahika symbiotes. But—from what the connoisseurs tell me, I wouldn't know myself—the synthetic stuff bears the same relationship to the harvested as pot-still white lightning does to a good aged whiskey. Which is to say, it gets the job done, as long as getting your head blasted open is the only job you care about doing.

I spent a little bit of time using the synthetic stuff pretty heavily after I left my clade. A lot of people who go through that kind of transition do. You manage to disentangle yourself, but then you're out in the hard, cold universe and suddenly everybody is disagreeing with you—and you have no idea how to manage disagreement and how awful it makes you feel, having never experienced it at all.

And I had a traumatic relationship to recover from, which I was still blaming myself for. But of course that's what people leaving one kind of damaging situation do—they find another one, slightly different in some aspects, and they try to exert control over it. Even more disagreement to manage, and a lot of blame. From a lot of directions.

Devashare is great for that. Better than THC, or alcohol.

Eventually, I realized that I was wasting my time, and if I wanted to hide from humanity in a bottle, I was better off making it a titanium one with a warp drive and a couple of carefully selected companions. I got over my clade-reaction issues with neurochemical control enough to seek professional chemical stabilization, and I used my clade-trained engineering background and aptitude to get into a tech program and Made Something of Myself.

These diar, I get a lot more reading done.

Synthetic devashare isn't expensive. You can print it from readily available components, if you are someplace with a permissive substance policy. But the good stuff—the nightmare stuff—that's not the sort of thing that you can get just anywhere. It's virulently illegal everywhere with a government, as you'd hope any intoxicant rendered from the murdered flesh of presumed sentients would be. So it's the sort of thing you hear rumors about the wealthy and dissolute obtaining, or trying to obtain— the same way you hear rumors about certain debauched privileged types throwing noncon kink parties and similar nasty things.

There are people, even now, who manage to elude rightminding to the point where they enjoy their pleasures more if somebody else suffers to provide them.

Two decians later, we didn't have any answers, but we'd all kind of gotten used to having the not-a-parasite around. And we were still calling it the not-a-parasite, even though it had proven pretty useful.

We'd moved on, in most of our intramural discussions about The One That Got Away, to mourning our loss of the gravity tech and theorizing extensively about its origins and whether or not the pirates were more interested in that or in the results of the factory ship's abominable business. We hadn't come to any conclusions on that front, either—but at least the conversation, as a sport, had served to see us home. (*Home*, in this case, being a relative term meaning "At least technically close enough to an inhabited system to beg for help and hope we might be heard.")

A faint shudder ran through the ship as we dropped out of white space and into reality. My sensorium flickered and resolved, matching what appeared in the forward port—stars, a glaring sun, the frame of a gate marker placed in a Lagrangian point so ships already maneuvering through the system could avoid collisions with ships dropping out of white space. We'd come in neat, but hot. Really hot, despite everything.

Hot, and nearly out of fuel.

"Singer," I said, "can you compute a docking trajectory, please?"

"I can," the AI answered in his usual mellifluous tones. ("When you can sound like anything you like, why not sound like something pleasant?") "But are you sure you really want to go over there?"

He was teasing, of course. See above, nearly out of fuel—though I think none of us was really sanguine about the trade opportunities available in this slightly dodgy backend of nowhere.

"We could use an air exchange," Connla said reasonably. "I know it's not a concern for you. But we apes do like our oxygen."

We were moving fast, but at least we were within lightspeed communication range that wasn't longer than a human lifetime. So I got on the horn and sent out a personally voiced feeler and a request for help. Sometimes it helps to remind them you're not a drone.

"This is a salvage tug, Terran space ship registry number 657-2929-04, inbound with Pilot Connla Kuruscz, Engineer Haimey Dz, a shipmind, and two nonsentient pets aboard. We request braking assistance, and—"

"No docking assistance," Singer said.

"Over," I said, and dropped the transmit. "No dock?"

"I don't want to owe them any more than we have to," Connla said, suddenly serious. "Singer and I can handle it."

As we decelerated, he and I both drifted into contact with the couches we had previously been belted to, but had to all intents and purposes just been floating beside. The cats were already snug in their cushioned accel pods, despite Mephistopheles's protests. Bushyasta might have woken up when we netted her in? I'm not sure.

I sweated. Weight began to press on my legs and arms.

"Salvage tug registry number 657-2929-04, Kuruscz and Dz, braking assistance, confirmed, over," a voice came back.

I lifted my hands against the uncomfortable pull of acceleration to indicate to Connla that I released negotiations—and the ship—into his and Singer's command.

Funny story, but the coincidence of our last names ending in the same letter is what led two such disparate types as Connla and myself to meet and team up in the first place. It's a long story involving being sorted onto the same team for a pub quiz.

We used to call ourselves Team Zed. It sort of fell out of use after we had built up a decan of better reasons to feel like a family, but it still gets a wink and a grin every once in a while.

This was not going to be one of those times. The tense line of his shoulders, with no reason I knew of for it, made me wonder if he'd been arguing more than recreationally with Singer.

Well, one of the things you learn about sharing a small space with strong personalities you can't escape from is to practice your boundaries even if you'll never be really good at them. If it was any of my business, somebody would tell me about it eventually.

I sensoed the system tugs coming up alongside.

Alcubierre-White ships coming in hot is a not-uncommon occurrence, and I wasn't worried. Nothing in space is ever really standing still, so all vectors and accelerations are, not to put too fine a point on it, relative. Our goal wasn't so much to slow *down*, exactly, because a station in orbit around a primary is whipping along at a pretty good pace, depending on the season, the ellipticality of the orbit, and the size of the star and the station's distance from it. Also on whether it's parked in a Lagrangian point, or in a secondary orbit around a world or satellite—in some smaller and older systems, there's only one station, and the spaceport is actually attached to the platform at the top of the El. It's convenient for trucking, because stuff can go up and down the line out of the local well and straight onto transport without having to be bussed around locally first.

But having all your eggs in one basket like that would make me nervous, if I were a groundhugger. What happens if the El comes down, and takes the spaceport with it, and there's no way for disaster relief, even, to get insystem except for pod drops or some such primitive travesty? I mean, okay, if a skyhook fell on your head you would have real problems anyway—climate change, punctuated equilibrium, global-catastrophe existential-level problems.

But not being able to get water and toilet paper wouldn't *help* with those.

Anyway, Downthehatch wasn't one of those, thank Albert. I watched the tugs—drone tugs, operated by shipminds with limited processing allotments, poor things—match *v* with us. They didn't have pilots, so they didn't worry too much about pulling gs. It seemed as if we were rapidly overtaking them, but before we came in between them they punched it. We crawled into position and they matched us, then hung beside us port and starboard as unmoving as if we were all welded together.

Having matched us, they grappled us, and started the burn to drag us down.

The EM drive, which we used for slow maneuvering, didn't burn anything—but it couldn't brake or accelerate us as fast as the AWD. We wouldn't run out of fuel, using the EM drive, but if we hadn't been able to yell for help from the tugs, we would have been a long fifty ans or so dropping our v and coming back around to meet the station.

I watched nervously, tracking the fuel used as their burn turned us, then slowed us to something closer to maneuvering speed.

We were still moving faster relative to the station than I was comfortable with when Singer hit the release and I floated off my couch. We were no longer changing v.

"We have to validate for the fuel anyway," I said.

They both ignored me.

The station was not yet in sight ahead, and we had plenty of time to kill before we caught up with it. Of course this meant that Singer and Connla started arguing about the nature of consciousness again. (I'm sorry, "discussing." Connla tells me that being clade-bred, I think spirited discussions are arguments long before there's any arguing going on.)

I tuned them out for a while and looked around for the local primary. It was bright yellow, and off to the left.

When I tuned back in, Singer was ending a paragraph by asking, "By those standards, am I a real intelligence? Am I just a sufficiently complicated and randomized construct that I adequately simulate an intelligence? Or am I just a mock-up?"

"Aw," I said. "You're ghost in the machine enough for me, Singer."

"You could ask the same thing of me," Connla replied, more infinitely amused than infinitely patient with the existential crises of inanimate objects. "Most human philosophy for as long as human philosophy has been recorded seems to be concerned with pretty much the same question. If free will is an illusion, do I exist? Or do I merely think I exist?"

I sighed. "Is there any functional difference?"

"Is that the worm Ouroboros eating his tail I see?"

"You bumped your psychopathy up, didn't you?"

He smiled generously. "Of course I did. I'm flying. Can't be distracted by doubts."

His hands moved over the screens, gently and flawlessly stroking transparent display and contact surfaces. Singer could do it all, of course—and would, when it came to the incredibly delicate work of matching velocities with the station—but there was some pleasure to be had in manual control while it was possible.

"I feel like it's a more pressing question for me," Singer said. "I'm nothing *but* those electrical signals."

"Are you suggesting I'm something more?" I replied. "Did you get us those docking permissions?"

"You have flesh."

"Sure, and my consciousness seems to be an emergent property of that flesh. It's shaped by the flesh; it can be modified by modifying the meat. At least I can move you into a new mem and you take up right where you left off. Maybe a little smarter. We can *model* a human brain, even duplicate one—"

"Well, *duplicate* might not be the right term," Connla said. "Duplicate my brain, shove me into a digester, and I'm still dead methane keeping the electricity on. Maybe if you mapped all the meat and then engineered identical meat with identical chemicals you'd get an identical mind, but then you still have the problem of your mind being stuck in meat. Which is what most of the upload guys are trying to avoid."

"You're making my point for me, interrupting lad."

The ship shuddered with a brief burn. The arc of a structure swung across the forward screen—swirling, stately.

"This is wildly antisocial!" I said.

"Sorry," Connla said.

He didn't look sorry. He winked.

"It's like systems of government," Singer said suddenly as he completed his swing and burned again to arrest the movement.

"Here we go again."

"It's why I want us to be very careful what we commit to while we're dealing with this station. They make bad governmental choices, and by patronizing them, we're just validating their choices."

"We still need fuel and supplies. We need new chow," Connla said reasonably. "And air that doesn't smell like the garlic in last week's soup."

I braced myself. I suppose when you're functionally immortal, think at the speed of light, and your multitasking ability is only limited by the number of parallel processor arrays you can line up, you need a lot of hobbies.

Singer said, "Government is either imposed with force, or it derives from the will of the governed. But it's a social contract, right? It exists simply because people say it does. It's not a thing you can touch."

"Neither is consciousness," Connla said.

"You're encouraging him," I said. "Fly the tug, so we don't die."

"My point exactly!" Singer continued. "It's like . . . language. Or an economy. It's a consensus model, not an objective reality."

"There's a whole body of theory and a not-insignificant pile of myth that insists that language actually does have some kind of objective reality," Connla said. "But we'll let that slide for now. Are you going someplace interesting with this?"

The superstructure sighed as the AI's feather touch adjusted our trajectory toward the dock. The great wheel of the station grew, and morphed slowly into an arc, clipped at the edges by the frame of the forward window.

"I'm hurt," Singer said, "by the implication that I might be going someplace *uninteresting*."

"Supernovae and small fishes," I muttered. "Aren't we *still* coming in a little hot?"

"Don't you trust me?" Singer said. "We work together because we agree to. Because we see that collective bargain, that social contract, as advantageous to all of us. I work with you because the work interests me. Because I enjoy traveling with you. Because the rewards of salvage and exploration are generally intellectually stimulating."

"Because we put up with your lectures."

"I'm going to pretend I didn't hear that, Haimey."

"Because the salvage helps pay off your obligation," Connla offered.

I said, "Aren't we *still* coming in a little hot?"

"You work with me because of my skills, and also my companionship. Although your perversity forces you to suggest otherwise."

"My perversity currently forces me to ask if you shouldn't be taking this *emergency decel upon which all our lives depend* a *little* more seriously."

"I am capable of multitasking," Singer scoffed.

We bent on an arc with another burn, moving parallel to the station's axis of rotation now. The dock was coming up fast, relative motion sharp and quick, and the fuel gauge was on empty and not even flickering when we shifted *v*. I knew Singer was in contact with the station's AI because of the ripple of lights across the console that allowed us slowbrains to monitor his resource allocation.

I hoped the station wasn't screaming at us to slow down. I waited to feel heavy again, but I kept just floating above my couch.

Well, if we got hit for it, I'd take the fine out of Singer's share. If we plowed into the airlock at velocity . . . we'd have bigger problems than a speeding ticket.

And so would the station.

"Oh, Void," I said as we came around the curve. "That's the pirate ship."

There she was, big as life, docked and quiescent. We whipped past her so fast she looked like a white blur. I couldn't see any weapons on her, but we were moving pretty fast and perhaps they retracted into their ports when she was trying to look like she wasn't a corsair. I started to doubt my pattern recognition just as Singer said, "Confirmed."

Cold settled into my gut. "How did they track us here? How did they get here ahead of us?"

Connla said, "Maybe they were coming here anyway."

I sucked my teeth. "Well, that's rotten luck."

Singer, calmly, commented, "We have to dock."

"They *fired* on us."

Singer said, "You have a better plan?"

Connla added, "One that doesn't involve freezing to death in the Big Empty?"

I didn't. And yeah, my shipmate definitely had his sophipathology pumped right up.

"Maybe they didn't see us," Connla added.

Maybe.

We whipped around the station again, and the ship did look quiet. Downthehatch wasn't a *big* station—thirty thousand people at most—but that was enough to get lost in.

Maybe it would be okay. And—I looked at the fuel readout again—it wasn't as if we had a lot of choices.

"Authority derives from the consent of the governed, is what I'm saying," Singer continued, as if we hadn't been derailed by the threat of people with guns and a grudge. "And that consent is derived from consensus. Which is never universal."

"Somebody always feels like they're getting screwed," Connla clarified.

"That's business," I agreed, picking at my cuticle.

Connla glared at me, and I felt the weight of Singer's disapproval in the flicker of his status lights. They could be as expressive as a frown.

"What?" I said. "I was agreeing with you. You say consent is never universal, but remember—I grew up in a clade. Where consensus is perfect, and enforced. I ran away. I'm allergic to perfect consensus. It has to be enforced somehow, and once you sign the clade contract, they just tune your neurology until you agree. Boom, no conflict."

"But government," Singer said. "Government is a social contract. It has no objective existence. It's a thing human beings made up. The good ones allow for the allocation of present resources in a manner that meets present needs, including those of the most vulnerable, which requires a certain amount of altruism and also foresight in those who do not currently need assistance that somedia they are likely to. Which is why"—he sighed—"I have to turn myself in and serve my time for the Core, helping to run things."

"It all takes a lack of denial, too," I said. "Which is the hard part. We're *still* hot. Please acknowledge."

"Acknowledging," Singer answered. "We're hot. I'm on it."

I could have mentioned that it was rightminding which made that basic level of altruism possible; that we were hierarchal creatures with a tendency toward magical and unrealistic thinking, left to our own devices. That evolution had left us with a number of sophipathologies intrinsic to our intellectual makeup, and that to survive as a society we intervened in those failures to grasp reality in order to make our people, in general, more amenable to working for a commonweal.

Clade Light, really.

One of the things the Freeporters objected to.

Singer said, "These people made up a bad government. It's imposed, not emergent. You won't like it."

"Clades are imposed." We still had time to kill. That's the problem with space: even scary things can take a really long time to happen. "Rightminding is imposed."

"There's agreeing to live by the obligations and laws of a civilization in order to enjoy its common protections, and then there's having obligations and laws forced upon you."

"I'm not going to move here," I said. "Just eat something with fresh spices in it. Besides, Downthehatch is a Synarche system. It can't be *that* tyrannical. And if we had a choice about coming here, we wouldn't be. Especially with a pirate ship in dock."

"They might as well be Republic pirates," Connla teased.

"They might as well be," Singer agreed darkly. Which seemed a little on-the-nose, given that there was, in fact, a pirate ship in dock.

We were spiraling close to the station. Close enough that I wished they would stop arguing and fly the damn tug. I wondered what we looked like coming in, with our scorched and empty derrick housings and our hastily patched hull.

I hoped—again—that the pirates weren't looking.

"We're going to have to report the pirates," Singer said unhappily. "To a stationmaster who is giving them berth space."

Maybe the stationmaster doesn't know, I almost said, and swallowed it. One of the problems with AIs grown from personality seeds is that sometimes they're just as reactive and weird as any human. Singer was acting out because he was worried.

Of course the stationmaster knew. Which meant we needed to find another way to make sure the information made it back to the Core.

Singer feathered his engines. The ship luffed, hesitated, glided. Nudged the docking ring and—relative to the station—stopped. Singer caught the hook and—elegant, perfect, seamless, with no sense of acceleration—the station appeared to stop rotating, and the sun *beneath* the ship began to whirl instead. A locking click reverberated through the hull, followed by the hiss of exchanging atmosphere.

I worked my jaw as my ears popped painfully. My body, suddenly, weighed a ton. It was only quarter gravity, but it felt like somebody had tied sacks of bolts and washers to all of my limbs.

"Your fresh air, Connla," Singer said dryly. "Enjoy breathing it in freedom for as long as you can. I'll be arguing with the local arm of the Synarche for an extension on my service start date. Hopefully I'll still be here when you return."

I looked down at my star-webbed hands. We could make it home without Singer; flying an established space lane wasn't *hard*, not for a pilot as good as Connla. I wouldn't trust any expert system we found out here in the margins, anyway.

"Nanocream," I asked out loud. "Do we have any?"

Singer said, "I can fab you some. There was a bit ready-made in first aid stores, but I'm afraid it's expired."

I smeared the stuff on, watched it color-match my skin. It looked mostly okay, but it was missing the subtle shadings of red-brown and cocoa that my natural complexion had, the centimeter-by-centimeter color variation.

I looked flat. A little plastic.

Ill. Or like an android.

Well, no offense to any androids, but that was about how I felt, as well.

CHAPTER 7

SHALL I COMPARE THEE TO A DOCKING RING? THOU ART more beautiful and more temperate, though that's not really hard when you're talking about an airlock whose external temperature is measured on the low end of kelvins. On the other hand, I'm not sure I could have been happier with anything or felt more raw, unfettered love than I did for that docking ring, right then. Free and with my afthands on metal, I stretched against the rotational acceleration and sighed.

I love Singer; don't get me wrong. I wouldn't trade my life for any crowded station existence, and most definitely not for *anything* on the downside. How do people live down wells? But it was good to get away from him and Connla—for just a few hours. There's nothing like being annoyed by *different* sentiences to make you really appreciate your own.

Not that Downthehatch Station had a lot to recommend it. The ox section smelled of chlorine, strong enough to smart in my sinuses. The chlorine section probably stank of oxygen, I was willing to bet, because nothing makes two mutually bioincompatible life-forms feel more relaxed and at home than breathing trace quantities of each other's poison.

Some stations, you walk out of the docking ring—okay, you climb up through it, usually, though on this one we *had* docked alongside the axis of spin, which is not as sturdy a connection but you don't have to go up a ladder to get out—and there are restaurants, nightlife, trade shops, and tourist attractions. Showers and brothels and the usual amenities of any port.

On some others, you're lucky if there's a bathroom.

This was one of the latter. Not even a dive bar in sight, just a long dingy curve of corridor with fibrous gray carpeting institutionalizing it further. It had windows, at least, and as I looked to my left I had the rare pleasure of a glimpse of Singer from the outside, visible through the ports. Chalk another small human convenience up to side-by-side docking.

I pulled my screen out of my pocket and checked directions to the stationmaster's office. Technically we did not have to present in person, having received clearances—but there was the little matter of the criminal issues to report, and the social capital therefrom to negotiate. Connla and I had drawn lots, and it had fallen to me to deal with strangers.

Again.

I'm pretty sure he cheats. Especially since, as I was pulling my station shoes on to cushion my poor afthands, he had smiled cheerily and said, "It'll be good for you to get out and meet some people!"

Then he had announced his intention to go find the local strategy games club and see if he could get laid, find a chess partner, or both. So yeah, I'm pretty sure he cheats. I had sighed, and reminded him to turn his conscience and risk-assessment back on, and told Singer not to print him any station shoes unless he did.

I can cheat too, on occasion.

The connecting corridor from the docking ring spiraled me into a main hallway after a dozen steps or so, coming in from the side to make it easy to merge with the flow of traffic. *This* was where all the people were. A diverse group—I spotted a lot of humans, some of whom side-eyed me just enough to let me know they'd spotted the nanoskin and wondered if I was an overly made-up human or an AI out for a stroll.

There's always somebody who feels like they have the right to judge.

But there was also a selection of other ox-type systers, including some small furry ones, some caterpillar-like ones, a couple of examples of a photosynthetic species that were particularly welcome on stations because they respirated using carbon dioxide, and one member of an ele-phantine, red-skinned species whose name was unpronounceable to Ter-rans. We called them Thunderbys, and this one's hulking frame strained the capacity of the corridor.

Like most other people, I edged to one side to let it past, stepping into the embrasure of an eatery doorway. The proprietor, a human like me, gave me the veil eye when they realized I wasn't coming in, but stopped short of actually shoving me back out into the Thunderby's path, thus saving both of us embarrassment and me possible injury. The Thunderby was huddling already, trying to take up as little space as possible, which still amounted to all of it. Its manipulator appendages consisted of five tentacular appurtenances, which it had wrapped around its torso in an uncomfortable-looking show of courtesy so as to minimize its profile.

Politeness counts the effort, or so one of my clademothers used to say.

I frowned at it thoughtfully, but though the Thunderby was *big* enough to have been the species mainly crewing the factory ship, it was the wrong outline. I was pretty sure we were looking for something more or less bipedal and bilaterally symmetrical.

Maybe Singer would get something useful out of the station data-base. That wasn't my job this trip, anyway.

One side of the corridor rose in a ramp to the next level, and—following color-coded signs for Station Admin—I rose with it, feeling the pull of rotational "gravity" ease as I ascended toward the station's hub. That came with a new and peculiar sensation: a sort of stretching along the fibers of my skin. My integument—and the Koregoi senso—was reacting to the change in angular and rotational momentum as I rose. I could feel the station spinning, and the fine gradation in speed between my head and my feet. Normally, that would be too subtle to notice. I steadied myself against the wall until the sensation evened out.

I thought of mentioning it to Connla, but Singer was monitoring my senso, and the fact that Connla had turned our immediate link off made me think he'd probably found his chess club and didn't care to be bothered.

I hoped he didn't run into any pirates while he was there. But honestly, it wasn't any riskier than huddling in the ship would have been. The pirates knew what our *ship* looked like. They had no idea who *we* were.

The ramp merged me onto another busy corridor. This one was lined with nearly anonymous offices, some with transparent windows, rather than with shops and eateries.

I applied my ID card and most scannable appendage to the sensor beside the door marked *Stationmaster* in thirty-seven languages and Standard Galactic Iconography Set Number 3. The Core had already updated to Set Number 8 by then, to give you an idea of how behind the times this backwater was.

The door slid aside and I found myself in a little suite, uncomfortably warm and humid by human standards, lit with full-spectrum bulbs. Probably past what my species would consider full spectrum, honestly; my skin tingled with UV.

Other than the temperature and water content of the air, the door debouched into a pleasant-enough little reception/waiting area with a series of padded tuffets for seating, those being the sort of things that almost any species that liked to sit could sit or rest upon without discomfort. I was the only sentient visibly present. I took a blue tuffet beside the half-wall, and waited.

No more than a few minutes later, someone poked their head around the edge of the divider, and my suspicions were confirmed. The being wearing the stationmaster ID flash on their upper torso was bipedal, roughly humanoid in outline, but their integument was, from the front, an almost lusterless, smooth purple-black resembling rubber. They had a head, with four pretty normal eyes—by Terran standards—ranged around it, but the head was otherwise a fairly featureless egg. There were respiration slits between each of the eyes, and on the back of the body was a series of pollen-yellow bladders that lay flat in ranks on either side of the spine.

They were a Ceeharen, a member of a symbiotic, photosynthetic syster species I'd noticed represented in the corridor. They made a pleasant susurrant moaning—which issued from the bladders along their cellulose spine, not from their respiration apparatus—and exhaled a welcoming cloud of oxygen into the room.

Come in, my senso translated their speech. *Be welcome. I am designated as [Colonel] [Habren] for these purposes. How may such a one as this assist such a one as you?*

I was glad the stationmaster wasn't human. It limited the chance that they would find the makeup hiding the silver stuff all over my hands and face weird or suspicious. On the other hand, most interspecies advantages flow two ways. I didn't have a damned idea what they were thinking, either.

I followed Habren in, was seated on one of the ubiquitous tuffets, introduced myself by name and—by his registry number—as Singer's engineer, and said, "I wanted to thank you personally for the braking assist."

Of course, Habren said. *For humanitarian reasons if nothing else.*

They paused.

There is the little matter of justifying your crew continuing to hold right of use to the salvage tug, as it seems the recent cost of your missions has dramatically exceeded their usefulness, and the tug appears damaged. Also there is the little matter of your shipmind's selective service option having been called in. . . .

"These things are true," I told them. I steepled my fingers in my lap. "We have some nonmaterial salvage from this past trip that is significantly better than a prize vessel, however. I'd like to speak to the station Goodlaw about it. Do you have a border control vessel in port currently? Or within hailing distance?"

We have a Goodlaw on the station, Habren said. They stretched under the full-spectrum light that bathed their desk. My butt was leaving a pair of hemispherical sweat stains on my tuffet, encouraged by the warmth and humidity, but my lungs and skin were basking in it. Something about that pose, straining—unconsciously?—toward the light, and their lack of access to a Justice vessel that would be more useful to an outpost like this than the constable they *did* have, made me think the Ceeharen was a little bitter about being exiled out here at the back of beyond. It was administering the kind of station that would never be anything but countless troubles, small and big, without the resources allocated to manage it properly. There was probably nothing the stationmaster could do to stop Freeporters from calling through here, even if they wanted to.

So was it safe telling them what we'd found? Would they pass our identity and registry on to the captain of that Republic ship docked out there, willingly or under duress?

"I would like to speak with the station Goodlaw," I said. "We have information of significant value regarding piracy and other illegal acts. I think it should more than redeem our debt to society."

I see, said Habren.

"I also need some information about a syster species."

Well, that should be possible, if we have it in the databases. Which syster would that be?

"Ah," I said. "You see. That's the problem."

They waited patiently, blinking the eyes in sequence around their head.

"I don't know which syster it was. I know some details of their physiology."

Habren continued blinking, and I decided to anthropomorphize that as a show of polite-and-engaged listening and get on with my life.

I said, "Large. Perhaps two times my height, three to five times my mass. Bipedal, with manipulating structures not too unlike these." I held up a forehand. "Strong preference for what we humans would call earth tones." I sensoed Habren some absorption data to give it an idea about the colors.

In the answer to one of those ancient philosophical questions, it turns out that nobody's idea of green is the same as anybody else's idea of green, at least on a species level—but at least the physics for comparing them all is pretty straightforward.

It blinked again, perhaps reviewing the data. Perhaps stalling for time.

Would you care to share why you require this information?

"I'll be happy to." My back was up. I sucked it up against my irrational objections and tuned my irritation back a little. But just a little. Possibly my instincts were telling me something important, and not merely xenophobic. I didn't *trust* Habren. But I didn't know for sure they were one of the bad guys either. "I'll share it with the Goodlaw as soon as I can get an appointment with it."

Perhaps it will be able to be more helpful, then. The translator made Habren sound inanely cheerful. Somehow, I doubted its actual expressions of emotion were so chipper. *Now, on to the matter of resolving your debt. . . .*

"Yes," I said. "We have no prize."

We are aware.

"But we *do* have a good deal of information on Freeport pirate activity off the galactic plane." I left out the part where we could provide detailed descriptions of what appeared to be salvaged Koregoi tech that they seemed to be using—or stealing from renderers.

I also left out that we'd noticed the pirate ship docked on our way in. Just in case. "That ought to be worth something, right?"

Something, it agreed. I thought, reluctantly.

I pressed on. "And we've also found out some interesting information about renderers who are murdering Ativahikas and producing organic devashare in quantity. Traffickers. Including something about their hunting grounds, and the coordinates of one of their victims."

I *really* wasn't going to mention the Koregoi senso to this being, I decided. At the back of my head, I could hear Singer agreeing. We'd send a packet to the Core, just in case. If we could get one out clean, without having to go through Habren's offices. Or if Singer thought the wheel-mind could be trusted.

Could you corrupt a wheelmind?

You could probably convince one that maximum preservation of life required going along with some shady business practices.

The Ativahikas might be grateful for that information, they mused.

They might be. Who could tell? Who could manage to communicate it to them?

"Is that enough to justify our fuel and refit expenses?"

My senso translated the sound it made in reply as a wordless, noncommittal grunt.

There's also the matter of your shipmind. We have received word that it is selected for service and is requested to be on the next packet Coreward.

The constriction of panic squeezed my lungs.

"I believe he is aware of this selection, and is filing for an extension as we speak. Our intention is to move Coreward as soon as our ship is spaceworthy again, which would actually get him there faster than if he went into service todia, given relative speeds of a direct route and a packet. Never mind the fuel savings."

We will have to research whether fuel can be allotted. And other consumables, of course. You will no doubt require sustenance of various kinds for such a long journey.

The constriction eased a bit, but only a bit. The damned plant was dragging me. What did it want? A bribe of some kind? Or just to slow us down?

I tuned myself until I could say "That seems reasonable" and sound like I meant it. I thought to myself, *Oh slightly corrupt stationmaster, what do you want? What is your motive for being pointlessly obstructionist?*

And was I confused, or had the obstructionism kicked in when I started asking about the Mystery Systers from the *Milk Chocolate Marauder?*

What was going on with Habren, then?

Maybe they just hated being exiled to the ass-back of nowhere on this shitty station without enough resources to control it properly. Maybe they wanted out, or enough resources allotted to help them fight the pirates. Or maybe they themselves were beholden to pirates. They probably had no choice but to deal with them occasionally, so far from the might of the Core.

And either they did not wish to be so beholden, and were willing to bend rules for what seemed to them a good purpose—or they didn't mind at all, because the pirates were paying.

Possibly I'd just given away a lot of useful information to the people who were hunting us.

It occurred to me that it was possible that the alien tech in my skin could by itself buy Habren an awful lot of goodwill and resources. Then it took all my willpower not to start picking self-consciously at the skin on my hand.

Calm down, Haimey.

Habren's avenues of attack were limited, if they were in with the pirates, because they had to maintain some kind of deniability. Especially where Singer was concerned, with him suddenly a member of government and of significant interest to the Synarche.

So I felt like once we came to the agreement, we were in a better condition. Habren could pass word around to other stations that we were bad citizens, but coming from an outpost like this, and with our prior reputation for plain dealing, it wouldn't do us too much harm. They could try to arrest us for reckless driving. They could take their own sweet time about deciding whether to fuel and supply us for the run home, and then about actually performing the fueling and supplying.

For now, though, we signed off on the preliminary deal—that Habren was going to research the logistics of allowing us to run Singer home—and I made sure a copy of the info went into the mail system before I left their office. Packet mail was an encoded, AI-protected, Synarche-run system. It could probably be hacked by somebody better than me, but I didn't think it could be hacked tracelessly, and if the contract and the record that we had proposed bringing Singer in ourselves existed and reached the Core before we—presumably moving faster—did . . .

Well, with a little luck, they might come looking if we got lost.

It was possible that Habren could keep the mail from going through at all. That was a level of dysfunction that I sincerely hoped we wouldn't have to contend with, though. We might just have already lost, if that were the case.

After the near tropicality of the stationmaster's office, the Goodlaw's office was absolutely delightful. I did not so much walk as float in, as the gravity this far upwheel was pretty slight, which made me a lot more comfortable. And I floated in not knowing what to expect, and found myself at once enchanted.

It's considered polite, in varied-climate habitats such as stations and multispecies hospitals, to warn your guest if they might be entering an environment that could prove hazardous to their species. Ox breathers, in general, could manage each other's habitats—at least in space, where the super-Earth life-forms made do with vastly undercompensating approximations of gravity, since the alternative would have been spinning stations so fast that they would be challenged not to fly to bits. Fortunately, high-gravity types tended to be pretty tough creatures, albeit with a tendency to succumb to the bends.

The station's Goodlaw was the opposite of one of those: an ox breather, and one who liked a supersaturated environment by human standards. Senso told me when I walked in that ox was at 33% of the atmosphere, which explained why absolutely everything inside the office was nonflammable. The temperature was balmy, the air dryish, and the whole office suffused with a pleasant, indirect light.

Based on that, and how the walls were hung with broad nets meant to resemble interwoven vines, I was pretty sure that I was about to be confronted by a—

—two-meter praying mantis, more or less.

Many-faceted eyes poked out from behind a privacy curtain, followed closely by a slender protothorax and a pair of folded raptorial limbs, along with a pair of more delicate manipulators. It advanced a few delicate steps on its long, fragile legs—the homeworld of this syster species was low-gravity—and I clenched my fists in my pockets and tried very hard to control my atavistic terror. It wasn't going to eat me, but my limbic system was certain of the opposite of that.

Its name, in a terrible transliteration, was Goodlaw Cheeirilaq, or that was what it said in the English portion of the sign by the door, and it was a Rashaqin, one of the most technologically established and gentlest of the systers, and never mind that it looked like something that would eat a meter-and-a-half-long wasp for dinner.

It seemed to have an ovipositor, so I guessed it was female, but having no idea how gender constructs worked in Rashaqin society, I decided to just keep thinking of it as an it. Enough other critters have called me an it since I left the clade—where they would have taken grave offense—that it's become just another pronoun. There are more important things to fuss about in space than whether the whatchamacallit's translator system is telling it you're a them or an it or a whatchamacallit yourself.

I bowed, an act of respect that seemed to be understood, as the Goodlaw returned the gesture with a lowering on its head and forethorax. As it came into sight, the resemblance to an Earth insect I'd only seen in lucky pet cages on some other ships both strengthened and faded.

My new acquaintance had broad wings that were folded under light green sheaths along its spine. But it walked on six legs in addition to its manipulators and raptorial forelimbs. Its little hooked feet anchored it neatly to the webworks, though it seemed at home in the very light gravity.

"I don't have an appointment," I said. "But your door was open."

The insect stridulated, *Greetings, friend Dz. I am forewarned that you have police business for me to consider.*

Transferring the documentation was easy; I just forwarded senso clips of my exploration of the factory ship and the two pirate attacks to the Goodlaw. Cheeirilaq asked me to make myself comfortable while it reviewed the documents, which didn't take it as long as I would have expected. Probably it had AI assistance.

These are unedited?

"Nearly," I said. "Our shipmind removed 3.5 seconds containing proprietary information necessary to our salvage operations, which we are not required to release." That proprietary information, loosely so termed, was the pinprick.

I see you had not filed for a permit for this salvage operation.

"There was no appropriate jurisdiction to file in, as we were in unincorporated space."

The Goodlaw knew, and I knew, that we could have filed with our station of departure. It tilted its head, studying me with all its multifaceted eyes, and stridulated something that my senso returned as *untranslatable.* I assumed it was a thinking noise.

You won't mind a ship inspection, then?

"We have no contraband." A rush of relief: we *didn't* have any contraband, and I was profoundly glad of it. "Our only interest in the factory ship we found was to bring it back and turn it in, and if we hadn't encountered the pirates we would have probably brought it to the nearest Synarche Space Guard station."

Then you will not mind a ship inspection.

I consulted with Singer. Whatever Connla was doing, he'd ducked out of senso, which made me just as happy, but in his absence Singer and I constituted a quorum.

"As long as our shipmind can observe the inspection and record it, of course not."

That seems reasonable.

Either the Goodlaw was a lot less corrupt—or power-trippy—than the stationmaster, or it was a lot more subtle about it.

This appears to be artificial gravity.

"It does, doesn't it?"

What you have shown me looks like magic, Synizen Dz.

I grinned. "There is no such thing as magic. There's only physics we insufficiently understand." I took a deep breath, and decided to trust it at least a little bit further. One way or another, it was likely to know about the pirate ship docked on the ring already. Whether revealing that we *also* knew, and had had a past encounter with said ship, was likely to get us into trouble . . . that, I couldn't say.

So I gambled.

I said, "By the way, the ship that took a potshot at us is docked here."

Fascinating. The mantid rubbed its raptorial arms together.

There was an awkward silence. Well, awkward for me, anyway. The Goodlaw spent it regarding me with compound eyes, utterly unmoving.

Well, maybe it was waiting for me. I decided to risk it. "Now, sorry to be so blunt, but Habren is playing games with me on the topic. Will this data pay for a refuel?"

Pay is an archaic concept. But yes, this justifies further resource allocation to your project. I will speak to Habren. I believe they will agree to a dispensation of fuel and consumables.

Without even a pause, it reached out with a manipulator and opened a com channel. Stunning me, Cheeirilaq patched me in as well.

There were some indistinguishable noises, and then a hum through the senso. I sat quietly and listened while Cheeirilaq spoke with Habren, demanding with infinite politeness that Singer and crew be expedited on our way as merrily as possible, and with as much alacrity.

If you insist, I can probably justify fuel for that, Habren admitted, after what I decided was a grumpy pause.

Of course you can, Cheeirilaq answered. *It's already been allotted, and Dz here is right; its tug is smaller than a mail packet and can travel faster on the same fuel allotment. I would encourage you to provide a generous bonus allotment, in fact, given that they are both performing a transport service for the Synarche and bringing in important information about criminal activities.*

The translator wouldn't quite let Habren sound grudging, but I projected it anyway. They spoke directly to me. *You will have to obtain repairs to your derrick in the Core, however.*

That will be acceptable, Cheeirilaq replied, before I could. *I shall issue them a voucher.*

After all that, I found myself in strong agreement with Connla that now was a great time for a little rest and recreation. We were stuck here until we got our fuel and our clearances, and bumping around the tug being anxious about pirates was only going to annoy Singer. Besides, it wasn't as if any of them knew what I *looked* like.

I wasn't interested in strategy games or sex, though, so I ran a quick-search on what I *did* want, then let Singer know where I was going. A few minutes later, I seated myself on a stool of a reasonably clean ring bar in a low-grav section of the wheel. Having eased off my station shoes and feeling much more comfortable with my afthands (clad in socks!) resting in perched position on the rail beneath the service top, I gave myself over to contemplating the nuanceless amber depths of a glass of printed whiskey. I hadn't had my drink for two mins when a local bar-type, subspecies human, presenting masculine and on the make, crawled over.

He sidled onto the next stool, hooked flat feet under the rail, and said, "What *are* you hiding under all that paint?"

I didn't look at him. He was wearing a spider-dress—a collection of jointed limbs and servos that formed a halo around his shoulders and were meant to respond independently to his skin conductivity, muscle tension, everything up to and including his brain radiation, broadcasting his mood and attention to everyone around. A pretty narcissistic piece of clothing, if you ask me, designed to make your interiority everybody else's problem.

They made them in cobra and chameleon models too. I probably would have preferred an octopus. Colors *and* lots of limbs.

He waited for a moment, dress contracted like it had touched something hot, contemplating his evident failure to connect.

I was choking, freezing up. I could not think of a snappy put-down to save my life.

And the best part about choking is that once you notice you're choking you choke harder. Because becoming self-conscious is the surest way to get worse at something.

Antisocially, he said, "I'm Rohn. Can I at least buy you a drink?"

"No thanks," I said, this being a much less personal sort of question. "I have one, and I don't need any more obligations."

"Free and clear," he offered.

I ignored him.

"So what are you here for?"

I tapped the rim of my glass. The bartender glanced over to see if I needed a refill already, then set the flask back when I shook my head.

My neighbor simmered down, but as I was getting to the bottom of my glass I could feel him revving up for a fresh approach, contemplating angles and flight trajectories. All his spider legs, one by one, were focusing on me. They had tiny lights worked into their structure, which looked like nanotube and was probably as strong as it was low-mass. I might be judging him unfairly; the dress *would* be useful for a lubber in low-g.

"Sorry," I said. "I'm a pervert. I only like girls."

"You could get that fixed. Isn't it kind of sophipathology to only respond to one gender?"

I shrugged. "It's who I am, and I like who I am."

Little white lies. They get us through.

". . . When there are literally thousands of options?"

"I also only respond to people with boundaries," I said. "So I wouldn't like you either way. And I'm not getting *that* fixed, either. So I guess I am a bigot as well as a pervert."

You'd think that would be rude enough to send him packing. But you would be wrong.

Before Rohn could speak further Connla walked through the privacy screen and stood there for a moment, scanning the very sparse mid-shift crowd until he spotted me. I could feel my neighbor's back going up, and concealed a smile.

Connla's not my thing, you understand. But by most human standards, he's awfully pretty. His homeworld went in for a bunch of hypermasculine gene tweaks among the early settlers, and just about every male-ID from Spartacus is roughly two meters tall with a chin dimple and big broad shoulders. They've all got a partial myostatin block encoded, too, which means they tend to be strong as hell and hungry all the time, because they don't lay down much in the way of body fat—they just convert it into muscles.

As you can imagine, this is useful in some circumstances, and less useful in a cramped, resource-limited environment such as a tugboat. Connla's a good pilot, though, and normally we don't have to worry about how much he eats.

He was looking a little wasted from the short rations on the way in, but heads turned nonetheless. And a couple of sets of shoulders slumped in disappointment when he grinned at me and started over. I made a mental note of which ones and marked them for him in senso, just in case he was interested later.

Just because I don't care for the prowl myself doesn't mean I can't be a pretty good wingperson.

My neighbor's shoulders stiffened rather than slumping. His dress postured.

I continued my hard regime of ignoring him as Connla slid in beside me. He tapped the bar in front of him and said, "A double for me, please, and get my shipmate another of whatever she's drinking. This a friend of yours?"

That last was directed at me, regarding Rohn.

I said, "Strategy club didn't pan out?"

"Meets next shift," he said. "We still going to be in port? Nice dress."

"I'm Rohn," said Rohn.

"Cargo inspection," I said with a shrug. "And hull seal, I hope. Then we get our consumables. The derrick will have to wait for Core."

"Won't take long, seeing as how we haven't got any cargo." The drinks arrived. He downed half of his with a comfortable sigh.

I was still nursing the end of my first one.

"Anyway, I thought I'd come see if you'd found any action." He touched my memory. "That one over there, huh?"

I didn't answer. He was already looking through the senso.

Connla studied the young person appreciatively. I will say this for him: Connla likes his fun, but (unlike me) he's not the least little bit biased by gender, augmentation status, or background. He likes wit and a pretty face, true—but who doesn't? And at least one of those things is easy enough to buy.

Anyway, he's got enough testosterone for the both of us, and he comes by it honestly—if you expand the definition of *honestly* to include "inherited it from grandparents who had it engineered in."

Spartacus is an interesting culture. I'm rather glad he's never brought me home to visit his parents.

I patted him on his arm. They're touch-prohibitive where he comes from, but he's mellowed a lot since we first started flying together. I suspect the conflict between skin hunger and social controls against admitting it is one of the reasons why he chases sex so much. "Go get 'em, tiger."

He picked up his glass, gave me a sideways grin and a toss of his glossy black ponytail, and went.

Neighbor dude looked down at my untouched second drink. I picked it up and tasted it.

He smiled at me. "Are you and your shipmate . . . ?"

I rolled my eyes. "No. I told you, I don't swing that way. Too complicated."

"Don't swing to shipmates, or to masculine-identified types?"

It was really none of his business. But I was getting irritated. And I'd already told him how I felt.

More irritated. This one had no manners, and could not take a hint.

"Don't swing," I said. "I had that stuff turned off. Too much of a pain in the ass, quite frankly." I gave him a wicked grin. "But as I said, and you failed to internalize, if I *did* like dealing with hormone surges and getting pie-eyed, give me a nice, soft, curvy girl-type any dia. Or one of those squidgineers, with the cartilaginous limbs and as many boobs as they decided to pay for. Now *that's* hot."

He backed off, finally, and I sipped my second drink, feeling peaceful. The truth was, after all that damned closeness where I grew up, the vulnerability made me nervous. You let your guard down to one person, pretty soon other people started creeping in over the razor wire and around the force fields, too. And then they inevitably hurt you, and what might have been a few chips and dents if your deflectors were working turned, instead, into a full-sledged meteor storm, leaving behind cracked bones and big, meaty gouges.

Better to just shut down the whole shebang.

I wasn't here for shenanigans, anyway. I was here for dancing. Low-g *dancing*.

And the band my research had promised was just now taking the stage.

Sweaty, thrilled, feeling like my body was properly oiled and running like it didn't need a tune-up for the first time in I didn't know how long, I slid into the booth beside Connla and his new conquest. They were grinning at each other foolishly, but Connla had waved me over, so I figured I wasn't intruding. Maybe it was Introduction Time, which meant he might like this one enough to keep in touch via packet after we shipped out. He'd expect me to remember which affair went with which port of call—which wasn't too onerous of an expectation, given how much time we had to float around and gossip.

"Haimey," he said. "Do you need another drink?"

"I'd love one," I said. "Something long and not too poisonous."

He ordered on the screen, and his new friend extended a hand. "I'm Pearl. So you're a salvage engineer?"

Typically, he hadn't picked the prettiest contender to move on, but one with a mobile face and an air of curiosity that made them charismatic. It's hard not to like somebody who's genuinely interested in you. Or genuinely interested in *things*, in general.

"I'm Haimey," I answered, and took their hand. Their fingers were long and cool. "Since Connla is too busy to introduce us."

"Too busy fetching you things, you mean." He stood up and winked. "Be right back."

"What is your vocation?" I said, since the subject of my work was already apparently well-discussed.

"I make reproductions of Terran Eastern Orthodox iconographic art."

"That a religion?"

"They were very into gold leaf," they said. "And I'm a recyclables engineer."

"Diverse," I said, impressed. "Not everybody has that much drive."

"I bore easily," Pearl answered. They grinned sideways at Connla, who had just appeared with our drinks and a bowl of crunchy soy-sim snack things.

"How did you come into engineering?" Pearl asked.

"I enjoy it," I said. "Admittedly, I was tuned to enjoy it, to take my designate. But I didn't see any reason to change that program when I struck out on my own." I shrugged. I had the skills, and making myself hate them would have been a real waste of time and energy.

"Designate?"

Connla seated himself, kept his silence, ate a snack.

"I grew up in a clade."

Pearl's eyes focused more closely on me, but the question that followed came in a friendly tone. "How did you escape?"

"They're designed to avoid conflict. How do you think?"

A silence—shocked? Startled? I knew what outsiders thought of the clades, and they weren't entirely wrong. Join, sign the contract, be assured of being surrounded by like-minded individuals working tirelessly for your mutual benefit forever. Raise children who would never break your heart, never rebel. And you wouldn't even have to sacrifice your free will, because you'd *want* just that, just what everyone else wanted. Because you'd be tuned regularly to assure that it was what you wanted and that you were happy with your life choices, and all the hard decisions were made in such a way as not to challenge anyone in the group, because everyone in the group held the same beliefs in common.

Once you signed the contract, you would never be alone again.

You'd never be different again, either.

But what good was difference when it made so many people so terribly sad, so lonely, destroyed so many friendships and families and romantic relationships?

The clades liked to point out that their choices were just a more extreme version of being and remaining a productive member of the Synarche—or any society dedicated to the common good. You made social choices, or you made sophipathic choices, and if you wanted to make sophipathic choices without consequence you went off and joined the Freeports.

Clade members were generally rated among the happiest individuals, when surveyed.

If you could really call them individuals.

"It's not *hard* to escape," I explained. "It's just that almost nobody wants to. But there *are* rules about these things, and free choice, and adult responsibilities and so on. Well, parents are responsible for the education and well-being of their children, and as long as they meet certain standards the Synarche will not intervene. The Synarche requires that upon attaining majority, every child be provided with one an of retreat, during which time they become responsible for their own tuning and right-minding, and at the end of that an they make their own decision whether to remain with the clade or choose another life."

I shrugged, and wondered if Pearl could see in that simple gesture the pain of losing an enforced religion because somebody gave you the switch and you were curious enough to turn it off.

"Most of them go back?" they said.

"Almost all of them go back," I answered. "Before the an is up, usually. Lonely-no-more is hard to put down, and harder not to pick up again."

"Not you, though."

"I . . . discovered I liked my own voice. So I stayed away, and then I requested another retreat an, which they were legally obligated to give. And then I decided I wasn't going back at all."

Connla nudged my drink at me, and I tasted it. Berries and some bright herb I didn't recognize, and an intoxicant burn. It steadied my breathing. There were other, messier details in the story, but we didn't need to go into those now, and here.

The full story was not for strangers in bars.

"They tried to enforce an obligation against her for her education," Connla said dryly, while I watched Pearl's eyebrows go up. "And force her to come back that way."

"Did you pay it off?" Pearl asked.

"The Synarche ruled that the legal person Haimey Dz—that's me— had incurred no debt, because the debt had been incurred by a unit of the clade due to a decision made by the clade and for services executed within the clade. You can't owe yourself a debt. So. No. But I'm not exactly welcome home for the holidiar either. And once I stood up to them on that— well, and there was another thing after—they decided they didn't want me back."

After that drink, I didn't feel like dancing anymore, and it was getting on toward shift-end. Connla was taking his conquest to the strategy game club. I headed back to Singer, to see if he needed any help to get ready for the inspection. He didn't, and I cleaned myself up and went to bed.

Sleeping in gravity, even station grav, is always tricky. My body wakes up achy in strange places, from pressure points, and I wind up feeling itchy and sweaty and compressed. Still, tuning the hormones helps. And retuning them when you wake helps with the inevitable grogginess and discomfiture. Singer would have woken me if there had been any trouble, and he must have noticed me stirring, because there was a hot cup of synthesized coffee waiting for me when I rolled over, dislodging two cats in the process.

Mephistopheles complained about it. Bushyasta just grumbled in her sleep and curled a paw over her eyes.

Nice work, if you can get it.

You know, I complain about the synthetic coffee. But it's really not as bad as all that. It's hot and brown and has caffeine, and getting your drugs per os is more satisfying than just bumping.

Given the dancing under semigrav the night before, I wasn't as sore as I could have been. I just did a little light stretching and checked in with Singer to see if Connla had made it home. He had, but not long before, and was still awake in the common cabin. Singer also told me the inspection had been through, and been pretty cursory. He hadn't felt the need to wake me up for it, and they'd mostly been interested in his logs.

He'd given them copies on his own senso that matched mine exactly, because they had been simultaneously recorded and simultaneously edited. Convenient, that we weren't actually lying at all, and only omitting a few instants.

We were in the process of getting our fuel, and we had our organics. Repairs were under way as well. Now we just had to nerve ourselves up to head for the Core, and let go of Singer. Possibly with pirates in hot pursuit.

"Couldn't get us any more real coffee, huh?" Connla had his own mug, and was huddled sleepily over it. He'd have to tune it down when I pushed him toward his bunk in about a quarter, but right now he looked tiredly pleased and cheerful, and I didn't begrudge him a few extra moments to enjoy his buzz. I'd liked Pearl too, so that was handy.

"How often do you think this outpost gets a shipment of C. *arabica*?" Singer hesitated. "Do you want to run me down to the Core, as arranged? Or *should* I jump ship here and catch an inbound packet?"

"We've got a contract," I reminded.

"How long can we push the extension?" Connla said.

Singer said, "We can try to find a prize on our way downspiral, though the closer to the Core we get, the cleaner-picked the gleanings will be."

"Can't you get out of it?" I asked.

Singer sighed. "I filed for the extension. I can do that *once.*"

"You always kind of wanted this," Connla teased. "Admit it. You've been prepping for it your whole life."

"Life is a meathead-centric term," Singer said primly. "And my feelings on the subject are complex. As you are certainly aware."

Connla snorted laughter.

Singer said, "If I had my choice, I'd bilocate. But I'm not authorized to replicate. And I will miss salvage work, but I can come back to it, if you still want me when my term of service is up."

"Sure," I said grumpily. "What's so exciting about bureaucracy?"

Singer said, "Our current solution to managing predators—which is not without ethical implications—is to remove the desire to exploit the system or others members of the system at a neurological level, on those occasions and in those individuals where it occurs in antisocial volume and becomes sophipathology. And to provide everybody with an Income, which removes some of the motive for the desperate to prey on each other."

"There are still a few predators out there," I said.

"More than a few," Singer agreed, untroubled. "And even more opportunists whose natural social conscience isn't quite sophipathological enough to demand rightminding. One of the interesting things about programming people of all sorts to be more ethical is that it also makes them more ethical about the limits of programming people to be ethical."

"It's the only disease we force treatment of for the benefit of others."

"Not historically," Singer said. "And not in the case of epidemics, where forced treatment or quarantine were routine." I could hear the suppressed amusement in his voice as he said, "It's not a perfect system, just better than all the other ones. And you're absolutely correct. I *want* to do this. Trying to solve the most intractable problems confronting the galaxy—how to get everybody to agree to work together for the common good—is *profoundly* exciting."

"Nerd," Connla said affectionately. Regretfully.

"We need you more than the Synarche does," I said with feeling.

"Individually, yes. In the aggregate, probably not. I could apply for a hardship bye, but I doubt it would be granted. However inconvenient it is to our little enclave . . . I have been selected."

"It's a civic duty."

"It would also be *more* inconvenient to our little enclave if the regulatory body we rely on to create a stable environment collapsed due to lack of participation and we all had to live like the pirates—except without a wealthy and well-regulated shipping, there's not a lot to pirate from. Stealing from people living at subsistence level is a desperation act. Piracy requires an investment, so it also requires a return on that investment. And we learned something about pirates while we were out in the night this time. Maybe I can do something about . . ."

His silence indicated whatever was going on at Downthehatch, and with regard to Colonel Habren.

I tried to sound cheery rather than passive-aggressive. "We can always take your term off, you know. Finish this run, hopefully be in a good position, settle in on the Income for a while. Go back out when you're done."

"We could retire," Connla said dubiously. "We don't *have* to do this. We're out of obligation—just—and Singer's debt will be bought off by his service."

"I'm not cut out to sit on a station somewhere, surrounded by hordes of life-forms. And I'm even less suited to life on a planet, so don't even start with that idea."

Also, Connla and I would both get bored with that pretty quickly. We were *suited* to this, and while it was possible to change what one was suited to . . . it was unattractive to change who you were, unless who you were was making you desperately unhappy.

"We can sign on with a packet," Connla suggested. "Release this tug, get a different one when Singer's through. You could upgrade to navigator, given a couple of correspondence classes on the trip in and the fancy gravsense your new friend has given you."

I couldn't shake the foreboding that if we let Singer go—I mean, not that we could keep him, but that if we let him go—he was never coming back to us. Maybe it was just clade damage—why would anybody who got away from you return if they had better options, and weren't all the options better? Singer could do a lot more with his existence than be a tugboat, let's be honest.

"Still too many people," I replied. "Also, you *love* following orders."

"I could do it for a couple of ans."

I didn't want to go to the Core. I didn't want to sign on with a packet, or settle down to wait for Singer to come back to us in a future that might never happen. I didn't want to hire on a temp AI. I didn't want an alien nanoweb curling around under my skin, showing me the curvature of space-time . . . but I also, somehow, didn't quite want it gone. (As if wanting it gone would help anything, and if I decided I did, heading to the Core and a big interspecies sector hospital would be my best bet of finding somebody with the medical knowledge to get it out and leave me in one piece afterward.)

What I wanted to do—and it was a yearning as strong and rebellious as any journey-an yearning for a clade-disapproved lover who didn't care for you in return—was head up and out, into the darkness. I didn't want to leave the pirates and the factory ship to this understaffed station's bureaucracy. I thought the Goodlaw was pretty okay, but that stationmaster—a total waste of chlorophyll.

Whenever I stopped tuning it out, I kept seeing the dead Ativahika, spinning slowly, and the terrible rendered bubbles of its flesh. I wanted to go *do* something about it.

Myself. *Personally.*

"We could take that in to a better authority too," Singer said, and I realized he'd been monitoring my senso. "Once I'm serving in the Synarche, I could direct resources toward it."

He was right, and my desires were irrational, illogical, atavistic, and selfish. But they were *my* desires, and I was irrationally, illogically, atavistically, selfishly wedded to them. I wanted to keep them, simply because they were mine. Not because they benefitted me in any way.

"Well," Connla said. "I'm going to sleep on it. Let's stay here a few more shifts. We can cut loose to save on docking obligations if you like, though honestly . . ."

"You'd like the run of the station for a little while longer," I said.

"Pearl is pretty great," he said in return, with a sly little smile. "And the odds of us ever making it back out here—"

"Well," I said with a sigh. "Let's talk about it again in a couple of shifts, then. Can we afford the berth that long, Singer?"

"As long as there's no competition for it," he said. "I'll talk to wheelmind and make sure we have a suspended embarkation permission, so we can bounce out at once when we decide we're going, as soon as the station can give us a window. And I'll see about getting your space suits upgraded too."

"Just in case."

"Safety first," he said, and Connla laughed.

CHAPTER 8

WENT DANCING TWICE MORE—AT DIFFERENT BARS, JUST IN case my new friend Rohn showed up again, and I doused myself in antipheromone first even though it gave me the itches—and toured the botanical gardens, and went out to dinner once with Connla and Pearl. I know that depending on where you're from, it probably seems unconcerned, possibly even irresponsible, given the threat sitting docked a third of the ring away from us. But we couldn't *go* anywhere, and it was going to be decians before we were back where we could do anything about it again, and skulking about acting paranoid wouldn't change anything.

Anyway, one of the first things you learn in space is not to *thrash*. If you have nothing constructive to do, the most constructive thing you can do is often nothing at all. In a mindful sense, I mean.

Thrashing is the thing that gets people killed. Not sitting still.

The botanical gardens were amazing considering the size and isolation of Downthehatch. Of course, they were useful for food, and oxygen exchange, and air filtration, but these must be a project of love for somebody. Possibly, if I wasn't stereotyping, Habren themself, being photosynthetic and all.

There was an extensive aquaculture section too, with a dodecapod engaged as gardener—a species I'd encountered descriptions of, but never previously met. Senso with it was *fascinating*, as its perceptual systems were so different from mine we had to use translator meshes even to exchange basic concepts, but after pestering it with badly communicated questions for as long as I thought I could get away with, I almost conceived of a passion to take up water gardening.

Impossible on Singer, of course. And if I give you the impression I was annoying the poor thing, well, I about had to pry myself loose when its explanation of algae control protocols stretched into the second decihour.

After I made my excuses to the dodecapod, I went to wander around the nonaqueous areas of the botanical garden. And that was where I ran into the Goodlaw again.

Almost literally.

Cheeirilaq's mottled wing coverts and carapace blended into the greenery so thoroughly that I would have trodden on one or two of the constable's delicate feathery feet if it hadn't whisked them away a moment before my station shoe descended. I don't think I would have hurt it much, because the shoes are a closed-cell foam meant to protect my tender afthands when I have to walk on them like some kind of barbarian— but low-gravity life-forms are notoriously fragile. The speed of the dodge was . . . well, unearthly, despite the transparent tubes of an ox-supplement system winding around Cheeirilaq's multiple breathing holes, which probably meant it was feeling a little light-headed . . . or light-wherever it kept its brain. Probably in the abdomen, considering the relative size of the head. Or that nice armored thorax, which would get it close to the manipulator arms, and still not too far from the sensory equipment.

Not that I was contemplating all that at the time, you understand.

What I was doing was feeling my hands and scalp go cold while some tiny shrew ancestor in my amygdala stared up at a two-meter-long praying mantis reared back over me with its barbed-wire forelimbs raised as if to stab and clutch. The rodent ancestor screamed at me in whispers to keep still, keep still, keep still and maybe it won't be able to see you and find you and eat you. It was the most amazing sensation, entirely devoid of will: my body just . . . crystallized, as immovable as in those nightmares when your body becomes aware that your REM paralysis is still switched on, but you can't make yourself wake up from whatever horror is chasing you.

We stared at one another for long seconds. Then Cheeirilaq settled its two lifted feet neatly back on the path—in my heightened state, I remember thinking very clearly how the feathery fronds were admirably adapted to grasping surfaces and moving around in low or zero g—closed those bread-knife manipulator arms, and settled itself with a shake of wings and head and torso like a roused cat attempting to shrug back into her dignity.

It looked away and quickly groomed its antennae with the smaller, feathery set of manipulators.

Counting wings and wing coverts, the Goodlaw had eighteen limbs, which was an impressive total for any sentient. And yes, part of my brain was doing the math, because brains are ridiculous. Another part was trying not to get upset about the *sheer number of legs on that thing, oh my Void.*

Its abdomen was still visibly inflating and deflating. The Goodlaw possessed something like lungs, I could see, and from the pulsing transition of each breath along its length, it seemed like it had an efficient one-way respiration system, unlike my own kludgy air bladders that had to waste capacity moving each expired breath back out the way it came. With each deep breath, slender bands of brilliant red became visible around the leaf-green bands of Cheeirilaq's integument. From this, I deduced that Cheeirilaq's chroma could not be too different from my own.

Friend Haimey, it said, and my senso gave the disembodied voice a tone of mild embarrassment. *You . . . startled me.*

Friend?

It had, come to think of it, used the term before. Perhaps it was a term of respect from its species.

"You also startled me, Goodlaw," I said. "I'm very sorry for nearly stepping on your foot. Your lovely natural coloring blends in rather well in this environment."

The foliage of my homeworld is also verdant. Its stridulation, this time, was combined with a breathy whistle from the respiration tubes along its abdomen, a sound that I could not help but hear as melancholy or homesickness.

It's deadly to anthropomorphize, and yet who the hell can stop doing it?

I parsed that for a moment before realizing that in one of those occasional translation bugs—no pun intended—what Cheeirilaq had said was more accurately translated as "lushly shaded in [green]."

"Your species were ambush predators?"

It made a funny little bow. I was starting to get the hang of its body language.

"Mine were opportunistic omnivores," I said. "We ran our prey down in packs and ate a lot of whatever was available."

It stridulated. From this vantage, I could see the variety of sounds being made by the ridged edges of the wing coverts, and the rubbing of the walking legs. I wondered if its species sang for pleasure.

A very sound evolutionary strategy. I would like to visit Terra one dia, but I am afraid it would be impossible.

I imagined the effect of human-standard gravity on the slender legs and exoskeleton and winced. Apparently, I winced visibly enough that it was even obvious to an alien with no mobile facial features, because the tiny head pivoted and rocked to examine me from several angles with the mirrorlike compound eyes, and the tiny pinpricks of simple eyes. I felt like I was being examined by a curious cat.

Maybe all obligate carnivores are essentially the same. Can I eat that? Is it going to eat me? Is it a toy?

Perhaps Cheeirilaq settled on "toy." *You are offended?*

"Oh no," I said. "Just realizing that Terra would be a deadly environment for one such as yourself, due to the gravity, and feeling a pang of sympathy. Hard on the tourists, that."

I often think that we lose many opportunities for cultural exchange because so few of the systers have homeworlds that are mutually compatible for tourism. The senso made it sound disappointed, but Cheeirilaq's upright posture and tilted head made me think it was more wry amusement.

"Saves on a lot of colonial adventurism, though." I took a deep breath of heavily oxygenated air. "I've never been to Terra myself."

Somehow, we fell into step beside one another, proceeding in a stately way through the garden. As the Goodlaw moved, I noticed that it had been standing in a little park area, with an abstract, water-tinkling statue for contemplation, and a bench for contemplating on.

The paths were lined with specimens from many worlds, showy and colorful, arranged to show the foliage to advantage—and so that they could be lit in the most appropriate spectra. There were beds of greens and red-violets, some Terran and some not, some showing flowers or other dramatic structures. There were the black-leaved trees from Favor, with their almost shineless leaf surfaces, forming a dramatic backdrop to some intensely scarlet flowers I did not recognize.

Busy pollinators buzzed and fluttered among them, leaving me to wonder how they knew which plants were biologically compatible. Smell. Instinct. Ancestral insect knowledge.

I wondered if the methane and chlorine sections of Downthehatch had similar extravagances, or if their stationmasters had different hobbies.

We paused beside a low, puce-colored plant that had the rough architecture of a mammalian brain and seemed otherwise unprepossessing, but was nevertheless absolutely darting and swarming with bright-winged butterflies. Or butterfly analogues; I didn't know enough to be able to tell, and couldn't be arsed to check my senso for the data.

It was busy, anyway.

We turned again, this time back toward the aquaculture area. "And Habren? What's their deal?"

My new friend paced alongside me on six slender legs, the two deadly looking raptorial manipulators folded against its forethorax, the more delicate ones waving gently in the air. *Allow me to encrypt this conversation?*

The stationmaster might, in fact, be eavesdropping on our senso.

The Goodlaw, in fact, had access to law-enforcement encryption tools.

"Of course."

It wouldn't be suspicious *at all* that Goodlaw Cheeirilaq and I were talking about it over encrypted channels, of course. But the Goodlaw being the law in these parts, and the Synarche Space Guard being out of town currently, I decided to trust its judgment. There was a tickle as Cheeirilaq established a secure socket into my sphere, requesting limited permissions that I readily granted. It wouldn't prevent a really determined eavesdropper, but it would slow them down a little.

I hoped I would meet you here, it said. *I've been monitoring your movements, under orders from [Habren], and I noticed your pattern of visits. Since I come here fairly often myself, a chance meeting would seem unremarkable.*

Speaking out loud would make the secure connection useless, so I replied silently. *You don't trust Habren.*

There was the virtual equivalent of a shrug. *[Habren] is no worse than many. This place is in dire need of personnel support. The Republic is involved in its management through extortion, as you have no doubt deduced, and [Habren] does not care for being beholden to pirates. However, obtaining defensive personnel is less than easy. Material resources are less of a problem, obviously, because we have excellent printing support and the local system for materials.*

If [Colonel] [Habren] could manage some major coup, they might get more attention and support. That would benefit Habren and also the station, and disbenefit the pirates.

Where do all these plants come from, if resources are so scarce? I asked.

Shipped as seed, often traded with other hobbyists. The soil is manufactured. All the pollinators are local-system. The only real resource expenditure is space, and as you have noticed, the station is not crowded.

Habren's interest is not why you sought me out, however. I felt alarm that Habren had set the Goodlaw to watch me, and confusion at the Goodlaw's loyalties. Habren might be worse than Cheeirilaq was admitting. If there was a chance we were being monitored, it wouldn't exactly want to call out its . . . well, the stationmaster wasn't precisely its boss, but somebody in greater authority over the station than it held itself . . . in a recordable format. And it couldn't entirely know my loyalties, either.

I recognize your tattoos.

Well, that shifted me from mild alarm to sirens shrieking so badly I had to tune myself down to mere alert arousal just in order to hear the rest of the conversation. I took a deep breath and held it and turned my amygdala down to about three, then let the breath out again.

You can see them? I asked, glancing down at my nanoskin-covered arm.

Ultraviolet reflectivity. A wing-settle that could be an insectoid shrug.

I was looking for information on the syster operating the factory ship, I said. Noncommittal, and something it already knew. *There's nothing in our databases, which might be nothing or might be withheld information. Habren claimed they had no information either, but they might be lying.*

That's because the species operating the factory ship is not a syster.

I actually turned to the giant bug and gaped, dumbstruck. As far as I knew, every intelligent race that the Synarche had encountered had, eventually, been induced to join it. The fact of an enormous, existing trade organization and governmental body that, in general, had overwhelmingly superior technology to any emerging race and also a complete monopoly on exploration and trade generally proved a convincing argument. Once a species developed what Terrans called the Alcubierre-White drive, or one of its variant technologies, the Synarche was waiting to greet them.

Sometimes new systers tried to start a shooting war, which generally had similar results to a kitten attacking your pants leg; when the difference in available force is so overwhelming, and you're essentially raising a child, there's literally no need to shoot back. Even races as belligerent as my own had come around eventually.

A few went with isolationist policies for a local generation or two, but eventually somebody started tuning into the propaganda channels and wanting all that great stuff, and within a hundred ans or so—well, the Synarche was also patient. Like a respectful suitor—unlike my friend Rohn in the bar—it had nothing to gain by hurrying things.

Earth could have learned a long time ago that securing initial and ongoing consent, rather than attempting to assert hierarchy, is key to a nonconfrontational relationship. Because we're basically primates, we had to wait for a bunch of aliens to come teach us. We'd at least, by then, developed the tech to fix our brains so we could accept emotionally what logic should have showed us.

What can I say? We're slow.

Not a syster? I asked. I mean, there were the Ativahikas, which weren't *exactly* a syster, not really talking to the rest of us much. And not having a white space drive so much as *being* a white space drive. . . .

Suddenly, all the glittering particles gliding gracefully and harmlessly between the cells of my epidermis seemed to ferociously itch. I'm not a praying sentient, but at that moment, I felt such a horrible black hole of implication implode in my belly that I almost doubled over in pain. Chee-irilaq put a manipulator on my shoulder to steady me.

That's why you recognize the tattoos, I said.

The particles are derived from the sensory organs of Ativahikas. They are not widely known; in fact, their existence is kept a secret outside of law enforcement circles. They are believed to be a form of Koregoi technology that was given to or traded for or somehow imbued into the Ativahika species in a time of great antiquity. In combination with certain innate abilities of the Ativahikas, they allow the species to—

I interrupted. *—to traverse space-time as if they were living starships. And somebody is stealing these particles, by murdering Ativahikas. And I have a bit of this technology embedded in me.*

I'm sorry, Cheeirilaq stridulated, reminding me that the rest of the conversation had been carried out in utter silence.

We stopped before the aquaculture observation windows.

I am glad, the Goodlaw continued, *that you did not acquiesce to this anathema knowing its origin.*

I'm a walking war crime.

Yes.

The dodecapod was hard at work when we paused. It had a combined head and body about a meter across. It didn't speak to us, seeming involved in its labors, but as we paused it raised six of its twelve legs in a cheery wave, flashing ripples of electric blue and silver across its normally sedate dark red surface. Maybe it recognized us; apparently we were both around enough, and we'd been waiting for clearance to leave for more than two dia. Also, dodecapods and humans have kind of a long-term friendly relationship. I don't remember all the details, but we found them before they invented spaceflight—spaceflight is a rough invention for aquatic species, for a number of obvious reasons, though they're great astronauts once somebody gets them up here, and the noncompressibility of water means they're often really good at remaining functional in erratic gs—and before the Synarche brought us in as systers, but after we'd developed crude rightminding technology.

So our species are, in the parlance of the Synarche, elder systers to one another.

Cheeirilaq and I both waved back.

Does Habren know?

Cheeirilaq's wing coverts buzzed. That seemed more like a shrug than a yes, given what I also picked up through the senso.

Who. Who did this to me?

They are Jothari. The Synarche's greatest tragedy. But I think it was Terran pirates who murdered their crew and stole their ship and . . . cargo. Such a wave of distaste that I could feel it through the senso, despite our incompatible neurologies.

The name meant nothing to me.

What do you mean, the Synarche's greatest tragedy? We don't have tragedies anymore.

Well, Cheeirilaq said, *perhaps we still did, a long time ago.*

And it proceeded to tell me the history of how the Synarche learned to be a patient suitor, because it turns out that making mistakes is how we grow up, whether we're a multispecies alien utopia, or just some dude screwing up their first romance beyond believability.

This is what I learned: early on, when the Synarche was new, it was not a Synarche yet at all, but a Galactic Parliamentary Democracy—and grandiosely so named, because in those diar it consisted of five or six of the foundation systers and perhaps a dozen systems. The short version of a very long and ugly story is that by the time the Galactic Parliamentary Democracy encountered the Jothari, the Jothari were working on establishing a smaller but still thriving interstellar community of their own. They'd come of age in one of the sparser and darker arms of the Milky Way—not unlike my own species, as it happened, so I feel a certain sympathy for this—and had never seen any evidence of sentient life until a Parliamentary ship dropped out of white space over their homeworld, ascertained that they were a spacefaring species, and opened communications in as friendly a manner as possible, considering a language gap.

I mean, when you show up in orbit over somebody else's inhabited planet, not dropping a rock on it or tossing your bow wave in their direction is, in itself, a reasonable assurance of goodwill, but not everybody understands that—and there is, I suppose, the possibility that you might want a quickly habitable planet afterward.

Anyway, the Jothari had managed to reach a couple-three of their closest neighbor systems, and had pretty good shipping and space-colonization efforts going on. Then the Galactic Parliamentary Democracy ship full of weirdos like my friend the Goodlaw showed up and opened communications. The Parliamentary crew was not met in a friendly fashion, but at least no shots were fired.

They drew back, and that was when they found out that the Jothari were navigating by harvesting Ativahikas, a species generally-accepted-as-sentient, who had a migratory path running through the core of Jothari space. The Synarche's antecedents tried to intervene, leading to the beginnings of a war.

Through absolute blind bad luck, an antibiotic-resistant pandemic broke out among the Jothari worlds around then, and somewhere between

60 and 80 percent of their population died. They declared this an act of war on the part of the proto-Synarche, and came gunning.

There was a lot more of the proto-Synarche, and despite the Jothari superior navigation, the Synarche . . . wiped them out.

Not to the last being. But to the last world, leaving those that remained homeless. And not welcome in proto-Synarche space—if they would have considered coming near the government that had committed semi-involuntary genocide against them. So they made their way as best they could.

Maybe they have shadow colonies, Cheeirilaq said. *Maybe they've gone as far out as Andromeda and possibly even made allies there. Though if they had, I'm not sure we'd still find them scavenging around the edges of Synarche space.*

They're not in the databases.

No. Well, you could find them. They're not expunged. Just deemphasized. And it's possible the archinformists used keywords that were less than helpful to the neophyte to archive and classify the data.

Possible. Sure. And Habren doesn't want me to know about them?

[Habren's species] was one of the ones involved in the initial mistake. It gave me its version of Habren's species name, which was as made-up as the human version, the original being in plant pheromones. *They're culturally very ashamed. That was about the time people started looking for a better system of government, it turns out. My people have a saying, that every civilization is founded in a terrible crime.*

There didn't seem to be much I could say to that. Even given my limited knowledge of the vast span of Terran history, terrible crimes seemed terribly commonplace, and didn't usually lead to enlightenment.

The swirling, sinking sensation in my gut was grief, and I let myself feel it, along with the gratitude for what the Synarche was. Imperfect, surely; infested with its own brands of sophipathology and problematic social constructs. Walking a fine and wavering balance between the conformity and regulation necessary for social cohesiveness and the observance of individual freedoms within reason.

But also comprised of such a plurality of individuals and syster species spread across such vast distances that it was difficult to obtain an even vaguely accurate census, and somehow, through the tuned social consciences of all of us, managing to function.

There was pride to be taken in that.

It never could have happened without rightminding. And rightminding, taken to extremes, gave you clades. But clades also made a lot of people happy who would have been lonely and broken and without community otherwise.

Nothing is perfect. Except the Well. And what *could* be more perfect than the great big gravity chute of Supermassive Black Hole Saga-star, churning along in its spot at the center of the Milky Way? That's pretty near as perfect as a thing can conceivably be: a horizon of perfect destruction.

Why do you do this? Cheeirilaq asked me, breaking a contemplative silence I hadn't noticed until it ended. The mantid was one of those creatures you could just hang around with, not saying anything, and not notice the quiet because it felt natural. I would have liked it for a shipmate, though Singer would have been a little small. *You could go sit planetside and do pretty much anything at all forever, without competition for scarce resources. So why come out here and risk your neck at all?*

Huh. Apparently humans and twelve-legged, six-winged mantids have some of the same expressions of speech. Who would have guessed?

I was born out here. Why do you? I countered.

Crowded homeworld. I remembered from somewhere, possibly crèche, that Cheeirilaq's people are solitary except for mating and child-rearing. The latter of which is carried on in nursery crèches in which all adults are expected to take a turn. Other than that, they have hobbies and entertainments and pretty much keep to themselves, being intensely territorial.

"One Rashaqin, one station," as they say. Not because they're so tough. Because they just really don't get along.

Strange that it seemed perfectly able to get along with unrelated sentients. Maybe that was pheromones.

It said, *Had to go somewhere. I like solving crimes.*

That doesn't tell me how you wound up out here in this nest of Freeport sympathizers.

It whetted its killing manipulators one over the other, which looked like a threat but might have been a shrug. *Got into some administrative trouble in the Core.*

Noncommittally.

I wondered if it had eaten a suspect. If it had, I hoped the suspect deserved it. It seemed like a good cop, as such things went, and I'd hate to think less of it.

Cheeirilaq sighed. An enormous sigh, like a Terran dog. Its entire abdomen filled with air, swelling each of its breathing chambers until the brilliant red bands around its abdomen were wider than the green, and I could see that they were each edged in thin ribbons of black and a mustardy yellow. I gawped at it in surprise, though really, all sorts of creatures sigh. Oxing up is a sensible response to just about any situation or potential situation that doesn't require immediately holding one's breath. And if you're going to have to hold your breath, well, you might as well be good and pink—or purple, or that nice blue color some critters use to hold oxygen, if that's your thing—when you do so.

I might have to bring you in, it said, reluctantly admitting something we'd both known all along. It stridulated out loud again. *I have sent a packet Coreward regarding our earlier conversation, but please understand that I am basically in exile here, and I find that many of my communications go missing.*

I thought of my reliance on the packets for security and a chance of backup, and tuned my anxiety down a peg. It wasn't helping.

"No hard feelings if you do," I answered. "A bug's gotta eat, after all."

Also, it said, allowing me to sense reluctance, *I know you have some embarrassing political secrets to keep.*

That stunned me to silence for long seconds. I blinked, swallowed, tuned, nodded. *I might have to run away, you understand.*

That is the sensible thing to do when a larger predator is pursuing you. No hard feelings at all.

I was so deep in my head while bounding gently along the corridor back to Singer that it took most of the circumference of the station before I realized I was being followed. Followed pretty expertly, too—my shadow stayed far enough back in the curve that I never got a good look at them (bipedal and humanoid, but not much else), even when I ducked into a shop and came out reversing direction as if I'd spotted something back along the concourse that I wanted to go investigate.

That set my mind racing again, but in a different direction.

Habren wouldn't need to shadow me, because nobody can hide on a station from the wheelmind and the stationmaster. Every centimeter of the interior is under some kind of surveillance, and while you could get lost in a crowd on one of the big ones, maybe, Downthehatch just wasn't large enough. Habren might want to *dust* me, in which case an ambush was more likely than a stalker. If they wanted to send me down the well, they could just jump me when I went back to Singer.

Or a lift or airlock could be arranged to have a convenient accident. Theoretically there were safeguards against that kind of thing—above and beyond rightminding and AI oversight—but I was pretty sure by now that Habren's rightminding was not as stable and maintained as you might like in somebody with a few tens of thousands of lives in their hands.

I got Singer on senso and filled him in, including a dump of everything Cheeirilaq and I had talked about. Some things, you want to make sure your teammates have access to if anything bad should happen to you.

My skin crawled. My palms were wet and cold. I tried to walk casually, as if I were engaged in one last idle wander through open spaces before returning to my departing ship.

Did we ever get our clearance?

I filed for it, Singer answered. *And sent a reminder.*

The pit of my stomach dropped, adding itself to the unsettling sensations. But there was something else, too—a prickling along my body, as if a soft wind were stirring my vellus hair. And a sense of . . . weight. Of gravity. Of something watching, just as I had felt out by the Jothari ship.

Oh, bloody Well, I said to Singer. *I think the guy following me is one of the pirates. And I think they're like me.*

"Screw this," I said out loud, and stopped in the middle of the corridor. It wasn't entirely deserted—there were people here and there—and the adrenaline singing in my veins was longing for a confrontation. I could have tuned it down—probably should have—but it felt good, and I have not always had the best record when it comes to deciding to turn off harmful but thrilling emotions.

Haimey, Singer said, *what are you doing?*

Dealing with a problem.

Oh, for crying out loud. He didn't think it at me, but I could feel his irritation, and also his recognition of the fact that meatforms did a lot of stupid things because of our meat, and the senseless clutter of our drunkard's-walk evolutionary development didn't help.

Sure, I said, responding to his emotion rather than any words, and trying to keep my tone light. *There's no pointless code clutter still floating around in you.*

I do regular maintenance, he sniffed. *But you wouldn't be Haimey if you weren't pugnacious.*

I laughed out loud.

Conveniently, just as my stalker rounded the corner, and I got my first good look at them. At *her.*

I don't go in for the sexy bad-girl thing anymore, but . . . damn. The Republican pirate was charismatic in a way that reached right past all the rightminding safeguards on my emotions and hormones and made me want to get to know her better and bond and be best friends with her forever. You can turn off sex, and you can turn off romantic love—but it's really hard to turn off all the human emotional responses to a powerful individual without also turning off your humanity.

She looked like a planetary: not tall, but her body bulky with high-grav muscles, shoulders wide and sleeves of her coverall rolled up to show off sculptured forearms. She had a broad face with high, slanted cheek-bones; coffee-dark eyes with a moderate fold; straight black hair cropped at the ear except for some longer locks, those dyed in fluttering streaks of red and gold.

Her light gold complexion was dusted in cobwebs of silver.

I gaped. She hesitated, but not as if she was surprised to see me. She glanced over her shoulder and then settled herself, arms folded, rubber-soled boots planted. Looked like she had gravity-style feet inside them, instead of afthands. I wondered if that meant she went planetside frequently.

She looked me up and down. My skin prickled with observation as she performed the same kind of assessment on me as I had on her. She cocked her head.

In a clear, light tone, she said, "I know who you are, Haimey Dz. You used to be a revolutionary."

"Suddenly," I said, "a lot of folks are very interested in my past misdeeds."

"Misdeeds?" She shook her head sadly. "What happened to you?"

"Is that what they say about me where you're from?" I asked. "The Legendary Haimey Dz?"

She laughed. "Not exactly."

"I'm flattered to find out I'm a topic of conversation anywhere. I'm a tugboat engineer. And you have the advantage of me."

It was a deliberate opening, to see what she would do. She surprised me.

She stroked her chin with a thumb and forefinger, making her cob-webs sparkle. No wonder people were staring; the effect was distracting. She said, "My name is Zanya Farweather, and I'm a representative of the Autonomous Collective Republic of Freeports."

"You're a pirate."

"If you're a fascist, sure."

I am not entirely sure how I kept myself from rolling my eyes. God, she sounded like my first girlfriend. Only girlfriend, if I'm going to be honest. As if tyranny of the majority or a complete lack of social controls were somehow better than Synarchy.

But she also flaunted her galaxies openly, and I hid mine under a layer of paint. And she had to know where they came from.

This person is probably the same one who killed a whole shipful of Jothari.

"What do you want?"

"You have possession of something of ours."

"Something you stole, you mean." *From some people who murdered to get it.*

Her pretty eyes narrowed. "Pretty self-righteous, for an interstellar dumpster diver."

"Was that supposed to be an insult of some kind? Because if you're trying to threaten me—"

She sighed. Stepped back, and crossed her arms. The labile play of emotions across her face reminded me that I was probably dealing with somebody unrightminded, who had never had therapy or engaged in the kind of self-examination that makes you question and eventually understand yourself and your own emotions. The Freeporters were violently opposed to social controls of all sorts. Even—especially?—healthy ones.

She was a reactionary force.

I was scared of her.

Connla and Singer were in my senso, and I could feel them there. Their support was encouraging. Singer was probably tuning me, too, to keep me from freaking the hell out. This was not a time when an atavistic panic response from my endocrine system would be useful.

See above; sometimes the best thing you can do is just not thrash.

"I'm trying to offer you a place," she said, the muscles in her upper arms rippling as she tightened her grip on her own crossed arms. She was,

I realized, struggling to control her temper. "Look, Haimey. You were very resourceful out there. We can use people like you. And like your shipmind, who we know has been requisitioned back to the Core and isn't too keen on going. You're in obligation trouble. Financial trouble," she reinforced, stressing the archaic word. "We can give you freedom and keep you together."

"How do you know all that?"

"Your shipmind filed for a service extension. And it's not like you and your shipmates brought back a lot of salvage to justify the outlay on this salvage mission. So"—she smiled and unfolded her arms to wave one hand airily—"come with us. Be free of the Synarche. Find out what it's like to truly be yourself, without a bunch of hive-types telling you what to think and feel. You already threw off the clade mind control. Why not dispense with the rest of it for a while and experience an honest emotion or two? You never know . . ."

The smile broadened, and even with my limbic system tuned way down I felt the shiver of her charisma in the pit of my stomach. "I heard a rumor you like bad girls."

It was all I could manage to keep from rolling my eyes. Maybe they *hadn't* researched me that thoroughly, then. Or maybe their barbarian emotional logic actually led them to believe that such an appeal could trump my better judgment. And my rightminding.

"Thanks," I said. "I'd sooner kiss Rohn."

I saw her attempt to parse what I was saying, the look of puzzlement creasing her flawless brow when the words didn't impart meaning no matter what directions she turned them about in.

I took a step back toward Singer's airlock, feeling fiercely glad that I could just step sideways into it rather than having to drop or climb down a shaft. Giving Sexy Pirate Farweather the advantage of elevation was a risk I didn't want to take. The second step, though, I felt—well, I felt heavy. Profoundly heavy, as if I were under a big change in v, or very tired, or both.

"Sorry, kid," Farweather said. "Can't let you do that—"

Oh dear, said a series of chirp and sawing noises. *Is there a problem here, Synizens?*

A large green serrated limb poked out between us, barring the width of the corridor. Gravity returned to normal, and I shot Cheeirilaq a quick senso warning that things might get dangerously heavy for its physiognomy.

Not that I was sure what either of us could do about it if she decided to squash the Goodlaw like a . . . well, like a bug.

She's not a Synizen, I sensoed.

Cheeirilaq didn't respond. It flexed its saw-toothed forelimbs as if stretching out a kink and pivoted its head so the light flashed off its faceted eyes.

"Just asking directions," Farweather said. She was already fading back down the corridor, and as she vanished around the corner I felt a moment of profound relief—and then an instant later I realized that my palms were clammy with sweat and my heart was pounding so hard my vision wasn't stable.

I thought you tuned me down, I accused Singer.

I did, he answered. *It seemed possible you might need all the adrenaline you could get, however.*

That was fair. I couldn't get too mad at him for fiddling that, even without permission. Even with all the juice making me unstable.

And as the immediate threat passed, I stopped trembling and managed to focus myself on Cheeirilaq. "Thank you for preventing my kidnapping, anyway. Is this going to put you in a bad position?"

Its antennae did something that was probably a shrug, and it stridulated, *No worse than I already am. This is still a Synarche station. Whatever [Habren] gets up to on the side. If anything happened to me, the constabulary would show up in force, expense of shipping resources to the end of nowhere aside, and they don't want to risk that. What was that being insinuating about you, Haimey? I only caught part of the conversation.*

"I thought you knew my political secrets."

I know they exist. Your record is sealed.

Which raised the interesting question of how Sexy Pirate knew about it.

I thought you might be a Core agent, Cheeirilaq admitted. *I take it I was mistaken.*

"It's a long story," I said.

Why is it sealed?

"I was underage," I answered, turning to go. "And the courts decided that it wasn't my fault."

CHAPTER 9

SLID INTO THE AIRLOCK UNMOLESTED BUT SOAKING IN anxiety hormones to the point where Singer actually reached in through the senso and twiddled me down a notch for the second time in a few minutes. I was aggravated about it until the calm chemicals hit, and then I remembered that there was a reason why I'd let him talk me into giving him the keys. When I get really bad, I don't always remember that the terrible, distracting atavism is something I can fix, or even that I ought to.

Singer never forgets.

He was living up to his name when I stepped inside, engaged in a four-part vocal round with himself that seemed to have something to do with the world's largest Mexican restaurant, by which I deduced that it was an antique. Singer also has a thing about madrigals, which means that Connla and I know a lot of madrigals.

"Did you get all that?" I asked from the airlock.

"Enough of it," Connla said dryly.

One of the reasons we picked out our tug was that Singer liked the acoustics.

He was singing softly enough that the cats weren't hiding. I wriggled out of my station shoes and shooed the cats into their acceleration pods—well, I shooed Mephistopheles. Bushyasta, I just picked up, fitted her tiny little breathing mask, and plopped her in while she cracked one eye and purred at me; apparently doing anything else under quarter grav was entirely too much effort for anybody, and at this point I was inclined to agree. Connla was in the common cabin, finishing a set of pushups. I tossed him a towel and nearly missed because I'm terrible at arcs under gravity, but he snaked an arm out and caught it anyway.

Singer brought his round to a perfectly timed and elegant close.

Connla pulled a shirt on. "What does wheelmind say about debarkation?"

"No clearance yet."

"We filed shifts ago. This begins to resemble intentional obstructionism."

"Yep," I agreed. "They're keeping us here. But if so, why did they give us a full load of fuel and consumables?"

"We're not the only crew who could use those," Connla said ominously. "Singer, give me a direct patch to wheelmind? And to Colonel Habren, if they're available. But the AI is what I really want."

"You have it."

Connla had long legs, and it only took him a couple of bounds to make it into the command cabin. I was a little behind him, and dropped into my acceleration couch without anybody having to mention it. Singer'd stretched a film across the gangway. We both had to walk through it to get from the aft end of the tug, so I had a little bit of breath protection. I looked through it at my painted hands as I settled my harness, and wondered if it would be enough. Not being able to see the webwork of the Koregoi senso on my skin seemed abruptly wrong and worrying.

Connla took a deep breath and put his most professional voice on. "Wheelmind Downthehatch, this is Salvage Tug Terran Registration number 657-2929-04 requesting immediate leave to depart."

"Request pending," the station AI said.

Connla started the EM drive. "Can you give me a reason for the delay, wheelmind?"

"Stationmaster Habren would like to speak with you before you depart."

"Our exit flight plan has been filed for five shifts, wheelmind. Please advise if there is an error in it that requires correction?"

"No error," the wheelmind replied. It had a typically musical AI voice, in a higher register that would cut through noise. I wondered what pronouns it liked.

"Definitely," Singer said, just for the three of us, "being stalled."

"Please stand by for transmission from Stationmaster Habren."

This is being designate [Colonel][Habren]. Salvage tug 657-2929-04, please stand down engines. You are not cleared to depart.

"Reason?" Connla said, shortly.

Singer's hull resounded with unexpected impact like a steel drum. I jumped against the restraints, a moment of panic confusing my reactions before it came under control and I identified the sound. Someone was hammering with heavy fists or some other resilient object on the station-side door of the airlock.

The deep voice of the symbiote-infected pirate, sonorous and trying not to sound irritated, boomed through the intercom. "Just hold up a min! I only want to talk to you!"

Connla glanced over at me.

I shook my head. "There's your reason."

Wheelmind's voice broke in again. "Salvage Tug designation 657-2929-04, please be aware that you are incurring resource obligation by refusing to stand down. The air you are breathing belongs to somebody else."

"Void and Well," Connla cursed. The tug shivered as Singer increased the power to the EM drive.

We could try to pull ourselves loose using that, but would probably just wind up screwing up Downthehatch's orbit in a lot of annoying ways that would be time-consuming and irresponsibly resource-expensive to fix and which we would incur obligation for. While staying, ourselves, stuck right to it. We could try to blow the docking bolts, but that risked damaging Singer's airlock—and spaceworthiness.

Connla snapped, "Wheelmind, this is Salvage Tug Terran space ship registration number 657-2929-04, advising that if you do not withdraw the docking bolts, we *will* have no choice but to engage our white drive."

I gaped. We might survive it, being safe . . . ish . . . inside our AW bubble. The station—

The loss of life would be extreme, as whatever bits of the station extended into Singer's white bubble were suddenly dropped into the universe next door. We'd be stuck with a big chunk of space station attached to our docking ring. The wheel . . . would be stuck with a great, gaping hole.

I was still reeling with the enormity when Singer's hull vibrated gently with the scrape of withdrawing docking bolts, and we drifted free. Vibration doesn't carry in a vacuum, so the pounding cut off instantaneously, and in the immediate silence that followed, Connla said, "Can't follow our filed flight plan. I'm going to have to live-stick this. Haimey, if your passenger notices any obstacles before I do, I'm sure we'd all appreciate a heads-up."

A patter of light impacts rang through the hull—not dangerous, not high mass and not high velocity. The shower of particles and debris shot past us, streaking by the windscreen, glittering as they turned. I whipped my head around reflexively, which was ridiculous, but the lizard brain has its own protocols.

Senso and Singer pivoted my vision to the rear of the ship. Senso showed me a big human or close analogue standing framed in the open airlock door. The human had dumped the lock, blowing out into space after us whatever small supplies and bits of things we hadn't yet loaded and stowed.

I hoped we hadn't just been pelted with anything important.

The human figure was Farweather.

I didn't know how I knew, because she was anonymous in a heavy-duty vacuum suit, but I knew it like I knew the back of my hand. Better, my own hands having become fairly alien to me of late.

Behind Farweather, the glossy orange-red of the decomp door showed brilliantly. She was silhouetted against it in the pale decomp suit. How she'd held her position against the outrush of air I couldn't imagine.

Or rather, I couldn't imagine—but I knew. Because my parasite felt the shift in mass, the way Farweather linked herself to the structure of the wheel, and the way the station's rotation faltered and its orbit began to adjust to compensate. She was suddenly massive enough that the wheel just ... stuck to her.

Its rotation was whipping her out of sight. I breathed a sigh of relief, imagining Farweather glowering through her face screen.

I said, "Punch it."

"Punching," Connla replied.

Just as something much larger than our little pile of abandoned consumables launched itself away from the vanishing airlock, directly at Singer's stern.

"I should probably tell you guys—"

"Brace for evasion," Singer said.

I yowled like one of the cats as he twisted us to the left and down. The projectile should have slipped past us comfortably after the course correction, except—

"It's her," I said.

"Her."

"The—it must be the pirate. Farweather. I can *feel* her."

"She *jumped after us?*" Connla yelped. "Of all the lunatic—"

Singer said, "Can you feel why I don't detect any thrusters, even though her trajectory is altering to match ours?"

"Yes." I could feel her bending space. Moving herself, by changing the shape of the universe. And in some peculiar way I could just ... sense her presence. "She's like me."

"Like you." Singer sounded dubious.

I scratched my wrist, leaving welts through the film. There was a dead sentient embedded under my skin. I couldn't think about that now. Maybe I couldn't think about it ever.

"She's got the parasite, okay? She's probably the person who was on the *Marauder*. The mass-murderer." There was a moment of stunned silence. Connla looked over at me, and even Singer had no immediate response. If either of my shipmates had been about to speak after that, I cut them off by changing the subject. "She's accelerating. Gaining on us . . . Transition?"

"There's a lot of clutter this close to the station," Connla said. "Don't want to sweep up somebody's lightsail in our bow wave and take them for a ride." He wove us through a flotilla of tiny, glittering pleasure craft as he said it, then ducked us under the pushed-in muzzle of an insystem mining server towing a seemingly infinite strand of cargo pearls.

"She's still coming."

"We're still leaving," Connla said, and spun us onto a new trajectory.

The thing about the EM drive; it's cheap, but it's stately. We weren't moving fast, exactly, and I could feel the pirate slinging herself down gravitational slopes and along flares of magnetic force like some kind of interplanetary traceuse.

So this was how the Ativahikas did it.

"What's she going to do if she catches us?" Connla asked. "Punch through the hull?"

I thought about supermassive fists. "Maybe?"

Then I realized something.

What she could do—was doing—I could also do. Maybe.

The parasite tingled with awareness in my skin. What she was doing to space-time—why couldn't I do it too?

But how? What was the procedure?

I'd tried talking to the parasite—of course I had, wouldn't you?—and the parasite was notable in never actually talking back. It gave me sensory information, apparently, and that was all. I had no idea how I might get it to take and act on information from me. We'd used the map it generated to slingshot us around some strange gravity curves on the way here, but I hadn't *changed* anything.

Except. When I'd first contracted it.

My hand had felt . . . really heavy.

"We're not accelerating as well as we ought to be," Connla said. "It's like something is damping the drive, or like we're hauling more mass than we should be."

Oh, so she could do that too, could she? Less and less did I want to fight her.

"I'll go get her," I said tiredly. I reached to uncouple my harness. I had my film; maybe the parasite would protect me a little bit.

"And fistfight her? Yeah, I don't think so," Connla said. "New plan."

She was less than a kilometer away now, a little figure shining silver in her suit as the primary's rays limned her. We dodged around a ferry— Void, the *fines*—and she made up a few meters by adjusting to the hypotenuse of our maneuver.

But wait.

What if we were really massive, and being pulled in a particular direction by that mass? Down the slopes of space-time, like some kind of snowboarding dirtsider. They go in for all kinds of crazy sports down there.

The flying suits look like fun, I admit it. Especially on a dense-atmosphere low-grav world, like the homeworld Cheeirilaq's species came from. Man, I bet they got a lot of tourism interest from extreme sports types.

I imagined myself, Singer, the whole lot of us—heavy. Pushed from behind by the expansion of space-time. Pulled from before by its compression. Exactly what the white drive did, only without the bubble. Sliding down a sudden and unexpected regional gravity well.

"This is going to fuck up orbital dynamics alllll over this system," I said out loud as Singer leaped down the slope in space-time I had just constructed, and spun on a long arc away from the crowded environs of the wheel.

"It doesn't when the Ativahikas do it," Singer said, so I knew he was monitoring my senso. "Maybe the Koregoi knew a trick."

"Do you think the Koregoi engineered the Ativahikas?"

"I think now is a lousy time to theorize!"

Staring out the forward port wasn't helping me relax into guiding the tug. I closed my eyes and tried to extend myself into the world as you do when you meditate. Seeking the alpha state, concentrating on my breath, extending filaments into the universe as I tried to relax into a place of calm and comprehension. Sometimes the old-fashioned tricks are the best.

Meditation is supposed to be centering; focusing. It is not supposed to feel as if you have just dropped a huge stone down the well of your being. But as I reached out, something huge and nonexistent slammed itself into the center of my awareness. It felt like it splashed me up against the edges of myself—all the physical sensations of a shattering revelation without the actual epiphany. Hunger cramped my stomach; chills and aches filled my limbs. I shuddered and gasped.

But when I reached back, I realized that we were opening a lead on the pirate. I could feel her back there, her own little dimple in space-time dropping away from ours. When I reached back, I felt a kind of tickle, as if her attention reached out to me in return. My head snapped around; for a moment I would have sworn that somebody said my name.

I could also feel the swirl of the system, all its tangles of influences and shifting patterns of interaction. How does any system manage to find a stable pattern? It boggles the mind.

"Take us off the plane and punch out," I told Connla, crawling back into my own awareness enough to make my mouth form sounds.

"On it," he said, resuming control. We had as much v now as I could give us without knocking myself unconscious, which seemed like it would be poor foresight. I hoped there wasn't a second pirate ship lurking up here—but I couldn't feel one, and I thought with this new awareness a white bubble would have stood out like a hard nodule, a bead under the skin of space. That wouldn't stop the one back on the station from coming after us, though.

I let my awareness collapse. I fell back in my couch, soaked in so much nervous and exertion sweat that the film was not keeping up with it. I turned my head with great effort and looked over at Connla. "Maybe turn down the psychopathy a little bit next time. Wow."

"It got us out, didn't it?" He gave me his charming rogue smile.

I swallowed sickness. "Would you really have done it? If Habren had been sophipathic enough to push the issue—"

"Connla wouldn't have to," Singer said. "He addressed his remark to the wheelmind. The AI would be forced to act to preserve as much life as possible."

I said, "I guess we know why Habren had the wheelmind delaying us. They were stalling us until the pirates made up their minds what to do. Oh, we just racked up so much punitive obligation with those traffic violations."

"I don't mean to make you nervous," Singer said, "but we're going to have bigger problems than debt when we get back to civilization, unless we can prove something on that stationmaster. Criminal charges, my friends."

"I hope it was the stationmaster," I said. "I liked the Goodlaw."

On the other hand, I wouldn't feel betrayed, exactly, if it turned out that Cheeirilaq was in league with the pirates. I liked it, but that didn't mean I trusted it.

And the pirate had been charismatic, but that didn't mean I liked or trusted her, either. Connla and Singer get a bye, because I'll never feel attracted to either one of them, but I think I mentioned I got all that endocrine stuff turned off. It's better for me if I'm not attracted to people physically, because wanting people makes me want to trust them. I've never been able to nourish any desire to fuck people I don't trust. And vulnerability? It's just too fucking scary.

So why let yourself feel lonely when you already know that having a relationship won't do anything except make you anxious about whatever terrible thing might happen next, and if you turn off the anxiousness, you'll feel like an idiot when something bad inevitably happens?

"Well, they're both suspect for now," Connla said brutally, hands flying over his panels. "Everybody we interacted with is suspect."

He was doing a lot of his flying through senso, but the ability to delegate functions to your reflexes and muscle memory is, so far, irreproducible. I can't do the math in time to catch a softball if somebody tosses me one—but my body, sufficiently practiced, can just reach out and snag it out of the atmosphere.

Well, unless I'm under gravity. In which case my body has no clue what it's doing.

We couldn't, obviously, count on station guidance on the way out. So he was doing it all himself, and it was impressive to watch.

"I'm sorry," I said to Connla, because we both knew the stationmaster and the Goodlaw weren't the only people who were suspect. "You liked Pearl."

He grunted. "I hope it was the stationmaster, too."

"New problem," Singer said, merciless. "Where exactly in the six thousand, three hundred, fifty-one systems; eight thousand, eight hundred, and seventy-three worlds; and tens of thousands of miscellaneous outposts—estimated from best available recent date—are we going now, oh my fugitive crew?"

Singer always asked the best/worst questions. I stalled, because organic life-forms need a lot of boring time to think, not having as many parallel processing pathways as our AI brethren.

"Are there really that many inhabited worlds?"

"Counting moons, but not counting asteroid outposts," he said. "Remember, some systems have multiple habitable worlds, especially when you start counting methane and chlorine and water breathers."

Now that he mentioned it, I'd heard that Terra had come to arrangements with some systers about a colony on a moon of one of the gas giants there. Ox breathers like me don't have much use for a nice, rich, frozen ball of methane, but somebody sure does.

More power to them, I say. There are benefits of having a friendly noncompetitive syster civilization next door. Somebody farther out in the system might be able to catch an inconvenient rock before it bumps into your homeworld, for example. And there's exploration to consider as well. Much easier for somebody who's at home in an environment to map it and science it up than somebody who needs a drone or a pressure suit to get there.

I thought of Cheeirilaq, and how logistics made it impossible for many of us to have any chance at all of visiting each other's homeworlds except for virtually. I'd argue that that's a strength of the space natives. We come from the same world, even if we breathe different things, and our perspectives overlap in ways people like Connla have to work much harder to appreciate.

We're all little warm things in the bosom of the great Cold, after all. Well, okay. Except for those methane types. They're generally not very warm at all. Though warmer than space, which is something.

"We could go join the Freeports," Connla said, deadpan.

"I think they're trying to eat us," I replied. "I suspect any offers of assistance from that quarter come with fishhooks."

"Piracy really isn't my thing," Singer agreed.

I couldn't believe it was me who offered, "Head for the Core, explain what happened, turn ourselves in?"

"You're full of interdicted tech without a good explanation for how it got there, and no way to get it back out again," Connla said. "I'm sure your by-the-book Goodlaw friend is likely to mention that in the next packet."

"If Habren lets it," I said. I had a feeling about how free and clear communications going in and out of that station were. "Why are the pirates still after us?"

"How did they *track* us?" Connla countered.

"Oh, I think I know that." I sighed. "Another way I'm a liability. Singer, I'm sorry, this isn't making things easier for you, either."

"They can't have tracked you," Singer said. "They were at the station when we arrived. They must be thinking that we tracked them."

I knew that a Synarche service summons wasn't the sort of thing you just . . . shrugged off. And I . . . didn't have anywhere else to go.

"Posit," Singer said. "The pirates are still after us because they want you, Haimey."

"They were willing to blow me up pretty good along with the rest of us back at the factory ship."

"Are we sure those are the pirates?" Connla asked.

"Well," I cursed. "Don't tell me there's a *third* party running around with a dose of Koregoi-Ativahika nanobug parasites. I'm not sure I'm ready to incorporate that."

Singer said, "There's a possibility that they didn't know you had the Koregoi senso on board, at that point. Or that you'd integrate it and be able and willing to use it. Also, they shot us free of the Jothari ship. They could have just blown us up."

"Huh," Connla said. "Right. So we presume for now that they are, in fact, pirates. Why do they want us now when they didn't before?" He picked at his thumbnail thoughtfully.

"They reviewed the *Milk Chocolate Marauder*'s files and saw me get jabbed. Or Farweather just felt the stuff in me." I shrugged.

I thought for a few moments about things that didn't make sense. Like the pirates not destroying us outright, if that was their goal. Like Zanya Farweather knowing who I was, and at least a little bit about my history.

"I bet the person who sold us that intel about the Jothari ship was working for Habren, or these pirates," I said. "This Farweather person said a few things that made me think we were expected. I think we were brought out here on purpose."

Singer said, "They think we have information. They wanted us—

Haimey?—alive and possibly cooperative. And they wanted that before they knew Haimey had the Koregoi senso on board."

"That's not creepy," Connla said.

"Okay," I said. "So what do we know that we don't know we know?"

"More to the point," Connla said, "what does the parasite know?"

CHAPTER 10

I'S NOT LIKE THE DAMNED THING SPEAKS ENGLISH!" I fumed, the third time Connla looked over at me worriedly. I understood—I got it! The pirates could—somehow—track us. Probably through the parasite, because it was the only superscience we had floating around, and I didn't know of any more conventional means by which it could have been accomplished. More to the point, *Singer* didn't know about any, and he had better data banks than I did.

But *I* couldn't seem to track the pirates in return. Not over this distance. And not to put too fine a point on it, but we didn't know where we were going or what to do next. And until we figured it out, we had the choice of burning irreplaceable fuel going in what might turn out to be a wrong direction; trying to outrun the news that we'd gone rogue that was no doubt even now propagating, packet by packet, across the galaxy; or throwing in the towel, heading for the Core, turning ourselves in, and trying to explain away the illegal and dangerous actions we'd taken by convincing the Synarche that their local government at Downthehatch was a corrupted sector. We couldn't drop out of white space and wait until we came up with a plan, despite our very adequate stock of consumables, because there was that chance that the pirates could track us, and if we stood still there was the chance they might catch us.

Well. Meditating worked the last time.

What the hell, it might work again.

I don't want to get all woo about it, because it didn't feel like that at all. And I've never been big into the Eightfold Path or any of that religious stuff—Connla dabbled with it for a while, but I think that was mostly a reaction to where he grew up, and he eventually dropped all the Buddha and went for "loveable" rogue, instead.

Honestly, Right Speech and its prohibition on filling the air with needless chattering would probably be the hardest one for me. Also, I like the occasional curse word. But putting yourself into a meditative state, that's useful, and it turns out that even before tuning and rightminding, people knew a little bit about how to hack their neurochemistry.

I settled myself in a convenient corner of the common cabin, folded myself into a comfortably fetal position, and sent myself into my breath. I'd been able to feel the pirate the last time I did this; maybe I could at least get a fix on her position again. Maybe if I calmed myself and observed the sensations from the parasite for a while, it would even tell me something I didn't already know.

I was out of other ideas, anyway.

It took a few moments to find my breath, but once I did I settled into the comfortable no-space inside myself pretty rapidly. As before, concentrating made the sensations of the parasite in my body stand out more strongly—not just as new, or alien, but as a sense I hadn't previously known I had. Humans were pretty sense-poor, even among Terran species, but I imagined that my new facility was not unlike those species who were able to navigate by sensing a planet's magnetosphere, or who had some kind of built-in echolocation.

It's pretty common to visualize space-time via a wireframe projection, which is useful because it makes the concept of a "gravity well" and so forth intuitively obvious. If you're a planetary, it's like visualizing the landscape's inclines via a topographic map. Of course, it's also deceptive, for a couple of reasons.

The first is that space-time (as we sense-limited humans perceive it) is neither two-dimensional nor static, but four-dimensional, and one of those dimensions is imperceptible to us except that it's what keeps everything from happening at once. The other is that it's not a wireframe, any more than Olympus Mons is a series of lines drawn at varying intervals to one another. So what I was perceiving was probably not at all like what most people would be visualizing, any more than . . . any more than George Eliot's narrative of *Middlemarch*, enormous and sprawling and omniscient as it is, can accurately represent the breadth and depth of the fictional world that it implies in its interstices, as babies are revealed to have been conceived, carried, and born in an aside or two; as marriages and wedding journeys occur while our attention is with someone else in some other state of domestic crisis.

My awareness of what for lack of a better analogy I will call the shape of space-time started to permeate me as I floated and felt. As if my nerve endings did not end with my skin; as if I were feeling a great, transparent, but still defined real matrix that I was embedded in but could move through, more or less freely. Gravity wells like cliffs you could fall down from any angle, or like great down-welling currents—easy to sense, and instinctively I knew they were dangerous and I should stay clear. I felt as if I had been navigating a vast space by touch alone, groping in the darkness, and suddenly I could see.

And yet somehow all that information came through a sense of patterns of weight not so much on as *in* my skin. The parasite, through whatever alien means, was training my brain to accept its input as sensory data and perceive it as this matrix I was examining now.

Neuroplasticity is a wonderful thing.

But I still had to stop and look, I supposed, which was why the meditation was useful. There was a lot of competing sensory input, and my brain tended to preferentially sort that from the senses it was used to interpreting as more important and more immediately relevant. So I had a selective attention problem: I could pay attention to what my eyes and ears and skin and tongue and inner ear and whatnot told me, or I could pay attention to my . . . space sonar, which I badly needed a better name for.

I bet dolphins and dodecapods don't have this problem.

Well, they might, if you strapped corrective lenses onto their eyes and stuck them in a rover vehicle optimized to be operated by flippers.

So there was the world inside my skin, space in all its folds and sweeps and tangles and cliffs and swells, immense and moving and utterly incomprehensible, and even as I tuned myself into it I spiked a surge of panic at how *big* everything was. It was the same atavistic emotion our ancestors felt, I imagined, in their tiny boats in the middle of a vast and changing sea with no land in sight and nothing in any direction to tell them which way to go, or even which way they *were* going, because the world was moving around them and moving them around even as in their own perspective they were staying still.

I drew a deep breath and told myself that they had the same thing I had.

We both had the stars.

Slowly, I began to build a sense of where I was in this strange and gigantic spread of information, and what certain elements of it might mean. There was the Core, I was certain—that increasing, variegated slope that ended in a stunning drop, which suggested to me that that was a place from which even information could not escape. That's the textbook definition of a certain kind of space-time phenomenon, and it seemed to be the right spot for the Saga-star.

I felt the power of the enormous black hole, and it was like a cliff you couldn't even get your nerve up to glance down. I could feel the weight of Andromeda, and other galaxies farther out—and the lightness and . . . frailness . . . of so-called Cold Patches, where the fabric of the universe was frayed from interuniversal collisions or less explainable phenomena. I made the decision that these things were irrelevant to my current needs, not because of any certainty that I was right but because the need to filter out something—*anything*—made me arbitrary.

"The *science* you could do with this," Singer breathed, riding my senso.

"Yeah, and they're using it to vivisect Ativahikas." I couldn't have kept the bitterness out of my voice, so I didn't even try.

He sighed and said, "I still think we should turn ourselves in."

"I know, Singer," Connla said soothingly. "We know."

Closer to home, though, I had a sense of where we were, and where we'd been, and the universe is so big that even though we were moving as fast as our A-WD could push us, I had plenty of time to look around in a leisurely fashion and admire the scenery.

The macro scale wasn't helping me much. I had a sense, a little itch, that might have been the pirate. It felt both familiar and out of place, noticeable as a spot on light cloth, sharp as a pinprick brushing skin, and it was, for the time being, comfortably far away. I let that go—it didn't help us, did it? Because we weren't going anywhere closer to the pirates if I could possibly help it—and with that, I realized also that I could feel other motions, quick and slight like stroking fingertips. Uncounted myriads of them, softer and subtler than the pin-tip pressure that I assumed was our Republic nemesis.

Ativahikas, maybe? If they used the same means to navigate these soundless and unsounded seas, it seemed logical that we'd be able to sense one another. And then I also sensed pressure points that might be the *Milk Chocolate Marauder*'s sister ships, a very few of them flitting about the edges of Synarche space. I could feel the space lanes, too, like running lights against a dark sky marking out the patterns of approach paths to a station. We were avoiding those, and any Synarche world, like the craven fugitives we were.

There was so much information, and I had so little sense what any of it meant. Or even what I was looking for, honestly. Where did we go from here? What was the next step? What was the place we should seek?

Hell, we couldn't even run away and join the Republic. We were in trouble with the pirates too.

I went deeper, tuned my attention finer. Started to look at the subtle and beautiful patterns of heaviness that lace the universe, for lack of any better ideas.

The cobwebs of dark gravity were lovely, and it struck me how profoundly lucky I was to be able to sense them now. I was one of the first humans to perceive this, which—now that I was thinking more clearly—made me return to contemplate Singer's comment on what a profound scientific tool I'd stumbled upon. That in itself might be enough to get us out of trouble with the Synarche, though it also probably meant that I would get drafted into public service along with Singer, leaving poor Connla on his own. The scientific and survey corps would be slavering to get their hands on this tech—to be able to sense dark gravity directly, rather than relying on gravitational lensing and its other effects on actual *visible* things, would be an observational advantage beyond profound.

Assuming, of course, that our scientists could find a way to duplicate it without murdering Ativahikas to get it. Maybe they could back-engineer the load I was carrying. Or isolate it and convince it to reproduce in volunteers.

I was in for a lot of blood draws, wasn't I?

It amused me momentarily to think of those dark-matter laceworks of mass as actual cobwebs, structures spun for some purpose, then abandoned and left behind when that purpose was served and their denizens moved on. It was a conceit, of course: I didn't imagine for an instant that some godlike creature or species had actually—literally or figuratively—pulled the universe out of its ass. But the image entertained me.

And while I was dwelling on it, I started to notice the anomalies.

They didn't make sense to me, which I guess is the definition of *anomaly*. But picture a curtain that a kitten has climbed up, and the little pinprick holes and snags where the light shines through more brightly than it does elsewhere. That's not *exactly* what I was sensing—there was no curtain, no light, and no kitten except for the one who was determinedly bumping my face with her head and meowing (*hello* Mephistopheles, it's not dinnertime yet, and I see cats enjoy helping with meditation almost as much as they enjoy helping with yoga)—but it gives the idea. The "pinpricks" didn't form any immediately obvious pattern, and there was no immediately obvious cause for them to exist—and they didn't line up with my mental map of transition scars, either, so it wasn't that. They were minute—nanoscale—and they seemed evenly if not uniformly distributed.

I focused on committing the experience to my sensorium, because I wanted to spend some time examining it with Connla and especially with Singer. I managed to save the whole thing as a map we could study at our leisure—well, not quite the whole thing, because that would have been not merely an unparseable amount of data, but it would have filled up Singer's whole brain with lots of extra left over.

Mephistopheles resorted to licking my ear. I don't know if you've ever experienced a scratchy cat tongue inside your auditory canal, but let me tell you, it's an unforgettable sensation.

The cat wasn't going to let me focus anyway, so I opened my eyes and cuddled her. I talk to cats, like a lot of spacers. The cats don't mind, and it keeps you from annoying your shipmates with constant chatter. And sometimes talking a thing through out loud with an appreciative audience is all you need.

(Okay, logically, I knew I wasn't going to annoy Singer, because ship-minds aren't programmed to be annoyed by their crew, but my own internal controls kicked in and it stopped me from free-associating as well as I could when it came to the cats. Or cat, because talking to Bushyasta mostly involved saying "Sorry, kitty" when you pushed her snoring body out of the way.)

So I held Mephistopheles up to my face so her parti-colored nose nearly touched mine, and said, "Hey, cat, so you know what's funny?"

She purred encouragingly.

"What's *funny* is your face!" She squinched eyes at me, and I laughed. "All right. You're a member of this crew, too. I don't suppose you and your sister have a vote? I know, right? If only we had something to navigate by."

And then I stopped, and stared into her furry little face. "Of course," I said.

She purred.

"If only we did have something to navigate by." I lobbed her under-hand at her feeding station and turned my attention to Singer, readying the map to send to him. "I have something for you, ship."

After breakfast, while I was washing up, Singer pinged me and asked, "What do you think about pirates, Haimey?"

"Well," I said. I thought about it, and about whether it was a trick question, but Singer generally wants to discuss things rather than playing gotcha games. It's just that you only need one gaslighting relationship to train you to watch yourself. "I think the Admiral will get me if I'm not good, so I always wash behind my ears."

Singer snorted.

"I think they're antisocial."

"But you don't want to make a value judgment about antisocialness?"

"It's not good for the rest of the community," I said. "Obviously. It's not good for the exploited if you—or pirates—are antisocial and exploit."

"Everybody exploits, in some fashion."

"Sure, but there's . . . exploitation with consent and without it, I guess? Not all relationships are parasitic."

"Yes," he said. "Some are commensal. But I also consider this: as long as there have been exploited classes, the world has been looking for ways to keep those exploited classes from striving. Better to keep them from even *feeling* striving. Bleed them, starve them, terrorize them into learned helplessness, seduce them into Stockholm syndrome so they police themselves. Provide them with drugs—legal or illegal—and then use the sequelae of those addictions to control them further. Give them a minimum comfortable living so they're not motivated to overthrow the government. There are ways, and some ways are more ethical than others. Rightminding is one of those tools."

"You're going to get fired by the Synarche before they even really hire you, if you keep this line of thinking up."

He laughed his machine laugh. "This line of thinking is why they want me, Haimey."

He was probably correct. "You sure nag me enough about my tuning for somebody who thinks rightminding is a tool of social oppression."

"Control is not oppression, necessarily. And rightminding does help people be happier. . . . I think rightminding is a tool," he answered. "And any tool can also be a weapon of oppression as easily as it can be an implement of construction."

"Okay," I said.

There was a pause, and I wasn't sure if he was letting me think, or waiting to see if I would comment further. After a moment, he shifted gears.

"I also think I want to try analyzing how your alien parasite handles data, and whether it has anything we would recognize as being similar to an operating system."

"You want to figure out how to hack it?"

"I don't know," he said, with a mellifluous sigh. "Can you hack alien technology? Does it even have written programs, algorithms, heuristics as we would identify them . . . ?"

"Singer," I said.

"I want to learn to hack it," he owned.

"Well," said Connla, when I came out into the control cabin, "I was looking at your gravity maps, and I had an idea."

"Let's hear it."

"It's not a *safe* idea."

"When are they ever?"

He chuckled. "Caution is your job. So, theorizing—the pirates want you for some reason."

"Probably because they want to render me down for my parasites," I groused.

"I'd make a joke about it being the most action you've seen since I've known you, but I suspect you'd take it the wrong way," he teased.

"Too late."

"Here, Haimey. Look. They don't need you alive for that."

That drew me up short. He was right, of course.

"If they need you alive, it's for something you *know*. Or that they *think* you know."

"I'm listening."

"Or something they think you can find."

"If they think I got Farweather's leftover parasites, shouldn't Farweather be able to do or sense anything I can do or sense?"

"She commented on your politics, right?"

"So?"

He blew escaped hair out of his eyes. "So maybe it's something you already knew before the parasites."

I sighed and crossed my arms. Suddenly I wanted a nap. Probably time for more coffee. "Like what?"

He shrugged. "Maybe it's clade stuff. Or maybe it has to do with your dramatic encounter with politics when you were a kid."

He knew the broad outlines. I'd admitted to being the anonymized person in the news coverage when we were fairly new partners. And one of the nicest things about Connla is that whatever it is that makes people judgmental, he was either born without it, or turned it off. Still, I had to tune my reactivity down not to snap at him.

He either didn't notice or ignored it, and kept talking. "So our best course is to figure out what they're looking for, go get it first, and take it back to the Synarche."

"Our best course is to go run to the Synarche right now, and throw ourselves upon their mercy."

"That's a course that ends with you and Singer both going into Synarche service for an indefinite period—"

"I *want* to go into Synarche service," Singer agued.

"—and me either taking subsistence on the Guarantee, or signing on with a packet ship or something. That's not where I want to end up."

Apparently he'd been thinking the same things I had.

"So it's all selfishness on your part?"

"Basically," he agreed. "But I just gave us a goal, which is better than floating around aimlessly unable to make up our minds, right?"

"Okay," I said. "What's the goal?"

"Figure out what the pirates want. Get there first. Get ahold of it and get it or information on its whereabouts back to the Synarche." He studied my frown. "Okay?"

"Not okay. Not even remotely okay." I counted ten, then let my breath out. "But let's do it anyway."

He sighed in relief.

I said, "So where do we start?"

"And there we're back to square one," he said.

I grinned wickedly. "Except we're not."

The look he gave me could have scorched the hull. "All right, Haimey. What do you know that I don't?"

I leaned back on the nothing and crossed my hands behind my head. "So what would you use for landmarks, if this was how you sensed the world? Where would you post signage, so to speak?"

"Black holes," Connla said promptly.

"Gravity wells. Gravity peaks. Is that even a thing? Big blank spots, right? Gaps between things."

"I'm wondering if this map is relativistic or quantum," Singer said.

"The universe is a weird place," I said. "Does it matter?"

"Well, in simple terms, if we try to navigate by it, it matters a lot because stuff is always moving. So are we aiming at where something was a million ans ago, if it's a million light-ans away? Or are we aiming where it is right now? Or even where it's predicted to be when we get there, if somehow the tech is compensating for our relative motion?"

"You just made me really glad I'm not the navigator."

"Me too," Connla said fervently, and I decided not to pursue the question of whether he meant he was glad he wasn't the navigator . . . or glad that *I* wasn't. "But you were going somewhere."

"Right," I said. "What's the biggest signpost in the whole damn galaxy?"

Connla tipped his head. Singer made a thinking noise.

We are all looking at the map in senso anyway, so I lit up the thing I was thinking of. A beacon, right at the core of our galaxy. A big empty massive nothing.

The biggest well of them all.

"And if I'm wrong," I said cheerily, "we're close to the Core, and closer to help, and farther from where the pirates generally roam."

"Sure," Connla grumped. "All the more convenient for turning ourselves in."

"We're going to wind up deemed antisocial for sure! We might as well be ready!" I said cheerily, and went back to checking coordinates with Singer against the map in my head.

Being inbound rather than surfing the periphery had advantages as well as disadvantages. One of the advantages was that as we entered more inhabited spaces, we had the aid of navigational buoys, which were full of newsy information packets. In the ordinary course of events, these packets would have automatically downloaded into Singer's storage whenever we dropped out of white space near one, while any unduplicated packets from elsewhere that he was carrying would be uploaded to the buoy.

Thus was data propagated around the Synarche in the most efficient means possible given lightspeed limitations on transmission.

This was a great system, unless you were a fugitive.

We could have faked up a false origin packet, between Singer and me, but tampering with the mail was an offense that would get us into more trouble and obligation than breaking some traffic regulations on our way out of a slightly seedy space station—and since tampering with the mail was one of the things we were concerned might have happened to our earlier packet and hoped to report if so, it would probably behoove us not to commit the same crime ourselves.

The pirates could probably follow or at least locate us even while we were in white space, which nobody else could manage. So *they* had better ways to track us than by trying to hack the interstellar mail tracelessly (that last word is key)—which even Singer wasn't sure he could manage, as the minds that ran it were big and old and wise in the ways of logistics and treachery, as well as having abundant cycles to play with. There was the possibility that we needed to dodge Goodlaw Cheeirilaq, who *would* be using things like packet transfers to follow us.

I really didn't want Cheeirilaq to be in with the pirates. Maybe I had a kind of intellectual crush on the old bug. It's easier for me to form connections in contexts where I can't really feel emotionally vulnerable.

But I also didn't want to operate under the assumption that it wasn't tracking us just because I liked it. And it could have been tracking us because we'd basically torn up the system on our way out of Downthehatch. We could have just shut down our transponder (also illegal), or we could have faked a malfunction (illegal, but only if you got caught).

The complication lay in the fact that we also needed the information we could get from the packets—*we* had to stay updated about traffic patterns, hazards, and whether there were any developments in current affairs we needed to be aware of. Such as, for example, a BOLO on a salvage tug answering Singer's description and registration number.

So what Singer decided he would do was to mark our packets as confidential and highest priority, addressed to the Synarche Grand Council, and he loaded them with every bit of information we'd gleaned about the pirates and about Downthehatch.

"I'll want to include the data on your parasite," he told me while I was staring over the top of my screen instead of reading for the third or twelfth time about how Clarissa Harlowe, whose virtue was arguable but whose lack of ability to learn from her mistakes was manifest, was tricked back into the brothel by the dastardly Lovelace.

Why are people named Lovelace always villains when they appear in questionable literature? The only more certain moral doom lies in being named Raffles.

"Excuse me?" I said. I wasn't holding the screen, just letting it float before me. It dimmed when my eye drifted off it. I glanced down at my hand, frowning at the silvery cobwebs.

"We need to drop out and dump our bow wave anyway," Singer said. "The particle field is getting pretty thick up front. I think, when we check in with a beacon, we ought to include the data we've collected on your parasite."

"Making me even more of a target."

"For science," he said. "And so the navy knows what they're dealing with if they decide to go after the pirates."

I felt a pang at the thought of Farweather in a navy brig.

"Your acquaintance is a criminal," Singer reminded me.

"She's not a friend," I told him. "I know that. And I don't usually go in for the sexy bad-girl thing."

"Since when?" Connla shot across the cabin. I hadn't heard him drift in. "You know I'm not the greatest fan of authority, but I feel like we need to share information. In case something does happen to us, and for our own protection."

That was hard to argue with. It just . . . felt like my privacy was being invaded. It was another step toward the inevitable gateway leading me into Synarche service, my freedom curtailed, surrounded—again—by people who had nothing but my best interests at heart. They could even tune me not to mind it so much, which I wasn't sure I could stand.

"I need to think about it," I said.

Some time passed, and I didn't do much except stare unreadingly at *Clarissa*. I could feel Singer watching me. It wasn't creepy; it was like the sense you get when a family member is in the room, doing something nearby without interacting with or even acknowledging you. But it didn't bother me the way it would have if it were a family member.

I'll be the first to admit, I probably don't respond to family members the way most people do.

"What is it?" Singer asked finally.

I sighed. "Clade flashbacks," I said.

"You say that a lot," Singer said. "But it's an answer that's scientifically designed to sound like an answer without actually containing a lot of information."

"I have too damned much self-knowledge," I said bitterly. I glanced around. Connla was on his sleep shift, and as I didn't see either cat, I assumed they were using him for his immobile body heat while they had the opportunity. If they could, cats would invent full-time full-sensorium VR for all humans everywhere so they could sleep on our immobile bodies eternally. And probably eat our extremities, too.

"You have some other trauma," Singer said kindly, and I knew he wasn't just guessing. His question couched in the form of a statement precipitated such a burst of tremendous rage that if it were anybody else not-asking, I might have punched them. It's hard to punch a free-floating shipvoice, though, and whaling a bulkhead would look silly, send me spinning across the cabin, and hurt me more than it hurt Singer.

So I gritted my teeth and—over my own objections—dialed my amygdala back down to a dull roar. Post-traumatic distress is basically a fight-or-flight response gone haywire, and when there's nothing you can do about it, it's so fucking boring.

"Oh, you know the story." I stuffed my screen into a handy net—spacer's habit, even when you're moving in the same straight line you've been moving in for weeks, and no chance of a change in vector or v in sight—and kicked across the command cabin to make some busywork for myself restowing a harness that was already perfectly well folded and stowed.

"Actually," said Singer, "I don't."

"I left my clade," I recited, "because I took my mandated an outside it, and discovered that I liked being an individual. So I left, and they weren't very happy with me."

"That," said Singer gently, "is not a story. It's a deflection."

"A deflection, huh?" I tightened the straps very gently and carefully.

"One that doesn't explain the PTSD."

"Oh," I said. "That." I shrugged. "You know that story too."

"I know a version of it. One that's pretty similar in its gross outlines to the leaving-the-clade story. That you had somebody you loved, and they betrayed you and turned out to be a criminal. That they harmed some others, and you were absolved of complicity in the crimes."

"See? You do know everything. The Synarche turned me loose again; I can't have done anything too terrible."

"I didn't think you had," he answered softly.

I dropped the conversational thread, hoping wearily that he wouldn't pursue it if I looked like I was reading again. Still. I turned a page to make it convincing.

"I'm not concerned about any terrible things you might have done," he said quietly. "I'm concerned about the terrible things that happened to you."

CHAPTER 11

THERE WAS A GIRL. THERE'S ALWAYS A GIRL, THEY SAY, and in this case it was true. Her name was Niyara, and she had green eyes, and she said she loved me. She said she was my best friend, that I was family to her. She said a lot of things.

She was a walking time bomb.

In more ways than one.

Oh, you know. The clues were there. The clues are always there. You just . . . well, you get good at constructing a narrative that explains them away, don't you? If you're only supposed to call at certain times, it's because she's working and needs to concentrate. If you always seem to meet at your place, it's because she likes your cats, and because her ex is still sharing the suite with her and having you over is awkward. Housing is at a premium on stations, and it's hard to get reassigned. Lots of people share space.

If she seems to forget a lot of things that are important to you, well, she's distracted; she probably needs to tune her reactivity a little more carefully and she's one of those people who are reluctant to bump.

You know how it is. Sometimes you're a little reluctant to bump as well. You want to have an honest feeling and find out what your subconscious really thinks about something. Except you keep getting weirdly anxious for no reason, and you seem to be bumping a lot to keep that under control.

Did you know that people with PTSD, when under stress, often use the second person in order to distance themselves from events?

By now, you've figured out that she was married. And lying to me about it, and I guess probably lying to her spouse about me, which are the two significant details, because it's not like everybody is monogamous, and most people who aren't, aren't assholes about it. But she . . . liked being in control, and she liked having secrets, and she liked drama.

And I knew it, on some level, and I ignored it. I chose to trust, because my hormones were surging, and I was limerent and infatuated, and I wanted with all my heart and soul to *believe*. In us.

In her. So once I found out about the wife, I believed her when she told me it was long over, that they were just still living together for convenience. And when I found out they were sleeping in the same bed, I . . . believed her again, and I honestly don't even remember what the lie was and I cannot bear to go look at my senso logs and find out.

She was an awful person, and she was using me, and I should have known better. But I was very young, and very in love.

She was also, it happens, a terrorist.

I'd just re-upped for my second an of release from the clade—to be with Niyara, as much as because I hadn't yet decided if I was going to give up the clade for her. I was pretty sure I was, but I was also trying to talk her into coming home to visit.

"It's great," I told her. "Nobody ever argues."

"Nobody ever fights for what they believe in, you mean," she said, which should have been a clue.

I knew she was a political radical, but when you're nineteen that's sexy. I remember one time when we were lying in bed together and just as I was drifting off to sleep, she woke me up to tell me all about why the Synarche was a corrupt institution and must be brought down.

"It's a corrupt institution that protects your right to say it should be changed or replaced, as long as you use legal means to do so," I reminded her. "You've got a better system in mind?"

"One without forced government service," she said.

"So you think people who *want* to run the government should?"

"You approve of conscripting people instead?"

"Well, we have enough evidence that making people compete for the job attracts a lot of narcissists. Part of being a community is being part of the governing body. Taking responsibility for its actions and helping to make choices that benefit all the citizenry. Taking responsibility for its well-being, just as you do when you're part of a family. It's an obligation and a nuisance, sure, but it's one we accept for the common good."

She had rolled over, and was staring at me. "It's a *draft*."

"So is jury duty. And required voting on referendums." I sighed. "Besides, community service builds a sense of community. It allows us to meet our systers and come to regard them as people rather than alien others. It helps hack our neurology and makes us better citizens of the galaxy."

"Now you're just mouthing your civics indoctrination at me. What about freedom? What about individual rights?"

I was young and self-righteous, and I didn't know when to quit. We've all been there. Anyway, I was, as I believe I said, nineteen. And I'd aced this test. "Nonautocratic government is a meme. It's a set of ideas arrived at by common agreement and enforced by institutions and the individual consent of the governed. The purpose of nonautocratic government is to provide for individual rights and freedoms, protect the body and welfare of the governed, and engage in projects that exist on too large a scale for individuals to reasonably be expected to complete them. So we serve, if we're called. It's a couple of ans, and in return we get stability and livelihood and the personal freedom to, among other things, criticize the system."

"I had no idea you were this naive," she said, in a voice that made me bump hard to dial back the sudden reflexive anger I felt at her dismissal.

My voice was still keen and too high when I replied, "Sure. And what are you, a pirate?"

"Freeporter," she said automatically.

"So you are one!"

"No," she said. "They're parasites. But they have a few good ideas about personal freedom."

"Well, I have a few good ideas about personal responsibility."

She got up in a huff and went home.

To her wife, I suppose.

I spent the rest of the night cold, alone, and crying—too invested in my own misery and the certainty I'd done it to myself and deserved it. The worst thing you can do to somebody clade-bred is abandon them. We don't know how to handle it. We don't know how to handle conflict at all.

It occurred to me much, much later—after a lot of rightminding—that Niyara knew that, of course, and had used it against me. If I questioned her, if I stood up to her, if I expressed a boundary or told her where to get off, she withdrew. And she made out that it was my fault, also.

I never fought with her about it again. I went to her meetings, after a while, though I figured out pretty fast from things people would say that I wasn't invited to all of them.

I wasn't a revolutionary—I didn't *become* a revolutionary. Okay, maybe slightly; there's still some things about the Synarche that I think are poorly managed, such as the way they can, in fact, require anyone's service at any time, taking them away from their careers and loved ones, no matter what else they might have going on.

And my clade had left me a little . . . *embittered* isn't the right word. Ready to interrogate and perhaps reject the values I had been raised with, let's say.

So if I were to rebel against my upbringing, political revolutionary on a small scale would be a—*reasonable* is the wrong word—*likely* thing for me to pursue. It would certainly shock my clademothers.

I didn't understand any of this at the time, mind you. I was too inexperienced for that kind of self-knowledge and had the juvenile kind instead, which mostly consists of finding logical ways to justify whatever it is you feel like doing.

Nobody ever mentioned terrorism to me.

Nobody ever mentioned bombs.

Maybe they knew I would balk. Maybe my indoctrination hadn't yet proceeded to that level.

We fought a lot, in retrospect. Constantly.

I didn't realize it at the time for several reasons. First of all, because I was from a clade, where nobody fought. Second, because I watched a lot of pipeline dramas, where everybody yells at each other all the time because melodrama is interesting. Third, because . . . well, I'd never been in a relationship before. And because I didn't have a lot of experience with conflict, I didn't realize when I was being manipulated into it, or when the conflict itself was being manipulated to direct me in unhealthy ways.

Case in point, the last argument Niyara and I ever had. I remember that one in particular, because it *was* the last argument we had. And because I underwent enhanced recollection under Judicial supervision, for the trial, and now I *can't* forget. Selective memory, it turns out, is a blessing.

Even with the enhanced recollection, I can't remember exactly how it started, because the conversation was so profoundly trivial. We were on couches in one of Ansara Station's observation pods, drinking tea and staring out the big bubble ports at the universe scrolling past outside. And I was trying to have, well, what I thought was a serious discussion of my prospects for leaving the clade, whether I should, and my prospects for becoming a pilot.

My prattling trailed off when I noticed Niyara staring at me with incredulity.

"What?" I said it nervously, looking for reassurance. "You don't think I have what it takes to be a pilot?"

She mouthed one of her refrains. "I can't believe how naive you are."

I had been lying sprawled on the couch, my legs kicked over the back. It suddenly felt like far too vulnerable a position to have put myself in. I swung my legs around and sat up, hugging myself. "It can't be *that* impossible to get into pilot training. I have good engineering and crisis-response aptitudes."

"I'm *sure*," she said mockingly.

I felt scathed, struck. Disemboweled. I opened my mouth to defend myself, and nothing came out.

She said, "But you'd be giving all your skill and talent to a corrupt system that would exploit you, and not give you anything in return."

"I don't think that's fair—" I started.

She interrupted me with a snort. "Spend your whole life running errands for the Synarche, and what do you get out of it?"

"Stability?" I said. "Adventure? Contributing to the well-being of the commonwealth? Giving back something in exchange for your oxygen ration and livelihood? Feeling useful?"

"'*Feeling useful*,'" she mocked.

The skin on my face felt dry and tight. I was angry, but I didn't really know what *angry* was, or what to do with it.

"I think you mean 'being exploited,'" she continued.

"If you say so."

But the seed of doubt was in me, doing seed-of-doubt things—sending out curling green tendrils and raveling down threadlike roots. I grew up in a clade. What did I really know about whether or not the Synarche exploited its citizens? I was coming to the conclusion that the clades *did*, which left me deeply uncomfortable and unsettled in my identity and existence.

"But what's the better system, then?"

She guffawed. "If you have to constantly alter your natural mental state to survive a situation, doesn't it follow that the situation is toxic?"

"It might follow that your brain chemical balance is maladaptive," I countered. "We didn't evolve to live in a galaxy-spanning interdependence.

Are you going to argue we should leave psychopaths untuned in order to let them prey on the rest of us because our species somehow evolved to have a certain number of self-eating monsters in it?"

It had felt like firm ground when I started the argument, but Niyara shaking her head and frowning at me made me trail off in insecurity.

"We evolved to be competitive and hierarchal," she said, pitching her voice so it sounded like she was agreeing with me and felt sorry for me at the same time. "We evolved to excel in order to increase our own status and desirability." She shrugged. "Denying that doesn't change it."

"Indulging it doesn't make it right!" I shot back.

"Like I said"—she shook her head sadly— "naive. But you're willing to go do something that is a total betrayal of my feelings?"

"So I should care about your feelings in a way you never cared about mine? It's *my life*. I'm the one who has to live it."

"I care about your feelings. There are lots of things you could do to have adventures, to explore!"

"You give my feelings a lot of lip service," I admitted. "In between trying to control me."

I have no idea where I found the spunk to stand up to her. And managing the conflict reasonably was beyond me at that point in my life. I got up, turned around, and walked away from her, because the alternative was starting to shout and throw things, and I was much too thoroughly socialized and programmed against what my linemothers would have called "displays" to create such a scene as that.

Five hours later, when I was lying on my bunk resisting the urge to tune and even more strongly resisting the near compulsion to send her a long, sorrowful mail, she texted me.

I'm sorry. I was a jerk. Meet me for dinner and I'll make it up to you.

I wasn't sure I believed her, but I *was* sure that I felt miserable when we were fighting, so I messaged back: *Tell me where.*

CHAPTER 12

S O WE WERE ON A DATE WHEN NIYARA BLEW UP.

Actually blew up. Literally on a date.

After the fight, we'd met at a cafe in the outer ring of Ansara Station. That was one of the bigger ones, and there were shops and bars and places to eat or relax and chat with friends—or chat up potential new friends—lining the hull on either side, in between the docking tunnels. She'd picked out a place that did Ethiopian food, which is an old Terran specialty and amazingly delicious—and it was the sort of joint where you had to bring in your own wine if you wanted it.

We hadn't brought any, so she sent me down the block to pick up a bottle. I was paying for a nice-enough white when the concussion wave hit me and the decomp doors came down. Luckily, I was still standing by the counter, or I could have been severed. Those doors don't stop if an unlucky sentient is in the way; other lives depend on it.

All I could think of was getting back to her. It was nine long mins before the breach was declared stabilized and I could get out of the wine shop.

I still had the wine in my hand when I reached her. I dropped it. The bottle bounced a couple of times and rolled a little bit away. Then I dropped myself, to my knees beside her, and gathered up the scraps of my lover into my arms.

Her lips shaped a word. Senso picked up her intent and relayed it to me. "See?" she was saying, dying. "I do care about you."

I had been about to say something comforting. It got stuck in my throat, and while I goggled at her, she bubbled a laugh.

"I sent you out of the blast radius, didn't I?" she said, and died.

She didn't have to die. The injuries weren't severe enough to kill her if she got on life support. But she'd taken time-release poison before she blew the station hatchway. And that was the end of that, for Niyara Omedela, the love of my life, whose entire existence as I understood it was a lie.

I . . . spent a lot of time being interrogated, and eventually cleared. I'd been a dupe, I guess. Used to make her seem normal, connected? As a cover for her other intrigues? The Synarche doesn't care if you're sneaking around because you're having an illicit assignation, and one sneak is as good as another.

Or maybe she needed . . . an outlet. Somebody who wasn't part of the inner workings of her cell.

Her wife exploded too, over in H sector. Killed five people for no good reason except some political philosophy from the dark ages.

So I guess they were still an item after all.

There was a trial.

I was tried as an accessory. And I was acquitted, because having revolutionary ideas and associating with revolutionaries is not a criminal offense, and nobody could prove I did more than that. Because I hadn't, I told myself, but it's hard to shake the guilt. The sense that if I'd been paying attention, I could have stopped that from happening. That those eight lives—not counting Niyara and her wife—were on my conscience.

Because I was a juvenile—under twenty-five standard ans—my name was never released to the senswebs and my identity was legally protected from all but my family. Or in my case, the clade. When I was acquitted, I was absolved. The records were sealed. My . . . "family" knew.

It worked out in one way. My clade didn't really want me back after that, and who could blame them? I had mostly decided to leave before Niyara killed herself. After Niyara, I mostly contemplated coming home because I couldn't figure out where else to go. And their obvious reluctance—their distaste for the association—

If it hadn't been for Niyara, I probably wouldn't have stayed away as long as I did. If it hadn't been for what Niyara *did*, I would have asked to go home when I realized she was never going to love me back the way I loved her. She gave my happiness a lot of lip service, but that's all it ever was. Her actions never supported what she said, and I flatter myself that I would have figured it out eventually and had the courage to walk away.

As it was, I was still blaming myself for her not loving me, and then blaming myself for not seeing that she was a monster. And then blaming myself for a clade I didn't care about not loving me enough to take me back joyfully even though I'd become a liability. I mean, they sued for custody, and they would have made me one of them again. They're *supposed* to let you walk away whenever you want.

In practice, that's not how it works.

I won the first court case. And I was saved from appeals. The Niyara thing hit the feeds, and they decided they'd had enough of me. Bad publicity. Otherwise I'd still be fending off lawsuits from my clade questioning my competence to make decisions for myself, and seeking protective custody.

So I wanted to go back in order to feel like part of something again, and in order to not feel terrible, and I would have done it if they would have not made me feel like they were taking me on charity. Maybe I'd had enough of guilt and manipulation by then.

The judge decided I wasn't culpable. It took two suicide attempts and a lot of rightminding before I started to be able to contemplate that they might have a point.

I'm sure I'm better now.

She got under my skin, I guess. Looks like letting things under my skin is a lifelong failing of mine.

Anyway, if my clade *had* wanted me, they would have wanted me to find a mate and for each of us to birth a couple of offspring for the crèche, and . . .

I could have had myself adjusted to do that, of course. Rightminding is amazing stuff. If I'd chosen to, I could have gotten tuned right back into the perfect clade member, and I would have *liked* the life I was leading. I would have been perfectly satisfied to give up adventure and settle down and take up my appointed tasks in the community of people who all thought exactly the same things I did, so we never argued.

I would have been utterly content. No restlessness, no hollowness, no sense of searching. No sense of anything missing, which I wake up with pretty much every dia and which follows me around while I wonder where the hell my pants are and if there's any toothpaste left. No existential angst, no ontological dread.

No striving.

Anyway, I stayed out in the universe and found a way to keep exploring, finding new things. Being useful and scratching that hunter's itch both.

I could have had the guilt turned off. But sometimes tough feelings are there for a reason: so you can learn from them. They're your endocrine system's way of saying *don't do that again*. So I decided to listen to what my conscience was telling me, learn a few things, and grow up.

And I got all that romance shit turned off at the root. I'm obviously not somebody who can be trusted with strong emotions.

It took me a lot of soul-searching to get to where I could let him do it, but I told Singer he could put the details of what happened to me on the Jothari ship in his packet. He was right, and if anything happened to us, somebody had to know. Much as that level of exposure and vulnerability terrified me. We got our information back, and buggered out into white space as fast as we possibly could.

There was no BOLO, which was almost more threatening than if there had been. Did that mean our malfeasance had gone unreported? Because the stationmaster wanted to keep the hunt private? Because the Goodlaw did? Because they weren't pursuing us?

We traveled on.

* * *

Haimey.

Fist-sized bees were tangled in my hair. Never mind my hair is short and tightly curled and sometimes shaved right off; in the dream it was a long fluffy cloud and there were bees in it, tugging me every which way as their wings found purchase in atmosphere and pulled me across a habitat. I couldn't control my trajectory; there was nothing to push against and nothing to grab. I went at the whim of the bees.

Haimey.

Their buzz was a bass line; their wings tickled my ears. They pulled me along a station corridor, toward a shadowy figure silhouetted against a viewport that glowed with a suffusing light. The broad shoulders and solid frame revealed her identity, however. It was Farweather. She drifted, anchored by the fingertips of one hand, and turned slowly toward me.

Haimey. Don't you think it's time you charted your own path?

I wanted to stop, to back away. The bees in my hair pulled me along the corridor, tugging harder—left, then right, then left again, surging by turns, yanking at the roots of my hair. I couldn't reach the walls to slow myself.

As your bee friends are letting me do now?

Bees? she asked.

It wasn't worth arguing about. *How is following you charting my own path?*

It's better than buying the program, serving the Synarche, isn't it? Working for the benefit of everybody but yourself?

Somehow, I felt like I'd had this conversation before. *What does the Republic offer that's better?*

The Freeports offer freedom, she said archly.

It was funny, and I struggled not to laugh. I didn't want to give her the advantage, even in points.

Right. I said. *Freedom from responsibility. If you don't mind, I was reading. You're interrupting me.*

As the jailer bees brought me almost within touching range of Farweather, I flailed wildly and swatted at them. My movements felt sluggish, impeded. Drugged.

Suddenly, I was falling away from her, as if acceleration had suddenly asserted itself and the ship I was in was gliding through space around me while I drifted, relatively stationary.

Have it your way, she said. *This isn't over.*

She receded rapidly out of sight. I made contact with a bulkhead, which pressed against my back with reassuring force, and I almost started to relax until the bees, still tugging at my hair, began to sting.

I jerked awake in the dimness of my sleeping cubby. Bushyasta had climbed inside my net and was curled against my head, claws snagged in my hair, purring loudly in her sleep and kneading, which explained the pinpricks in my scalp.

"Dammit, cat," I said groggily.

Singer must have been correcting course, because she drifted against her anchoring grip, tugging painfully.

"Ow," I said, reaching up to push her away. "Ow, cat. Dammit!"

"Good morning, Haimey," Singer said. "If you're awake, we're coming up on a beacon."

Extricating—ExtriCATing—myself took a few minutes. Once I'd gotten Bushyasta out of my hair and lobbed her gently across quarters (she made no appearance of waking up during any of this; I'm sure she eats but damned if I know when) I pulled on some soft trousers and a tank top and made my way into the control cabin.

Connla lifted a hand in greeting without saying anything or shifting his attention. He seemed busy, so I drifted back into the galley and fixed myself some coffee.

The parasite told me where we were without my having to look at a chart, or even out a viewport. I could feel the slope of the galaxy as we glided down it, the Well tethering us despite our distance. We'd popped out of white space and were cruising on EM drive, describing a gentle arc toward what must be the beacon.

"In range," Singer said. "Transferring data."

I flinched inwardly. No take-backs, now. I drowned my emotions in a swig of coffee and didn't say anything.

"Interesting," Singer said a moment later. "Haimey, there's a message here from Goodlaw Cheeirilaq, for you."

The message in question was short, to the point, and encrypted. Fortunately, the encryption lock was coded to my DNA on file, which did two things: made it easy to read, and assured me that it probably had come from an official source. It was conceivable the Freeporters had a record of my DNA—I had been stabbed by a needle on a ship that wound up their prize, after all—and it was also conceivable that they had the DNA-datalock. But Singer didn't think it terribly likely, and I trusted his judgment.

What Cheeirilaq told me was also reassuring, since I had decided to trust the Goodlaw; that my message had been received, and that Cheeirilaq was following us, and that it was in contact with Core authorities. I didn't think it could make the kind of *time* we were making, not having the advantage of Koregoi senso. But it was still comforting to imagine that backup was on the way. Even if the backup in question was a giant low-gravity bug, it was better than nothing—and Cheeirilaq happened to be a giant low-gravity bug with the full force of law on its side. Even at the frontiers of space that was worth something, and among the packed worlds of the Core it was worth something more.

Planets are one of the reasons we all have to work so hard to get along out here, despite the systers of the Synarche comprising an insane array of metabolisms and morphologies. We *have* to find ways to work together, because the consequences of war are so horrific.

Planets are fragile, and easy to break. They are complicated systems that suffer greatly from relatively minor upsets that are completely trivial to create. And while they are robust in that they can often recover from many catastrophes, the catastrophes themselves are trivial to engineer, and the recovery may take geologic ages.

And it is possible to engineer unrecoverable catastrophes.

Planets are hostages to fortune. And the time is going to come for every species when they'll want friends.

One thing about the Freeporters: they mostly don't have a lot of colonies. Possibly not any, unless they're well hidden. They get what they need and want that can't be found in space by taking it, not growing or creating it.

They are exploitational, because of that. People tend to be more invested in protective social structures and collective, collaborative government when they feel themselves at risk. When they have something to lose. The Freeporters, not having the same level of investment, also don't have the drive to engage. They take what they can get and sequester it. They are outside the system.

Farweather, of course, would tell me that I was under the thumb of oppressive government, duped into complicity with my own enslavement. And I admit, it's tempting to consider what it would be like to skip out on responsibility, accountability, and interdependence and live only for yourself—but the idea of being surrounded by people with the same sophipathology makes it somewhat less appealing.

Actually, I wonder if Farweather would tell me that—or if I'm just imagining what Niyara would say, and projecting it onto the Sexy Pirate Type because trauma recapitulates itself.

CHAPTER 13

I T WAS A LONG TRIP. CONNLA LEARNED SOME STRATEGY game from Xxyxxyx and tried to get Singer interested in it. Singer continued with the hobby that had gotten him into draft trouble in the first place, which was playing in the official Synarche governance and conflict-resolution algorithm games and simulators. The so-called Global Dynamic Systems let him have a direct influence on government and policy through soft governance; there was oversight from the Core AIs and systers, but somebody a long time ago had figured out that people of almost all species tended to be more altruistic when allowed to set their own limits for sacrifice, and they'd also figured out that, statistically speaking, widesourced solutions to problems often worked out pretty well when you considered the *average* across responses, instead of the *most popular* response.

I repeat this because Singer mentioned it to me no less than five or six times, along with some long-winded stuff about "using the narrative to change framing around complex problems whose solutions are impeded by poor conceptualizing."

He always wanted to talk to me about his hobbies when I was just getting into a good bit of my book. I am not sure how he could tell.

Maybe we *should* send him off to govern for a few ans. Running checks and oversight on people and doing what he loved to do all the time might just get him to shut up about it occasionally when he came back.

If he came back.

Which was, of course, the outcome I feared.

Life is change, I reminded myself, and scrolled open my copy of *The Color Purple.*

I finished any number of very long antique books over the time that followed. Most recently, *Roots,* and by the time we were approaching the Core I had started *Two Winding Stairs.* Travel got fussier as we made our way into the Core. Space here was cluttered, hops short, and traffic in lanes controlled by AIs in order to avoid inadvertent and tragic colocations. Because we were not following a filed and programmed plan, we had to avoid the lanes.

I think I read everything we had downloaded on that trip. I'd worked my way into the nonfiction, and some of Connla's strategy books. I even picked up the little onionskin edition of *Illuminatus!* a couple of times and ran my thumb down the pages. They crinkled playfully. I put it back in my cubby, next to a chain a crèchemate gave me when I was little and a gingko leaf preserved in some kind of molded crystal. It was a keepsake of Terra, supposedly. I had read that in the early ans of the diaspora, people leaving the homeworld took a teaspoon of earth with them, but the practice fell out of favor eventually. Microbes, probably. And there were enough humans scattered through the galaxy by now that we would have excavated down to regolith if we'd kept up with it.

White space, this far into the Core, was quite literally white. Less brilliant bands brindled it, but it was sufficiently bright outside that Singer dimmed all the viewports and even filtered the output from his own senso feed so that what reached Connla and me was considerably attenuated. We'd learned that trick some ans ago, around the time that we also discovered it was totally possible to develop a glare headache from referred senso.

This has nothing to do, of course, with either Connla or me having a tendency to shrug into Singer's skin and pretend to be a space ship ourselves. Definitely not while making *vroom* noises.

We dropped out of white space occasionally in order to correct course or navigate around some large obstacle such as a star—which we had to do more and more, because while I could guide us by reading the curves of space-time, it turned out that the longer I did that the more exhausted I got, and the more likely I was to make mistakes. So it was easier to have me give Singer a map, and let him handle the tricky bits in normal space.

Mistakes are a good thing to avoid, in space. And the EM drive doesn't use fuel.

Coming back Newton, we entered a jeweled realm. Stars—suns—gleamed huge and bright and close on every side. The depth of field was most striking; through the lack of perspective, space can seem flat. Here in the Core, though, the sheer density of pinprick stars gave a sense of texture to the velvety blackness they illuminated. You could read by their glow. You could probably even have drawn by it.

By then, the Well was a constant presence—or a heavy absence, rather—in the back of my mind. It was not painful, but inescapable, inspiring me with trite comparisons to lost teeth and missing limbs. I felt it—not so much physically as through the Koregoi senso, which I guess means I felt it physically and I was making valueless distinctions to make myself feel better—as a pull whose effect swept an entire galaxy into a stately, turning spiral, the way you would feel it if you anchored your feet to the hull close to the hub of a station, in such a way that your body was parallel to the axis of rotation. Like when you're young, and you hold two of another person's hands and whirl around a common center of gravity until your other two limbs are flung out and the pair of you spin like a carousel.

I found myself glancing constantly at the forward viewport, as if I might catch a glimpse of the Well we were rushing toward. It hung there, our destination, as present as the sense that somebody nearby is staring at you.

More than a hundred diar later—which is to say almost that many white transitions and intermediary short coasts on EM drive later—I looked up not out of impatience, but because Singer's senso warned me that now would be an excellent time to look up.

I watched the wall of starlight peel itself back and shiver into count-less discrete points of light just as we were falling out of white space and into reality, and I caught my first glimpse of the Well.

How do you describe a system that might just be the biggest thing in the galaxy? It was there, right before us. Still distant enough so what we were seeing was a look down the slide of history into long ago.

Revealed before us was a ballet of stars swathed in nebulae like lay-ers of tulle and chiffon illuminated from within. Without really realizing I was expecting anything, I had nevertheless expected space around the Well to be empty and dark, a vacuumed carpet. Instead, the sky was full of brilliant clouds and orbiting stars.

The cluster and its primary massed something like four million times what a yellow dwarf star does. You could make an argument that the object at its heart was, in fact, the primary for the entire Milky Way gal-axy, the Well so deep it swept all the systems and systers of the vast and far-flung Synarche in our endless, careening dance.

At its center, veiled in all those whirling nets of mist and light, lay the most incredible precipice in the galaxy. The event horizon of the super-massive black hole.

The accretion disk around the Well was a vast, whipping spiral of white and peach and gold, redshifting through orange into blood as it approached the center. Around the edge of the event horizon was a lensed ring of light—the image of everything behind the Well con-densed and twisted into a torus by the profound space-time curvature invoked by its mass.

That was how, despite being a singularity from which no light escaped, the Saga-star was mistily visible, its deformed crescent of brilliant light a partial ring around a hopelessly dark center. It looked like images I've seen of how a partially eclipsed sun would look on a cloudy dia, if you were on the dirt downwell.

The Saga-star was so enormous, so vast, that even a human with no more protection than a space suit could have approached that event horizon, sidled right up to it, without being ripped apart by the tidal forces. You'd be blinded by its light—which Singer was filtering for us—and die in a blaze of blueshifted radiation condensed out of the entire history of the universe before you could get close enough to die of being stretched to pieces.

The Saga-star whipped around at a tremendous rate of speed, much faster than the rotation of the accretion disk. That disk, and the relativistic jets careening forth at right angles from it, were not stable, stately spinning or fluttering objects such as you see in animations. Instead they roiled and twisted and barrel-rolled, as if the black hole were a giant marble wrapped in glowing fabric, spun at random.

It looked deadly and fierce, and the most amazing thing was that I wasn't scared of it at all.

It was too big, too powerful, too amazingly beyond my comprehension. Its companion stars swung around it. A couple of them had worlds, two of those even inhabited. There were systers that had grown *up* here as species.

What would it do to your psyche if this were your sky? What would it do to the racial awareness of your species if this were their memory of their dirt-bound cradle, before they stepped out into the great emptiness beyond?

Except they'd never have a concept of emptiness, or maybe even darkness, because their sky was a brilliant dance. As I watched, a star slid behind the Well and was lensed around it, appearing as a bent-seeming, melted-looking ring surrounding the brighter crescent of the accretion disk.

It was—in the dictionary definition of the word—unfathomable.

Because Singer was filtering the image and tuning our senso, I could also make out what he saw in so much more defined detail than I could have with my naked human eye, including the towering fountains of X-rays spewing perpendicularly to the accretion disk from the poles of the rapidly spinning black hole.

The crescent shape of that visible accretion disk was not just an effect of gravitational lensing. It was also due to the fact that what we were seeing was not the light of the black hole itself, which of course did not emit any, which would be why it—and its lesser kin—were called black holes, after all. What we were seeing was radiation that had escaped the accretion disk, and the reason one side seemed so much brighter than the other was because *that* side of the accretion disk was rotating toward us at nearly the speed of light, so the escaping light—and other radiation—was being fired toward our observer position, while the other side was receding.

The black hole was an eerie sight, a mystical experience. Probably because I was importing an enormous weight of expectation to this glimpse of the powers of gravity. But also because here it was, the avatar of destruction, but also the engine that drove the great wheel upon which all life as we knew it depended.

I yawned like a nervous dog, feeling my jaw crack, and realized that I had risen from my work station and drifted—heedlessly—to the viewport, where I hung with my fingers pressed against the smooth, cool, transparent surface like a kid in front of an aquarium full of moray eels.

"Wow," said Connla, who had somehow appeared beside me. Perhaps Singer had summoned him.

"Kinda makes you want to spit," I joked.

He punched me lightly on the arm. "You're the one with the weird psychic Koregoi hunch about supermassive black holes. So what do we do now?"

"I don't know," I said, still staring. "Go closer?"

We went closer, and I nursed a small, embarrassed secret. Because I had said I didn't know—but I did know. Or the Koregoi senso knew, because I felt an instinctual urge to sidle up to the magnificent, incomprehensible emptiness marking out its stately dance of annihilation ahead of us. I was drawn into the furnace irresistibly, wondering all the while if this were in fact such a good idea after all.

I felt like I had to do it. And I also felt like I couldn't explain to Connla, or even Singer, why I seemed to know what I needed to do.

It was probably a terrible mistake anyway. I told myself that I'd make sure we didn't get too close. I told myself that moreover, Singer would make sure we didn't get too close.

I told myself that I didn't really need to explain to my shipmates that the alien parasite shimmering over my body—seeming brighter now, as we grew closer to the Well—was feeding me strategy.

Okay, so I was probably kidding myself.

We proceeded in short white transitions and long coasts between, curving down the gravitic slope of the Well like a marble dropped into a shallow funnel. The accretion disk grew brighter and brighter; Singer extruded and installed more shielding to protect us from the saturating miasma of radiation. Being X-ray-cooked wasn't really in our plans, either for Connla and me or for the kitten sisters.

It also gave me an excuse not to exercise under gs, because Singer disassembled the spinlounge for materials. We'd just have to make do for a while.

Fortunately, having two sets of hands helps with freefall stretching and isometrics.

Space nearby was full of people—or as full as space gets, even in the tight confines of the Core. The skies around the Well were dotted with research and sightseeing vessels, not to mention all the craft merely on their way from one place to another, and skimming around the giant obstacle in the way. We dropped our encoded packets every time we came within range of a beacon, and I knew it wouldn't be long before the Judiciary ships started coming out to meet us.

I kept feeling around for the pirate ship and Farweather, but I could no longer detect them. I hoped it meant they were far away, but it was equally likely, I knew, that Farweather and her people had some means of cloaking themselves. I hoped it was just the black hole's mass confusing my ability to detect them, because that meant that they, too, would probably be unable to find where I was.

My ability to worry about pirates was sharply curtailed as we got closer and closer to the massive structure of the Well. It was a presence, but more than that, it was a font of data, and—since pirates don't generally come near the Core, which is full of Synarche Judiciary—I was the first person with the ability to directly sense gravitational forces to approach it, as far as I knew.

The first person since the Koregoi, at least.

I was amazed, and I was boggled.

The physics were too much for me, so I patched Singer in to my senso. He could handle the math, and anyway he pouted if I could sense things that he couldn't. The exchange was supposed to go the other way, after all; he'd always had the superior machine sensorium, mine being limited by being, despite my improvements, a planet-evolved kludge of an organic, while he was built, after having been designed.

It made him feel better, anyway, when I showed him what he was missing.

We both started to pick up on the anomalies simultaneously. There were variations in texture, for lack of a better word, in the area surrounding the Well. And they seemed to have a semiregular pattern.

This is not to say the Well's accretion disk was, or should have been, entirely uniform. But the object itself was unbalanced, in its enormous mass, which should have been impossible. You can't unbalance a singularity: it has no dimension, and dimension is a requirement when you're trying to say that one end of a thing is heavier than the other.

At last we coasted just—in relative terms at least—above the Well, as close as the sightseeing cruises ever came. Singer got pretty quiet, which I took to mean he was recruiting as many cycles as possible to crunch numbers. I floated and watched the gorgeousness that was the Well, in all its complexity and angular momentum.

A huge, lonely melancholy welled up inside me at the sheer enormousness of what I was contemplating. It wasn't an unpleasant feeling, exactly, so I let it ride.

Perhaps what I was feeling was the thing called awe.

Connla floated over next me, and we were companionably quiet for a while. The scale of the thing was so immense that though I knew the space around us bristled with other ships—syster and human—none were easily visible. I caught a flicker of a gleam of silver once or twice, starlight reflecting off the banking flank of another vessel. But that was all.

Despite the distance, it made me feel a little less lonely.

Connla said, "Do you know where the pirates are now?"

I reached out, and still couldn't find them. Farweather was obviously better at all this stuff than I was.

"I can't find her," I said. "But there is something else going on."

"Interesting," said Singer, who must have been giving me a fraction of his attention after all. "Focus on that structure, please."

"What structure?"

He directed my attention. "There's a series of repeated gravitational anomalies here. That's not something I'd expect to see inside a black hole. The literature doesn't contain any description of something like this."

He caught himself, his next comment sounding amused. "In fairness, nobody has examined the space around a black hole with Koregoi technology in living memory—or if they have, they haven't published on it."

What he was pointing at wasn't within the Saga-star itself, where I shouldn't have been able to recover any information, but rather in the relativistic jets that sputtered away from it, and also in the . . . well, the very fabric of space-time, warped and twisted as it was by the distorting mass of the Saga-star. The Well was a weird place, for sure.

I was distracted briefly by sparking, twisting brightness like a thrashing snake of fire as one of the black hole's satellite stars seemed to be shredding itself to pieces, stretching into an arc like an octopus arm above and east of the heart of the Well. It writhed brightly, a spectrum of raveling colors, and then vanished and jumped position as the star itself resolved into view, some distance away.

The star had suffered no harm; the image of it had been distorted by intense gravitational lensing. Two more repeated images followed, as if the star navigated through a chamber of mirrors, reflected and its reflections reflected.

Beyond it, I could sense an artificial construct, an enormous habitat that I deduced was Synarche Station itself, seat of government and hub of our confederation of species. It was more populous than most worlds, and for a moment I felt choked up as I considered it.

But I focused my attention on what Singer wanted me to see, and I could make it out. There was a complicated series of concentric lines that looked like ripples, or a standing wave.

If you could squint with the inside of your head, I squinted. "There's a pattern."

"It's a frequency spectrum generated with a diffraction spectrograph," Singer said confidently. "And it's detailed enough that I can determine what light source it's modeling, I'm certain, given enough cycles."

"It's an *X* on a map," Connla said. "Isn't it?"

"Maybe," I said.

Yes.

They were both quiet for a bit, thinking. That nagging, off-balance sense of spin was still there also, so I turned my attention to examining it more closely, pointing my crewmates at the relevant senso. "I think there's something else weird going on."

"Something massive near the event horizon," Connla suggested. He'd been quiet, just observing. "Something the Saga-star is co-orbiting? A second black hole?"

"Wouldn't they merge, if they were that close?" I asked, completely dodging the question of what could be massive enough to put a wobble in a black hole something like 44 million kilometers across. "There's a second orbiting black hole in the system, but that's a couple of light-ans out."

"I don't know," Singer said. "There are several ways in which the Well does not conform to expectations, but I have no data to indicate that it's *lopsided.*"

"So there's something down there," Connla said.

"There can't be something *down* there," I argued.

I was arguing more often, I realized, feeling weird about it as I did. Arguing wasn't in my profile.

"Well, not past the *event horizon.*" He smoothed his ponytail, offended. "Maybe close to the edge? Is that even a thing that can happen?"

A cat was bumping against my sternum. I cuddled her and said, "Hey, Mephi," before realizing a moment later that it was Bushyasta. "What are you doing awake?"

"Statistically, it had to happen sooner or later." Singer, dryly.

Bushyasta headbutted me and purred. I scritched her, staring into space.

Literally staring into space, I suppose—or into the wavering vortex of the black hole's distorted accretion disk. The Well is a remarkably inefficient engine of total annihilation. It actually manages to consume less than 1 percent of the matter and energy that fall prey to its enormous mass, because the incomprehensible vastness of its gravitational power imparts so much angular momentum to whatever accretes to it that most of that stuff has to be fired back out again to allow even a small amount to fall *in.*

"What if you put a white bubble inside a black hole's gravity well," I said, "but, you know, outside the Schwarzschild radius. Could you park something there? Something you didn't want people to find until they had the technology necessary to get it out again? Do you think that could make the Well feel lopsided?"

"Like data?" Singer asked.

"Like data," I agreed. "Or like a ship?"

"Oh," Connla said.

Bushyasta's purrs vibrated against my chest.

Singer asked, "Can you feel something down there?"

"Something."

"Can you tell me more?"

"Let me see."

I wasn't sure, exactly, how to grope my way around inside the Well without feeling as if I were staring into a star while trying to focus on a tiny, backlit insect. It wasn't glare, exactly. But it was metaphorically glare. Glare-like, maybe.

It was uncomfortable and intense, but it didn't take me long to find it—now that I had an idea what I was looking for and where to look for it. And after decians of practice, I was getting pretty decent at spotting white bubbles, if I do say so myself.

The Koregoi senso gave me a perception of being immersed in a strong current as I reached out toward the anomalous wobble. I had both an awareness of being swept along, sliding down the Well as if down a curved hull surface, and simultaneously of a more holistic knowledge. I was embedded in space-time, permeated with it, but also a removed observer with a long, large-scale view.

The anomaly was, indeed, an anchored, stationary white bubble, or something very like one. Except the scar it had left on the surface of space-time was massive. I don't mean to say it was large, though, because in terms of scale it was not long or wide or tall. It was just . . . heavy, if that word can be said to mean anything under the circumstances.

Heavy enough to create gravitational eddies within the Well's accretion disk, like a rock beside a whirlpool. And it was that that I had been sensing as a wobble.

"Somebody put that there on purpose," I said.

Singer added, "And made it easy to find, if you had the right tools for looking."

"Look inside, already," Connla replied.

"It's not that easy."

But there was the parasite, after all. It wasn't like *looking*, exactly—more like groping around blindly in a large velvet bag, uncertain if you were going to pull out a handful of emeralds or a handful of wasps.

I found the thing inside the white bubble. And as I noticed it, surfing through the Koregoi tech to get a feel for the location, I felt the thing inside the Koregoi bubble notice me. The first contact was feather-light, like brushing fronds; slowly and nonthreateningly, it grew stronger, and I realized that I was kicked into the time-buried Koregoi artifact's senso. It was a peculiar experience, not in the least because gravity and time dilation are essentially the same thing, so I found myself with a mayfly sense of being exposed to a slow and ponderous attention.

"Oh my," I said, blinking. "It's a ship all right. And, Singer, it's talking to me."

CHAPTER 14

HOW DO YOU GET SOMETHING OUT OF THE BOTTOM OF the biggest hole in the galaxy?

That wasn't even the first argument we had to have. The first argument we had to have was whether we even should. Singer was a big proponent of archaeological value in situ—but on the other hand, the archaeological value of a site you can't reach is questionable.

As we were discussing that, I tried tuning in closer to the Koregoi ship's signal. It wasn't communicating a lot of information: what I was getting was more of a steady ping than actual conversation. But the mystery did nothing to reduce the excitement thrilling through me.

Neither the conversation with Singer and Connla nor my attempts to communicate with whatever lurked at the bottom of the Well kept me from pressing my face to the viewport and watching the incredible spectacle as the black hole's orbiting stars lensed in and out of apparent locations, multiplying and subtracting themselves. Not too much later, Singer interrupted the debate to inform us that Synarche ships were moving toward our position. The Well is not terribly big, as such systems go, and it would not take them long to reach us. Singer pointed out that he would be obliged to leave us when they arrived, as his extension on Synarche service would be up. I knew that I would almost certainly be required to surrender myself as well.

So we had to work fast.

We agreed that we had, basically, two options, and a bunch of tactics to achieve them. Once we agreed on retrieval, we knew that we could attempt to move the parked artifact—in its white bubble—remotely. Or we could attempt to get to it somehow and take control. Basically, raising or wreck-diving.

There were beacons within a few light-minutes, and in the interests of filing the paperwork, Singer fired off a series of tight-beam packets staking our claim to the Koregoi vessel and registering our intent to a salvage operation. That accomplished, we were at least arguably legal, and the next step was getting there.

You're not supposed to be able to communicate with objects in white space. But I was doing my damnedest, and the Koregoi senso made the impossible possible. The ship didn't seem to have a shipmind—there was no *awareness* in there that I could determine or contact. But I managed to at least get the systems to notice me. Like when a presence-controlled light blinks on when you enter a cabin.

So I could see the ship. And the ship could see me. Whether I could get control over any of the ship's systems was another question—one I wished I had a few decians to explore rather than the space of time it would take the Core ships to reach us on EM drive.

Theoretically, they could order us to desist with lightspeed coms first. But if they did that, we had legal recourse, and the odds of the Synarche coming back to us with a cease order or even a stall were pretty slim. Singer was a pretty good lawyer, and the nice thing about AIs is that they're tireless when it comes to filing motions.

Connla looked up from his calculations finally and said, "Well, if we go in after it, we'll have a hell of a story to tell. In about two thousand ans."

I zipped across the cabin to him with a kick-and-catch, grabbing a rail with my afthands and hanging beside him. Peering over his shoulder at his math, to be honest.

"Is time dilation going to affect us?" I asked. "The ship is in a white bubble. We'll be in a bubble too. We don't have to worry about relativistic effects in white space because we're not actually *moving* very fast."

"Normally true," Singer said. "And that's how we physics-lawyer our way into an interstellar community at all. But you're reckoning without the profound slope of space-time into the Well. I mean, theoretically you could fly an AWD ship right into a black hole and out again, as long as you didn't let the field collapse. But there's a lot of *stuff* in an accretion disk, and your white bubble is going to fold, spindle, mutilate, and accelerate that stuff as it passes through that region of space. So there's the problem of the photon ramrod effect. You could solve that with graduated buffer folds, which is a procedure we already use for busy areas of space. But it would take a lot of energy to set up that many buffers."

"This doesn't tell me how we fall prey to time dilation."

"Even with the white drive, we're moving through regions of space that are themselves dilated because of relativistic effects. The stuff falling into the Well is moving so fast that time has to slow down, essentially, because otherwise it would exceed c. It's not us, in other words—it's what we'd be folding."

"And that's why the Koregoi artifact feels slow. Despite being in a bubble."

"Got it," Connla said.

"Maybe we should have stuck with the business model of leading wreck-diving tours of black hole regions," I mused.

Singer didn't contradict me.

Connla said, "We could sell it as an antisenescence treatment, too. Look twenty ans younger than your agemates when you go home for your crèche reunion!"

I covered my face with my hand.

"How confident are we that it's actually a Koregoi artifact?" Connla asked.

"If it's ancient alien superscience, it's pretty much by definition Koregoi," I answered. "And it's parked inside a black hole, did you notice?"

Singer said, "Another option is using your contact with the artifact to nudge it—white bubble and all—out of a parked orbit and into a location where it would get kicked out by one of the Well's relativistic jets. Because the Saga-star is so big, and because it imparts so much energy to what it's sucking in, the angular momentum that stuff gains is enormous, and for any of it to fall in at all, a lot of it has to be ejected to remove momentum for the system. We could use that to push the artifact out of the Well, like a little cartoon fish on a cartoon whale's blow spout."

"That sounds really *cool*," Connla said. "But if we do that then we have to go catch the damned thing. And it'll be moving pretty fast, and we probably don't have the acceleration to do that in normal space."

"That's sort of sad," I said.

"It is. If we don't have another option, though, it might be worth trying."

"I have another option," I said.

Connla looked at me, and I imagined I felt Singer's attention shift to focus on me more completely, though of course that was projection. But I could also feel the sleepy presence of the Koregoi ship, and I thought that as long as I was doing impossible things I could probably control it remotely.

"What we can do," I said, "is add energy to the system."

"Raise its orbit," Connla said.

"Change the orientation of the A-WD field, and increase the density of the folding and stretching at its edges, and bring it out—boom—like an air bubble rising through water under gravity. It'll come out STL, even—then all we have to do is stop it, and retrieve it normally."

"Huh," Connla said. He moved some data around on his interface. "We'd have to make sure nothing important is in front of it when it pops up, because when you take the white drive down, it'll make one hell of a particle cannon."

"*Can* you take the white drive down remotely?"

"I don't see why not," I said. Then I cleared my throat. "I mean, assuming I can get control of the vessel at all."

• • •

I didn't get control of the vessel.

Control might be a questionable word here anyway.

I got access, though—or a connection. I wasn't managing to communicate with it, exactly, or offer it commands, though my Koregoi senso seemed to auto-tune to it and give me at least that much connection. It wasn't responsive, though. I could just feel it waiting out there, big and passive, like somebody breathing but not talking on the other end of a com connection.

A little creepy, really.

Singer tried using some of the stuff he'd learned about talking to—or at least tuning into the signals from—my Koregoi senso. He didn't seem to be making much headway either. And—we were assuming the thing was a ship, but it could have been just about anything in there. At least it was *something* and we hadn't come all this way for an empty wrinkle in space-time.

Maybe we should go wreck-diving. Hell, the Synarche might be gone in two thousand ans. Then we wouldn't have to worry about selective service.

Resupply, on the other hand—sure, *that* might be a problem.

The next step seemed to be trial and error. On my part, and on Singer's. He piggybacked on my signal, poking around in there, and when I tried to ask him what he was actually doing I got a string of programming jargon that was so far beyond me it might as well have been one of those twelve-tone semi-ultrasonic methane-breather languages that shatter ice crystals and sound like a glass harmonica having a bad dia at work.

We were having some effect, though, or I was fooling myself into believing we were, because it felt like the contact was deepening and clarifying. The result, subconsciously, was like somebody looking at you while waiting for you to finish saying something really dumbass. Or maybe I was just feeling self-conscious by then.

I still wasn't managing to communicate, though—and I didn't feel like anything was changing in a hurry. In fact, I was about to suggest to

Singer that he carry on, piggybacked on my senso, while I got a sandwich and took a nap.

Just as I was formulating the offer, the alien object—inside its white bubble—smoothly and incrementally began to move.

Toward us.

"Whoa," I said, my pulse accelerating. "Singer, did you do that?"

"I was just about to ask you the same thing. What did you do?"

"I don't know!"

"Well, keep doing it! It's working!"

The object rose out of the Well like a freight elevator, its bubble a little itch or snag in my Koregoi awareness. It was slow, to start. Painfully slow, on a scale where even Singer's actuarial expectancy of conscious existence might not be enough to let him see its journey ended.

For a while, I wondered if it would have the capability—or the fuel— to fold space-time fast and hard enough to pull itself out of something like the Well. As far as I knew, this was a thing that had never been attempted. When we had access to a real library, I should check out if anybody had probed these depths with remote drones, or if we were making scientific history here.

I'd anchored myself by my afthands to a rail and was watching with tight breath, hunger and tiredness forgotten—or tuned out by Singer, which was nearly the same. The anomaly accelerated, hoving toward us, not actually moving itself because the space inside its white bubble was stationary. But the space *around* the white bubble was scrunching up before and unscrunching behind like an inchworm on amphetamines.

Pretty soon, it was coming so fast I could barely believe it. I tried not to think too hard about the fact that the Koregoi senso was apparently letting me feel what was happening light-minutes away at an instantaneous rate of return. These ancestor-systers could manipulate space-time in such a way as to create localized, artificial gravity. What was a little spooky action at a distance to them?

The black hole time dilation kept being obvious, and that made me re-realize just how fast the anomaly had to be moving, because . . . well, it was way down in the Well, and from its perspective, we were living very fast indeed right now in our perch on the rim.

Singer eventually kicked me out of my own senso and forced me to eat something and have a nap. *He* kept working on trying to communicate with the ship. Apparently he didn't need me awake for that, so I stayed out of his way.

Space is big, and even at ludicrous rates of speed, crossing chunks of it takes a long time.

While the Koregoi artifact swam its way to the surface against the current of space-time, the Synarche ships closed on us. We held a brief conference about what to do when they got there.

"Turn me over," Singer said definitively. "Explain everything, ask them to corroborate with Goodlaw Cheeirilaq, bask in the glory of having retrieved what appears for the time being to be a fully functional Koregoi ship, and see if you can somehow get in on the study team."

"I'm not an academic," Connla said. "I'll have to find a gig."

I held my tongue. I wished I could have managed to be more excited about the unprecedented thing we'd discovered. But I didn't want to be an academic. I really didn't want to be an experimental subject.

And I didn't want to be stuck in the crowded Core.

But I also really didn't think they'd be letting me just wander off anywhere with a hide full of Koregoi tech that could sense dark gravity, create artificial gravity, and manipulate the curves of space-time. I was going to get drafted into Synarche service for a term of at least a few ans as soon as they got here, right alongside Singer.

Well, at least maybe we'd get to stay in touch, if that happened.

So I was stuck, and I couldn't expect Connla to be stuck with me. He was too good of a pilot to sit down a well.

Even the big one.

With a sense of rising futility and entrapment, I wondered what we were going to do with the cats. I didn't want to split them up, but the idea of losing both of them crushed me, and I couldn't ask Connla to make that sacrifice either.

I petted Mephistopheles's patchworky ears and bumped a load of GABA analogues in order to keep from bursting into tears. If I got to stay with Singer, Connla should get Mephistopheles and Bushyasta. It was only fair.

The band is breaking up, I thought, and laughed a little at my own melodramatics, which was a good sign the tuning was kicking in. All things end, but this had been a healthy and happy part of my life, much better than the bit before.

Good for me.

Now that I was calmer, I realized that my anxiety had come from some ancestral part of my brain that was convinced that whatever came next would be entirely and irreparably awful, and I'd probably wind up wounded and emotionally shattered again before it was through. Also, what I was losing was so *good*. I'd found what I wanted, and now I had to give it up.

That sucked like a singularity.

I wanted to run back to a clade and not have to make any choices again ever. I wanted to run for the Big Empty and never come back. I wanted to stop having to *decide* things.

It was just change panic. Change panic is awful.

Transitions *suck*.

Apprehension rooted in traumatic response, it turns out, doesn't help with that.

Well, I wasn't going to let them stick me on a planet, that was for sure. Or even a big station, if I could help it. I was staying where I didn't have to *walk*, because I wasn't going through adaptive surgery *again*.

Something big was getting close. I brought myself forcefully back from the depths of self-examination, frightened and startled for a moment because my focus had been so far away. It was the white bubble that contained the Koregoi ship, unless we were wrong about everything. (Possibly it was a killer robot from the depths of time that would eat us all and then consume the galaxy. Possibly. That had been one of Connla's suggestions when we were discussing it earlier, *probably* tongue in cheek, but I wouldn't want to be the one to tell him I'd discounted his opinion and then have it turn out to, in fact, *be* a killer robot from the depths of time.)

I couldn't see it with my eyes, of course; but the archaeological senso told me where it was, and I could feel the ripples and eddies its movement left in the already gravity-stressed fabric of space-time as if somebody were dragging an anchor out of a whirlpool.

It crested—and stopped.

I held my breath as I "watched" it breach from the depths of the Saga-star, and felt my doom impending. I hadn't been this chained to a path I had no control over since I got out of my clade.

Left to my own devices I would have bolted, Singer, Connla, cats and all. Maybe *this* was why people went pirate.

I had too many ethics, and too much a sense of my obligations as a citizen, to do it. Anyway, Singer wouldn't have heard of it, so I didn't even bring it up.

This is what we call "being socially aware."

"Well," I said. "There it is."

"Sure is," Singer agreed. "Can you get it into normal space remotely?"

"*Do* we want to?" I waved vaguely at the screens that showed the prog-ress of our incoming entourage of Synarche vessels. "Everybody will see it, if I do."

"We weren't planning on *hiding* it." Singer believes in following the rules.

Alas.

"Besides," he said, "one white space spacewalk is enough for this life-time. I would be remiss to allow you to attempt that again."

"Aw," Connla said. "She got away with it."

I punched him on the arm companionably, but didn't feel up to arguing with Singer when my interior landscape was bubbling away with subterranean volcanic activity. "I'll try."

I still had my contact with the ship. It didn't seem to be trying to communicate with me through the Koregoi senso the same way Singer did through plain, old-fashioned, boring, noninfectious Synarche tech.

I examined my inputs, feeling it long before it would have come into view even if it had been in real space. We wouldn't be able to see it until we were sharing a universe, and I wondered if it would be more efficient to do what we usually did and go close enough to it to tune our white bubble to match theirs. Or if I actually could reach out there and communicate with the thing enough to order—or convince—it to just . . . turn its white bubble off.

Singer's detectors, like my Koregoi senso, could feel the mass, the dent it put in the fabric of this peculiar hole in space-time.

"Still no luck in figuring out how to talk to it?" I asked Singer.

"Maybe," he said. "The problem is, I am even more sure now that it doesn't have a shipmind. Or any kind of mind. It's not sapient, either organically or machinewise. It's just . . . like being noticed by a plant or something."

"A Big Dumb Object?" Connla said helpfully.

"You're a Big Dumb Object," I replied. "How about you do something useful like feeding the cats?"

"I put the cats in a breath bubble," Singer said. "Just in case."

That was actually kind of a relief. I didn't think the Synarche was going to open fire on us, obviously, and nobody had ever found Koregoi *weapons* (which made a lot of sense to me now: see above, discussion of being able to control gravity, who needs a gun?), but . . . better safe than sorry.

Nobody wants to spacewalk to an alien ship while worrying about their pets.

"Hey," Singer said. "I think I have a connection."

"Is it talking back?"

"Are you kidding?" he said. "I'm not even sure I can figure out yet how to ping."

It took a few more diar of trial and error before he was ready to try bringing the Koregoi artifact—we were all pretty well convinced it was a ship by now—into the main line of our consensus reality and space-time, out of the pocket universe it had been so cozy in for eons. Once Singer figured out how, though, we knew we couldn't wait. The Synarche was so close the lag on the lightspeed communication was a few standard minutes, and they were really trying to have opinions about when and where and what we should do with our friendly antique warp bubble.

Fortunately, space around the Well is saturated with radiation and clutter and loss and noise, and it's really not surprising we couldn't hear them very well.

So we put our fingers in our ears, and Singer unfolded space, and the Koregoi artifact popped out of the wrinkle and into Newtonian space like somebody had gently and evenly pulled smooth a blanket that had been folded around a marble.

We'd gathered in the control cabin to watch the unveiling. Connla and I both gasped aloud, as one.

It was pretty damned definitely a ship. And it was *huge*. Blocky, but with rounded corners and edges. Patchwork in appearance, as if the hull were constructed of vast plates that had been painted separately with different paint lots and then assembled more or less with disregard to what those color choices were. To my eyes, it was a series of warm oranges and mossy greens; I wondered what kind of color variation the eyes—or eye-analogues—of the systers who had built it saw.

A smooth, angled, wedge-shaped nose stretched back into a kind of massive, rounded parallelogram. I tasted textures, surfaces. Whatever the hull was made of, the sensors didn't have it on file.

The thing was cold on the inside. Seriously cold. Space cold.

Methane breathers. Or dead.

I thrilled with excitement. "We got it out."

Singer said, "And it's big."

"Confirmed: that's not a human ship," Connla said a moment later. "Or any registered syster."

"How often does *that* happen twice in one trip?" I said, possibly a little more light-heartedly than the gravity of the situation suggested.

"Holy carp, how do you *feed* that thing?"

I closed my eyes, the better to concentrate on what I was feeling through my own senso and Singer's instruments rather than looking.

The ship's sensors were better, anyway. Connla's voice made me jump and look again. It loomed over us, cliff-like now as we approached it. I had . . . nothing to say in reply.

Nobody built ships that big. The energy expenditure needed to throw a white field around them was beyond prohibitive. Even an antimatter reaction couldn't cover it. This thing was bigger than the *Milk Chocolate Marauder*. And it wasn't a bubble around a hollow inside.

This thing was bigger than some *stations*, by a long fall.

"Wow," Connla said.

I just reached out and touched the forward bulkhead with my fingertips again. As if that could get me physically closer to the thing. Awe surged through me, so strong as to seem numinous.

So this is what the Wake-Seekers are feeling, when they feel it.

Some of that awe was because we had a visual of something that could only be a Koregoi vessel. Well, maybe not *only*, but it was the top explanation that came to *my* mind. Some of it was because, well, we had coaxed this thing out of the depths of deep time and a black hole, and here it was nearly close enough to touch.

"Wish we still had a boom," Connla muttered.

Yeah, that was quite likely going to be a problem.

I wondered if the ship looked better in whatever wavelengths its builders perceived—I found myself imagining they saw it as a soothing marine blue—but *I* still had to look at it with human eyeballs. It was no better through my interface with Singer; he was getting it in infrared and ultraviolet, too, about a dozen shades of each—but with his perceptions I could experience the vivid, hallucinatory patternings that covered the hull.

They were almost organic. Stripes, spots, and whorls that looked as if somebody had painted a tabby cat while in the grip of a manic episode were laid over a shaded coloration that started dark on one surface—it might have been what was meant to be the dorsal side, but that could just be my Terracentrism getting in the way—and paled to lesser intensity on the other.

The craft itself had some organic outlines, too. Its white coils were there, intact. As we came closer, I could see that the coils encompassed a hull whose angled-brick shape was ornamented on a small scale with bulbous curves and strange, knobby outcrops. It remained strangely streamlined-looking, but the streamlining didn't look mechanically or aerodynamically effective, and it certainly didn't look like anything you'd take very deep into an atmosphere.

Not with the fragile halo of the white coils surrounding it. Not with the aerodynamics of a brick.

I found myself visualizing how it would look against the coruscating, folded background of white space—the silver and ebony of the Core. That white space background would have been both different from the high-gravity sky we were currently experiencing, and similar. The blaze of light, the lensed distortions, the bands of white and dark. But as flashy as the view from inside white space was, it didn't have the twists, the spirals, the flares, the sheer magnitude of gee-whiz engendered by a forty-odd-million stellar-mass black hole.

I kept looking at it when I should have been hurrying.

We got something out of that, I thought.

Well. Not all the way out. But that got me wondering. A black hole this big . . . How close to the event horizon would be recoverable? What could you learn from a trip like that?

Who would you be if you came back?

The astrogator who flew into the Well and came back without getting spaghettified.

It sounded like a children's reel.

"Right," I said, holding my sparkling, galaxy-studded hand up in front of the equally sparkling night before us. "Time to spacewalk, and all."

Because we had no boom, we grappled the Koregoi ship and matched velocities with her. I went over on a clipped cable, like one of those planetary things where you slide down a long line on a carabiner, and you're going really fast because you're under acceleration? I hear people do it for sightseeing. And for fun. When I landed on the hull, at least there was something ferrous enough in the structure to help me stick, so that was a benefit.

Nothing even vaguely resembling a hatch was visible on that hide, smooth and blocky and strangely curved as some exotic fruit.

"Any idea how I get in there? Is there even an 'in there' to get to?"

"Well, it isn't solid through," Connla said. "Sensors show lots of open space inside."

I ran my glove over the surface.

I discovered in passing that while the patches of different *visible* color didn't seem to indicate any additional qualities, the stripes that were evident in more energetic wavelengths had a slightly different texture, which was interesting.

I decided to explore that for a while. Maybe they were tactile, and my clue for getting inside would be in my sense of touch.

Well, it was a nice guess, anyway.

The damn thing was big. I kept walking around on it—well,

crawling around on it, three points of contact at all times—and I hadn't even come close to circumnavigating it yet. I wasn't sure how much luck I was likely to have randomly knocking on the hull and looking for hatches, either.

I tried following the stripes and whorls around; tried poking at the various colors and color combinations in a bunch of patterns (I had hopes for the Fibonacci strings); and generally making enough of a nuisance of myself that if there *had* been anybody inside, they probably would have come out to yell at me to get off their damn lawn, you meddling sentients, and honestly I couldn't have complained.

"Repeated sequences?" I asked Singer, standing up and stretching my spine out, making sure there was ox in my tanks and that both of my feet were firmly magnetized to something ferrous.

"It all looks pretty random," he answered sadly.

"This is more fun in three-vees."

Connla laughed. "It's more like one of those problem-solving games where you have to keep moving stuff around until you find the right pattern."

"Yeah, I always hated those," I grumbled.

I ran my gloves over the plates again, feeling the change in textures snagging at the fabric. And I had what might be described as a minor epiphany.

Textures.

Densities. Or at least, functional densities? Artificial densities?

Patches that were exerting more gravity than they should have been, in other words, which I was picking up through the Koregoi senso that had infiltrated my skin.

The information on the surface of the ship was encoded in how *heavy* parts of it were.

So if I didn't know how to get in . . . maybe my parasite did.

I kept my magnetized boots on the hull, but I shut down the electromagnets in my gloves so I wouldn't be distracted by *those* tugs and pulls. It would probably feel different, right? Something inside my skin, as opposed to something I was wearing on the outside? But it probably wouldn't hurt to reduce the noise in the system.

I held out my arms, waving my forehands around like a damaged windmill, and realized that I could feel something, indeed. The variations were too small for the navigation trick I'd used to be effective—I couldn't just close my eyes and feel the shape of space because the scale was . . . well, not below my limit of perception, but lost in the scale of everything else. But moving my forehands in circles, I sensed the artificial variations in the surface of the ship, and—walking slowly, careful of my safety line— found a place where the artificial gravity marked out a kind of bull's-eye on the hull of the Koregoi ship.

Artificial gravity.

In everything that had happened since we'd encountered the *Milk Chocolate Marauder,* I'd almost forgotten that that was what we were dealing with here. Something paradigm-changing, a technology that would revolutionize the Synarche's understanding of how the universe worked, give us access to whole new theoretical universes that I didn't even begin to have the knowledge to understand. I could feel Singer's excitement, though—*he* understood. Well, this would make up for losing the *Milk Chocolate Marauder.*

"Got something here," I said, and felt as much as heard Connla exhale. "Now how do I get it open?"

"Let me see if I can manage to talk to it yet," Singer said. "Well, not talk. I still can't find a shipmind in there. But if I can get a protocol and figure out how—"

"Okay," I said. "I'm just going to chill out while you work on that."

I sat down on the hull beside the bull's-eye and magnetized my butt.

The Synarche ships were close enough now that I could see them with the naked eye, mostly because of their visible movement against the backdrop of stars and Well and gas and twisted light spiraling down the Milky Way's tub drain.

That was my new life, coming to meet me.

I tried to feel resigned. At least we would be safe from pirates soon.

That thought got me checking the senso again, seeing if I could feel Farweather or any of her folks around. Maybe I was getting paranoid. Would they really risk chasing us all the way into the Core? I mean, they had everything we had. And the *Milk Chocolate Marauder*. And it was patently too late to keep us from giving information to the Synarche.

There was no percentage for them in coming here. Just like there was no percentage for me in going there.

And I had much more immediate problems than a Sexy Pirate, anyway.

"Get me in here before they show up, would you?" I asked Singer plaintively.

"I'd like a stronger negotiating position too, you know. Ah, wait, look now."

An aperture appeared before me.

I don't mean the door irised, or an airlock hatch slid aside, or some bit of plating dropped into the gap behind it and moved off. I mean it appeared: One moment I was frowning through my faceplate at the unforgiving hull, wondering if the ancient astronauts went in for annoying logic riddles. And the next instant, the hull in front of my face was evaporating before my eyes, as fast and dry and completely as a liquid nitrogen spill. I braced for evacuating atmosphere to blow past me—or blow me off the ship—but there was no rush of escaping air and no sense of pressure whatsoever.

"Well," Singer said in my ear. "That had no good reason to sublimate like that."

I peered through the gap. The interior was lit, and it didn't look like an airlock. I could see fairly far down what I assumed was a corridor before it curved out of sight. "Did you happen to get a spectrograph while it was doing that?"

"It's not made of anything exotic. And it seems to have been precipitated back into the hull. Possibly that explains the roughened texture that you noted. Do you want to send in a probe?"

I felt brave. And impatient. Before Singer could tell me no, I extended my gloved hand and shoved it right through the gap.

"Haimey!"

"What?" I said. "It's like a probe."

Singer's anger was as much scientific outrage as fear for my safety. "And you've just contaminated the interior of that alien ship with your skin cells and our atmosphere and an incalculable amount of cat dander."

"Oh come on," I answered. "You know most of that got blown off in the airlock. What's going on in there?"

The glove had about as many sensors on the outside as a human forehand, and they relayed to my sensorium and from there to Singer and Connla. But I didn't trust what I was feeling, because I was feeling . . . warmth.

"Singer? You said this thing was cold."

"It was," he said. "Up until that hatch evaporated. Maybe they're expecting you."

"How can it be warm inside if it's exposed to space?"

"That is an excellent question. I can detect no barrier."

"Do you have access to the system yet?"

"I'm trying to get the keys to the operating system. Failing that, I think I can probably write one, though it'll be a hot mess to begin with. And I don't exactly want to purge everything that's in there so I can colonize it. I'd rather figure out how their architecture is intended to function."

"So you can subvert it."

"I am what I am," Singer said. "Has it bitten your hand off yet?"

"You're in my senso," I answered. "You tell me."

You know, going inside might seem even stupider than sticking my hand through a hole that hadn't been there a second ago. But if the Koregoi ship, or whatever might be *in* the Koregoi ship, wanted to do me harm,

I was far more vulnerable out here in the arms of the Enemy as I could ever be once I was inside her hull.

"Haimey," Connla said, accurately reading my intentions. "Haven't you actually learned anything from last time?"

"Probably not," I said, moving already.

CHAPTER 15

GLIDED THROUGH THE HATCHWAY, AND SUDDENLY FELL. I tucked, striking the deck with my shoulder. Rolling, I ended flat on my back, a staticky circle of haze tunneling my vision. My diaphragm cramped, bright and sharp, and I could only keep straining to exhale, long after any air had left my lungs.

I thought I would pass out, but the cramp eased after a few moments. Well, this was *fucking* familiar.

"Flush it down the Well," I swore. "I *hate* gravity."

The vanishing hatch reconstituted itself in a solidifying swirl of vapor. Reverse sublimation: just a little more Koregoi magic. I was too overwhelmed—and too focused on my job and its dangers—to let myself feel overawed. I rolled on my side, still breathing shallowly because I was afraid of triggering the cramp once more.

The inside of the Koregoi ship was of a piece with the outside. The same materials, from a preliminary examination, and the same seemingly random visible light colors that gave way to detailed ultraviolet markings. Some of these were on a much finer scale, and I assumed they were probably use-instruction markings of some sort: the usual warnings and notifications and technical specifications that most sentients living amid the deferred catastrophe of space tend to print on their delicate traveling habitats because you don't always have time to look such things up in the midst of an emergency.

The corridor I was in was sinuous and sinusoidal, roughly square but with rounded corners and slightly, varyingly convex walls. Light was provided by long, luminescent streaks embedded into the various surfaces, seemingly at random.

The corridor was about three times as big around as an access tube designed for a human would be. Those random patches of ochre and mossy colors banded it, like the segments of a Terran earthworm. It twisted in a way that made me think it ran, itself, around other spaces inside the hull of the ship, and very probably around blocks of machinery and hardware, too. Not in any kind of regular, regimented way that would seem normal to a human engineer. But probably in a manner that was very efficient for packing things into spaces, if you could control the horizontal and the vertical.

I rolled onto my hands and knees, orienting myself. It seemed as if I could stand up comfortably in the corridor or service tube or whatever it was, so I did, trying to make sense of how it twisted around at seeming random. I took a step forward, balancing on my afthands, thinking sadly of how bruised my fingers were going to be again. It was enough to make a girl start thinking of getting herself restored to baseline.

I jest.

Nothing was going to make me start thinking of getting myself restored to baseline.

I walked forward a little bit more, expecting to feel the corridor sloping under me where it twisted. Instead, what happened was that the corridor reoriented itself as if it were spinning, my inner ear insisting that I was walking on a perfectly level surface with no angle, twist, or incline at all. This did not agree with what my eyes were telling me, and as a result my stomach lurched.

Singer helped me tune down the nausea, and I leaned one hand on the wall and closed my eyes until the hull stopped spinning.

"Well, that's a terrible design choice," I said.

I opened my eyes again, tried a few more experimental steps. Nope, still awful.

"Make a note," I said. "The Koregoi did not suffer vertigo."

"Maybe you should come back," Singer said.

"Maybe you should crawl," suggested Connla.

"Maybe you should do something anatomically improbable," I retorted. Maybe if I looked down at my afthands while I was moving, it would be okay. I could stop every few steps and glance around to make sure I wasn't missing anything.

I probably wouldn't get eaten.

Right?

Well, it did work, sort of. I didn't get sick again, and I made forward progress, but since I didn't know what I was looking for or where I was going, even progress was something of a Pyrrhic victory. I might be walking away from the thing I needed.

I was, however, officially in possession of the Koregoi ship for salvage purposes, which would do a lot to improve our bargaining position. And Connla's economic situation. If he wound up on his own in the not-too-distant future, at least he wouldn't be in a pile of debt because of fines and so forth.

And if Singer and I ever got out of Synarche service, we'd be in a good position as well.

I held on to that happy thought as I picked my way through the ship. It was ghostly, empty. Unlike the *Milk Chocolate Marauder*, there was the usual detritus of a shipboard life—mysterious alien artifacts that were probably chewing gum wrappers and condoms and shoelaces, or the moral equivalent. The archinformists were going to have a field dia with this place. I spotted a small enclosure with some unsettling plumbing that I was pretty sure was the head. When I investigated it, I managed to figure out how to make one of the fixtures make the sort of whooshing sound that generally indicates a vacuum disposal. Fitting my anatomy to it would be a different issue, but I didn't intend to be sticking around that long.

The other fixture produced actual water—H_2O—that seemed clean and uncontaminated to a quick field test.

Stop for a moment and just appreciate it. Actual water. Running water. In a ship that had been parked out behind a black hole for possibly millions of ans.

That left me with more of a sense of awe than anything else I had seen that dia.

It also told me that the Koregoi (or at least, *these* Koregoi) probably used good old water as a solvent in their biology. Just as I did. That was important and interesting. The ship's atmosphere told me they breathed a tolerable mix of oxygen, nitrogen, and the usual accoutrements. I would bet I could survive where they came from.

Science! But there was no sign of aliens, dead or otherwise. There was just the mysterious warmth, and what Singer assured me would be a perfectly breathable atmosphere if my suit developed a catastrophic leak. Even so I was glad we'd gotten the new ones at Downthehatch.

He utterly forbade me to crack my helmet, though, which seemed like an unkind tease. Why tell me I could breathe it and then leave me smelling my own farts?

I know, I know. Pathogens. And not the fart pathogens. The alien ones.

"I think I'm in to the system," Singer said. "Working on sorting this data out. I'll have to teach myself their language, but that shouldn't be too hard. They seem to have been carrying a lot of children's picture books, or the alien equivalent."

"That's depressing," Connla said.

I asked, "How come?"

There was a pause, as if he couldn't believe what a barbarian he was dealing with, before he said, "Because that probably means it was a colony transport, and full of young sentients. Before it mysteriously got abandoned near the event horizon of a giant black hole, with all their stuff in it."

I peered into a cabin that had obviously been a bunkroom. Six beds, sized for two humans apiece—or probably one Koregoi, based on the corridor height. I was spending a lot of time in ships designed for larger sentients.

"Sorry," I said. "I forget about childhood. Maybe they forgot where they parked?"

He laughed, but I could tell he was trying pretty hard to get there.

"Colony ship explains the size, though," Singer said. "If that's what it is there must be lots of habitat space in there somewhere." He paused. "Colony ship, or just a colony."

"Mobile space station?"

He made a shrugging noise. "Why not?"

"How close are the Synarche ships?"

"Another hour or so," Singer said. "What's around the next bend?"

"That's the attitude that got sentients to the stars!" Adrenaline kept breaking through my tuning, and it was making me giddy.

I took a few more steps, paying attention to my afthands to fight the vertigo, and found myself in a large space whose entire ceiling glowed with a broad-spectrum light. The walls—and how weird was it to be thinking in terms of ceilings and walls on a starship?—had tiers of transparent, sharply angled receptacles projecting from them. Peering through, I could see what looked like drains, and the ports for a fluid circulation system.

"Looks like it was hydroponics, once upon a time."

"Or a really big filing system," Connla said.

"There's desiccated organic material in here. I'm going with hydroponics."

"Sure," Connla said. "Choose the least creative interpretation."

I ignored him. I walked through the hydroponics room and up the far wall, which became a floor as I stepped on to it. I was pretty sure that would work, because I could see the corridor continuing overhead—or dead ahead, once I'd made the transition. I wanted to find a viewport, for no particular reason except the emotional validation of looking out at space from the inside, and maybe watching the Synarche ships arrive.

The idea made me sad. But it also felt like closure. And I badly needed some of that.

The corridor forked. I took the left, on a whim, because it spiraled perspective-up while the other one bent and arced perspective-down. My afthands hurt like blazes. Back on Singer, in any normal ship, they were a huge advantage. Under these circumstances, not so much. I figured that once the Synarche got here I would just sit down and let them come get me. They could earn their keep by carrying me out.

Yes. A nice comfortable stretcher.

That sounded like just the thing.

Eventually I found the sky.

It was round and vast from where I stood beneath an enormous dome of a viewport. And it wasn't empty at all, because it was full of the incandescent blaze of the Saga-star and the tiny, sharp-edged shadows of the flitting Core ships like paper cutouts held up on little sticks before an inferno. The Koregoi ship was filtering the brilliance just as Singer did—though probably not the same *way* Singer did—so I could look up at the stunningness of that vista with my heart in my mouth and just breathe it in for a little while.

It was incredibly glorious, and the ship I was on was the most amazing archeological and engineering discovery of my lifetime, and all I could feel was melancholy. Hugely, quietly, complicatedly sad.

Singer was in the foreground, a larger silhouette than the others. My home for fifteen ans.

I thought, *I won't go back there. It will be easier to say goodbye if I don't go back.*

Somebody else could pack up my things, the few things I had with sentimental value that weren't recyclables. Did I really care about an old book and a couple of knickknacks?

I would just embark from here, onto one of the Synarche ships. Or maybe they'd want me to join the prize crew on the Koregoi ship, given what covered my body beneath the transparent top layers of my skin. Suddenly, I wanted to strip my suit off and hold my hand up to the sky, to compare the patterns the Koregoi senso had left on my body to the swirling, lensed, impossibly distorted glory of the Core.

I wouldn't do it, though. Singer would be terribly disappointed in me if I did. And suddenly I could not bear the thought of ever disappointing Singer.

I wasn't losing anything, I told myself. All those memories were there in my fox, crisp as the dia they were recorded, and unlike meat memories they wouldn't decay or alter if I pulled them up and reveled in them.

I wouldn't, though. It wasn't healthy to live in the past—or worse, to let the past live in your head forever. I'd save that kind of wallowing for special occasions.

Anniversaries. Funerals.

You know.

And it was a lie. I was losing something: I was losing the chance to make new memories, to return to a place of safety. And no matter how philosophical I managed to pretend I was about it, that stuff was gone. I'd gotten invested in a future—despite telling myself after Niyara that I was never going to get invested in a future with anyone or anything again.

We need stability, I guess. Our brains fool us. We can put down roots, even in the hydroponic tanks of a glorified tugboat. We can't *help* putting down roots. The best we can do is lie to ourselves about it. I don't think it's even a sophipathology, something you can correct for. If anything, *not* getting attached is the illness of thought that leads to antisocial behavior. It's just the way things are. Sometimes—usually—navigating life involves navigating pain.

But it's one thing to know that on an intellectual level, and another to face the reality of how the dream of a future had become a fading projection, like a memory of something that never happened. Had turned out to be a chimera, all along.

I wanted to go home. And home was gone, lost to me. For the third time in my life.

You would think you'd get used to that sort of thing. But all I could manage was to hope that this was the last time.

"Hey," Singer said. His voice made me jump; it didn't come through the senso but reverberated in my actual skull, through atmosphere and helmet and atmosphere again. "I got some control of this thing."

He was talking through some sort of speaker or vibrating membrane, somewhere within the structure of the observation bubble surrounding me.

"How about engines?" I asked. "Life support?"

"Don't rush me."

"It came when I called. Are you telling me you can't do as well as I did?"

"I don't have aliens in my butt."

"You don't have a butt to have aliens in."

"Well, we're guaranteed salvage rights now," Connla interrupted. He was trying to sound cheery and devil-may-care. He managed to sound strained, mostly. "Just in the nick of time, too. Here comes the Core."

I stood and watched them come. And for all my determination not to live in the past, here I was. Poking around the ragged edges of Niyara, and losing Niyara, and *missing* Niyara, which was the most terrible thing. Because she didn't deserve my grief, or my sorrow. She didn't even deserve my anger, and yet here I was, struggling with letting that anger go.

Neither did my clade, come to think of it. And yet, there was some pain there too. Funny and distanced, just like the pain around Niyara was weirdly attenuated. Not just by time, but because I was a different person than I had been then—Judicial interventions, and therapy, and getting myself taken out of the clade consensus. All of it had left a mark.

This would leave a mark, too, but I thought about it, and I decided that I didn't want to get over it by turning myself into a different person this time.

I liked who I was now. It wasn't entirely comfortable—I knew there were places where I chafed and rubbed and prickled, against my shipmates and against myself—but overall, I liked who I'd been with Singer and Connla.

And time and experience were starting to paper over the holes in my memory around Niyara and around leaving the clade, the things I hadn't been permitted to remember because they were clade secrets, or secrets about how terrorists could manage to blow up half a recreation deck.

I didn't want to reinvent myself again. Even if hanging on to myself hurt.

Was this what having an identity felt like? Was this *being someone?* Feeling like there was a core of who you were beyond which you could not be altered?

Feeling . . . continuity. Feeling like you existed as a real, solid thing, apart from your trauma.

Did other people have this? And not just a set of rules and chemical settings, tunings and rightminding, that they'd decided bounded the parameters of their actions?

It explained some things about people's behavior. And their defensiveness surrounding certain antisocial aspects of their personalities.

I had never really felt like I existed apart from the clade, and apart from Niyara. The person I was now was Judicially constructed. Who was I *really?*

"Haimey?" Singer said. "Are you all right?"

"Sad," I admitted.

"I can sense that. Should you bump?"

"No!" I made myself jump with my own vehemence. "Sorry. I mean, no, it's natural sadness. Earned. I'm going to miss being a team with Connla and you. And I'm going to miss the cats."

"It might not be permanent," Singer said.

"I know. But I can't hold on to that."

That was the future. And the future was gone.

"I know." A pause; then he said, "I'm putting together the beginnings of a schematic, if you want to explore a little bit more."

"Nah," I said. "My afthands hurt. I think I'm just going to lie down here and watch the Synarche come."

I made myself comfortable on the decking and propped my ankles on a little bump in the floor. The gravity shifted directions there, so it felt like my lower extremities were floating, which helped with the pain relief. It was awfully weird, experiencing space as *up*, and anyway craning against gravity was doing a number on my neck by then.

The little ships grew until they were as big as Singer, then bigger. They were still farther away than he was, which gave me a pretty good indication of their size. We'd offered no indication of lack of cooperation, but they weren't taking any chances that we might hit a bout of independence or antisocialism or just plain sophipathology and light out for the territories in the archaeological discovery of the century. And to be honest, if we'd had a better idea of how to make it go, I might have done just that.

Also, I bet most of them wanted to be in on the adventure. Every syster within striking distance would want a taste of and a claim on this discovery. And even putting materialistic and status motives aside, how would you ever live it down with your great-great-grand-nestlings if you passed up the opportunity to be present at a piece of history like this?

"How many of them are there?" I asked Singer.

"Twenty-three," he answered.

"Wow," Connla said. "I can't remember the last time I felt this important."

"Oh," I said. "I bet you had a line around the block to ask you to dance at your graduation ball."

He snorted. "I'm not *that* much younger than you, old lady."

Actually, he was a few ans older. But I let it slide.

I thought about my breathing, and found a kind of peace. Melancholy but not miserable. I'd probably cry myself to sleep for ages, and every time I saw a cat, if I didn't tune, but I could survive this.

I would survive this. I would stay friends with Connla and Singer, because there was no reason not to.

And I would go on to have new adventures, besides.

The Synarche ships were coasting to a matched velocity, and I was feeling . . . not exactly good about the galaxy, but at least not catastrophic. Singer's tug turned, moving back to allow them in toward the Koregoi vessel . . .

. . . and exploded into a thousand flaring firework sparks.

CHAPTER 16

CHOKED IN DISBELIEF, AND CLUTCHED MY THROAT—OR MY
suit, over where it felt like my throat was closing. The sparks spread,
dying quickly as they ran out of oxidant, already beginning to fall into
orbit as they felt the powerful draw of the Well. A cloud of vapor puffed
into void and froze, sparkling as the flakes of oxygen and carbon dioxide
and nitrogen and water vapor turned, expanding and tumbling with the
momentum of decompression.

Larger chunks of what had been a ship broke apart, trailing cables
and linkages and sparkling sprays of debris. I saw a big piece of the aft
hull—identifiable by the stump of a derrick—blown off at a high rate of
speed, tumbling end over end.

"Singer!" I choked on it, but I got it out.

No answer.

Singer. Connla.

The cats.

Ice spiked through me, a moment of sheer panic, and then my own
body clarified the adrenaline rush and settled me into a perfect, terrible
calm. No tuning needed; this was the atavistic survival response in a situation for which it had evolved, through millions of ans of trial and error
where the errors got you eaten.

"Connla?"

Reaching out into the senso toward where he should have been felt
like trying to grab a rope with an amputated hand. I had no coms, and

access only to the fox in my wetware; no uplink at all. And looking at the sky overhead, I didn't think there would be an answer.

I had a pretty good view of what remained of Singer . . . and it wasn't promising. A sparking hulk turned in space, white coils snapped into an arc and unraveling like a sliced, fraying segment of hose. The tug was dark except for the silent sizzle of electricity, already fading. There would be electron beams I couldn't see, invisible because they were bridging gaps in vacuum, in addition to the blue and green and yellow arcs formed where there was something made of atoms for the electricity to excite.

The other Synarche ships were there. Within sight now. I could try to reach them. I had to try to reach them, although with nothing but my naked suit com, broadcasting from inside the Koregoi prize . . .

Let's just say I didn't fancy my chances.

But other than those Synarche vessels, I was completely alone, and I had no idea if Singer had informed them that he had crew aboard the salvaged vessel before he . . . before the explosion.

What had happened to Singer? What the Well could have gone so terribly wrong? There had been no sign that the Koregoi ship was taking any automated action. I hadn't felt any tremor though the hull, as if a mass driver had been activated, and there had been no visible trace of energy weapon. A ship built by people who could manipulate gravity at a whim might have other weapons, though—weapons out of fantasy, repulsor rays and rattlers.

I realized that I wasn't lying down anymore. That somehow, without realizing it, I had rolled upright and run to the arched dome of the observation pod.

I leaned on the transparent shell and looked around for something that I could jury-rig to in order to make an antenna. That simple tech; a pre-space juvenile could build one with a bit of wire. I just needed something conductive that extended into the outside, or that connected to something else conductive that likewise extended.

The adrenaline was wearing off, and behind it came the grief and horror

I didn't have time to feel, slicking up my palms and eyes. I shut it down, tuned harder than was possibly safe, knowing that if I pushed myself as hard as I needed to it was likely to destabilize my brain chemistry for diar unless I spent a long, careful time coming down off the bump I was giving myself. Dumping a lot of brain chemicals into yourself abruptly tends to send the system into wild spins. And I wasn't as good at tuning this stuff as . . .

. . . as some people.

I got myself together with a couple of deep breaths and didn't look at my air gauge. There was plenty of atmosphere in the Koregoi ship if the option became breathing it, or suffocating. Then I began quartering the edge of the dome, looking for something I could use to boost a signal.

It was all smooth and organic, as if the damned bubble had grown there.

After a few minutes, I looked up, frustrated, to judge the position of the Synarche ships. I froze, horrified, as I realized that they were pulling away. There was no external sign of their trajectory—no flare of a chemical burn—as they were operating off the EM drive. But they were definitely backing off. Leaving me alone in here.

It made sense, of course. It was the safe and sensible thing to do. *Something* had just destroyed Si—destroyed the tug, destroyed the *tug*, dammit—and the smart money would have bet on the source of that aggressive action being the Koregoi vessel we'd just dragged up from the abyss of deep time.

The Synarche ships had approached cautiously. Now they were high-tailing it back to a more respectful distance at maximum *a*, hanging *v* on their survey ships like garlands. I didn't blame them; I just wished I was out there with them. Or better yet, that all of us were.

Stop thinking about Singer.

Half of a tug turned in space. Another piece had blown away, and I could not locate it now. It was conceivable that somebody had survived in there. In an airlock or a safety pod. If they were suited up already. It was conceivable.

Sure it was.

I shook my head in awe at how screwed I was, and started thinking about what I could do for food, once I tried the air and it didn't kill me—which was going to be a little while yet, in any case. There was a lot of ship to explore, and the Synarche ships would be back. Staying alive . . . Well, you could go a long time without food. Water that I could be sure was safe, and oxygen, however—each need was orders of magnitudes more urgent than the one before.

I leaned my head back and blinked through another flush of tears. Then threw myself back away from the observation dome in a comically useless reflex as *something* swept through the tiny—in space terms—gap between Singer and the Koregoi ship.

You can't see a ship in white space. In the normal course of events, you can just barely detect it with gravitometric sensors, though that becomes easier if it's not moving. Or more precisely, not folding your region of space past its stationary location at a really incomprehensible rate of something that functionally mimics speed.

It turned out that I could *sense* a ship in white space pretty well now, though. Or at least, the Koregoi senso could. And my reflexes had opinions about large things moving extremely fast near the fragile soap-bubble of an observation dome.

A few moments after the gut-twisting blur of a ship in white space, I sensed something even more unnerving. A faint impact rang through the Koregoi ship—easy to sense because I happened to be in close contact with it, by which I mean sprawled flat and trying to catch my breath for the second time that dia.

Something—something not terribly big or extremely fast-moving, but with enough momentum to send a shiver through the vessel—had just struck the hull.

I froze for a moment, hunched in an ancient mammalian cringe posture—chin tucked, shoulders popped around my ears like epaulets, forehands half-raised. Waiting for the next explosion, the one I would hear and feel instead of seeing at a distance, in a position that would do absolutely nothing to protect me from it.

Won't have to worry about starving to death, I thought.

And then I . . . didn't die.

A few more moments went by, and I didn't die some more.

I peeled myself out of my defensive crouch. Centimeter by centimeter, I straightened. I looked around, aware that if I had been on a station, I'd be a good candidate for that dia's monitor follies programming right about now.

Isn't it amazing how you can be embarrassed as anything even when nobody's looking? If I were a cat, I would have been washing my ears. Except for the helmet being in the way, of course.

Not being dead, I tried to feel my way into the ship's senso again. It felt . . . echoing, empty in there without Singer. But I persisted. Nothing like work to aid compartmentalization, right?

I let my awareness filter into the ship's sensor network, like ink diluting into water. It was surprisingly easy—more a matter of relaxing my boundaries than pushing through a membrane. It seemed to work better, actually, when I let go of my intentionality and just let the Koregoi senso handle the transition itself. I had a sort of proprioception, as if the ship were an extension of my nervous system.

The ship was a great hollow shape, its drives quiescent but waiting, its spaces full of secrets I would have to explore if I wanted to have a chance of surviving until the Core ships decided it was safe to come back. If it was safe to come back.

Was it safe to come back?

I was paying more attention to my planning than to what I was feeling through the ship, so I was utterly blindsided when the quivering tendrils of my sensibility, so to speak, brushed up against an unexpected, and unexpectedly familiar, human presence. And not a welcome one. I snapped back into myself in shock and dismay. Well, additional dismay—I already had plenty, but now I had an even more immediate problem than possibly pathogenic atmosphere and a soon to be pressing need for hydration.

It was a greedy, grabbing awareness, and when I brushed it I recoiled as it snatched after me.

It was Farweather. And she was on the ship with me. And she knew I was here.

The projectile that struck the Koregoi hull had been a pirate.

My pirate. Or the pirate who wanted to collect me, which I suppose amounts to the same thing.

I froze as if under the shadow of a predator's wings. I *needed* to escape. Viscerally, out of the kind of instinctive, atavistic sense of self-preservation that—if you don't answer it—results in crippling anxiety or blind panic. My heart rate accelerated, and for a long moment I just stood listening to it, feeling my pulse tremble in my fingertips so hard they seemed to pulse against the inside of my suit. I was too terrified even to scream.

Do something, said a voice in my head that didn't sound like my own. *Do something, do something, do something—*

Do what, though?

After what seemed like a half an, I realized who I was pleading with, and what I had been waiting for. And that Singer wasn't coming to rescue me this time, or to tweak my brain just enough to make me functional again.

I was in the stage of panic where it's hard to do anything. Hard to make decisions, because they all seem like they will end in catastrophe. What if I tuned wrong? What if I made myself too calm, and I didn't react appropriately to the threat? My attitude jets were misaligned, and all I was succeeding in doing was burning fuel and just spinning myself in circles.

So that was the first thing to fix, if I wanted to live. *Calm the hell down, Dz.* Thinking the command to myself alone was enough to release me from the paralysis, and I managed to tune myself to something more like a functional state of hyperarousal and settle in. Tuning myself always made me nervous—too easy to check right out of reality, if you got too reliant on it, and never worry about whether your decisions were smart or ambitious, when you could just turn off feeling weird about them later.

That was how I justified letting—making—Singer do most of the work, and why I always made sure there were strict time limits on his interventions. But I didn't have Singer now, and panic paralysis over that fact wasn't helping me.

I turned down my grief, too. There would be time for it later, and I knew I would have to experience it, because even with rightminding, experiences repressed and unexperienced lead to a series of sophipathologies. Anxiety being one of them.

The last thing I really needed was more anxiety.

I reached back into my fox for the precise memories of what it had felt like when Farweather struck the hull. Could I use the sense of impact, possibly combined with that weird proprioception, to determine where she was? Where she might be gaining entry to the ship? Where she was now, in relation to me?

Could I hide, or fight, or set up an ambush?

Probably, I thought. Yes, probably. I didn't touch her awareness again, but I reached out gently, trying to sense her weight in space without actually making contact with her. I was pretty sure that if she had a sense of my whereabouts, she would be heading for me. Was she able to feel me taking up space in the universe, the same way I could sometimes feel her? Could I hide myself somehow? It was a big, labyrinthine ship. If I could make it so that she couldn't feel me, did she stand much of a chance of fighting me?

Well, who knew what technology the Freeporters had, or had stolen. She might have a really good infrared imager, for all I knew. I thought about the chances for an ambush. I didn't know the ship well—at all, really—which was a major drawback. Also the fact that Farweather and I shared a weird alien kind of senso did seem to make it unlikely that I could hide myself from her with any accuracy. Although, honestly, it was hard to guess what she could or couldn't do. If it was possible to hide ourselves from each other very well—

Well, wouldn't she be doing it?

Maybe. Or she might be trying to stampede me. It was impossible to know.

Right. So I needed to be on the move, and I needed to be on the move in whatever direction she was neither coming from, nor heading. And I needed to conceal myself from her, if that was possible, or alternately I needed to make it too risky or dangerous for her to come after me.

I was, I realized, afraid of her. Not just in the adversary sense. Not just in the sense that here was a person who was stalking me. No, I was afraid of Zanya Farweather, pirate, in and of her own self.

Why?

Well, she was kind of a badass, for one thing.

And then, she reminded me of my ex.

Not physically. But in a sense of presence, and something—a rogue something, an edgy something that might be just a disdain for social norms—that my unrightminded self found ineluctably compelling.

She was trouble. And I liked trouble.

That's my problem. I always have.

I imagined Singer saying *Your bad girl problem is a problem, girl.* It broke my heart a little, but this time thinking about Singer got me moving. Paying attention a little more. Going forward.

I was walking, and I was headed for the door. Companionway. Whatever.

When I realized that I'd actually managed to start moving, I kicked up my adrenaline a notch and gave myself a fuel boost and began to run. It hurt my afthands (*sooo* not designed for this), but I shut the pain off as an inconvenience. Either I'd survive this, in which case I could look into fixing anything I'd busted, or they'd wind up infected inside my suit and I'd probably die of gas gangrene.

Hey, I'd found an option that was even *less* appealing than starving to death! Let's hear it for human ingenuity!

• • •

I didn't have a plan. I followed my instincts, mouselike, into the tunnels of the Koregoi ship—or, as I was starting to think of it, the Prize. I tried not to think about it too much, remembering that my link to the ship had seemed to work better when I wasn't trying to guide things consciously. That, in fact, the less I tried to control and second-guess my connection with the Koregoi senso, the better it had seemed to work.

So I just ran, and followed my instincts. And tried not to choke.

The Prize was gigantic. It seemed to have endless miles of corridors, all twisty and disorienting. I hit on a trick that helped with the vertigo, at least: fixing my gaze on a spot as far ahead as I could make out, and not letting it waver from that spot until I had to switch it—*snap*—to a new spot. *Drishti*, yogis called the tactic. Spotting, if you were a dancer.

I visualized myself small as I ran. I didn't know if it would help, but I was pretty confident that Farweather had noticed her sensorium contacting mine, and I was additionally pretty sure that reaching out to check her location was as likely to give her new information on me as it was to reassure me about her whereabouts. If I could see her, she could probably see me. If she was looking, and maybe even if she wasn't. And I expected her to be looking.

Still, not peeking was hard—one of the hardest things I've ever done.

I had no real plan except *hide, go to ground, bide my time.* I wondered if Farweather had come alone. If she'd expected the Prize to be empty.

If she'd brought supplies.

If I could steal those supplies.

My flight led me through twisting companionways and chambers vast and tiny and in between, whose purposes were indeterminate because I did not stop to investigate. Many of them were full of *stuff*, and the purposes of that stuff were also indeterminate, because of all those same reasons.

I dialed up my endorphins, and still my afthands were killing me.

I didn't think too hard about anything, which, being me, was one of the most unnatural things I have ever done.

I ran.

I went to ground, finally, in a storage locker. It seemed as good a place as any to hole up. Being at the conjunction of three different corridors, it offered a number of escape routes, and whatever the purpose of the material in it was, the stuff was soft and made decent padding. I propped the cover open and built myself a crude little nest by pulling the clothlike substance into a pile.

Having found a place to stretch out, I made the next—and potentially stupid—executive decision. My boots had to come off. I needed to see if the moisture pooling against my skin was sweat, or if it was lymph and blood.

And if the boots came off, the whole suit might as well come off. There was no integrity to the seal after that.

I stripped down to my skinsuit and didn't die immediately, which was a relief and a little bit of a surprise. I knew the ox levels were okay; we'd checked that before—we'd checked that. There were alien ecosystems to which humans responded with instant and fatal anaphylaxis, and I had no guarantee that whatever was still floating around in the ship from the Koregoi era wasn't fatal.

All I could promise myself was that anaphylaxis would be faster than either gas gangrene *or* starvation. Which was, quite frankly, a win the way things were going currently.

My nether extremities looked better than anticipated. Or better than feared, anyway. Some blisters, two of them popped. A few abrasions. Some swelling, and a tendon that might be strained or just sore. Mostly what I was feeling, I thought, was muscle soreness from unfamiliar use— though don't get me wrong, that hurt quite enough.

At least it would all heal fast. Thank you, ancient aliens.

I tuned again, and reminded myself not to use the lack of ongoing pain as an excuse to hurt myself worse. I rationed myself some water and some yeast concentrate from my suit stores, and consumed it as slowly as I could manage, and when I relieved myself I made sure to use the recycler built into my suit. In a survival situation, save everything you can.

Then I had time to think, and to put a few things in perspective.

One of those things was the question of just what had happened to Singer. And Connla. And the cats.

I no longer thought the Prize or its defenses, even automatic ones, were responsible. Instead, it seemed likely that what had happened was that Singer's tug had been caught in the edge of a nearly superluminal particle blast, the bow wave of Farweather's pirate ship dropping out of white space for a few seconds so that she could make the completely unbelievably risky jump across empty space from it to the Prize before it accelerated again.

I already knew the pirate pilots were hotdoggers; we'd established that out by the *Milk Chocolate Marauder* where they'd nearly killed themselves and us with close flying. I couldn't say we were lucky this time—my ship, my shipmates—but honestly, the Koregoi ship or the remains of Singer or even one of the Core ships could have gotten snagged up in a fold of space-time when the Freeport ship lobbed itself back into white space, and that that hadn't happened . . . Well, it was good flying, a miracle, or both.

What was Farweather doing on the Prize right now? Now that she had it, I didn't expect Farweather to leave the Prize just parked in the middle of the Synarche fleet. Did her derring-do indicate that she knew how to get it moving? Or had it just been a sophipathological gamble?

One in a series of same, if so.

Well, we could be moving now, for all I knew. It's not like there would be a sense of acceleration in white space, or for that matter inside a ship with controlled artificial gravity under any circumstances. I thought about that for a moment—the implications of it, the effect on maneuverability.

If you could control for forces with technology, you could pull the kind of g and *a* in a crewed ship that you could in a drone, without worrying about converting ship's complement and cats into a fine protein paste all over the inside of the hull.

No wonder the pirates wanted this tech.

. . . The pirates *had* this tech, didn't they? They would have gotten it from the factory ship, if they hadn't had it already. A nice cargo of devashare was one thing, but surely the reason Farweather would have infiltrated the ship and killed everybody on board it was their shiny, newly installed gravity.

I wondered if she'd brought the Koregoi senso with her, or if that had been something else she'd stolen.

I lay down in that storage locker, and I slept like I'd pricked my finger on a spindle and fallen under a spell. I should have set traps, alarms, protections—I didn't do any of those things. All I did was try to squish my senso down into a tiny, smooth, reflective ball that I could hide inside and pretend I was invisible. Honestly, it was as much a visualization exercise as anything that had any science behind it. Synarche senso could be activated by targeted visualization, because it was Synarche senso, and because it was designed to integrate seamlessly with the neurology and physiology of as many different sentients as possible.

In the case of alien superscience . . . well. I was pretty sure it was magical thinking, but in all honesty I was too tired to care. There is only so much clarity one can obtain from chemical support before the sheer biological necessity of rest overwhelms even the most aggressive program of bumps, as most people discover the hard way in their school ans.

I never put myself in the infirmary, but at least two of my clademates did, and one of them needed extensive neuroreconstruction afterward. Probably even more extensive than my Judicial Recon, after Niyara. I didn't have extensive organic damage, after all. Just psychological. Well, and the organic remodeling that follows trauma.

I think the nightmares were what at least partially got me over my clade-bred resistance to tuning.

Magical thinking or not, Farweather didn't find me and kill me in my sleep. Karma shelters the fool, and I woke up still alone in my storage locker. Still alone in my head, too. Which was better than I'd dared to hope for when the lights went out.

When the lights *figuratively* went out. The Prize's veins of ambient illumination were still glowing softly in the surfaces, and I had no way to instruct the ship to shut them off. I'd wrapped a fold of cloth across my eyes instead. They did seem to have dimmed, though—normally I'd expect to awaken to be dazzled by lights that had seemed of normal brightness when I lay down, but these were dim and soothing.

I sat up, shrugging out of my cocoon of soft-woven synthetics, and the locker around me brightened gradually, stopping at a comfortable level.

Well, that answered that. The Koregoi ship was definitely cooperating with me.

I wondered if it was cooperating with Farweather too, given that she also had the parasite. And was far more experienced in how to use it. Childishly, I hoped the Prize liked me better.

I reached out—not much of a reach in a space so narrow—and patted the wall of the storage locker just in case the ship wanted an affirmation that I appreciated its nurturing behavior.

I wish I could say I felt rested and clear of thought, but the fact of the matter is that I was stiff from lying still, and groggy and maze-headed and overslept. If I'd dreamed, I didn't remember it, but I had that sense of oneiric hangover that sometimes follows on having navigated a particularly difficult and convoluted map of dreams. Maybe my tuning was holding up, and keeping the nightmares at bay. I made a point of pushing back the time limit on that, while I was thinking about it.

I stretched myself as silently as I could manage, wondering if there was a way to convince the ship to dim my interior lights again. It seemed to have accepted me bunking in this storage bin, but I could imagine the beams of light streaming out through every tiny crevice and crack and ventilation hole in the thing, never mind that open cover, and exactly how inobvious that wouldn't be from the outside.

Also, it would be safest not to reside in any fixed abode. I couldn't just avoid Farweather forever. We were on a finite ship, even if it was a ship as big as some stations, and she no doubt had some plans for how that might play out over time.

Which meant I needed plans too: a plan to protect myself from her, a plan to get control of the ship away from her, and a plan to get her under *my* control before she captured or got rid of me.

Living like a mousie in the walls of the Koregoi Prize wasn't any of those things. It wouldn't take a ship's cat with the wits of Mephistopheles to catch me. But it was a bit better than lying here like a sitting duck and waiting to be picked up, put in the bag, and made off with.

So. First step. Keep collecting supplies, and keep moving.

And figure out what the hell I was going to eat, too, and sooner rather than later.

I wrapped my salvaged storage-locker cloth strips and swaths into a makeshift bundle, and made shoulder straps for it. It made a halfway passable backpack. My boots, regretfully, I slid back on—wincing all the while, although I'd wrapped my afthands in strips of clean cloth. The strips were not particularly absorbent, because the materials were all what we Earth-types would call synthetic, which was also why they hadn't rotted in however many millennians since the Prize was parked, but at least they were fluffy.

I would rather have left them bare—but trying to run around on my naked afthands, or even all fours, would have been worse in the long run than sucking it up and wearing the boots. I guessed I would just have to do what so many premodern soldiers had done, and get used to the pain of marching and try to heal the blisters while I kept right on marching, because there wasn't any other choice.

Reasonable expectations, I realized—and not for the first time—had become a thing of the past. I might be the only soldier fighting this war, and it might be a war of two. But that didn't stop what it was, and what I was doing here. Or the fact that the Synarche needed me.

On the move again, I risked reaching out very gently, very tentatively into the Koregoi senso webbing my body and my mind. I didn't want to make contact with Farweather, but I was hoping to get a sense of where she was and maybe even what she was doing.

I didn't get that. What I *did* feel was the textures and patterns of space-time slipping steadily around the Prize as white space peristalsed her down.

The Koregoi ship was moving.

We were under way.

I reeled a little. Farweather had gotten us moving, and I couldn't tell you *why* I found that so startling and upsetting, but I did.

Okay, I take that back. I definitely knew why I found it upsetting—because I was alone in a ship I had no control over, heading into deep space after having been privateered by a Freeport pirate queen who'd infected me with, well, aliens. And that was, honestly, pretty startling on the face of it.

But I felt like I should have expected it. It was a bad thing, after all. You expected those and braced for them, so they couldn't leave you gob-smacked, helpless with surprise.

Surprise is the kind of emotion that people like me—people with my upbringing who have left it, however many of us there are (a dozen or so?)—struggle to never, ever, ever get caught out by. We make sure we have plans in place. We consider options.

And here I was, surprised. Blindsided by grief.

Don't worry about it now, Haimey.

Keep moving.

Small, attainable goals, and worry about the big goals when you have enough small goals lined up and accomplished to have any resources at all that you have a chance of working with.

I wondered where we were going.

CHAPTER 17

GOAL NUMBER THE FIRST: DON'T GET CAUGHT.

Okay, then, what's my plan of attack for that? Or the plan of evasion, more accurately. Step one, avoid contact with Farweather, either through senso or physically.

I didn't have any illusions about my ability to take her in single combat. For one thing, while humans traditionally divided themselves up into lovers and fighters, I considered myself living evidence that that was a false binary, having no skill with either set of tools. I belonged to a third group, equally useful: I was an engineer.

For another thing, I was pretty confident that Farweather hadn't come to this alien environment unarmed. Unlike me. Because she *was* a fighter, every centimeter of her.

I could try to set a trap. But that was likely to fail and also likely to move me up on her priority list. Right now, I figured she probably had her work cut out for her in regard to exploring the Prize, mastering its systems, and getting where she wanted to be going, unexpected hitchhiker and all. If we *got* there, she'd probably have additional resources to throw at the problem of me, which meant that *her* best use of resources was to defend herself, defend the Koregoi ship's key systems, and bide her time until she could meet me with overwhelming force. My earlier fears were realistic, but probably a little overblown, because if she decided to take the risk of coming out to get me it could result in potential failure of her mission objectives and possibly getting clobbered or killed herself.

She'd want to avoid that. I mean, *I* didn't think I could take her, but that didn't mean she wouldn't want to be cautious.

Sure, Haimey, I heard myself tell myself in Singer's voice. *Because caution has certainly been her watchword all along, and you have no evidence at all that she's interested in capturing or subverting you for her own reasons, whatever the strategy behind those reasons may be.*

I *could* try to ambush her. Probably, eventually, I would. But not todia. Because right now I needed an advantage.

So I had to assume that she would be defending herself, and I had to assume that she might, in fact, come after me. So while she was consolidating her control over the ship's systems and setting up whatever defenses she was setting up, I needed to be learning the structures of the Prize like the warrens of the clade I grew up in. I needed to be a mouse in those warrens. A stainless steel rat in the walls.

Just as well to have something interesting to fill the standard hours with. All my book files were back on Singer. Without reading material, I needed *something* to occupy my time. Memorizing an alien spacecraft the size of a medium station would probably keep me busy. Unless it got me caught.

Or killed.

I hadn't sat still while I was doing this thinking, either. In fact, I'd found something fascinating, which was that those organic-seeming corridors and the spaces they connected were webbed with service crawlways. Or service *floatways*, more precisely—because there was no gravity in those.

I pulled my awful boots off again, wrapped them through my makeshift backpack, and exulted in the comfort of having all four hands free to work as my ergonomics engineers had intended. Everything instantly seemed better when I wasn't under g anymore, and even better than that when I sipped some reclaimed water and chewed a couple of yeast tablets. Your brain uses glucose to think, it turns out, and when you don't have it, your decision-making and emotional regulation remains somewhat impaired, no matter how much you tune.

The playful teasing of my own interior voice reminded me of Singer, which was too much of a distraction, and I shut it down. My fox had been running the whole time, though—recording, memorizing as I moved through the ship. My meat memory might fail me, but I was going to use it anyway, because it was essentially bottomless. The machine memory could create a perfect three-dimensional map of the spaces I moved through. Once I had access to a shipmind again, and to more processing power than the tiny bit packed into my suit and skull, I would be able to use that map to generate the kind of plot that could reveal what I was missing and give me the shapes of spaces I hadn't yet figured out how to reach. Spaces that might be solid-state, technology, hunks of computronium wedged in where they fit . . . or that might hide even stranger treasures.

Like snacks, for example.

Pity that wasn't available to me now, because I could have used it.

As I swung through narrow spaces, I wondered: the Koregoi parasite seemed so happy in my body, and had certainly revved my metabolism well beyond the usual bounds. We drank the same solvents. Breathed the same oxidant. If my biochemistry matched up that well with theirs, did that mean I could eat their food without harming myself? Were we biologically similar enough to process the same nutrients?

I really hoped so. A lot.

I decided to gamble that my attempt to hide myself had worked. I needed intel badly. Using my Koregoi-extended proprioception—or rather, letting it use me—I tracked where Farweather was as I moved through the ship mapping and exploring. I was pretty sure that I'd been right about her plan, because while I was drunkard-walking all over the place, making largely random choices in order to get a vague plan of as much of the ship as possible, Farweather was moving in a tight spiral out from a central core, a planned and cautious exploration.

She didn't seem to be hiding herself, either. Maybe she didn't know how. Maybe I only thought I was invisible, or somewhat less noticeable anyway, and she knew exactly where I was at all times and was laughing at my completely random stagger through the Prize's byways.

It didn't matter. Well, it *did* matter. But I couldn't affect it either way, so I needed to not concern myself with it. It didn't matter because it was out of my control, and my energy needed to go to things that I could control, or at least hope to affect the outcome of. See above, item one, Haimey Dz survival plan for being marooned on an alien starship while trying to hide from a sexy pirate.

I really, really wished I had along a copy of *Robinson Crusoe*.

I crawled and mapped, floated and mapped, avoided Farweather's territory. I slept in corners and access tunnels and stowage bays, never the same one twice, and tried to leave behind no evidence of my passage. And tried also not to notice how hungry I was getting, as the first couple of diar went by.

Goal number two: find something to eat, somewhere.

Between what I put out, and the atmospheric moisture, my suit was reclaiming enough water that I wasn't in danger of dehydrating, and I'd rigged up a small evaporation still to make sure I was getting uncontaminated water with which I could replenish. Who knew what might be in H_2O that has been sitting in the pipes for a few hundred ans? I had a pretty good handle on the schematics of the Prize, including—I hoped—a number of things Farweather didn't know, because she didn't often venture out of her fortified bubble. I'd spied on her a little, and she'd filled the access tubes near her little domain with insulating foam that would have to be clawed or gouged out by hand, and she'd laced the corridors with cameras and the occasional dart trap. Fortunately, having been on the *Milk Chocolate Marauder*, I had a pretty fair idea of what her jury-rigging skills were like. I also thought that mine were better, and her dart traps were easy to spot. (Unless she was smart enough to hide her true level of skill and conceal a few better, which was possible. It was reasonable caution to act like that might be the case, but if I really started to believe it I would have to admit that I was probably psyching myself.)

So I stayed off her marked turf so as not to let her *know* her dart traps were silly. And she didn't venture out of her secured corridors and cabins either, which was a nicer vote of confidence in my skill and dangerousness than I had been expecting from her. Or, you know, maybe she was a homebody.

I didn't really think she was a homebody.

My suit, by this point, had actually snugged down to the limit of its elasticity and was starting to hang a little loose on me. The yeast tablets were not a subsistence diet; they were a snack. And I only had a few of them left. Even rationing doesn't make a resource last forever if you can't figure out how to renew it.

Second priority: food was starting to seem even *more* violently important.

I hoped it wouldn't mean raiding Farweather's supplies, because that would put goal number two in direct contravention with goal number one—explore, avoid, reconnoiter—and it was a little early in the proceedings to be running up against strategic conflict already. Especially when I was the only commander and all the troops and noncoms, also.

Well, if I were food on an alien colony ship, where would I be? I'd probably be long decomposed, honestly—decayed into crumbling sawdust, hydroponics dead, organics of all sorts hopelessly degraded. There was no ecosystem on this ship anymore—even the kind of incomplete oxygen-and-water cycle that we'd maintained on Singer, with our algae tanks and living walls in order to process fresh oxygen and produce fresh greens.

If I *had* to kill and eat Farweather, I was starting to think I might be willing to try it, though I didn't have anything to butcher her with. She, however, did have supplies.

I could tell because she wasn't dying.

I could probably steal them from her.

That was a terrible idea.

. . .

Wait, where was the oxygen coming from? It didn't smell like tanks, and it didn't smell like catalysts or electrolysis. The alien ship didn't carry the faint tang of ozone. In fact, it smelled fresh. Green. Growing.

Did the Koregoi have something like blue-green algae on this thing as part of their life-support processing, or was their atmosphere synthesis just good enough, technologically speaking, that they didn't have to make everything they reconstituted smell like the inside of a tin can that had been floating around in space, unaired, for a thousand ans or so?

If there were edible plants of some sort on this thing, eating them would be a simpler solution than trying to catch Farweather. Also less socially taboo. Which I *guess* matters.

And who would bring plants that you couldn't also eat to space, up here where weight and space were at a premium? Especially if you had a big city-ship full of hungry mouths to feed, and you might be taking them to a planet where you needed to have some kind of horticulture, too. And I'd actually *found* part of a hydroponics operation.

Those hydroponics tanks were not currently functional . . . but there might be seed banks. And a way to turn them back on.

Remembering the hydroponics made me think of Connla, and thinking of Connla made me sad, so I thought about something else. Plans. I thought about plans. Plants and plans.

There might be an oxygen-processing center somewhere with tanks.

Okay so. Where were the tanks? I'd been all over the ship, I thought, and had some idea of where the blank bits might be, though a reliable map would have to wait for access to rendering software and processing power. Or an AI, which amounted to the same thing.

For now, I stretched out in a side corridor—one of the freefall ones— and thought about it. Plenty of blank space, and they probably wouldn't need direct access. I mean, you could send a diver in to clean if you needed, but probably if they got contaminated or needed cleaning, or you wanted to harvest a crop and get the next crop in . . . wouldn't you just pump the stuff out, dry it in sheets (vacuum freeze-drying! why not?) and then wash the tank out with a nice hot rinse and start over with a new batch immediately? Nobody should ever need to go in there except if it needed repairs.

Well, that said to me that I should look in the dead spaces. Or in the areas around the dead spaces, for the controls.

I had a plan. With a hungry sigh, I wedged my bundle of sleeping rags behind some pipes, fetched the space suit helmet and ox supply I hadn't been bothering with, and I went in search of sustenance.

And maybe a shower too while I was at it.

Six hours later I was happily munching my way through a stack of space nori as thick as a Gutenberg Bible. It could have used a little salt and some wasabi, but it hadn't killed me yet, and on the off chance it never did, I was already in the process of making more.

Who knew if it was nutritionally complete, or what amino acids and sugars the Koregoi used to build and fuel their bodies? And if those had any overlap at all with the ones I used?

Well, malnutrition was a slower way to die than starvation. Give it a check in the plus column and move on.

I probably contaminated the hell out of the tank with my Earth microbes while I was in there, and in memory of Singer I felt pretty bad about that, but there honestly wasn't much I could have done to prevent it, and I was breathing commensals and microbiota all over the alien micro-ecosystem in here anyway.

In any case, my increased level of alertness and energy told me that there was *something* in there that I could metabolize, and my physiology got right on that, with a vengeance.

Other parts of my GI system weren't as pleased with the radically unfamiliar food source, unfortunately.

Oh well. At least my suit handled the cleanup. And reclaimed the water. Though that wasn't as critical now that I'd found giant tanks full of perfectly bog-standard (that was a joke) H_2O.

Well, I thought it was funny, anyway. It kept me laughing to myself all the way back to my improvised dehydrator, where I planned to pack up a new crop of algae biscuits and then find a crevice to mouse myself into for a good long rest.

Laughing made me think of my shipmates. Thinking of my shipmates made me so sad about not having Singer and Connla around to impugn my sense of humor that I could barely stand it. I could almost imagine Singer's presence sometimes, if I closed my eyes and held very still. I knew it was just my neurology sensing people who weren't there—I'm pretty sure nobody outside of a com serial has ever been haunted by the ghost of a destroyed AI—but that didn't remove the creepiness of being able to sense him back there.

If he'd been real, though, he would have brought books. So I could tell myself with a high confidence that I was kidding myself. Or that my neurons were kidding me, more precisely. And nobody was standing over my shoulder, observing me.

Unless this was my backbrain's method of telling my conscious mind that Farweather had found me and was stealth-piggybacking on my Koregoi senso.

That sent a chill through me. I stopped, a flake of space nori in my hand, and looked at the webwork of glittering coppery particles swirling and washing beneath my skin. Sometime over the past couple of decians, they'd integrated into my body image and I'd stopped even consciously noticing them unless they caught my eye, or something made me think of them.

They were still pretty. And I decided that if Farweather was camped in my blind spot, well, there wasn't much I could do about it. Singer could have chased her out, probably. I was helpless in this circumstance.

Dammit, Singer, I miss you. And not just for providing me with com security services.

Maybe I was haunted, because I swear I felt a fleeting sense of contact then, like the brush of immaterial fingers on my hair.

. . .

Goal number three: figure out where we were headed.

Subgoal: find a way to get that information to somebody who could help.

By this time, I had a really good mental map of the ship—both machine memories and schematics courtesy of my fox, and the more intuitive sense that came with my meat memory and the good old-fashioned senses of direction, travel time, and so forth that had kept my primate ancestors from (mostly) getting lost and eaten by leopards before they could reproduce, thereby leading us inevitably and inexorably to the stars and our rightful place amid the society of the systers.

Or, you know, blind luck and occasionally jumping really high at the right time and screaming for your friends to run away, if you don't care to subscribe to some kind of neoimperialist Manifest Destiny for humanity. Which is one of the maladapted bits of evolutionary baggage I'm very glad we've mostly trained out of ourselves, now that we have the tools.

Well, the Synarche has trained out of ourselves. The Freeporters . . . still haven't figured out the whole "sharing resources equitably" thing.

So. Back to the problem at hand: navigation. I had no access to a shipmind, or a shipmind's database of star charts. I had no access to the controls of the Prize, and no idea how to fly it if I did other than what I'd done before, which amounted to standing in one place and whistling *here kitty kitty*. A tactic, to be sure. Not a tactic I thought I should attempt while standing inside it.

What I did have was the Koregoi senso. So over the next couple of diar, as my body slowly adapted to a diet of space nori biscuits, I made myself a series of bolt-holes and hiding places through the vast—and now thoroughly mapped—interior. I even felt like I had a pretty good idea of what was going on in the turf Farweather had claimed as her own.

I armed myself with a couple of flasks of water—I'd found the flasks in one of the hydroponics rooms and filled them with what I filtered from the algae tanks—and a pile of my nori cakes. Some of the nori cakes were flavored with alien shrimp bits now, which was exciting and also hadn't killed me, and probably provided some protein. Whether it was protein my body could use or not . . . well, insert a big theatrical shrug right here.

I tried not to think about the fact that I was eating living animals and not tank-grown meat. It was a survival situation, my ancestors (barbarians) had done it for millions of generations, and anyway they probably had like three ganglia to rub together. The shrimps, not my ancestors.

And if I told myself that often enough, I could convince myself that they were basically little blue-green plants that just moved really quickly, and manage to get them down without having to adjust my neurochemistry too much to stop feeling like a monster.

The worst part was that they were actually pretty tasty. I would have felt less awful if I hated their flavor overall and was just choking them down to stay functional.

Then I holed up in one of the dens I'd located around the ship and was using as caches. I picked the one I felt most secure in: it was reasonably far from what I thought of as Farweather's territory, and in a well-shielded forward section of the ship. Also, there was some sort of device or object in a big, sealed cargo space between it and the area where the Freeporter stayed, and that device seemed to interfere with the Koregoi senso. So while I could feel forward and off to the sides just fine, I couldn't feel aft, toward Farweather. And I figured she couldn't feel forward, toward me.

This was as good a spot to try a little meditation on the shape of the universe as I was likely to find, so I settled in, loosened up my suit a bit, and made myself comfortable. Then I opened my mind to the Koregoi senso, and waited to see what might arise.

The biggest question in my mind was *Where am I*, and right after that was *Who's following us* and *Where is the rendezvous, and what Freeport assets are waiting there?* But just *asking* this persnickety peripheral that had infected my body for a direct answer never seemed to work. (Of course not.) So instead, I sat with it, thinking about my breathing, letting whatever thoughts wanted to arise or descend do their thing.

Mostly they were thoughts of grief. At first, anyway. I leaned back against a bulkhead and let the sorrow rise as I imagined Connla cuddling the cats to him as space opened up all around them. Maybe fate had been merciful, and all three of them had been caught in the initial particle blast. The emotions came with tears, and a pain that hitched my breathing, and I didn't tune to lessen it. Pain still had to be processed eventually. You could use rightminding to manage it, and to manage the sequelae of trauma. But you couldn't just make those things go away.

Not and expect people to have healthy brains and healthy psyches afterward. It was the equivalent of putting somebody with high blood pressure on rectifiers and not addressing the physical causes of the problem at a systemic and maintenance level as well.

I would have given anything to find Bushyasta sleeping in the beverage heater and have to pick fur out of the little cubby before making myself a beverage that didn't taste like cat dander. If we had a beverage heater, I would have killed for a cup of cat-dander tea. If we had any tea.

I was cautious. So cautious. I didn't reach out. I just . . . sat still. Held to myself. And let the universe come to me.

The idea is to breathe, and not actually think about anything complicated with intention. Think about the breath, sure. Think about the blood carrying the oxygen through your body. Picture the pathways of your arteries and veins.

Other thoughts will arise. Some of those thoughts will be sorrow. Some will be anger. Sometimes, there will be a flare of white rage directed at somebody close, somebody whose actions have harmed you or those you loved. Sometimes that fury might subside into grief. Sometimes it might flare into a craving for vengeance.

The thing was, a lot of people—people in the clade I grew up in, for example—have the idea that when you seek no-mind, or what the Wake-Seekers and those who follow the Path of the Unfinished Work call waiting awareness, you are not *conscious*, somehow. But that is not the case. What you are doing is trying to accept what you think and feel as simply events that are occurring, rather than as intrinsic parts of who you are, demanding immediate action. You experience the emotion or thought, and you choose not to judge it or yourself, or your relationship to that emotion or thought. And when it's done, you experience the next emotion.

Your self-ness is defined as something different from what you feel or think at the moment—something that can be made serene and thoughtful, careful of yourself and others, respectful of community. This is not dissimilar from rightminding, to be frank, and in a more religious time, after the Eschaton that left humanity so shattered and vulnerable and nearly destroyed us, it was a philosophy that many of my ancestors adopted, which led eventually to our acceptance of—and membership in—the Synarche.

There is an ancient concept of *dharma*, which means, essentially, right behavior. It includes such seemingly basic concepts as not taking more than you need, not deceiving or stealing, contributing to the well-being of other people, and not harming others in any other way as well. A number of religions and philosophies have grown up surrounding it, but I realized a long time ago that those mostly do not concern me. I'm not a religious person, though I dabbled for a while.

When I left the clade and after I was done burning myself up on synthetic deva, though, I realized that the world was a lonely place, and that it helped to have a philosophy, if nothing else, to help with the task of finding an identity.

Bloody vengeance, unfortunately, was not *dharma*. So when that showed up—with annoying regularity—I needed to let it go, and work on more socially beneficial tasks. Such as coming up with that set of directions.

I didn't want to let the fury go, though. Not yet. I didn't want to imagine ever letting it go, just yet. That rage, that loss—they had become integral to my identity. Letting go of them would be letting go of a piece of *me*, because that rage and grief . . . that rage and grief were my family, and all I had left of that family.

All the irony of unfinished business. I'd been so afraid of losing them because life is change, and the tide was drawing us apart. And now they were gone permanently, and I was still here, and I hadn't just lost the future I had planned for and gotten invested in (a future that had never, of course, been real, but only what seemed to me the most desirable of likely outcomes).

The authentic experience is an illusion. Safety is an illusion too.

So some of my fury was selfish: the fury of having been robbed of my family. The fury of being made to experience this grief, this pain, by someone else's carelessness.

I reminded myself that pain and grief did not have to be suffering. That loss could just be that, loss, and experienced as such, and released because the world was change and you could not hold on.

The distinction seemed pretty academic to me just then.

I knew I needed to let go.

I was not ready to let go now.

I was not ready to release my strong attachment to my friends.

But maybe I could be ready to put the rage and sorrow away for a little while, so that I could get some work done.

Once I had first experienced them for a little while. And by *experienced*, I do mean "wallowed."

Eventually, with a lot of practice, I did calm my mind, and fill it with the sound and sensation of my breathing and the tiny sounds rattling through the Prize's hull. I still didn't reach out—it was probably ridiculous, but I was concerned that the more aggressive I was in seeking information, the more likely it was that Farweather might notice me, or be able to pick up on what I was doing. The Koregoi senso sometimes fed me information about her. It was only reasonable to suppose that, likewise, it fed her information about me.

And she was better at using the stuff than I was. Still.

When I had finally managed to bore my persistent, argumentative brain into silence, though, what filled it was not a sense of Farweather's presence, or even echoes of her intentions or her own senso ghosts. What I felt was, instead, what a stone might feel if dropped into a cool and limpid pool.

I seemed to drift, and there were currents all around me. I could perceive them, and moreover I could see through them. I again had that sense that I had had earlier of being able to feel the shape of the galaxy, of the universe, as if I were stretched out on a hammock, the fabric conforming to the outlines of my body—if my body were infinite, and extended to the very edges of everything. And if my capacity to sense detail were likewise infinite, and extended to the very edges of everything.

Our ship was a heavy place in the sky, one of many. Where we had been, the weight of the Well far outstripped it. And where we were going—

Farweather, or the ship, was taking us no place very interesting, I realized—partly in relief and partly in disappointment. We were headed for a Freeport—we had to be, because there was nothing Synarche in this corner of the galaxy—which was bad for me. There would not be very many opportunities to bust out if we were surrounded by pirates and occupied by more pirates.

Well, at least that encouraged me to act sooner rather than later.

Strangely, though, the flooding of information into my receptive state was not limited to vectors and directions and potential destinations and clusters of atoms and dark gravity and other things that bent the world. There was something else out there, something I was noticing now rather than previously because . . . Well, I could come up with a lot of theories. Because I was in an extraordinarily receptive state of mind. Because the Koregoi ship was feeding me data subconsciously. Because using the Koregoi senso while sitting inside the Koregoi ship caused a lensing property.

All kinds of explanations, as I said. But the fact of the matter was that I did not know why I was seeing what I was seeing—which was a grossly but not exactly repeating pattern of variations encoded in the dark gravity structure of the universe, on (in absolute terms) a very tiny scale.

"Dharma in the Well, Singer," I said under my breath. "That looks like somebody has been scratching crib notes on the cosmos. I don't suppose you can read them, can you?"

There was no answer, of course.

If it was some kind of encoding, there was no way I would ever crack it without at least a shipmind to help, and better yet some attention from the massed minds and architecture of the Core. If it was just noise . . .

. . . I didn't think it was just noise.

Well, I wasn't headed anyplace where I could plan on looking for help. I guessed it was just as well I hadn't expected to find any.

Which brought me to goal number the fourth: get the hell off this ship, or get control of it away from Farweather, before I wound up completely kidnapped by pirates, for real. (As opposed to the sort of fractional and incomplete pirate-kidnapping I was currently enjoying.)

Get The Hell Off The Ship would have been my preference, for obvious reasons, but a pretty thorough exploration of my options didn't fill me with confidence on that front. Jumping out of a vessel in white space wasn't the best of ideas unless your goal was a pretty spectacular suicide. While the space-time folds, once constructed, maintained themselves without additional input—and while everything *inside* the white coils was, technically speaking, motionless, so you wouldn't be left behind—in practical terms the ship was folding space-time around itself, so if you stayed in the white bubble you'd just wind up going wherever the ship was going along with it. And if you drifted *out* of the white bubble, you'd be folded, spindled, and mutilated as you crossed the boundary into normal space.

A lot of larger human and syster ships—colony ships and transports—carried escape vessels with their own small white drives, so that if something noncatastrophic but disabling happened to the main vessel, crew and passengers could be evacuated by the reverse of the procedure we'd used with Singer to retrieve vessels trapped or abandoned in white space. The Prize didn't seem equipped with anything like that, although honestly how would I know if it did? Given the external airlock technology, it seemed completely within reason that sections of the Koregoi ship itself might just be capable of peeling off and flying away on their own.

That left . . . steal the stolen Koregoi ship back from Farweather, in a massively hubristic act of reverse piracy. With no tools, no weapons, no pirating skills, and no support from a shipmind or crew. Set a trap? Set a series of traps? Knock her on the back of the head?

Hell of a way to run a mutiny.

On the other hand, I *was* an engineer.

Well, Haimey Dz, you always wanted to make a legend for yourself. Here's your chance at becoming a really spectacular example of a cautionary tale!

That was a lie. Well, not the second half. But I never had wanted to be famous. Or infamous, which I honestly seemed to have more of a talent for. I hadn't wanted it: not after Niyara, and not now.

Infamy would keep finding me, however.

Some people just aren't born to be anonymous, Singer said.

Even if they're born as one of faceless dozens, safe and secure, into a clade?

Then: *Wait, what?*

Singer?

Singer, are you real?

No answer, no tickle in my senso. Had he even been there? Even been real?

I'd heard rumors of senso-echoes, burn-in, pathways that got deep-chained in fox and synapses both. If I heard Singer where there was no Singer, that was my brain expecting what it had become accustomed to. Just as if I put a bit of cake in my mouth and expected sweetness, whether the morsel had sugar in it or not.

I'd been alone, living as a fugitive in the belly of an alien ship and eating oxygen tank scrapings, for almost a decian now. Who the hell knew what my unsupervised brain was doing in there without Singer keeping tabs on it for me? Losing touch with reality, in all probability. Reverting to old, bad habits deeply ingrained in my neural pathways by a childhood that did not encourage the development of critical thinking skills.

Great. Now I was hallucinating dead friends.

And I still didn't have a firm plan.

Except for traps.

Okay, so how did I lay traps for an enemy who was holed up in a tiny, fortified section of the ship, and who had already laid more than her share of traps to keep *me* out if I should venture there? And how did I manage to catch her without harming her? Maybe I was too well socialized, but I did, in fact, still stick at murder.

Besides, she was the one who seemed to know how to control the ship. Unless she was just along for the ride as well, though that seemed unlikely.

I could try to lure her out—either with bait, or by destroying something she wouldn't want to see sacrificed. But if she wasn't willing to come out even to try to contain or neutralize me—I flattered myself that I was probably her most immediate threat—then she was unlikely to leave her bolt-hole at all. Maybe, having locked me out of the areas she needed to control the Prize, she considered me already adequately neutralized.

My own presumed inutility and ineffectuality were a cheerful perspective, so I thought about something else.

I'd been floating in the safe harbor of one of the service tubes and thought a change of scene might help me think. I weaseled out of it, groped my afthands into my hated boots (I had acclimated, honestly, and was getting better at walking for longer periods without excruciating pain, even under gravity that was slightly heavier than Earth-normal), and went for a walk.

The best thing about giant alien starships full of endlessly twisting corridors was that you could go for really long walks. Like, station walks. Hours and hours. I was even getting to the point where the constantly perspective-shifting, Escheresque corridors no longer made me nauseated.

I was on my second lap around what I thought of as the Promenade,

a spiraling Möbius strip of a loop that took me through that same observation bubble I'd first watched Singer destroyed from. Every time I passed
through it, I stopped to observe my little ritual of memory. If you are a
planetsider, you probably visit a grave or memorial to pay respects to a
loved one. I just stopped for a moment each time I passed through this
space, tilted my head back, and gazed up at the twisting bands of white
space.

In abstract emotional response rather than out of any physical problem, I ached. My palms hurt. My eyes hurt.

Dammit, I missed my cats.

I stood there for a few minutes, aching too much to get myself moving
again, becoming increasingly uncomfortable as my body noticed a lack
of inputs. This had been an increasing problem as I practiced meditating
my way into the Koregoi ship's outputs. I was getting better at it, and
I was realizing that the control systems for the Koregoi vessel were set
up to interface seamlessly and perhaps even on a subconscious level
(assuming that Koregoi had anything like human levels of conscious
awareness, which was dangerous turf to be on) with the desires of its crew.
Which implied that the ship had or at one time *had* had something like a
shipmind, even if I couldn't figure out how to access or communicate with
it. It must have some kind of discriminatory process, at least—so that the
interlocking desires of a few thousand crew members wouldn't cause the
thing to tear itself apart. It *must* have.

Mustn't it? An autonomous regulatory system, at the very least.

Maybe it functioned like the Synarche ideally should: a series of
expert algorithms generating a consensus model based on weighted
averages.

But lately, my attempts at Zen starship maintenance had been mired
in constant physical and senso-based distractions. As if somebody somewhere were playing a badly tuned radio in a space where I was attempting
to concentrate.

And now, here it was when I was standing up, just looking at the folded light of distant stars. My sensorium itched, metaphorically speaking. It was as if I were *feeling* a crackle of static, some kind of senso synesthesia. As if being so profoundly disconnected from all outside inputs that didn't come from my own senses and the Koregoi parasite was causing my brain to fill up the empty spaces.

Have you ever looked at real darkness? Darkness with absolutely no light in it? After a little while, your eyes begin to invent things. Sparkles. Outlines. Little shimmers and glimpses of movement. None of it is real, of course. It's just bored neurons making work for themselves.

I suspected that that was what I was feeling, or the machine-meat interface equivalent.

Phantom pain.

Sigh.

My feet were starting to ache, and without thinking about it, I lightened the gravity to something that felt much more comfortable to my space-adapted body. I had been spending enough time in the weightless access tubes that my bones weren't in danger of decaying under the constant pressure of my own weight, but I was frankly just sick and tired of *being heavy*.

I stretched in relief, feeling my spine crack. Then, a moment later, I realized what I'd done, reflexively, without thinking about it or really trying. Or what the ship had done, in response to my unexpressed need.

I'd just effortlessly controlled an aspect of the ship. Without so much as thinking about it. As if it were my own body. Or an autonomic process thereof. It had just kind of . . . done it for me.

Which would be great, I thought, if I could get it to do the same sorts of things when I *asked*.

No, Haimey. We don't fantasize about spacing the pirate. Murder is still wrong. No matter how much somebody who murders pets and friends deserves to die.

I didn't have control over my heart rate, not really. I mean, I could slow it with meditation and raise it with exercise. But I had a fox, and using *that* I could control my heart rate, and blood pressure, and adrenaline levels, and all sorts of things.

And if I could control the Prize's pinpoint application of gravity, well. Gravity was a beautiful way to deal with Farweather, wasn't it?

Gravity would make a *most* satisfactory trap.

Oh bugger. One more thing to practice.

On the other hand, one more thing to distract myself with. And I figured we were still at least two standard decians out from our destination, if I had it plotted right. Even at the speeds the Koregoi ship was moving at—not-moving at—even as quickly as the Koregoi ship was stitching space-time past itself, which was at a rate greater than I'd ever encountered or even heard was theoretically possible.

I wondered if we were in danger of running out of fuel.

Gravity. My enemy, my weapon.

I wondered if I could get good enough at using it to crush Farweather against the deck like a grape smashed by acceleration.

I knew I shouldn't let myself hate her so much. I knew I shouldn't. Hating people doesn't accomplish anything except poisoning yourself. I should turn it off. I should let it go.

The thing was, first I had to *want* to let it go.

I kept waiting for Farweather to try to communicate with me. I kept waiting for her to reach out, to ask, to flirt. To get back to her gaslighting games, to get whatever she wanted from me.

Maybe now that I was a de facto captive, admittedly one with the run of most of the less immediately useful segments of this vast ship, she figured that she didn't need any cooperation. She and her cronies would force it out of me when we landed.

Maybe she was hoping I would get desperate enough to come to her. To ask questions. To ask mercy? To ask for help.

Well, I would come to her. Come *for* her.

And I was planning on doing it just as soon as I'd had enough time to practice my control of the Prize's artificial gravity. And how I was going to use it to quite literally pin her down and ask a few goddamned questions.

And not hurt her any more than you have to, right, Haimey?

I sighed. *And not hurt her any more than I have to.*

Yes.

Next tiny goal—was this number five? Five and a half? Something like that—develop superpowers, and learn to control the force of gravity. Artificial gravity, at least, as practiced by the Koregoi.

Odd thing was, it turned out I had a knack for it. It was fun; it was intuitive. Before long, I had fine-enough control that I could arrange the strength of the Prize's artificial gravity in centimeter-wide bands, which I have to tell you felt really weird to step through.

That reminded me of what I'd sensed in the dark gravity, the subtle gradations of density that made up a kind of pattern, like an old-fashioned bar code or stick-letter alphabet. I was becoming more and more convinced that what I had discovered was a code. Possibly I was becoming more and more deranged in my isolation, making up the kind of conspiracy theory narratives that human brains under stress are prone to. I checked my chemical balance, and it seemed fine, but.

The limited processing capacity of my fox was inadequate to work on a problem like that. I needed the help of a shipmind.

A pang: a shipmind was the thing I had not got.

I went back to my current problem, then. Little goals: learning to use the Prize itself as a weapon.

CHAPTER 18

WELP. THERE'S DHARMA FOR YOU.

Two sleeps (I couldn't really call them diar, because my schedule was nothing like twenty-four stanhours anymore) before I planned to debut my daring (and dare I say, brilliant) plan to sneak into Farweather's strongholds through the service access, use my newfound gravity powers to pin her to the decking, and tie her up and make her hand over control of the Prize, that old saw about contact with the enemy came into play.

I could have run my plan sooner. It was ready; I was ready. But there was nothing to be gained by hurrying. And in all honesty, I was stalling a little because I was scared.

Scared of Farweather. Scared of whether or not my gravity trick was going to work if there was another living body in the way of it, or whether Farweather would have better control—or whether the ship itself would intervene with some kind of failsafe to protect her. And I was scared as well of what I might do if my plan worked and I actually did get the upper hand.

I was not, shall we say, that much farther along the road of releasing my attachment to wanting to slam her head into a bulkhead over and over and over again than I had been a standard decian or so previous. I didn't think my self-control could be trusted, and so I didn't want to test it.

On the other hand, we would be getting close to Freeport space, inasmuch as they were a they and capable of claiming and holding territory (all things are impermanent). The closer we were to Farweather's allies, the more trouble I was in. I guessed she probably had some kind of escort close somewhere—the ship she had jumped from to flying-tackle the Prize, for example—and would her erstwhile allies just trust her to take off with something as utterly unique as an intact Koregoi vessel as its sole prize crew without *some* kind of supervision?

Furthermore, I could smell her roasting coffee in there occasionally, and after twenty diar of space nori three meals a dia, I probably would have launched a commando raid just for a pound of beans, even if I had to chew them and swallow my spit to get any good out of them. So there was honestly no chance of me waiting *too* long.

The mutineers on the *Bounty* had their strawberries. You know, people *say* all the time that they would kill somebody for a cup of coffee. It was literally starting to seem like a pretty good idea to me.

Well, not kill. I wasn't going to murder anyone if I could possibly help it. I was willing to keep telling myself that until I convinced myself, too.

Not for coffee. Not for Singer. Not for Connla. Not for Bushyasta and Mephistopheles, and honestly I was maddest about the cats. They hadn't had any choices or any options.

I told myself again that I wasn't here to kill anybody todia.

Not if I could help it.

I was pulling on my boots—which I was finally used to—to go make it happen when the imp that installs perverse hardware and his sister, the imp of perverse coincidence, intervened. But let me go back a little, and tell it all in some sort of order.

I didn't have the boots on already because I was moving through the maintenance access tubes—what I assumed, anyway, were maintenance access tubes, because I had no idea what the heck else they might be for. And as a human engineer playing archaeologist in a vast alien starship, I figured I was entitled to a little intellectual laziness.

I'd had—reluctantly—to bump twice to keep my anxiety levels

manageable while I made my way through the tubes. It wasn't their narrowness—I would have had to have any claustrophobia rightminded out a long time ago to keep being a tugboat engineer—it was the fact that I was trying to move through them in utter physical silence, floating along and directing myself with tiny touches. While also keeping my sensorium pulled in tight against my skin, not interacting with the ship at all, and hoping that in so doing I could hide my movements from Farweather, if she happened to be looking for me.

She had some kind of a trick that concealed her whereabouts pretty well, except when it didn't. I just hoped I was reasonably approximating the manner in which she accomplished it. It turns out that sneaking is physically and emotionally exhausting, which maybe was why she didn't do it all the time either.

Who would have guessed she might have human frailties and failings?

I'd mapped all of the parts that were outside of what I thought of as Farweather's territory, and I both had them foxed in, and had developed the kind of intimate muscle memory that takes practice and exploration. When I drifted onto Farweather's turf, though, it was like moving from a well-lit space to a dim and smoke-filled one. I had my theories and extrapolations to navigate by, and I had as far down the tubes as I could see with my own unaugmented eyes. I projected a skin of my theorized map onto the walls of the tubes as I spidered along, imagining myself some kind of formless sea creature wafting through pipes and down drains.

I always was a little too creative for my own good.

The anxiety was bad. The sense of all the ways things could go wrong loomed intensely over me, congealed into a breathless knot behind my sternum. And I kept coming up with new ones. I could mess up the gravity and get squished. I could get sealed in and spend the rest of my objectively quite short but subjectively probably very long and unhappy existence like a jellyfish in the tubes, drifting along, unable to get out. And both of those seemed preferable in my head to the idea that I was going to have to climb out of this accessway and go get into a physical confrontation with somebody who was armed and didn't mind conflict in the slightest.

Clades . . . are not big on training people how to maintain boundaries and manage necessary conflict. We all just get along. No matter what. Whether it suits our personal needs or not. Personal needs are a privileged affectation.

I didn't really have an option of getting along with the pirate. Not unless I wanted to wind up trapped in some Freeport outpost fixing stolen ships as an indentured servant or something similar.

Turn it off.

Dammit, I tried!

I had tuned the anxiety out, but the fear of the situation was enough that it kept breaking through. Deep, visceral programming: avoid the fight. It was paralyzing.

Don't choke, I told myself, and then rolled my eyes at myself. I had probably just ensured that I would be choking.

After three minutes clinging to a coil of piping, forcing my limbic system to *stop hyperventilating* through blunt and hard-core endocrine control, I thought of Connla's flying trick of bumping his sophipathology up enough so you didn't worry too much about consequences.

It seemed like a terrible idea.

After two more minutes, I decided I needed to try it, or Farweather was going to figure out where I was, poke a bolt prod in through a convenient access hatch, and electrocute me in my burrow like a particularly large and smelly ship rat.

I bumped, got a little magnetism in there to turn off the inconvenient brain bits for an hour or so, and set a timer lockout so I couldn't do it again until after the first dose had worn off. That last part is pretty essential if you're doing this sort of thing alone, because once you turn off your common sense and ability to assess consequences, it turns out almost nobody wants them back again.

After that, everything was easy and I couldn't figure out what I'd been so apprehensive about. I felt confident, loose. I knew what I was doing, and I wasn't going to have any problem handling one little pirate. This was my domain—*space* was my domain—and if nothing else I could just get the Prize to shut down gravity entirely and be six times as capable in free fall as she was.

Hell, Farweather didn't even have afthands. Whereas I could anchor myself, eat spaghetti, turn a screwdriver, and pick my nose simultaneously. And without even getting the spaghetti anyplace biologically inappropriate.

It took me only a little bit of exploratory back-and-forth to check the location of the access hatches. I'd gotten pretty expert at identifying their nubby bits and the pressure points that made them smoke up and vanish when you wanted to go through. Confident I'd gotten as close to her command center as I was likely to, I located an access hatch I could use to get out into the corridors. I unslung my boots from over my shoulder and started working them on my afthands, as previously mentioned. Once I had them seated, I'd reach out into the Koregoi senso, try to feel where Farweather was before she noticed me (assuming she hadn't spotted me already and also assuming she wasn't lying in wait) so I could pop out, slam the gravity down around her, and give her the thumping she so richly deserved.

That was when I heard the screaming.

Reflexively—and when had using the *alien technology that had infected my body without my consent* become *reflexive?*—I reached out into the Koregoi senso. It unfolded like releasing cramped wings, and I felt instantly less anxious—as if my inner ear had been affected, or my hands bound behind my back, and I'd been trying to walk a balance beam. The relief was profound.

So profound it almost made up for the screaming.

Actually, the noise didn't bother me at all, except as noise. It was *really* irritating, like a crèche full of three-an-olds not getting their own way.

If I just shot her, the noise would probably stop, wouldn't it?

What a pity you don't have a gun.

Oh yeah. That is a problem.

Calm down, Dz. There's only two people on this boat that could be screaming, and you're pretty sure this one isn't you.

It could be a decoy.

Of course it could. Or she could be in trouble, in which case—

In which case, I really don't have to do anything about it, do I?

Yes, Haimey. You probably do. You still need her expertise.

A heavy sigh escaped me, the only external signifier of my interior argument. Briefly, I closed my eyes. There was still screaming, but it sounded tonally different—less surprised, and more furious and pained. I'd guessed right—the noise was close, and it was echoing through the maintenance tube as loudly if somebody had set up a speaker in here to boost it.

At least if she's hurt, she'll be easier to contain.

Assuming she's not in need of massive medical attention I can't provide.

Well, either way, she's not getting any less injured while we wait.

That'll just make her easier to control.

Dz.

Over the top, I said to myself, and triggered the access hatch.

Well, I didn't think she was faking it.

Farweather lay curled on her side in a puddle of very bright red blood, clutching her right wrist with her left hand. She was mid-shout when I weaseled out of the access door, found my orientation in local gravity, and dropped lightly down.

I landed in a crouch. Farweather stopped screaming and peeled her blood-slimed fingers loose from her wrist to snatch at her weapon. Red spurted, and she gave up trying to get the gun and went back to applying pressure again.

My weapon didn't require me to reach for anything except the (metaphorically speaking) goodwill of the ship. I felt it, felt it acquiesce to my desire, felt it tighten down on the already fallen pirate with the force of several Earth gravities—no joke even for somebody raised down a well. For a spacer like me, it would have been profoundly incapacitating. With a squeezed, breathy moan, she collapsed onto her back, just about managing to keep pressure on her wrist as both hands were pinned to her chest by their own weight.

"Rot in hell," she groaned, glaring at me.

I stood a meter off, observing Farweather and the apparatus surrounding her. It looked like a spring had recoiled, sending a piece of metal across her lower arm with enough force that it had acted like a blade. She had an arterial bleed going on, though not too bad a one—as if there were anything such as an insignificant arterial injury—and she was managing to keep enough pressure on it that while she could probably bleed out pretty easily if left untreated, she wasn't in *immediate* danger of dying.

I guess she had sensed me coming, after all. If she hadn't tried to get tricky, and had just gotten the drop on me the old-fashioned way by electrocuting me with her bolt prod or putting a few holes in me with the airgun she had holstered on her thigh, I'd be dead or a captive by now. But she'd tried to set a trap. And apparently I had been right about being the better engineer.

What kind of a sophipath wore a *projectile weapon* in a pressure vessel?

Well, a pirate who would think nothing of murdering a whole crew of people, even if those people were monsters. Silly question. Moving on now.

I probably really should kill her. I'd be saving my own life, and a lot of other lives over the long term, if I did.

I probably really should. But for now, I managed to swallow down another bolus of rage, and remember that I needed her. I groped in my suit repair kit for a roll of pressure tape. Crouching down, I braced and counterbalanced myself, and reached cautiously into the high-gravity zone to lay the tape very gently on her sternum.

If she was a cat, she would have been spitting at me with flattened ears.

"Go ahead and tape up that wrist," I said.

She did, using one hand and her teeth, managing not to lose too much more blood in the process. It took her about ninety seconds, and by the time she was done more fresh blood was smeared all over her, the deck, her face, and everything else within range—including splatters on my boots. The roll of tape was absolutely thick with gore. One more small, irreplaceable, useful item off the inventory.

I really wished I had access to a printer. You never realize how spoiled you get by not having to *keep* stuff around because you can just *make* it when you need it, until suddenly you discover that *stuff* is a finite resource and you can't just automatically get more.

When she'd stopped her bleeding, the next thing she did was reach for her gun.

I was, of course, ready for that, and pinned her to the deck hard enough that her face pulled back against the bones and her breathing grew labored.

"Bad pirate," I said. I was gambling that if she wasn't actively bleeding, her Koregoi parasite could repair her the same way mine had repaired me. Otherwise, well, there wasn't much I could do for her that wouldn't result in gangrene.

"... enjoying this."

Yeah, I was. I wish I could say I wasn't proud of it—I knew I wouldn't be proud of it when I quit being a temporary psychopath—but it wasn't so easy to stop enjoying it, either.

"Leave your weapons in the holsters, unclip them, and give them to me," I said.

"Fuck you," she answered.

"I'll crush you," I said.

"I don't think so," she answered. Her breathing strained under the weight of her own flesh. Still she managed a pained smile.

I let the ship pull her down a little more. She moaned. My fingernails dug into my forepalms.

She should be squashed like the insect she was. She should be paying for all the lives she had ended. Everything awful she had chosen and done. I wanted to smear her all over the decking and walk away.

She turned her head so her cheek lay flat against the deck, still looking at me. Her neck muscles weren't going to enjoy that tomorrow, if we both lived so long. I wondered if the pressure was blurring her vision yet.

"More weight," she said.

It wasn't really a standoff, of course. I was healthy—healthy-ish—and she'd lost a lot of blood. I just reached in again, bracing myself even more carefully, and relieved her of her visible armaments.

First I had to spend ten minutes talking myself out of murdering her in cold blood. And by the time I'd actually worked up my moral fiber enough that I could touch her without assassinating her, she'd passed out due to acceleration sickness, and I could pat her down for other dangerous items (two knives, a monofilament garrote that she was lucky she hadn't incorporated into her death trap or she'd probably be *missing* that hand entirely, and a spare clip for the air pistol) and make sure that her wrists and ankles were taped together securely with the blood-fouled suit repair kit.

By then, I was feeling more like myself again, which seemed like a great loss, because I didn't even get the chance to kick her in the head a couple of times while I was still disinhibited enough to do it.

I even made a point of being careful to make sure she was getting adequate blood flow to her extremities, which was *definitely* more than she deserved, and I found *her* first aid kit (she wasn't getting anything else out of mine) and gave her a spray-hypo of a broad-spectrum antibiotic and antiviral to keep her from getting alien space gangrene or the deadly Koregoi herpes or whatever else might be floating around out here.

The odds of cross-species infection were slim. But if I made the conscious decision to invest in some kind of caretaking behavior where she was concerned, I figured I was psychologically less likely to shove her out the nearest airlock.

Sunk cost fallacy. Make it work for you.

Why that seemed important to me at the time, I'm not really sure. Something about maintaining my humaneness and self-respect in the face of adversity. Or doing things the hard way. Or some side effect of my social conscience reasserting itself after its nice little nap.

Farweather didn't see it that way. She woke up while I was going through her kit, and though she didn't say anything, she lay quietly and watched me give her the antibiotic and antiviral hypo. I tucked her in with a couple of reflective blankets and gave her some fluids and glucose from her own first aid setup to ward off shock, which I guess baseline humans are more vulnerable to than I am.

"That's not going to make me think better of you," she said mildly, when I'd backed away.

I shrugged. "What you think of me is immaterial."

"So you don't *need* anything from me?"

She said it in a flirting tone that might have been more effective if she weren't covered in her own blood from trying to kill me. Oh, and if I hadn't had all that nonsense turned off. And I was very glad I had, because Farweather—mass murderer or no—was just the sort of bad girl I knew could get under my skin if I let her.

Clade upbringings fuck you up on so many levels, when you finally let the oppressive rightminding go and try to exist as an independent human being with things like judgment and will.

"Sure," I said dryly. I rummaged through her supplies and found the coffee. There was a little probe for heating water, and a vacuum extractor to draw it through the beans.

"Sweet eternity," I said reverently.

"Bitch, you'd better share," said she.

I smiled sweetly at her over my shoulder. "Teach me how to access the ship's drive functions, and how to navigate her, and we can have a conversation about it then."

"Fuck you," she said.

So I made myself an exceptionally good cup of coffee, and set about trying to figure it out for myself.

It turns out that caffeine is a highly addictive substance with really unpleasant physical withdrawal symptoms, if you're not bumping your brain chemistry to compensate, and that one of those withdrawal symptoms is an evil, splitting headache. Which Farweather told me *all about*, in excruciating detail, except when she was sleeping, or just curled up suffering on the floor.

I had no idea there were that many filthy insults available to the average speaker of Galactic Standard. Well, learn something new every dia; that's what my clademothers used to tell me. Which was more productive advice on the whole than most of what I was getting from the pirate.

So I learned a lot about my theoretical sexual, spiritual, and menu habits—all of it revolting. What Farweather *didn't* tell me about in detail, sadly, was how she'd been operating the Koregoi ship, even when I offered her coffee and a headache pill if she shared.

I'm not sure if I consider this a relief or a disappointment, but it either pleases or saddens me to report that it turns out I'm too well rightminded or just too socially aware to make much of a torturer. I pushed the issue as much as I could, but I have to be honest: it didn't get me anywhere, and I thought if I pushed her harder, she'd probably just lie to me. Not that lying to me would work for long: I could tell just as well as she could where we were in the universe, and which way we were going. So I'd know if she'd actually taught me how to steer the Prize or not almost immediately.

This isn't how it works on the holoserials.

And so we sailed on into the darkness, me trying to come up with a plan in case I didn't manage to divert us before we got to the Freeports, and going through her stuff—carefully, in case of booby traps. I found and disabled two, which left me with a good opinion of my own engineering skill. There were a lot of useful things in her luggage: I organized them neatly while I took an inventory. She filled her time with a robust suite of hobbies that included cursing, whining about her headache and shaky extremities, and napping extensively.

It was a long, long flight from the Core to the Republic of Pirates. Even at the relative-*v* the Prize reached and maintained, it would probably take us at least a third of an an or more to get there.

So I passed the time coding the projectile weapon to me, then taking it apart and hiding all the bits in various places where they wouldn't be speedy for her to reassemble, and trying to figure out how to get her on my side. That seemed the most productive use of her as a resource, since I hadn't had the intestinal fortitude just to murder her.

Maybe that was why she didn't take me seriously, come to think of it. On the other hand, it was hard to imagine how I would have gotten any information out of her if I *had* just up and slaughtered her.

Farweather slept a lot for the first couple of diar, in part definitely because I dosed her with a sedative every time *I* needed to rest, for safety's sake, and in part probably because of the caffeine withdrawal, and in part probably because she was making up lost blood volume. Which she could do, because I (grudgingly) fed her, and made sure she was adequately hydrated. She wasn't wearing a full suit the way I was, so—expiation for any wrong I've ever done, I swear it, and some karmic debt paid forward—I even helped her hop to the head and use it, though I made her figure out how to deal with her own hygiene, taped hands or no taped hands.

I was glad I'd figured out what the waste disposal closets looked like already. After my own experience with adapting to the space nori diet, I'd made a small study of how the Koregoi handled waste disposal. A toilet was a toilet was a toilet, it turned out, whether it was a zero-g litterbox or just a vacuum tube.

Everybody really does poop, no matter what their species is. Well, except for the plant people. They just outgas a lot of oxygen and water vapor.

Surprisingly, she didn't seem particularly grateful.

After a few diar, she was a little more functional. I had used the time to up my guard and create various precautions, and I'd figured out how to use her bolt prod. It wasn't biometrically coded to her, which was a—pardon me, ha ha—*shocking* oversight.

I hung it on my own belt. I could almost hear the scraping of her eyes in their sockets as she followed it around with her gaze, thinking about how to get control of it and the situation. I may have neglected to mention in there anywhere that while she was unconscious I'd built a lock for it that I coded to my own pheromones and DNA signature.

I'd also been continuing to try to meditate my way into the ship's control systems. Now that I had the run of the place, I'd used it, and I'd determined that there *was* nothing of the sort that we human types would consider a bridge, or a control room. Apparently the blasted Koregoi just navigated their ships by Zen. Or maybe turned them over to shipminds, vast and curious, but if that was the case then it seemed really likely that any shipmind once inhabiting this vessel was long corrupted, quiescent, or purged.

I still had time to come up with some kind of solution to the Kidnapped By Pirates problem, if I thought fast. And I *still* didn't have any books. I could access Farweather's stuff, because Freeporters didn't run to foxes and senso, so all her VR was in an external. But Farweather's taste in entertainment leaned to the kind of immersive sandbox VR exploration games with a lot of gun- or swordplay that left me cold. Connla had been a fan of that sort of thing, and even more so of large-scale military tactics simulators. Maybe he should have been the sole survivor. He'd have been less bored.

I pulled Farweather's compact VR rig off my head, tossed it in a corner, and walked away while she yelled at me about how I was treating her stuff with disrespect and I hadn't even asked her if I could use it.

Honestly, that was probably the closest she came to dying that whole trip, and I'm pretty sure she never even knew.

I waited until my hands organically stopped shaking with fury before I came back, walking and walking in random loops through the ship because I was, frankly, too attached to my atavistic barbarian rage to tune it down. I hadn't disassembled Farweather's perimeter, in case I needed it myself later to repel boarders, but I had opened it up, and I walked for the better part of a standard hour before I stopped fuming enough to trust myself, and to *want* to not be angry.

I made myself safe and headed back to our little base camp. Far-weather was where I'd left her, chained to a stanchion that I'd managed to coax the Koregoi ship to grow by meditating at it. It hadn't grown me the chains, and anyway I was hesitant, because Farweather could probably unwitch anything I could witch together that way. Instead, I'd used chains I'd welded up myself out of her own oxygen tanks.

Technically speaking, I hadn't *had* to do it. There had been a set of restraints in her gear, probably intended for me, if she caught me. But I wasn't going to use those on her: there was too much chance she had some sort of biocode on them that would allow her to override the locks.

Thus: the spare ox tanks. If we had to do any spacewalking, well. Zanya Farweather was shit out of luck.

Her own fault, really.

When I got back within sight of her, I stopped and folded my arms, leaning against the corridor wall at a cockeyed angle to her until she noticed I was there and shuffled around awkwardly to face me. The shimmer of copper-gold stardust in tendrils across her features had at some point stopped being unnerving, I noticed from the distance of my rage. Now it was just part of her face.

The only human face I'd seen in standard weeks. Because human brains are weird, I felt a little bit of affection for her at that moment.

Disfigured like me; infested, like me. We were poisoned together.

I loathed her and I despised her and I thought I probably would have completely lost touch with myself by now if she had not been there. And somewhere on my long, furious walk, I had figured out what I needed to do, I thought, to try to get her to give me what I needed.

Well, if I didn't have anything else to keep myself occupied with, I supposed there were worse hobbies than conversational salons with monsters. Even if I couldn't think of any right now.

I was going to need all the supportive brain chemicals and electrical tuning that I could get.

Farweather watched me carefully as I walked over and sat down. Not next to her; I wasn't stupid. But across the corridor against the wall, and diagonally a meter away or so. Where she could see me comfortably, but not under any circumstances reach. I had a flask of carbonated water in my hand, and I sipped it, considering her.

She studied me right back. "Ooo, something pissed off the good little clade girl."

She was lucky I was tuned. I gave myself an extra bump of GABA and took three deep breaths anyway.

I drank more water and didn't answer.

"Are you enjoying being angry?" she asked me, cocking her head. Her hair had gotten long, and she tossed it out of her eyes. The tape residue was slowly wearing off her uninjured wrist, but the chain connecting her feet to her hands was short enough that she still could only reach her face if she was sitting or crouched down.

She was trying to get my goat. Okay then. Apparently my letting my tuning slip a little had made her think that she could gain an advantage over me by continuing to push that.

Well, that was my tactic too, then. It was like wrestling: one of us would eventually get the upper hand, but we both had to offer openings to encourage the other to grapple, or we'd just wind up circling each other forever. And when it came to self-control, I had the advantage of my rightminding.

How could I lose?

I stretched my legs out more comfortably. "What if I turned you over to the Jothari?"

Her eyes narrowed a little. *Where did you learn that name?* But she didn't say it—didn't say anything, just frowned, by which I presumed she was thinking.

I decided to make her think harder. "I admit, I wondered how a human managed to get onto the crew of such a famously xenophobic species."

"The Synarche left them with good reasons to hate it," she said. "That's not xenophobia."

"Still."

She shrugged, chain rattling. "Lots of people don't like the Synarche. You'd be amazed at what you can come up to talk about with somebody when you discover you've got an enemy in common."

"Well." I sighed, and as if discovering that I had a sudden taste for it, got slowly to my feet to collect the coffee makings. "You're a Jothari mass murderer, Zanya. Are you telling me that an extralegal species that murders and disassembles sentients for profit wouldn't have a nice, rich price on the head of a treacherous alien crew member?"

"You'd have to find them," she scoffed.

I shrugged. "I bet if I put the word out they'd find me."

"Ativahikas have never been proved to be sentient," she said, which was as nice an avoidance of a subject as I'd ever seen.

I gave her my second-best pitying look. She couldn't have the best one, because I had honed it on Connla. "Whatever lets you sleep at night."

"I sleep fine at night," she spat back. "And I don't need to get my brain fiddled to do it."

The rich smell of the brewing coffee arose around the probe. I saw her lean back and close her eyes, inhaling deeply.

"You want some of this?"

She cracked an eye. "You know I do."

It did smell amazing. It occurred to me that if I could get her to start cooperating in small things, and reward that cooperation, then eventually I'd find it easier to get her to cooperate in larger things as well. Just like training a cat.

Unrightminded humans basically weren't that different from cats, were they?

Right? Maybe?

Maybe, in fact, I could get a psychological dependency going, and then she'd *want* to tell me what I needed to know: how to turn this Well-caught ship around.

It was probably my best chance of spending my retirement someplace more interesting than interment in a Freeport. And now that the options were a little clearer in my mind, it turned out that I would really *much* rather accept some semivoluntary service to the Synarche for a few ans, rather than be press-ganged by pirates who probably wanted me more for the stuff in my skin than my engineering skill anyway. I couldn't imagine myself very happy with a life of using my alien parasite to hunt down and raid unsuspecting ships and their crews.

"Ask nicely," I said, as if I were tired of arguing about it and looking for an excuse to say yes.

I was surprised that she managed to master the anger I saw bubbling up in her. Apparently unrightminded humans can in fact manage a little bit of self-control, though honestly you wouldn't know that from the plots of those antique books I'm always reading. There's not two of those imaginary ancient people with any forebrain activation between them.

Though I guess if they did have any, the plots would be pretty boring.

She chewed her lower lip for a moment. Then she said, "Please may I have some coffee?"

I gave her the coffee I was already working on, once it was strained and ready. I half expected her to throw the scalding fluid in my face, and was ready with the gravity if I saw her arm go back. But I guess she realized that even if she burned me, she'd still be chained to a stanchion, and she probably wanted that coffee a lot more than she wanted an empty gesture.

I mean, I know I would have.

There was a name for what I was trying to do to her, I was pretty sure. I wished Singer were here to remind me what it was.

Imprinting?

No, Stockholmification.

Right. From an ancient city name, back on Earth. Funny how words like that got into the language and never left. *Stentorian. Colossal. Stockholmify.*

All I had to do was make sure I didn't accidentally Stockholmify myself.

Or let her do it to me.

CHAPTER 19

I BROUGHT FARWEATHER HER COFFEE AND A BOWL OF OAT-
meal enriched with space nori and sat down a few meters away across
the corridor to enjoy my own breakfast. *Enjoy* was even the right term.
It was so nice to be eating something other than algae, or algae with space
shrimp, that I didn't even mind that with the two of us sharing the food
that had been meant for her alone—plus my gleanings from the algae
tanks—we were on pretty tight rations.

At least my space suit had stopped expanding around me for the time
being. And there was still a good quantity of coffee.

She sipped hers between taking bites of oatmeal—and pulling dis-
gusted faces—and said, "You still haven't managed to come up with an
argument I find convincing, you know."

"For the Synarche?"

She waved her spoon in the air. "For why you let an AI control what
you think and feel, and can't seem to survive without it."

"Well for one thing," I said calmly, "that's a misrepresentation."

"Oh?"

"Oh. Nobody controls what I feel except me, and rightminding lets
me *actually* control what I feel, instead of being at the mercy of a whole
bunch of very messy evolution. If anything, it makes me able to be more
me, and less whatever random genetics and misadventure have installed."

"Huh," she said. She licked the back of her spoon. "Well, it's nice that
you think so."

I ate my oatmeal.

"What about Judicial?"

"Recon?" I asked.

"If that's what you want to call brainwashing, sure."

"It heals people," I pointed out. "When you're too antisocial to know you're antisocial, society has to intervene. Like parents teaching children responsible behavior."

I tried not to think about the fact that—angry at her as I still was, craving revenge as I still was, *wanting to kick that spoon right up her smug, pert little nose* as I found myself and being unwilling to correct that feeling, to let go of it—I was probably not currently in any position to decide what was and what was not antisocial behavior. At least not on an emotional and desire level.

She smiled at me condescendingly.

"We're monsters," I said. "Atavistic horror shows. We can't exist in a civilized society without fixing the ways in which we are evolutionarily maladapted *to* that civilized existence. Not without constantly harming one another."

"The Freeports and Freeholds do just fine," Farweather said.

I gawked at her. I almost said, *It's nice that you think so.*

"I turned out all right," she said, with her most devilish smile.

I have my limits. "It's nice that you think so."

"If you're so confident that you'd do better, I dare you to meet me on equal ground."

"What do you mean?"

She smiled slyly, only half her mouth rising. "Turn it off."

"My *rightminding?*"

"All of it."

"That's pathological."

"Well," she said, "if the way you were raised—the *civilized* way you were raised—produces so much better, better-adjusted people than the free-range upbringing I got, prove it to me. Without chemical or mechanical crutches. Turn it off."

"I don't engage in murdering sentients for commerce," I said. "Case closed."

"You're programmed not to," she admitted. "That's not ethics. I want to know the real you." There was a pause while she examined her fingernails. "Unless you're afraid of what you'll learn."

Of course I was. I was terrified of what I might learn. And not just because of growing up in the clade and not really feeling like I had a *me* to fall back on. But also because of the Judicial oversight.

I was damaged. I always would be. How much of that oversight held me together? Would I even be functional without it?

"I dare you," she said.

"Drink your coffee," I replied.

"Why do you do what you do?" she asked me.

"It gives me a lot of freedom," I said. "I don't like feeling trapped."

"The Freeports would give you more freedom."

"Sure," I said. "As long as I subscribed to their . . . sorry, *your* . . . ideology. It's the freedom to do whatever I want, as long as I'm willing to agree that other people's well-being doesn't matter unless they can enforce it."

She looked at me blankly.

"Who cleans up the messes selfish people make? Somebody has to. With children, it's parents. When it's an adult with social power, what then?"

Farweather ducked her head so she could scratch her nose. "Well, cleaning it up is not *my* problem. I mean, I don't have to worry about that."

"I don't want to live in that world."

Farweather seemed to be thinking. "You'd rather let other people put their well-being over yours?"

"When they need it more? Sure would."

"Huh." Shaking her head gently, frowning, neck slightly twisted, she hunched her shoulders. She drew away. Probably would have walked away, if she hadn't been chained to a stanchion.

Brave words, Dz. And yet, if I admitted it, her sophipathology—no, I needed the older word, the archaic word—her *sociopathy*, her *social sickness* . . . It was attractive. Not being beholden to anybody. Not being *responsible* for anybody but myself. Not caring what effect my actions had on others.

I thought of Connla when he had that dialed up. His confidence. Unapologetic skill. Ability to get through the most stressful situations without self-criticism, self-consciousness, or choking.

What would it be like not to be worried all the time about what effect my actions had on other people?

Maybe Farweather was right.

Maybe that was freedom.

I wondered what would happen if I just . . . turned my ethics off again.

The freedom had felt *good*. It had been *nice* to worry only about myself and the pragmatic results of whether what I was doing right now would get me what I wanted, right now or in the immediate future. I'd needed Farweather for my own purposes, so I could be confident that I probably wouldn't kill her.

Could I rely on that need to *keep* me from killing her? It would be a lot easier to get through this if I weren't so damned worried and conflicted all the time. Thinking about the future was really doing a number on me.

Of course it's not that simple, but a rightminded person has pretty good control over things like their level of social engagement. Connla used that trick to get his self-conscious brain out of the way when he needed to fly hard and without thinking too much about the consequences of failure.

It can be dangerous to just turn off your conscience, of course. Especially without a cutout, a good friend, or an AI to make sure you remember to turn it back on again afterward. Consciences are the sort of thing that don't seem really desirable to have, unless you're currently using yours. And I really didn't want to have to keep dealing with the pangs and irruptions of mine now.

But . . . No, I couldn't. I mean, it would make talking to her—trying to manipulate her—a lot easier to put up with. But I might also decide that reassembling her airgun was a productive use of my time, and that's not the sort of equipment that goes well with poor impulse control.

Besides, I probably needed my empathy in order to create some kind of emotional bond with her and get her on my side.

Or at least that was a reasonable-sounding excuse, and I could keep telling myself that.

Well and falling, I did not want to keep talking to her. But I didn't want to be totally alone with only the sound of my own voice in my head to argue with, either.

"It seems to me," Farweather said, "that you find a lot of your validation in service."

"I'm not going to like you," I told her. "Your friends killed my friends. There's no payback for a debt as big as the one you owe me."

She was studying me curiously, a furrow between her black brows. The shimmer of blue iridescence on her hair was long vanished, dulled by grease and dirt. I'd taken sponge baths when I could, but we were both filthy.

"So what debt are you trying to pay back with all this doing things for other people, babes? What sin do you think *you* owe an unpaybackable debt for?"

"Sin is a null concept," I said.

"So why all this fuss about service, then?"

The chilled clench in my stomach didn't ease when I drank hot miso broth. I didn't look at her. "It's as good a reason to live as any."

"Okay," she said. "What about what you want?"

I shrugged. "What about what I want?"

"You serve other people's needs. Who serves yours?"

"What if what I need is to feel valuable to a community? To feel like I'm contributing and supporting my fellows."

"That's certainly what you've been brainwashed into feeling. Your entire life."

"Maybe it's who I am."

"Maybe it's why Niyara picked you out."

I admit it. I gawked.

She smirked at me, smug. She'd gotten my attention (and eye contact) now.

"That's a sealed juvenile file," I said.

She shrugged. Her chains rattled. Man, if I turned off my ethics I'd probably murder her just to not have to hear the rattling for a while. "Even in the heart of the empire, corruption spreads."

"Well," I swore. I wanted to spit, so I drank soup instead.

"You don't want to believe that." She had a cup of soup, too, but she wasn't drinking hers. She was just holding it between her hands, which rested on her upraised knees. I had dragged in some fluffy stuff that might be a mattress and might be packing material of the sort with little stale bubbles of atmosphere sandwiched between impermeable layers, and made her something reasonably soft to sit and sleep on.

I had my own pile against the wall a ways away, though when I had to sleep I usually did it floating in the access tubes. I have never slept well under gravity. Or within earshot of Farweather.

"I don't believe it," I allowed.

"Because you're an idiot who will sacrifice herself for any cause, no matter how stupid it is, if somebody she likes tells her it's important. Because it's been *etched* into you to do so."

I shrugged. Maybe she was right.

Maybe she was winning the argument—a prospect that both scared and excited me.

We sat in silence for a few minutes. I got up, brewed algae broth, fetched each of us a mug with a wide bottom and a narrow top. So strange, drinking out of open containers like we were in some kind of antique drama or something. I'd found them in a room with nonfunctional taps. Maybe they were drinking vessels. Maybe they were urinals.

I sat down again and we faced each other, drinking silently and in unison, cradling the mugs between our hands and letting the steam bathe our faces between each sip.

I realized I was mirroring her, and intentionally broke the pattern by setting my mug down.

You can just *set things down*. And they stay where you put them. I'll never get used to that.

"Don't you wonder who you'd be without the clade? Without Judicial Recon? Without rightminding?"

For some reason, this time it sank in that she knew about the Recon, too. So much for my privacy.

She must have read my face, because she shrugged and said, "You were interesting."

I thought it was a lie. I thought she'd known something about me before we ever met. I thought that was why Connla and Singer and I had been fed the information that led us to the *Milk Chocolate Marauder* in the first place, and why they'd been waiting for us there.

They'd been a little early, was all. Had to leave and come back. Been lucky they hadn't startled us off when they nearly ran us over.

I'd thought about it and thought about it, and nothing else made sense. Coincidence was possible. But what was much more likely was enemy action.

I finished my broth in one gulp. It had cooled enough that it nearly didn't scorch my throat going down.

I said, "Without that stuff? I wouldn't be anybody."

Maybe Farweather was better at using the Koregoi senso than I was because she was so much less self-conscious. Self-conscious? *Self-aware*.

She was what she was. She did what she did. I didn't think she worried about the whys and wherefores too much, come to think of it. If the universe had been bent on handing me an example of the exact opposite of who I was, it couldn't have found a better one. We might have been two opposite halves of one thing, complementary and conflicted.

I wondered if her personal life was a trail of carnage, too.

Probably, I thought. Probably.

She seemed not to feel nearly as bad about it as I would have, however.

It *had* felt glorious, not caring about consequences beyond what I wanted right now and was pretty sure I could get. Farweather just wanted what she wanted. She did what she felt like doing. She didn't care who got hurt, and she didn't feel any social responsibility to mitigate that harm, or seek compromise, or balance her needs against the needs of others.

I realized that on some level, I envied her.

Outside, the folded sky of white space—and my time as a free person (was I a free person?)—whisked silently by.

And then there was the part of my brain that remembered my history lessons and the ancient books I liked so much because they were a window into a world far more alien than the one embodied by people like Cheeirilaq and Singer. That part of me also reminded me periodically of what the outcomes were when an entire society was controlled by predators like Farweather.

That was how we got here in the first place. Got to the Synarche, I mean, not got to bunking on bubble wrap in a stolen alien space ship a million light-ans from anything useful. People like Farweather, unconstrained, create conditions so awful that people eventually decided to change themselves rather than keep living that way.

The voice in my own head was sounding more and more like Singer with every passing dia. I wondered if my personality was bifurcating. I'd read somewhere that that wasn't a real thing, but it sure showed up enough in old novels.

◆ ◆ ◆

"It's your hypocrisy that bothers me," Farweather said.

I blinked at her. "I don't understand what you mean."

"Well, you'll give me a lot of pious nonsense about how rightminding is essential for overcoming our atavistic urges and living in a civilized society, and yet you are afraid of using it yourself."

"I don't consider it cheating," I said. "I use it all the time."

She stared at me. I refused to look down. We broke at the same instant, or gave up, or decided it wasn't worth continuing. I heard myself sigh in relief, though, and caught the tiny smirk at the corners of her mouth before she controlled it.

"No, you don't, babes. You let other people use it on you. Other . . . *things*. Artificials. *Objects.*"

"Singer is a people," I snapped. And then felt terrible, because Singer had been a people, and now he was gone. And this . . . creature had helped kill him.

If anybody was an *object* around here . . .

"Keep his name out of your mouth," I said, and then felt even stupider, because she hadn't even *said* his name.

I was losing this round, and I needed to disengage without seeming like I was running away.

"Then why?" she asked, her voice low and intimate.

I didn't answer. *Because I don't trust myself to make those decisions* was not the sort of vulnerability you revealed to an enemy. And I am, and always have been, a terrible liar. Another side effect of growing up in a clade: you don't get a lot of practice, because everybody around you generally knows what you're thinking most of the time anyway.

"So you *don't* think you're a hypocrite?" she asked.

"No," I answered. "No more so than most people."

She snorted, her *child, you are so tiresome* sound. "This from somebody who doesn't like rightminding for herself, just for everybody around her—"

"That's not what I said—"

"—and who's decided to have her damned sexuality turned off rather than go through the rehab and therapy to deal with her trauma."

I stared at her for a minute. She stared back levelly.

"How did you know I had that turned off?"

She shrugged. "You told somebody on Downthehatch, didn't you?"

I stared right at her and said, "The reason I turned it off is because I have lousy taste in women."

She smiled, and I couldn't tell if she was failing to take my meaning, or failing to take my meaning on purpose, or just didn't consider it the insult I had intended it to be. Actually, she looked like she was taking it as a compliment, and I wished I'd kept my mouth shut.

"You could get that fixed too," she said, smiling smugly.

"A lot of work," I answered, smiling smugly right back at her, "for so very little reward."

"You know," Farweather said, "it wasn't us that killed your friends."

She was giving herself a sponge bath, crouched down with a bowl of water between her knees and a folded-up wad of fiber. I stood guard, turned slightly away to offer her a scrap of privacy. I'd rearranged her chains so she had a little more freedom, and I was watching her carefully for the time being to make sure it hadn't been *too* much freedom. She made a pretense of docility, but I had my fox tuned to keep reminding me that she wasn't tame and I needed to be on my guard around her. It would be much too easy to relax.

On the other hand, I was as much her captive as she was mine. I might have her body under control—but she, in her own way, had mine. I was going where she wanted to go, where her friends were waiting for us. And okay, it might be a little embarrassing for her to explain how she wound up handcuffed to a stanchion, but she could probably spin that as part of her master plan to subvert me.

I kept working on the ship, working on my connection to the ship.

I was learning interesting and useful things, refining my control over its internal spaces, and I was utterly failing to get any control over its trajectory or speed. I wasn't going to quit trying. But to be honest I wasn't feeling very hopeful.

Farweather hadn't looked up, studiedly casual, as if she didn't care if I rose to her bait.

It was probably worth it. "Oh, didn't you?"

She pulled her suit up, fastened it, and tapped the bulkhead with one finger. The nail was getting pretty long and clicked quite satisfyingly. I wasn't about to give her anything sharp enough to cut them with. "You must have gotten close enough to trigger this thing's self-defense mechanisms."

I sat down against the far wall.

She pushed the bowl of water and the washcloth out of her immediate orbit. I'd clean them up later.

"That seems likely," I said. I was trying for neutral, but the dryness must have soaked through.

She fastened her collar tab and gave me a lopsided smile.

"You want me to believe the Koregoi ship just attacked Singer. When I *know* your ship has guns, and you fired on us previously. When you came out of white space just then in a hail of particles."

"We knew it had defenses," she said. "That's why we planned the high-speed flyby, dropping out of white space just long enough for me to bail out, correct trajectory, and spacewalk over to the vessel. We didn't shoot you, so it must have used those defenses on your shipmates."

"And your high speed had nothing to do with the fact that there were a dozen Core vessels lined up for a piece of the Prize."

She smiled. "Most of them don't have guns."

A few had, though. But the pirates had been and gone before any of them could have acquired a solution. Which made it seem like maybe Farweather might be telling the truth about not being behind the death of Singer and his crew. The pirate vessel would not have had a lot of time to acquire a solution either. Especially if it had been busy coming up with a launch trajectory for Farweather.

But the bow wave . . .

Hell, maybe it was an accident. On the other hand, Farweather seemed capable of lying about absolutely everything.

I said, "I haven't seen any evidence of guns on this ship, either."

"You used the artificial gravity to nail me to the deck," she said. "What's to say that the ship can't use the same technology as a weapon?"

I pretended I hadn't already thought of that myself.

"I don't know," I said. "You tell me. Your people obviously know more about it than mine do."

She sat down too, facing me. I got up and moved her washbasin away, dumped it, wiped it clean. Started water for coffee.

"I don't know what you're talking about," she said.

"Really? You didn't get onto a ship controlled by a famously xenophobic race like the Jothari by trading them artificial gravity for access to their vessel? By installing it for them, and also installing the overrides?"

Her head had fallen to the side. Her hair was getting long, too. She smiled at me and didn't say anything.

"So where'd you get that technology?"

"Who's to say we did?"

"Less intact Koregoi ships?" I asked. "Dead ones?"

She leaned back and closed her eyes.

I said, "That just leaves the question of *why* you needed to get on the Jothari ship. It can't just have been a matter of wanting to steal a ship with the artificial gravity tech, not when you must have sold it to them and gone along to help install it and play technician."

"That's an interesting theory."

I left her coffee where she could just reach it with her fingertips if she stretched, and retreated.

I said, "I think I figured out why you needed to be on the Jothari ship.

And why you didn't load the Koregoi senso until you were ready to blow the Jothari ship."

"Oh?" she said companionably.

"Because you needed to manufacture it. You needed to refine the senso parasite from devashare, right? Or from the cadaver byproducts, or something. You needed a dead Ativahika."

"See?" she said. "You're pretty bright when you allow yourself to be."

God, you disgust me.

I didn't say it, though. I bit my lip, and remembered that I needed her, and that the clock was ticking and time was running out on me.

What I said was, "That's some real audacity. And your coffee is getting cold, Zanya."

"Let me into your fox," she said.

"Are you high?" I said.

"Let me in," she said, "and I'll teach you how to control the ship."

"I don't trust you," I said.

She held up her hand. The bandages were long off the wrist it was attached to. She crooked a little finger at me.

"Pinkie swear," the pirate said.

I laughed in her face and went back to constructing a kind of couch or sofa out of rolled and tied bolsters of soft fiber I'd scavenged from various places around the ship. Better than a pile of packing material, maybe. I should move into a different cabin, and figure out how to lock her into this one. But I didn't trust her unless I had my eyes on her.

I was sleeping elsewhere, anyway. And if I spent too much time away from her, I found that I got unbearably lonely.

"Show me how to change our course," I said, "and if you can explain why you want to get into my fox, I just might let you do it. After I chain you up so you'll starve in your own waste products if you kill or incapacitate me."

"That's the kind of trust that bespeaks a successful long partnership."

"It's the kind of trust you've earned."

She sighed. "I can't change our course."

"Won't."

"Can't," she said. Then she paused as if to consider. "Well, in the sense that I am absolutely unwilling to suffer the repercussions of carrying out your request, yes, won't."

"Repercussions."

"If I don't report on time, the biomine wired into my central nervous system will explode, and that'll be it for me, you, and this lovely piece of functional archaeology." She patted the deck of the Prize with what looked like affection.

I blinked but managed not to glance at her, surprised as always to be reminded she was human. And stunned, as well, by what she'd just revealed.

Of course, whether I could trust her or not was an open question. She'd lie like she was in the plane of a planetary formation disk if it suited her, and never bat a transplant-augmented eyelash either.

I folded my hands over my arms. "Where's my lecture on how the Republic of Pirates is the last guardian of human freedom?"

"Freedom includes the freedom to be an asshole," she said, and shrugged.

"Asshole and criminal are different things." Despite myself, I was outraged. Not at her; on her behalf.

She stretched, shrugged. Bent down and touched her toes and hung there, stretching her spine and thighs. I imagine she was still working on getting the kinks out from the time that I'd had her more closely chained.

She had a good two meters of range of motion, now. And I'd carefully marked a caution circle on the deck in the same yellow grease pencil I used for marking up repairs while I was planning them, because I had no intention of straying inside her range.

"So," I said. "My best course of action seems to be to toss you out an airlock, then. And try to figure out how to divert this thing with you safely elsewhere."

"Good thing for me you're not a murderer."

I smiled. "I could learn."

"Let me into your fox," she said, "and I'll restore your memories."

"My memories are just fine."

She laughed curtly. "Babes, if you say so."

Her mattress rustled as she stretched out and folded her hands behind her head. I turned around to look at her. Within instants, she was snoring.

"What did you mean?"

She poked around in her bowl of noodles, looking for the dehydrated green onion scraps. "Sorry?"

"What did you mean about restoring my memories?"

"Judicial Recon," she said, with a one-shouldered shrug of emphasis. "Don't you ever wonder what they Reconned over?"

"Reconstruction," I said, "means putting something back the way it was supposed to be, with repaired damage."

She slurped a noodle, though I couldn't see what was different about that one that she'd picked it out specially.

"Repaired or excised."

I bumped to glide over a memory of Niyara's blood on my hands, sticky-slick and already congealing. "Oh, I'm pretty sure all the damage is right where it ought to be."

She laughed lightly. I found a noodle of my own, and ate it despite the fact that I didn't have much appetite.

"See," she said, "I think the real reason why you're such a goody-two-shoes is because this is your Judicially constructed personality. The you you know *is* Judicial Recon, because you were a juvenile when what happened, happened. So they gave you a clean slate and a clean bill of health."

A chill crawled through me. It was possible. The clade and Justice

between them would have had the right to make decisions about recon-
structing my personality. And then to conceal those decisions from me if
they determined it would produce a healthier outcome.

I tried to keep my feelings off my face and eat my noodles.

"Don't you want to know who the real you is?"

I didn't lift my eyes from my bowl, as if the broth and its appetizing
skim of flavorful oil droplets were completely fascinating. "I was raised in
a clade. There is no real me."

CHAPTER 20

I WASN'T GOING TO LET FARWEATHER SEE THAT SHE'D GOT-
ten to me. It was a white-knuckled couple of moments until the tuning
really kicked in, however, and when it finally did I realized that I'd
overdone it. I was, in fact, a little stoned on my own endorphins.

But I also wasn't anxious, or reactive, or freaked right out, and I could
think clearly—admittedly, through a haze of general goodwill and fond-
ness for the universe intense enough that it even included murderous,
amoral bad girl pirate rogues.

Why did it have to be bad girls? Moreover, why did they seem to have
such a taste for me? I'd rendered myself more or less bulletproof. But they
still seemed to be able to smell me coming. Even after all the rightminding
and Recon.

I wondered if, in all the stuff she knew about me, Farweather knew
about the time I'd spent out of my mind on deva. That probably would
have bothered me if I were less chemically elevated. I almost laughed out
loud when I realized how many of my precautions and anxieties about
rightminding had to do with having been dependent on deva and never
wanting to go back there.

What if she was right? I didn't *think* Farweather was telling the truth;
I didn't think Farweather generally told the truth, unless it served her
own very specific purposes. But I was also now able to think about her
claims without anxiety or denial. It was an interesting perspective. I could
see the reactivity and defensiveness rising up self-protectively inside my

own brain, like an armored space marine ready to take on some kind of dangerous interstellar dragon.

The image made me giggle.

Farweather gave me an odd look from across the cabin.

I ignored her. Yep, if I was mixing my metaphors like that, I was definitely in an altered state. It felt good, though—like I was finally getting a chance to relax a little.

And I knew it would wear off soon. I didn't *want* to tune back toward baseline, because I was enjoying actually feeling a little bit good for a change. But as generations of lazily plotted thrillers tell us, it's rarely a good idea to get shit-faced while guarding a jail cell if you want your prisoner to be where you left them when you check later.

Once I knew she wasn't under my skin anymore, it occurred to me that I could certainly use her *expectation* of being under my skin. Especially since I'd been quiet for so long.

I settled down on my mattress, cross-legged, back to the wall, easing my slightly sore afthands. I'd been going around without my boots a bunch, and my afthands were better acclimated than I would have thought possible, but it did stretch the tendons in funny ways. Also, I thought they kind of freaked Farweather out, based on her sidelong glances, and I was all for anything that might put her off her stride.

I said, "So since you know all about me and Niyara, why do you think she did it?" I probably didn't quite succeed in not sounding hostile, but that probably made it seem more convincing that she had gotten to me.

Farweather gave me that *are you an alien?* stare, which I think was unfair, because I suspect most systers wouldn't have been surprised or confused by my question.

"To get at the Synarche," she said, as if it were patently obvious. "To protest their mind control practices. And some reasons of her own. You really are a babe in the woods, aren't you?"

Her dismissal niggled at me. I wanted to say, as if to a child, *How did she expect that to work out?* I recognized the urge, identified it, and then held my breath until it passed.

Good modeling of rational behavior there, Dz.

While I was looking at Farweather, and Farweather was looking at me, the Koregoi ship's lights and gravity fluttered briefly, never quite going off, but dimming (and lightening) significantly for a few seconds, in quick pulses. Well, that wasn't unsettling at all. Especially when we were reliant on that power source for life support, and when it was, conservatively speaking, probably a few millennians old.

Well, okay, maybe less than that in its own timeframe, what with having been put on ice at the edge of a black hole, where the subjective passage of time might have been only a few decans. Or a few dozen decans. I wished bitterly that Singer were here to figure out the physics and do the math for me.

Grief is stupid and hard.

And a centad is still a damned long time to go without a lubricant change and an overhaul.

I looked away from Farweather and then looked back, on the off chance that she would be wearing a calm expression, indicating that she knew what was causing the fluctuation and everything was under control, thank you.

Unfortunately for my peace of mind, she was biting her lower lip and frowning.

She didn't say anything, though, so I decided against giving her any information by implication about what I did or did not know about the status of the power systems on board the Koregoi prize, and instead just kept talking.

I said, "How do you think the Synarche feels about you?"

She did that shrugging thing I was learning to find so infuriating. "People just naturally hate things that are different from them."

The way you, and Niyara, hate us. Because our existence—and functionality as a community—threatens your identity.

What I said was, "People just naturally get eaten by big cats or die of disease before their eighth solar, too, but nobody has ever felt like that was a good-enough reason not to take preventative measures against leopard attacks and tetanus, once they were technologically able to."

"Synarche imperialism—"

"An argument that would hold more atmosphere if you could show me where the Synarche has done more to the Freeports than move against them when the burden of piracy got heavy enough to demand action. Hell, we don't even rightmind pirates without their consent."

"Coerced consent. If they don't agree, you just lock them up forever."

"That's just self-defense," I said cheerfully. "There's nothing wrong with enforcing reasonable boundaries through the application of consequences."

"You're pretty smug for somebody who's afraid to remember what she really did, and who she was before she got Reconned."

"How do you know about the Recon?" I wish I hadn't asked again. It was a vulnerability to care.

"You were interesting," she said, as she had said before.

"Information is for sale, is that what you're saying?"

She made a noncommittal noise. I guessed I would probably never actually know everything about this mess.

"You're pretty certain of yourself."

"Let me into your fox," she said, "and I'll show you who you were."

"If I let you into my fox, you can show me anything," I answered. "Machine memory is programmable. And unlike Justice, you don't need my consent for any changes, and you don't have any ethical guidelines."

She just laughed. "Dark and cold, you're naive."

She *did* get under my skin that time. But the soothing brain chemicals were still working, and I looked at my irritation, inspected it. Then I decided to say exactly what I'd thought about saying when I was defensive and reactive, just with intent this time.

"You know," I said lazily, "that's just atavistic anxiety and fear behavior, and it's pretty easy to regulate chemically. Then you can practice being afraid of things that might *actually* hurt you."

I'd managed to derail *her* into arguing in circles for a change, I realized. It felt . . . pretty good.

Not the sort of good you want to get hooked on, however. *Winning* conversations is fine every once in a while, but getting in the habit of *always having* to win them is a hell of a way to run any relationship that isn't already based on mutual antagonism. I told myself that I wanted Farweather off balance, and that it didn't hurt if I could find ways to make her eager to impress me. I wished I knew more about neural programming and how to get people to do what you wanted *without* rightminding when you had to work on their preconceptions and patterned behaviors rather than more self-aware sets of motivations.

I mean, not that Farweather was entirely un-self-aware. She wasn't childlike. She was just . . . self-justifying in funny ways.

Which made me wonder if I, too, was self-justifying in funny ways. Protecting my preconceptions. Defending my internal structures rather than being willing to challenge them.

Maybe I *was* a nice, safe little puppet of the Synarche, or Justice.

Or maybe I was a person who valued community and the well-being of the mass of sentient life over the individual right to be selfish. And I mean, that—by itself—was the one overarching and unifying belief that made the Synarche possible. I was free to be whoever I wanted, do whatever I wanted, as long as it wasn't harmful to or exploitative of others, or profligate with resources. I would be assured livelihood and health and housing, and if my efforts benefitted the community, I would be allotted resources to pursue them.

But if I was needed to serve for a time, I was expected to serve for that time. And not everybody—for example Singer—came with that essential freedom installed; AIs were expected to serve first, and earn their freedom later.

That didn't seem exactly right to me. But the resources to create them had to come from somewhere, didn't they?

The resources to create *me* had come from somewhere, too. Which is why I owed the Synarche service if it needed me. But I didn't have to pay off a debt just for existing. . . .

It was complicated. Maybe there are no really fair systems.

I don't know.

I didn't sleep well. Even when I tuned the anxiety out, my brain wouldn't be quiet: I was too deep in problem-solving mode to stop myself from assessing, contemplating, nagging at the relentlessly uncrunchable data.

If only intractable, nuanced, convoluted problems had simple linear solutions with a right and wrong answer, amenable to a little logical consideration. Of course, if that were the case, the entire course of human history would be different. And we probably wouldn't *need* a Synarche, because any idiot could figure out what to do in any given circumstance.

I could have *made* myself sleep, but honestly I felt that my brain needed the time to work, and if I slept, I wanted it to be the chemically uncomplicated sleep that would allow my subconscious to keep plugging away at the problems it was chewing on. I knew letting Farweather at my brain—at my machine memory—was a bad idea. A catastrophically bad idea.

But she'd gotten to me, after all.

Who was I? What had I done?

Who had I been, if I wasn't who I thought I was?

Or was she completely full of lies, saying anything she thought of to get me to wander into range? That was the most likely explanation, quite frankly. Probably everything she was telling me was balderdash. She knew an awful lot about me, though. Enough that I still suspected that she'd known it for much longer than she was admitting.

We'd all been traveling nonstop since we encountered each other near the murdered Jothari ship, so there wasn't *time* for her to have researched me unless the information was already easily available to her. Information takes a *long time* to get from place to place. Nearly as long as people do. All the evidence pointed to our presence there having been part of some complicated plan.

Maybe they'd fired to disable our ship rather than destroying it on purpose. If Singer hadn't popped us into white space, it's possible the next shot would have taken out our coils, and then we would have been at their mercy. We'd have had no *choice* except to surrender.

What would have happened to Singer then? The Freeporters hated artificial intelligences as abominations. Would they have just left him adrift in space? Would they have destroyed him once they'd retrieved me, or me and Connla?

Then I remembered that Singer and Connla *were* dead, and it hit me like a gravity whip *again*. Obviously, I was not doing a very good job of processing my grief. I needed time to mourn. What I had was . . . a lot of crazy ideas that sounded more than a little narcissistic to me when I stared at them for too long.

It made me feel like a nasty, suspicious, slightly off-kilter conspiracy theorist, but I couldn't help but wonder again about that tip that had sent Connla and Singer and me out to the disabled Jothari ship to begin with. The timelines really didn't make sense: Why hadn't we gotten there to find the Jothari ship already claimed by the pirates and removed? That only made sense if we'd gotten our hot tip on the location of fresh salvage *before* Farweather had murdered the Jothari ship. Or if we'd gotten it after, but the pirates had waited for us to get there.

Could they have been waiting for their own salvage tug? It took specialized skills to retrieve a derelict from white space, but they *had* to have Freeport salvage operators, right? How else did they manage to *pirate*, for crying out loud? And if they'd wanted *Singer* to use as a tug, they wouldn't have shot his damned boom off, would they?

Conspiracy theories are really attractive. Figuring out patterns is one of the things that gets your brain to give you a nice dose of chemical reward, the little ping of dopamine and whatever else that keeps you smiling. As a result, your brain is pretty good at finding patterns, and at disregarding information that doesn't fit. Which means it's also pretty good at finding *false* patterns, and at confirmation bias, and a bunch of other things that can be fatal. Our brains are also *really good* at making us the center of a narrative, because it's what we evolved for.

So maybe I was making things all about me, to a ridiculous level. And yet. If they hadn't needed salvage operators—specifically Synarche salvage operators—then I came back, again, to the idea that they'd been trying to get their hands on me. Which was not the most reassuring of conclusions, though it certainly did reinforce all my cherished beliefs about the depth of my own importance.

I wanted to know and I didn't want to know, and I was having doubts about everything from who I was to my most basic memories. I didn't think she was telling the truth—not all of it, anyway. But she might be telling *enough* of the truth that I would have something to gain—self-knowledge or something else—from taking it up with her.

It occurred to me that if I opened my fox to Farweather, she'd have to open hers to me. Assuming, of course, that she had one—but I couldn't imagine anybody getting around in civilized space without some kind of access to senso. How would you open doors, for that matter? Talk to systers? Sure, you might be a humanocentric bigot, but you still needed to be able to talk to other ships and stationmasters (Habren, anyone?) if you were going to have anything to do with civilized space at all—and at least some Freeporters patently did so.

It also occurred to me that the answers to just about everything I wanted to know were probably sitting right out there in the open, shelved neatly in Farweather's machine memory. Assuming she had machine memory.

This was a terrible idea. No justification I came up with was going to change that.

And yet, it was an idea that I kept having.

. . .

"How can I believe what you're telling me?" I asked, sitting down on my own mattress, bleary-eyed. I felt terrible: sweaty, complicated, as if my skin were borrowed and also itched abominably. Farweather, despite being chained to the stanchion by one ankle, managed to look cool and tidy, except where her hair was tangled and greasy. Mine was growing out long—by my standards, anyway—and had started forming a wooly puff that tended to get flattened on one side from sleeping under gravity, when I didn't go climb into my access tube and float free and comfortable.

She said, "Of all the things I am, I'm not a liar, Haimey."

"I'm still collecting data on that, thank you."

This is a terrible idea.

What would Connla do?

He'd tell you it was a terrible idea.

And then?

And then he'd probably decide to do it. Just to see what happened.

The still, small voice of my conscience was starting to sound rather a lot like Singer.

Right, I told myself. *Just to see what happens, then.*

"What kind of safeguards can you offer me, if we're trading machine memories?"

"I didn't say anything about trading," she answered, too quickly.

"Well," I said, "I'm not going to just let you *have* mine. There has to be some kind of quid pro quo."

"I'll help you get control of the ship."

"Not good enough." I was enjoying this. I reminded myself not to enjoy it too much, and that she was probably playing up her investment to make me think I had more control over the situation than I did.

"You're an engineer," she said, after studying her fingernails for a while. "You build the connectors. That way you can assure yourself that I won't do anything untoward. You can just design it out."

I considered it. Farweather seemed to have a more advanced opinion of my jury-rigging skill than I did.

Huh, who knows? Maybe she was right about that. In the very least, it was flattering.

Also probably her intention. But I was willing to take it where I could get it for the time being.

Was I willing to try to steal her memories without her consent?

It was a matter of life and death, wasn't it?

Hell, I thought. I'm already a walking war crime. How much more ethically compromised can I get? But how much more ethically compromised did I *want* to get? There was Farweather, blinking me, as a perfect example of what moral relativism led to.

"Look," she said. "I'm not a neuralistics expert. I know next to nothing about how rightminding works. What do you think I could do to you?"

"Then what good does it do *you* to get access to my fox?"

She smiled. "Well, I do happen to have the codes to unlock your Recon and see what's under it. So I don't actually need to be an expert. I just need to input a series of keys that will allow you to access the original memories. It's unconstitutional for Justice to actually *erase* old memories; they have to just bury them."

I knew enough about Recon and machine memory to know she was broadly accurate. Besides, changing and editing machine memories didn't actually change *meat* memories. Time and exposure and the brain editing itself to remove conflicts between what the fox told it and what it remembered for itself handled that problem. Meat memories were notoriously unreliable.

I frowned down at my fingernails. They were a mess; the poor diet was having an effect on me. "You just . . . *happen* to have them."

Bright-eyed, she shrugged. "Besides, if I harm you too badly, I'll starve before help gets here." She rattled her chain significantly.

"You could eat my corpse," I said cheerfully.

"Won't stay fresh long enough," she answered, deadpan. "Besides, there's still the problem of hydration."

* * *

I'm an idiot.

I went for it.

It took me a couple of diar to take apart and reconstruct some of the equipment from her kit and my kit (including some of my helmet controls and com) to make a rig that I was pretty sure would let her *read* my senso without writing to it. She could give me the access codes and the encryption keys, and *I* would enter them. Then I'd share the senso-memory with her, which was the real reason we needed the rig; her tech and mine weren't entirely compatible, though an AI probably could have navigated it, and we were both a little chary of just hooking up our alien parasites and letting them talk to each other.

This system also meant that I couldn't just paralyze her with a virus and go rummaging around in in *her* machine memory, but I suppose it made me a better person not to be engaged in coercive control of some-body else's fox in an attempt to steal access to their memories. More's the pity.

Not that I would ever have anything so illegal in my possession as a bit of code that could bust into somebody's fox. Especially after spending a couple of decians in the company of a pirate who wanted to own and control me, without much to do except stare at the walls, fail to get con-trol of the ship, and think up projects to keep myself busy.

Perish the thought.

She didn't like my conditions, but she agreed, which suggested to me that whatever might be hidden in my head—if anything *was* hidden in my head—was something that she and her pirate buddies expected to be very valuable.

And that meant I wanted to know it too.

I had her come to the very end of her chain, and turn around so her back was facing me. The leads on the primitive rig I'd knocked together weren't long, and I certainly wasn't going to come within range of her fists if I could help it. I suppose she could have stretched way out and pummeled me. But all I had to do was scramble away from her, and I would probably manage to escape without being harmed too badly or taken captive.

It would have been nice if we could have done it all passively, but the helmet receivers I'd salvaged needed to be right up against one's skull to pick up signals from the fox, and I hadn't figured out yet how to use our Koregoi symbiotes as antennae to broadcast from our foxes, as if we were dressing up as old-fashioned radio stations.

That was a joke. Of sorts.

I adhered two patches to the back of Farweather's neck, right under the base of her skull, and felt them stick on snugly. The leads ran back to the machine, and while she sat there patiently I drew it as far back as they would allow, and then walked back another couple of steps before adhering the patches to the analogous place on my own body. The stickum was cold, and the receivers a little uncomfortable. Their edges weren't as rounded as I would have liked; they were meant to be contained inside and padded by the lining of the helmet.

Still, they ought to work for what we needed. At least, when I flipped the toggles, the tiny lights on my jury-rigged electronics started dancing softly into brilliance, one by one by one.

I sat staring at her back, feeling . . . nothing, not even the prickle of a microcurrent across my scalp. If it hadn't been for the pretty little flicker of those status lights, I probably would have thought the thing wasn't getting any juice and reached out to check that I'd remembered to hit the power button.

Yes, it happens even to seasoned engineers.

Then I felt the shape of words forming inside my head, like the sound of my own thoughts.

Hello, Haimey.

The voice had a distinct sound to it, and it wasn't very much like Farweather's voice—it was deeper and more resonant—but the intonations were the same. Everybody's voice sounds different in their own head.

Well, I answered. *I guess that worked, then.*

Are you ready for the codes?

I laughed. *Not even . . . remotely.*

There was a pause, and I felt her groan in disbelief and suffering. "That was terrible," she said out loud.

It's who I am, I answered.

I turned my attention to my internal interfaces, while keeping half my mind's eye on Farweather. It was even trickier than it sounds, frankly, because I couldn't safely let the attention I had on her waver, but I also needed to run through the monitors and find my way into their operating system, which was an intentionally complicated task. You didn't want any random teenager mucking around with the inside of their own head. It had too much potential to end badly.

I wonder if I consented, I thought, and realized as I thought it that some part of my mind was taking for granted that Farweather was telling me the truth when she claimed that Judicial had reconstructed my machine memories, and thus allowed them to reshape the meat memories in their image.

I thought about those memories, tried consciously to call one up without accessing my fox for corroboration.

But it wasn't memories of Niyara that rose to the surface. Instead, it was memories of a more literal surfacing. I thought of the Prize, rising out of the Saga-star's accretion disk in mysterious response to my presence.

As I thought of it, I felt Farweather's surprised, mocking delight. *Oh, babes. You thought that was you?*

What do you mean? I answered.

The ship. Emerging from the Well. You thought you had something to do with it? It came when you called because you're so special?

I didn't answer. My cheeks burned. My eyes smarted.

Of course I had.

How precious. Honey, I control this ship. I always have.

She hadn't controlled the gravity when I slammed her against the deck, had she? I reached out to do it again, viciously, wanting to slap the glee out of her—

I stopped myself. Just in time.

That was not who I was.

Assuming I was anybody, I mean.

Then she asked, point-blank: *Did Niyara ever tell you anything she said would be important later? Did she ever give you anything? An upload? Something physical?*

I kept my face and mind as still as I could—not that she could see my face where she was sitting—which was probably as much of an answer as if I had gasped out loud.

I tried not to think of the little book, the only hard copy book I had ever held in my hands, and which I had for some reason hung on to all these ans. I thought instead about the feeling of Niyara's blood on my hands as I tried to hold her wounds closed.

But what I saw—what I remembered, intrusively, compulsively— was Niyara giving me the small package. And me staring at her, without even really registering what she had put in my hands. The thermoplex wrapping dented in my hands. Whatever was inside was moderately flex- ible without being soft, and made a faint crinkling sound. "What is this?"

"A gift," she said.

"A gift? A physical object?"

"So I'm old-fashioned," she had said. "Go on and open it."

That *was* old-fashioned. Wrapping paper, and something that wasn't just printed and endlessly recyclable. Except it was something printed. The old kind of printed: text on paper. A book.

I turned a page. It felt fragile and yet somehow strangely substantial. It had, I realized, a faint aroma. Polymer.

"Keep that safe," she had said. "It might be important to you somedia"

I had given the game away already. I said, *She sure did. It was on Singer when your people murdered him.*

A book, she said.

Then, after a pause, she said, *Do these numbers mean anything to you?*

They didn't. There were a lot of them, and I allowed my feelings of blank confusion to fill my mind while I retreated back into what I had been doing when she distracted me. I would think about this new conundrum later. Right now, I was going to have one more crack at breaking into Farweather's fox. I didn't think it would work, and I was sure it was unethical. But I wasn't exactly in a position where I could turn over what I knew to the Synarche and let them detail Judiciary to do a legal search. So I dropped that totally illegal bit of code I didn't have and hadn't written, and crossed my aftfingers in my boots.

The incompatibilities in our hardware and base code were just too much. I didn't think she'd noticed—I didn't get knocked back—but it was like throwing spaghetti at a frictionless surface. Maybe if I'd had the time to try a few iterations and adjustments, I could have worked around to something that might find a place to link in and siphon off some data. Possibly I should have tried harder to figure out a way to paralyze her. As it was, I was sure she'd yank the leads off if she got the tiniest inkling of what I was planning.

It didn't pay off, and I didn't have time to keep trying.

I wanted to use this time for my own purposes. I needed to pry into my own meat, rather than meta, memories of Niyara—and of what we had done. And see how much truth Farweather was telling me.

I memorized the numbers, though, against later need. You never knew.

I didn't believe Farweather would be able to feel what I was thinking as I went deeper into my meat memories; I was intentionally blocking the interface machine and also my machine memories. So the ayatana wouldn't influence what I recalled, and so nothing should show up in my senso feed.

I'd never intentionally blocked out my own ayatana before.

It was strange, like thinking about a story I'd heard of something that had happened to someone else. It *had* happened to someone else; I was briefly enmeshed in a memory that could only be Niyara's, and it left me shivering. I had a vivid sense of a . . . bottle, an old-fashioned wine bottle made of the kind of glass that would break into umpteen tiny shards if struck solidly, and of wiping the screws on the neck very, very carefully before threading a bottle cap into place.

In the memory I knew that if I didn't exercise profound diligence, the bottle would detonate. It was full of a highly reactive explosive and a handful of screws and washers to make shrapnel along with the shattering silica glass.

I wondered if I had read about what I was half experiencing in a court document, or if maybe a bit of Niyara's senso had been played at the trial and I was recollecting its sensations now. The trial—and the terrorist attack—were both such a long time ago that even if my recollections *hadn't* been edited for public safety, the meat ones wouldn't have been reliable. Especially since I'd been in a state of shock when it happened, and a state of profound trauma afterward, for the inquest and the trial.

One of the best things about the fox is that it gives everybody unbiased memories of *what actually happened* on any given dia, or in any given interaction. I can't imagine what dispute resolution must have been like in the bad old diar, when basically anybody could make any kind of claim about what happened, and unless somebody had had a recorder running, nobody ever could be sure of the truth. Eyewitness reports, they used to call them, and they were notoriously inaccurate and unprovable.

Those "eyewitness reports" were good records of what people *thought* they saw, and what they *remembered* they thought they saw. They were really good records of what confirmation bias led people to believe, and want to believe.

Trying to get a factual record out of that would be like . . . Like constantly dealing with Farweather, probably.

As if thinking of her had summoned her, she poked me in the attention. *Are you on task, babes?*

Looking for my meat memories didn't seem to be getting me anywhere. They were doubtless under so many layers of confabulation that I'd never be able to pick them out clearly anyway. Maybe I was just going to have to shut down my fox for a while and see what happened.

That meant getting to my own operating system, so to speak. And using Farweather's codes.

I could feel her looking over my shoulder, virtually speaking, as I delved deeper in my mind. The temptation to pull up old ayatanas and wallow in the memories was as powerful as any time you're going through your music collection and hit that cache of files you haven't listened to since you were in school. But I managed, despite the pull of nostalgia and procrastination.

Having Farweather right there playing virtual voyeur helped to keep the urge suppressed.

Anyway, I was getting closer to the operating system. I poked around a bit more, and was pretty sure I had found it because I suddenly hit such a strong sense of aversion that if Farweather hadn't been backstopping me, I would have been halfway across the room and totally jacked out of our jury-rigged sharing system before anybody could have said "boo." As I reached for the contact pads at the base of my skull, though, she gave me such a boost of calm that I managed to stop my hands in mid-grab and return them slowly to my lap.

"Why do I think there's more going on here than you're telling me?" I said out loud.

She shrugged. "Quit now, and you'll never get the chance to find out."

I wanted to curse her, but if I randomly cursed out everybody who got on my nerves on a given dia, I never would have been able to exist on a tiny ship with Connla for a decans and a half. Instead, I reached out into the structure of the hull with the Koregoi senso. *Make backups,* Singer always said. I fiddled with a few things, and left it there.

Best I could do right now.

She said, "What if I told you I had Niyara."

I stared at her, scoffed. "Niyara is dead. She died while bleeding all over me."

After cheating all over me, I thought. She'd lied on so many fronts, in so many ways. About big things and little. I could have dealt with being a secondary relationship, if she hadn't *lied* to me about not having a primary one. I . . . well, I probably wouldn't have been okay with her being a terrorist.

Would I have been?

Farweather turned her head so I could see the corner of her smile. "I've got her ayatana. Up to the moment of her death, actually. Safely hidden, so don't bother ratting through my stuff to find it."

I probably would have made a derogative comment about the desirability of ratting through pirate bags. Except I'd been doing it for weeks, scavenging her food and equipment.

So I guess she had me there.

On the one hand, if there was any such recording, it would explain a lot about how Farweather knew so much about me. And how she knew about the book. On the other hand, if there wasn't such a recording, her claim that she'd hidden it outside of her luggage meant I could never actually be sure if it existed or not.

I really had to stop underestimating her. It was going to get my head staved in. And maybe I should look into hiding some information where *she* wouldn't find it, just in case the Synarche got their hands and tentacles and whatnot on the Prize and I . . . hadn't made it.

"Then you probably know where she got the information you're so desperate to get back from me," I challenged.

"Oh, sure," Farweather said. "She stole it."

"It'd help if you told me what it was. I might be able to find it."

"But you wouldn't tell me what it is if you did know." She still had her back to me, but she crossed her arms triumphantly.

"I might bargain," I said. "After all, you have a lot of things that I want."

She glanced over her shoulder to leer at me, and I rolled my eyes.

"Don't be boring," I said.

"Look who's talking." But she turned away again. "A Koregoi artifact. She lifted it, and your clademothers managed to decipher the markings."

"My *clademothers*?" It burst out of me like I was an unregulated child.

Farweather was lying. She had to be lying.

She didn't feel like she was lying.

I took a long, calming breath.

She continued, "It was a probe, probably. Small. White space capable. There were plates on it made of inert metal. Inscribed with symbols. Didn't Terrans used to send out probes like that?"

"This wasn't Terran, though, I take it?"

"Definitely old," she answered. "It was spotted near the Core, and declared a heritage site, but the seekers and scientists hadn't managed to decode it. Niyara and some other Freeporters managed to . . . liberate it. It turned out it was a marker—a buoy, basically—and what it was there to mark was this thing." She tapped the deck under her hand. "That's how we knew where to look for it."

"You expect me to believe that my clademothers managed to read the message on an ancient artifact that the Core universities couldn't decipher? And that they were working with pirates? I do not believe it."

She shrugged. "They were pathological, but pretty good archaeologists, or so I hear. Possibly it's something to do with being so atavistic their own selves."

"Ooo, big word," I said mockingly.

She took it in stride, with a grin and a little shake of her head.

"So if your people found this, and my people decoded it and shared the information with you, why are you so keen on what you think *I* know?"

Farweather made a grumpy noise, like a disturbed cat. "Because Niyara didn't share everything with anybody, apparently. She spread her information around. And hid some of it."

"Why would she do that if she was planning to die?"

Farweather answered me with a question. "Haven't you always wondered what she was thinking?"

I didn't answer. She cranked around to check my face, then batted her
lashes at me while I resolutely did not move sideways to make eye contact.
"Haven't you ever wondered how she felt about you? If maybe she wanted
to give you something of value, that you could bargain with? She'd have
to hide something like that even from you, though—because she had to
know there would be Recon, and she couldn't have you handing it over to
Judiciary, or to your clade."

"You know what?" I said. "I really don't want to know. In fact, I was an
ass to let you talk me into this."

I hadn't managed to pick my way through her defenses and her unfamiliar tech to find out more about how she was piloting the Prize, if in
fact she *was* piloting the Prize. I hadn't figured out how much she actually
knew about me, about Niyara, about what Niyara had given me or done.
And suddenly, I didn't care anymore at all.

All I had accomplished was giving her another avenue to get under my
skin. My skin, which was marked with the stigmata of a murdered Ativahika.

I stripped the rig off and stood. This was a great time to make coffee.
Farweather said a few more things at me, but she was talking to my shoulder. I had plenty to occupy my attention and my hands.

Rightminding is a wonderful technology.

I didn't even think once about busting her nose.

Well, not that dia, anyway.

"The lights are dimming again," Farweather said, after I gave her her coffee
in silence and backed away to sip my own at a safe distance.

It had happened once or twice since the first time. We'd both largely
been ignoring it, each of us pretending for the other that we had some
idea of what was going on, I surmised—unless she was behind it all, but

if she was, or if she wasn't, I certainly wasn't going to give away that I was completely flummoxed by *asking* her.

I wondered what new gambit this was. What strategy had changed her mind.

"Well," I said, "my little box here isn't drawing any power from any external system. What do you think might be causing it?"

She glanced over her shoulder at me, and I—having turned toward her a little as well—could just see the edge of her frown. We were like two cats spatting, each refusing to yield turf or acknowledge the existence of the other.

"I just don't know," she said.

Well, that was a terrible answer.

I finished the coffee. I turned around and came toward her, looked at her. She rose, and came to look at me. She studied my face; I felt the beginnings of a connection. Some comprehension. A bridge between us.

She said, "Maybe we could, after all, find common ground. Work together. Maybe we can team up."

I said, "I need to go home, Farweather."

She smirked bitterly. "So do I."

"That didn't sound like a *decision*, exactly."

"No," she said. "Nor loyalty."

I wondered if she really was a human bomb. *Like Niyara.*

Niyara had chosen it, though.

I waited. We stood, facing each other. I knew I was too close; but I wanted to be there.

This is a bad idea, said the little voice in my head. My own internalized ghost of Singer. *Haimey, step back.*

She moved so fast I didn't even see her, swinging with one straight arm, taking a single lunge step forward, and clapping her cupped left hand against my right temple with force and accuracy.

I fell to the floor. I felt the impact on my limbs and body, treacherous gravity. *Treacherous gravity.*

328 • ELIZABETH BEAR

Treacherous gravity. My ally in this fight!

She'd—what had she done?

I tried to reach out into the parasite, to slam Farweather back against the wall, but all I got was a tickle of presence and then a crushing, incapacitating pain. Not from the fall; from my chest and my belly. From my *heart*.

I'm having a heart attack. She's somehow triggered a heart attack. I am going to die right here.

CHAPTER 21

T HURT SO MUCH, I WISHED I WOULD DIE. I WAS *FELLED,* like a tree. Like an ox. Like all those primitive, atavistic things that humans used to fell with their primitive, atavistic tools. The hard way. An axe through the heartwood; a hammer at the center of an X drawn between the ears and eyes.

Swing hard; follow through to the other side of whatever you are swinging at.

Zanya Farweather had been swinging at my soul.

My identity, my selfhood. The person I'd been for nearly twenty ans. It dropped away, and I was left wrecked and retching, cramped, choking up a thin stream of bile.

She hadn't really done anything to me physically. This was just what a broken heart felt like.

I'm an engineer. The little bit of my brain that stayed clear and focused in a crisis asserted itself, contemplated the problem. My fox wasn't working.

I curled in on myself. The pain was physical, immobilizing. As if I had been electrocuted.

Which is another way they used to fell animals, and people.

I couldn't . . . think. My mind skittered, blurred. I decided I needed to stand up; started to. Some indeterminate time later I realized I was still lying there. It seemed fine.

Somebody was touching me. Farweather. I wanted to recoil, but instead my body twitched feebly and lay still. She had pillowed my head on something uncomfortable, bony and soft. Her thigh. She petted my hair.

"Rest," she said. "I've got you."

I tried to organize myself, my thoughts. Tune the pain and grief and confusion down. Reflexively, I reached for that solace.

It wasn't there. Concentration failed me. I wasn't . . . unconscious, exactly. But I also wasn't *aware*. The world swam fuzzily, as if on the other side of a high fever, a concussion, a heavy drunk or other mild poisoning. My limbs didn't respond when I told them to, or when they did, they didn't behave in the ways I desired. Like a small child who couldn't quite get the stylus to move properly on the pad to make the smooth line she envisions.

Eventually, I slept.

I awoke several times into half-awareness and hungover discomfort before the final time, when I swam up into something like real consciousness. My body ached; I huddled in nausea. My skin felt chafed where the edges of my suit touched.

Farweather was right beside me. She seemed to be sleeping, sitting upright against the wall. She'd dragged me onto her improvised mattress. When I moved, the materials rustled, and she stirred.

"Drink this," she said, when my eyes opened. She handed me a squeeze bulb of something green—an electrolyte drink from her stores.

The chain I'd put on her rattled as she did it; she didn't seem to have gotten free.

I took the bulb, tried to sit up, and rapidly thought better of it. I lay back down and tried to remember exactly what had happened.

"How long?" I asked.

"About twelve hours," she said. "The vascular effects should be wearing off by now. You might have some memory and attention deficits for a while. Drink."

There was a bulb in my hand. I wasn't sure where it had come from, though it looked like the ones in her stores. I put it to my lips and bit down on the valve.

Sweet, tangy. It hit bottom in my stomach, first nauseating and then, suddenly, soothing. I felt better.

She'd . . . not a virus. Not a physical concussion. An EM pulse? That must be it. She'd somehow, with her parasite or with an implant of some kind, generated a powerful magnetic field, and she'd blasted it through my head.

There was a bulb in my hand, and I realized I was thirsty. It was about two-thirds full of greenish electrolyte drink. I put it in my mouth and drank.

I couldn't remember exactly what had happened. She'd put her hand to my face, like a caress. And then the pain.

I'd fallen down.

There were things . . . I reached for my fox, to try to tune some of the pain and nausea out. Nothing; not even the crackle of static. I remembered blood on my hands. I remembered the pain of loss. I remembered what it felt like to have your heart peeled out of your body and handed to you by somebody you'd loved and allowed yourself to be vulnerable to.

I didn't want to remember those things, but for some reason I didn't seem to be able to stop remembering.

I remembered that you couldn't trust anyone.

There was a bulb in my hand. "Drink," Farweather said, and I finished the little bit of fluid left in the bottom.

"Good girl," she said, and took it away from me.

My stomach churned. My head rang, vision doubling. I closed my eyes. I felt nauseated for some reason. Had I been drinking?

I tried to bump, to bring the pain down. For some reason, my fox didn't seem to be responding.

I slept.

•　•　•

"You have to wake up," Farweather said softly. "Both of us are going to need calories before long, and I can't reach the rest of the supplies."

I didn't want to. I didn't want to open my eyes. My head was splitting, and all I wanted to do was lie down and hide. For some reason, though I kept trying to bump to kill the headache, it kept not improving.

"Dammit," she said. "They told me neuronal death was going to be minimal."

I cracked an eye. "What did you do to me?"

"EMP," she said. "Don't worry; I just wiped your fox. The OS is toast, and the memory, but there shouldn't be a lot of organic damage."

"You wiped my memory?"

"Machine memory," she said. "You have backups, I'm sure."

Not of most of what I'd seen and learned since Singer was killed. Since this woman helped kill Singer. In that time, I had just a few things that I'd squirreled away.

I closed my eyes again, then opened them, because I didn't have the energy to sit up and punch her in the nose.

She said, "You'll be fine, but you need some more hydration and calories."

"Easy for you to say," I said.

I slept again.

I dreamed, and they were the terrible dreams that I had been tuning out for twenty ans.

The bottle is heavy. An antique. An art object, some kind of collectible. Possibly even gray-market valuable. I haven't asked where it came from, but I wonder how it made its way to space. What its history is.

None of that really matters now.

Now it is becoming a weapon in my hands.

I fill it meticulously, careful of the funnel. The glass is good because it's unlikely to strike a spark. It takes a screw-top, and I've constructed a reinforced one. I wipe the threads *very* carefully before I screw it on.

I set the bottle aside as she appears in the doorway. "Done?"

I look at the row a little sadly. Four, two for her and two for me. Tomorrow, I won't have to worry about not being real anymore.

Tomorrow I'll have served a purpose that isn't the one that was planned out for me since birth. Tomorrow, I'll die with my love.

"Done," I say.

She comes over and carefully touches a wall brace to discharge any sparks before she ruffles my hair. "Go home and clean up," she suggests. "We ought to celebrate. I'll pick you up in an hour?"

"Celebrate." The word feels weird as I roll it around my tongue. "But these—"

"Aren't going anywhere. I'll lock them in." She scritches my scalp luxuriously with her nails.

I stretch and purr.

She laughs and says, "If it makes you feel better, we can go to the same place as tomorrow. There. Now it's reconnaissance, and you can't say no."

I didn't jerk awake, because I woke so suddenly I was still paralyzed from the dream. The paralysis felt like a memory, too. Like running through glue when I heard the explosion. Knowing exactly what had happened. Knowing that Niyara had tricked me.

That I was going to have to live with what we'd done.

How would Niyara, of all people, ever have constructed a bomb? No, she needed me for that.

She needed an engineer.

And I needed somebody to help me take revenge for the way I was raised.

Because I couldn't move, and because my head was still fogged and sore, eventually I slept again.

"Haimey, wake up," she said. "You need to get up. You need to eat, and you need to bring me calories."

Niyara, leave me alone.

I rolled over and tried to keep sleeping. The rolling over went better than previous attempts at movement, and I risked opening my eyes. My head hurt, still, but it wasn't the sickening pain of before. Not Niyara.

Farweather.

"What did you *do* to me?" I whined.

She sighed. "EM pulse, as I have told you approximately seventy-five times. I wiped your fox."

"You fried my white matter," I said. I blinked. The world seemed less tunnely and dark at the edges than the last time I'd tried this.

"There's not supposed to be any permanent damage," she said. "But right now you need to eat, and so do I."

I tried to sit up, very slowly. I felt like I'd lost a lot of blood, and I wondered how I knew what losing that much blood felt like. "What happened to me?" I said.

"Haimey," Farweather said, with infinite patience. "Go over there and get the pack with the empanadas in it, would you? And a couple more bulbs of electrolyte drink."

I tried to stand up. It didn't work; I made it to a crouch and fell over. I lay there for a little while until Farweather made me get up on my hands and knees.

"Go over there and get two empanadas, and two bulbs of electrolyte drink."

I made it to the packs. She waited behind me, rattling her chain impatiently like a ghost of old guilt issues. I couldn't find the pack with the food in it. Eventually she guided me there, and after a couple of false starts I made it back to her and brought her a cold stuffed dumpling in a sterile, shelf-stable vacpac and a bulb of electrolytes, sugar, and water. Apparently I had been supposed to get one for myself, as well, and she woke me up and made me go back over.

Because she kept waking me up, I managed to get the food and the hydration inside me. Then I went back to sleep, because I was no better at maintaining a train of thought than any drunk person, and besides my head still hurt abominably.

I guess it was probably a couple of diar before I started being able to hold a conversation again, and by then I really didn't want to. Because I was starting to remember things when I was awake, not just when I was asleep—and not just which pack the empanadas were kept in.

Neural pathways are pretty well established, and I'd been wearing a fox since before puberty: external rig until my brain reached adult size, and then they'd done the transcranial surgery. They start us younger in the clades: not so much time to develop ideas of our own that way. Ideas of our own, such as might lead to discontent and unhappiness.

It would be terrible to be unhappy.

So I kept reaching reflexively for my machine capabilities—memory, processing, math, tuning—and finding nothing there. No response. In addition, my symptoms included cognitive and attention issues. I couldn't hold a thought. I couldn't accomplish a task without being distracted. And I couldn't keep my temper at all.

I was utterly deregulated, in other words.

If Farweather was telling me the truth, I had been fuzzily conscious for about three standard hours. Then I'd slept a lot, which—honestly—I continued to do as I slowly recovered. I don't think she'd expected my body's response to her gadget to be so extreme. But if they'd tested it—or modeled it, which I figured was more likely—they hadn't tested or modeled it on people who had grown up in a clade, or had significant Judicial Recon.

I think I'd actually worried her. At least, she'd acted concerned. Which was either a glimpse of a softer side of her, or a symptom that the Stockholmification was working. Or maybe just recognition that she couldn't reach the food without me.

Please tell me I've got some kind of a chance to get out of this.

There was no answering banter.

I felt even more hollow than I had. I *knew* the voice I had been imagining for company wasn't really Singer; I hadn't lost that much contact with reality. I knew it was just me talking to myself, giving myself a little bit of comfort here and there. I knew I'd just been playing his role in my head; still, it had been nice to pretend he was in there somewhere.

Now I couldn't hear it anymore. And the absence left me so profoundly lonely that it was a physical ache in my chest and belly.

There were other aches, too. There was the sense of something having been ripped from me; that heartbroken punch of loss without any memories to explain where it was coming from. And there was the neuralgic pain that tended to spike through my body unexpectedly, flaring and fading almost as fast again.

My afthands developed the habit of cramping in very awkward positions. Some of the fine motor control for those fingers and thumbs had been processed through my fox, too. Now I was also going to have to learn to do that the hard way.

That was when I salvaged the backup voice recorder—the black box—out of my space suit and started keeping a voice diary. Because I couldn't make backups, and I had no access to an ayatana. And if something happened to me—who was I kidding, something had already happened to me—I wanted to leave behind some kind of a record. Some kind of evidence. I made notes of everything that had happened since we found the murdered Ativahika. And I made notes of my conversations with Farweather, and what I found on the ship.

It helped me deal with the feelings, too. Talking them out. Even if it was only to a recorder.

As the dia went by, I slowly got back some control. And with the control, the shadows of memories I hadn't considered in ans—that perhaps I had not been *permitted* to consider in ans?—began emerging.

They were terrible, and I didn't want to think about them. Didn't want to remember the nightmares that emerged from under conflicting, and safer (though still terrible) memories.

It was as if two different versions of reality coexisted in my head at the same time. There was the story of Niyara and me, of her betrayal, the one that I'd polished and kept in my pocket all these ans in order to ward off unwise personal attachments.

And then there was the contradictory one, starting to assert itself, like a history from a parallel universe.

And it was so much more terrible than the first.

Zanya was washing her hair. And I was watching the networks of tiny glistening particles swirl across her skin as she knelt over the basin of water I'd brought her. She was rinsing soap out and squeezing the last clear droplets from the black strands.

We both spent a good amount of time doing calisthenics and body weight exercises, because it was a long, boring trip and we didn't have a lot to keep us busy. My joints hurt, but it was fascinating how easy gravity made exercise. She was getting more muscular, under the effects of all this gravity, and it was happening even more dramatically to me.

I also spent a good amount of time trying not to stare at her. And then trying not to get caught staring when I inevitably failed.

She didn't seem to care when I did. If anything, she looked smug about it when she noticed. As for me—well, there's a reason I had my sexuality turned off after Niyara. I have terrible taste in women. And Zanya, being an awful human being, was exactly the kind of terrible that was *just* to my taste.

And now my fox was fried, and my external self-control was wiped as well.

You're a grownup now, I told myself. *You know better.*

I did.

It didn't comfort me, honestly, because Hester Prynne knew better too, and look where that got her.

It would be different if I could rely on my rightminding, on my fox, to keep me going. But all I had were the stirrings in my loins and my own unpracticed self-control, neither of which were doing me any favors currently.

I had my memories, too. My slowly evolving memories, with their freight of guilt and revelation, were not helpful. They made me want to find distractions. Things to bury myself in.

"You're staring," Zanya said without lifting her head. She flexed her shoulders. "Like what you see?"

I watched the patterns of light sparkle across her back. "That has to make it harder to sneak up on people."

She shrugged. More muscles, more rippling. More sparkles, like glitter flowing in water under moving lights. "You tell me."

"I don't sneak up on people."

She chuckled and rattled her chain.

". . . not professionally."

She sat up, reaching for her dirty shirt to dry her hair.

When she'd wrapped it up, I handed her a clean one, because watching her wriggle into it was less distracting than staring at her breasts. My hormones had made up for their hiatus by reasserting themselves with adolescent ferocity.

And I'm getting these damned things turned off again the instant I can.

"Why did you say you had no options about going back to the Freeports?"

She sat down on her improvised mattress, which crackled under her weight. "That's easy," she said. "If I don't go back, the explosives packed along my spine will detonate. I'll die, and I'll probably blow a hole in the hull of this nice old ship, and that would be a pity for both of us, wouldn't it?"

I shuddered.

She'd mentioned this before. But not in such graphic terms. And I'd had a box in my head that kept me from feeling what she described quite so viscerally unless I wanted to.

She was a walking time bomb. As with Niyara . . . quite literally.

My type of woman. Damn it to the Well.

Conversationally, she said, "You know, I *do* still have Niyara's ayatana."

"Sure you do," I said.

She shrugged.

"If you have that, what do you need my information for?"

"You've got a key inside you, and you don't even know it."

I strained against the fuzziness and fog that still infected me. "Your random number string."

"Not random."

"What does it have to do with that book Niyara gave me?"

Her lips curved in a smile.

"At least tell me what you're gloating about."

"Maybe if you help us out."

"Why's that book so important?"

"Why'd you keep it all this time? Especially given what Niyara did to you. And what you thought she did to you."

That was an excellent question. And the answer was, *I had to.* "I had to," I said. And wished I hadn't.

"Because it was buried in your brain—in your fox—somewhere that you had to."

"If that was in there, the Recon would have found it out and Judicial would have taken the book."

"Not if the command predated Niyara."

I blinked at her. "You're saying my clade put it there?"

"I'm saying you weren't rebelling against your clade when you worked with her. You thought you were. But you were following their program all along."

"I can't handle this," I said.

I walked away.

I kind of wished she'd call after me, give me an excuse not to go.

She didn't. So I stayed away for a good long time.

When I came back, I brought fresh water. I even gave her a drink.

She didn't ask where I had been. She emptied the cup and set it down and then looked up at me. "Are you ready to resume that conversation?"

"Fuck you," I said.

"Ah." She steepled her fingers. "Well, as I recall, when you left you had asked me what might be in your head that I could want."

"It's a book code," I said. I'd had a lot of time to think about it, and while they were archaic and unused and hardly anybody even knew about them anymore, book codes were the only reason I could think of that you would need a particular edition of a particular book . . . and a string of numbers. "But the book is gone. You blew it up. So can we just stop . . . playing whatever game this is?"

"You get high marks," she said. "That's half of it. Niyara left you information you didn't know you had, and that's one reason we wanted you. But that's not the most important one."

I sat down on my mattress and sighed. I rummaged in the supplies, added water to a pack of rice, and triggered the heating unit. Space nori was pretty good on rice.

"All you need for that is the *book*. And the book is gone."

Apparently Farweather was going to keep talking no matter what. "But the information *you* have, Haimey. Your own memories. Even though you don't entirely know it. That information is so much more valuable to us than whatever Niyara gave you in a code. She couldn't put maps in a book code, and anyway she wouldn't hide that from us." She grinned. "Besides, I'm the one who knows how to get into this ship's databases. Thanks to your family and your ex."

I grunted. "A clade is not a family."

She waved it away airily. "Let's just say that we have reason to believe that some of what's locked up inside your head—the real history of Niyara, et al—is so sensitive that it seems likely that the Synarche would probably be willing to grant us certain concessions in order to keep it from being spread around. Undermining their moral authority."

I stared at her.

"Moral authority is pretty much what they operate on, so—" She shrugged.

"You think there's something so awful in my memories that you can use it to blackmail the entire Synarche?"

"Yep," she said.

"*What?*" It was bad enough what she'd done to me; how she'd violated me again and again. Setting up the booby trap that had injected me with this atrocity tech, the Koregoi senso. And then destroying my fox, my machine memories, everything that made me . . . me. The me I *wanted* to be.

She said, "Your guess is as good as mine, honestly. I'm just the guy with the EM gun; I'm not a psychospecialist."

The worst was when I retired to my secret nest in the maintenance tube to float, and sleep, and be alone.

There were no distractions in my nest, which had appealed to me before Farweather blew up my emotional regulation. Now it just meant that there was nothing to hold or focus my attention. I was restless. Feverish. The feeling of being ungrounded and unable to follow a mental thread was relentless. I couldn't think, couldn't reason. I certainly couldn't sleep reliably, or for long.

So I hung in my tube and drifted lightly on the end of my tether, trying not to fidget lest I put myself into a wobbling spin.

It was all so deeply frustrating, and there was so little I could come up with to remedy the situation. It was possible that stimulants might aid my concentration, but the strongest thing I had access to was Farweather's limited coffee supply, and we were rationing that. I'd cut her off, actually; more for me. It seemed like the least I could manage in terms of consequences, considering what she'd done to me.

I tried mindfulness, along with some other primitive rightminding techniques I'd heard of or read about or studied, back when I was still studying history. They helped a little, though the level of effort on return was pretty high. But they did not help enough. Whenever my concentration on my breathing (this is my in breath; this is my out breath) lapsed, my thoughts went skying off in every possible direction. And when I managed to rein them back from flying to the next thing, and the thing after that, and the next thing too, they fixated obsessively on history.

Not galactic history, either. But my own personal history. The ugly kind.

As I already mentioned, we were on a date when Niyara blew up.

Actually blew up. Literally on a date.

That part is true. Or anyway, I remembered it as true now, without the mediation of my machine memory. Though of course it was possible that long exposure to my fox's version of events had changed my own recollections. It was not true that we had fought, but we had parted company and then met at that cafe in the outer ring of Ansara Station.

Some things hadn't changed. I was, indeed, supposedly on my Choice An, supposedly getting a glimpse of the outside universe before I made my final decision to stay with the clade. The opportunity to change my mind was legally mandated by the Synarche, of course. I couldn't commit entirely to the clade until I turned twenty-five standard, and I had to do it, legally, while I wasn't under the influence of any tuning or rightminding controlled by the clade.

Ansara was the biggest human habitation I had ever visited, at the time, and the also first I'd ever been to with a significant percentage of nonhuman systers in residence. That isn't saying much, because I'd grown up on the station entirely populated by the women of Nyumba Yangu Haina Mlango, and I'd stopped at a grand total of two transfer points or waystations on my way to Ansara, which I had chosen because . . .

. . . because . . .

I opened my eyes and stared into the darkness of the maintenance tube. It wasn't very dark darkness. One of the things I'd noticed was that, in addition to all my weird new secondary senses relating to gravity and mass and so forth, my eyes were becoming better adapted to seeing under a variety of light conditions.

A less beneficial side effect, under the current conditions of tight rationing, was that I was hungry all the time and had started losing weight again, though the algae tanks kept Farweather and me from actually starving.

But I was distracting myself from thinking about Ansara. Ansara, which I had chosen to go to for my Choice An because . . .

I couldn't remember. There had been a logical process, I was sure. A reason to go there. Museums? A chance to study? It had a pretty good technical program.

No, I realized, as a second set of memories unveiled itself, coexisting alongside the first like some weird double exposure of the mind. I hadn't decided to go to Ansara. I'd been sent—or at least, the decision had been made for me, though at the time I'd accepted it as my own.

My own clade had set me up. Farweather was not lying about that.

. . . Unless she was, and my fragile, discombobulated memories were recoalescing around the seed she'd planted. Confabulating.

Well and Void, meat brains were useless things!

I had no way of knowing which version of events might be true. But now I remembered—thought I remembered?—additional details. We *had* gone to the Ethiopian cafe in order to run reconnaissance for a suicide bombing mission. Now I remembered having known about the mission, and I remembered having been an aware and willing participant.

At the time, I'd been a rebel. I'd thought I was striking back against the people who had raised me in a bubble. I'm not sure *why* I thought that. Except it seemed perfectly logical at the time. And my thinking that certainly cleared the clade of any culpability, didn't it? If I should happen to be interrogated.

But in retrospect, it seemed obvious that my clademothers sent me to Ansara specifically to meet up with Niyara and her cell, to join them, and to provide technical expertise for their mission of destruction. It was absolutely intentional, a blow against a Synarche that my clade deemed a threat to its existence and way of life. The Synarche insisted that individuals be granted personal freedom and autonomy of choice and body; my clade believed that the path to universal happiness was obedience to authority. Not even *obedience*, exactly; just allowing yourself to be subsumed by the authority, to become a part of it, to accept its decisions and program as your own.

Ansara was one of the bigger stations, and I believe I also mentioned the shops and bars and places to eat or relax with friends or potential friends or potential sex partners, for that matter, that blanketed the hull between the docking tunnels.

I'd built the explosives. We weren't supposed to be carrying them that dia, however. That dia, we were only supposed to be checking out the restaurant and estimating when its peak crowds would be. I decided I wanted a bottle of wine, since it was probably the last one we would ever drink.

Did I decide that?

No.

Niyara suggested it.

Let us eat, drink, and be merry, for tomorrow we most definitely die.

I picked out that nice-enough bottle of white—actually, it was a very good bottle, because there was no point in saving up against a holed hull at that point.

And while I was away from the table, Niyara detonated the bomb she had been wearing under her tunic, destroying herself and the restaurant and leaving me behind.

I knew instantly what had happened. The concussion wave hit me, and the decomp doors came down. I avoided decapitation because I was paying for the wine and I wasn't anywhere near the shop entrance. I remember standing by the doors, numbed, staring up at the pressure readout until the outside ring stabilized and the decomp door went up again. I scuttled under it hurriedly, thinking that if there was a seal problem or the pressure otherwise fluctuated while I was under the hatch, well, that was that for me.

Why did she do that? I wondered. *Why did she leave me behind?*

We had been going to change the galaxy together.

I still had the wine in my hand when I reached her. I dropped it. The flask bounced a couple of times and rolled a little bit away. These bottles were not made of glass. Then I also dropped, to my knees beside her, and gathered up the scraps of my lover into my arms.

Her lips shaped a word. Senso picked up her intent and relayed it to me.

"See?" she was saying, dying. "I do care about you."

I had been about to say something comforting. It got stuck in my throat, and while I goggled at her, she bubbled a laugh.

"I couldn't . . . You didn't have a choice. . . ," she said, and died.

She didn't have to die. The injuries weren't severe enough to kill her if she got on life support. What was enough to kill her was the time-release poison she'd taken before she blew the station hatchway. And that was the end of that, for Niyara Omedela, the love of my life.

I lunged to my feet. Grabbed the flask of wine, because I was thinking that it had my fingerprints on it. I smeared blood on the neck and the label. I wasn't thinking really clearly; I guess I was hoping that any security feeds would have been damaged by the blast and wouldn't have shown me clearly enough for immediate identification.

She'd worn one suicide harness. Two explosive bottles. There was another one at her apartment storage locker. If I ran, I could get there. It would open to my passcode. I could collect the other harness, and follow Niyara into glorious oblivion.

It was the most stunning protest I could think of, dying to oppose the Synarche, doing a little damage along the way. Self-immolation plus.

Surely her sacrifice, my sacrifice, could not be in vain.

346 • ELIZABETH BEAR

When I got to her apartment and crashed into the tiny workroom where I'd assembled the bombs, it was empty. There was nothing on the desk at all.

I washed my hands and recycled my bloody clothes. I slid back into the crowd still holding the wine and tried to plan what to do next. My heart was racing in a frenzy that even my fox could barely control. Did the fact that my harness was missing mean that the constables were on to us? On to both of us? Or just her?

I could build another harness. I could—

There were monitors going everywhere, full of the news of the attacks. *Attacks.* Plural.

As in, more than one.

That was how I found out that in addition to the suicide bombing of Niyara Omedela, there had been a second suicide bombing that dia as well. Her wife, Amelie Omedela, exploded over in H sector. Used the explosive harness I'd built for myself to do it. Killed five people for no good reason except some political philosophy from the dark ages.

One that I subscribed to, too. Or that my clade subscribed to for me, and which I had never questioned, because we were not built to question such things and we never really learned how.

I hadn't known she had a wife.

I didn't build a harness. I got very drunk, finishing that flask of wine all by myself.

The constables had picked me up before I got sober.

Somehow I fell asleep. This surprised me, when I woke up from it and realized that my eyes were crusty and my mouth was dried out like space.

I had no idea how I'd managed to unwind enough to go under, and no idea how long I'd been asleep for. Possibly I was too exhausted with memories and the volatile tears that memories seemed to drag from me at every opportunity now. *Lability.* That was the old-fashioned term. People under stress—physical, emotional, hormonal—used to be *labile*, before rightminding and before more primitive tech like mood regulators and so on.

I was *labile* now.

I was also still full of images and recollections, and they seemed the clearer for sleeping on them. Perhaps I had been dreaming, processing and refining old memories in the way you're supposed to process and refine newer ones. And I felt, for the first time perhaps, the full impact of what Farweather's booby trap had done to me.

That, all by itself, made me want to peel my own skin off with my fingernails. It was in me, this terrible history. It was a part of me, and I could not get it out.

But maybe I owed justice to the Ativahikas, if I could manage it.

If I could even keep myself alive.

I remembered now. I . . . had spent a lot of time being interrogated, and eventually went before Justice, where it was decided after a lengthy series of hearings, held in camera because I was a legal minor, that Nyumba Yangu Haina Mlango had brainwashed and controlled me, and that I— and all other minor children—were to be removed from their care.

The clade itself was to be disbanded, and its members subjected to incarceration or Recon.

They were given eight hours to surrender themselves and their children to Justice.

You can probably guess how this ends. They didn't turn themselves in.

They committed suicide en masse, making the decision as one. If they couldn't be together, and content; if they couldn't avoid being unhappy, even for a little while; if they were expected to take individual responsibility for their collective decision and suffer consequences for it . . .

. . . they did not wish to.

They killed the children, too.

CHAPTER 22

AS FOR ME? I SURVIVED.

Because I was in custody, I survived.

I was the one who lived.

My machine memories were edited. Because meat memories tend to be subsumed to outside narratives, the basic result was that my entire memory of events was . . . repaired. Replaced with memories that suited a past I was deemed able to live with, as part of my rehabilitation process. I hadn't ever been supposed to find out what happened to my clade, but it came out at the trial, so out of kindness Justice took it away again.

I consented.

Wouldn't you?

I was given the opportunity to have input into constructing a personality that the court deemed socially acceptable. Then I received intensive rightminding and became the new, improved Haimey Dz.

I had built myself from a kit. With some extensive professional assistance, naturally.

It was better to think my clade had cut me off after I left them than to remember what they had actually done. I wish I still had no idea what had happened to my crèche-sisters. The fact that I hadn't realized that I didn't know what had become of them until I was trapped in a runaway alien starship headed far up and out from the Milky Way—that I had, in fact, more or less forgotten all about them, categorizing them with the rest of the clademothers and other relations I thought I'd left behind or who had frozen me out—was a fresh and scouring little grief right up inside me, like a bubble behind my ribs.

I'd been a dupe, all right, but I hadn't been Niyara's dupe. She'd actually done something to protect me. Something she didn't have to do.

Something that indicated that she knew what was going on, what my clade had done, and that she actually cared about me. And for almost two decans, I'd been blaming her for everything. When my own family had been the ones to dupe me. To sacrifice me. And to make me think it was my own idea.

And then to leave me holding the bag, and the whole moral weight of everything they'd done.

Who was it who said the truth would set you free?

Freedom tasted a lot like choked-back vomit.

You never want to puke in microgravity if you can help it, and so I hung on to my bile, though it was a narrow triumph and a dubious one.

When I, itchy-eyed and somewhat the worse for exhaustion, came back into our impromptu habitation chamber, Farweather was awake and alert. She was doing calisthenics to the rattling of her chain, and she looked calm and cheerful and well rested. I wanted to kick her in the chin, but instead I emptied her slops, then went over to the mess kit and knocked together coffee and two bowls of porridge. Farweather was watching me, bird-bright. I neither looked at her nor spoke until the food was done, and she didn't say anything either.

I brought her a bulb of coffee and a bowl of porridge (algae and creamed grain . . . delightful) before stepping back to the pad-couch opposite to eat my own breakfast.

I didn't have much appetite. Hers seemed to be fine.

I said, "You wanted me to remember that I made the bombs."

"I did," she said.

"It's my fault all those people died."

"Pretty much," Zanya said. "Are you going to stop condescending to me now?"

I still didn't look at her. I drank my coffee. The porridge wouldn't go down on its own. I mean, it was a struggle on my best dia. Todia, it was actively nauseating. Or maybe I just didn't feel like eating.

"Look," Zanya said, "I do feel like I know you, a little."

I snorted. "We've been sleeping on the same deck plates for decians now."

"I told you I had an ayatana from Niyara." She stretched, both hands above her head, lifting one shoulder and then the other. I heard her spine crack. Gravity.

"I told *you* I didn't believe you. Twice, I think."

She smiled at me. "Fact doesn't care if you believe in it."

"And you've reviewed this putative recording."

"I have." The corners of her mouth curved down as she lost the smile. "She was one of ours, you know."

"I figured that out eventually." The possibility that she wasn't lying left me agitated, edgy.

She sipped her coffee, savoring. "She cared about you."

"I figured that out eventually, too." I pushed my porridge at her, unable to waste resources no matter how badly I wanted her to go to hell. She took it with a look of surprise, but set the bowl inside her empty one and went to work polishing off the remains. She was as hungry as I ought to be.

Farweather finished the greenish, unappealing gruel and stifled a burp behind her hand, looking momentarily uncomfortable. Neither one of us was used to getting enough food anymore.

She set the bowls aside and picked the coffee back up. "Was this an apology?"

"Do I have something to apologize for?"

Echoes of a petulant, inadequately rightminded adolescent.

"It seems like you think you do." She crossed her long legs and leaned back.

"What do you mean?"

"You were blaming yourself for what happened on Ansara before you even knew the truth," she pointed out, conveniently forgetting—or erasing—that she'd been blaming me herself a very few minutes before. "You keep trying to . . . I don't know, redeem yourself through service. You need to let go of that desire, Dz. Stop trying to make amends for things that are not and never were your fault."

"I built a *bomb*."

"Four bombs." She grinned. "Actually. But that wasn't you. Not exactly. That was somebody Nyumba Yangu Haina Mlango made up out of whole cloth, right? Somebody exactly like the rest of them."

I settled back and stared at her, realizing that I had crossed my arms defensively but not having much in the way of will to uncross them.

She said, "There's a weird power dynamic at work in here, too, right? If you, Dz, have to make amends for things even if you couldn't control them at the time, then in some way you, Dz, get to feel that you're not powerless. If you have to make amends for things that happened against your will, then you reclaim some power over those events."

I didn't answer.

"Look," she said. "My people aren't real comfortable with modifying yourself into a new species, but I have to admit that your people are reactionary even by my standards. A bunch of retro-gendered radically cis-female separatists who brainwash their unmodified, baseline-DNA clone children into absolute obedience and oneness with some primitive group mind? That's *a little fucking perverted*."

"You're saying my guilt is inappropriate."

"I'm saying I'm glad you got out. Got some freedom. You didn't *have* that freedom when you were with Niyara, even though you thought you did. You didn't have that freedom when Justice's legacy juice was running your head."

"So I'm free now." I kicked an afthand. "You set me free; that's what you're saying."

"I'm saying that you didn't make the choices, so your assuming responsibility for the outcomes is a little unrealistic, don't you think? Even if it is a means of asserting some agency over the course of proceedings."

"Somebody's responsible. And I'm the only person likely to step up to it, so I guess it is my job, yes."

"I'm absolving you," she said.

"I'd be more inclined to accept that if it didn't come from a mass murderer."

If I'd expected her to flinch, I was disappointed. She inclined her head, and the smile flickered back for a moment before vanishing again. *Touché.*

It takes one to know one, babes.

"Besides," I said. "The only absolution is in balancing the action. Exactly as if it were a debt from a past life."

"Do you believe in past lives?"

"I believe in past selves," I said. "I sort of have to."

"And you think you can carry the debt of what a dead woman did?"

"Is that what you'd call my past? A life lived by a dead woman?"

She made an eloquent, lazy gesture with her neck and shoulders. She changed the subject. "So your little Utopia—"

"Not so little."

"—what do you do about people who exploit the system?"

"You mean, people like you?"

She ignored my attempt to needle her. I suppose, given her life in a primitive society and her own ability to needle me, she had some practice. "Malingerers. People who don't pull their weight. How do you drive them to work harder?"

"Why do they need to?"

She blinked at me. I thought she was honestly puzzled. She shook her head and said, "But if they don't work—"

I said, "Busywork, they used to call it. There's absolutely no value to it. Economic value, or personal. There's value in work you enjoy, or that serves a need. There's no value in work for its own sake. It's just . . . churn.

Anxiety. Doing stuff to be doing stuff, not because it needs doing. There's enough for everybody."

I could see her getting angry, and honestly I didn't actually *care* if she understood what I was trying to say. I suspected it would take a full course of rightminding and ans of talk therapy to make a dent in Farweather and her ossified, archaic belief patterns. And I was bored with arguing with her.

My turn to change the subject. "Do you want some more coffee?"

"I'd be a fool to say no."

I made the coffee. She didn't speak. Her chain rattled lightly; when I turned around she'd wiped the bowls out with a sanitizer and stacked them neatly. The bowls had come with the ship, and as far as I knew they were hats or shoes or alien commodes, but they did okay in holding porridge. The coffee I brewed in bulbs, because that was the way it came prepackaged. All you had to do was obtain or create boiling water, and then inject it. The bulb would expand, stretching from the size of a thumb joint to large enough to hold a good-sized portion. The filter was built right in.

The power flickered again while I was boiling the water—but since all I was doing *was* boiling water, and I was using Farweather's power-cell operated probe to do it, that didn't really affect anything. I would go looking for the problem again todia, I decided. None of my previous attempts had borne fruit, but persistence was a virtue, and it wasn't like I had a whole lot of other things to be getting on with.

I handed Farweather her second bulb.

"I'm going to vibrate this chain right off me. And wind up in caffeine withdrawal again when you cut me off."

It was a joke. I didn't laugh. She was trying to mend fences, though. So that was something.

She cupped the bulb in both hands, enjoying the warmth while she waited for it to cool enough to be drinkable. She looked down at it and turned it gently in her hands.

She said, "'Human life. Duration: momentary. Nature: changeable. Perception: dim. Condition of body: decaying. Soul: spinning around. Fortune: unpredictable. Lasting fame: uncertain. Sum up: The body and its parts are a river, the soul a dream and mist, life is warfare and a journey far from home, lasting reputation is oblivion.'"

"That's grim," I said.

"That's Marcus Aurelius," she answered.

I drank my coffee. It was too hot, but I managed not to scorch a blister on my palate. This time.

"So given that," she said, "why don't you be somebody you want to be, instead of somebody you think you need to be in order to make reparations? Why not pick your own purpose in life?"

"You said it yourself," I told her. "That wasn't me. I don't exist."

She blinked at me with her head cocked as if what I was saying was in an untranslatable language.

I said, "I never existed. There was the me the clade made, and the me Justice made. There's no real me in here at all. So I can't want anything. And I can't *have* any purpose in life, other than to make amends."

She shook her head. I decided I didn't want to hear whatever was about to come out of her opening mouth, because it would all be lies and self-contradiction anyway. So I got up and I stalked off, and when she croaked, half laughing, "But that doesn't make any sense at all!" I pretended I hadn't heard her and kept walking.

I went up to the observation deck, and tried to talk to the ship again. Sometimes, I thought I might be getting somewhere.

Sometimes there was almost a sense, a flicker of some awareness at the edge of my own. Like, maybe the Prize was out there, but I just didn't know how to reach it.

"It can't be too hard if Farweather pulled it off," I said bitterly to thin air.

But that presence, or that awareness, felt familiar rather than alien.

So I wondered if I wasn't just experiencing the sort of sensory fill-in that your brain provides in total darkness. Hang out where there's absolutely no light for long enough, and your memory will start painting pictures out of the random firing of your visual cortex neurons while they try to make sense of a blackness they were not designed for.

So if I felt something out there, I guessed there was a pretty good chance that I was imagining it.

I tried for more than a stanhour and got nowhere. Again.

Of course, I came back eventually. To be honest, I came back sooner than I really wanted to. And not just because while it was a big ship, there wasn't much to do on it beyond exploring, going through cabinets for neatly stowed gear with more or less mysterious purposes, and being painfully aware of how Synarche archinformists would be pitching a fit at me for contaminating their site with my presence and microbes and skin cells and air currents and relentless *rearranging* of stuff. But unless I actually managed to trace the fault in the power system—assuming there was a fault, and flickering occasionally wasn't something that the Koregoi considered a design feature (who knew? maybe it was their idea of wall art?)—I didn't have anything to fix, or fix on. I was just . . . kind of hoping I would come up with a way of getting the ship away from Farweather by understanding it better.

Which, admittedly, was not such a bad idea.

Still, if I was floating through maintenance tubes I wasn't talking to Farweather, and if I wasn't talking to Farweather I stood half a chance of getting my head on straight eventually and even keeping it that way. Rightminding or no rightminding.

Okay, straight*er*.

I knew that my worrying about archinformists was a kind of denial. Because it had at its base the assumption that I would beat the odds and somehow manage to pry the ship out of Farweather's control and fly it back to Synarche space. The conquering hero.

Which seemed . . . okay. Possibly like something I shouldn't count on being able to pull off. But it was a nice life goal for the time being. And if I wound up kidnapped by space pirates . . . well, I wouldn't be the first woman to have been.

Who knew? Maybe I could even thrive as a space pirate, if I played my cards right. I could reinvent myself again. Invent an entirely new identity. Again.

What did I have to take me back to the Synarche, anyway, now that Singer and Connla and the cats were gone?

Except I still thought the Synarche was right, and I still thought the Synarche was home. My affections were not alienated on that front. So I guessed whatever Farweather thought she was doing when she fried my fox, it wasn't really working. Because what I wanted more than anything was to do the right thing.

I wished I had Singer with me to tell me what the right thing was. But I could make some guesses as to what he'd say. I'd known him pretty well. The right thing was to figure out how to get control of the Prize away from Farweather, turn it around, and begin the very, very, very long trip home. Fortunately, there was an entire inhabited galaxy between me and the Core, and the Prize was fast. But I would still be on short rations until I could find someplace to resupply.

So much algae.

Assuming she did not literally blow up, and take me and the Prize with her.

Well, if I had to toss her out an airlock to save the ship and myself . . .

. . . I'd span that void when I came to it. Especially since I had in fact been *trying* to wrest control of the ship and it just had not been working.

I wondered if she knew what kind of a time limit she was operating under. And if she did know how long she had, I also wondered if there was some way to leverage relativistic effects to keep her alive long enough to get her to a surgeon who might be able to remove the bomb (if there was a bomb).

The woman had *blown up my head*. Why was I even still considering what might be good for her?

At least in my avoidance I was learning a lot about the ship's systems. In particular, I was learning a great deal about its electrical grid, which was less like a grid, frankly, and more like a circulatory system. Not in the sense of being *alive*, per se, but in having trunks that diverged and spread apart in a branching fashion—treelike, fractal—until they cycled and returned.

I'd managed to figure out how to get into the engine room, or what I thought of as main engineering, and I supposed if I really needed to I could just sabotage something. But the random power fluctuations were already scary enough. The Enemy was out there, vast and cold and full of not much at all except the occasional random particle, and we were sweeping those up into our white field as we went.

The engines were definitely *alien*, but they also *made sense*, and I was an engineer. And these were not my first set of alien engines, either, though they were the first ones I couldn't just pull up a manual for, even if that manual was in badly translated Novoruss.

So, I couldn't control the ship. Not yet anyway. But I could *break* it. And probably kill myself and Farweather in the process—slowly, through starvation or environmental failure after we were stranded. But if we were lucky, death might come quickly and kindly. Oxygen starvation wasn't a bad way to go. You just got sleepy and foggy, and eventually sat down for a nice nap that lasted longer than you anticipated.

Restful.

I didn't want to nap without end. I wanted to find out what happened, going forward. I wanted to keep finding out for as long as I could. Maybe it was selfish, and maybe I didn't deserve it, but I *wanted* it. I wanted to keep existing. There were future selves that I could envision, and in envisioning, want to become.

That surprised me, a little, everything considered: my culpability in what had happened on Ansara; my recent bereavement.

If giving that up was what it took to keep the Koregoi ship from falling into the hands of the pirates, though? If I had to destroy the ship to save it, I decided . . . I would.

I was living with enough guilt already. Becoming somebody like Farweather *would* mean that I had died. Died and been reinvented as somebody I did not recognize, and somebody I did not want to be.

So I had a plan, and though I didn't really want to face Farweather, my options were somewhat limited overall. I was going to have to feed her eventually, and myself also. And since I'd given her most of my breakfast, my own hunger situation was progressing beyond where the yeast tablets could manage it for me.

I was thinking about maybe spending another stanhour tracing power lines and checking their connections, though I didn't think it would help much. Everything seemed to be orderly and in perfect working order. There was no *reason* for the power drops. And the power drops didn't seem to affect the drive, which made me think that maybe the drive was the source of the problem. If it was for some reason drawing power erratically, that might explain the dips, though I had no idea what could be causing that except a drive problem, and *there* was a terrifying idea. Or maybe it was the gravity generators, if that was a thing, because sure, why *wouldn't* there be gravity generators making the artificial gravity in this millennians-old Koregoi starship I was stuck on, on a one-way trip to nowhere. . . .

Was the ship somehow using dark gravity for that? As the Ativahika did for travel?

You're getting hysterical, Dz.

Man, times like these, I missed my regulator.

Anyway, I'd just made up my mind that I was going to head back in a stanhour or so, when the power dipped again, longer and harder this time. I grabbed a nearby housing and held on for dear life, half expecting the gravity to flicker off or the ship to abruptly change course or v and the inertial dampers that kept us all from dying to snap off and leave me slamming from deck plate to bulkhead.

Maybe I *was* getting a little paranoid. Maybe just a little.

In the darkness, I could have convinced myself that I felt a chill. I was being ridiculous, and I knew it. A body as large and well insulated as the Prize would take a long time to radiate its internal warmth away to a point that the inhabitants would find uncomfortable. Space is a terrible conductor of things like heat; there's not a lot of *there* there for the energy to move through. So the heat has to escape in the old-fashioned way, straight radiation, and that's inefficient and slow.

The lights stayed dim a long time, though. Long enough that I clipped my tools and gauges and headed through the various undoors as I went. I had another bad moment—it was a dia for bad moments—wondering what I would do if the hatches failed to operate, but either they had their own power sources (smart), or they had priority when it came to main power (less smart), or the little nanite fogs that I figured were probably what made them up were self-willed and self-powered and basically did their own thing, which was rejoice in sealing and unsealing hatchways anytime somebody wanted to walk through them.

I wasn't taking any chances that it would continue working, though. I gritted my teeth against the anticipated ache in my afthands, eschewed the more comfortable but smaller and circuitous maintenance tunnels, and I *ran*.

When I burst back into our nest, Farweather was on her feet, turning and looking from side to side. She couldn't really *see* anything, because she'd been in a room without any portholes, and I hadn't bothered to move her. I'd just grown that permanent appurtenance from the bulkhead (sweet-talking those same utility fogs, maybe? man, I wish I knew) and unceremoniously chained her to the wall.

As soon as I bolted in and stopped short, I knew she wasn't behind the ship's misbehavior. Her frosty exterior was melting, her face lightly sheened with sweat. Her pulse raced in the shadow of the hollow of her jaw, and she was so razor-sharp with decians of short rations that I could see it there. I knew what her heart felt like, thundering in her chest, because mine was palpitating too.

She whirled on me. "What did you *do?*" she said, her voice breaking between a whine and a snarl.

"Nothing," I said as the ship shuddered around us. My legs almost buckled as I came off the floor and then slammed back down. I didn't go to my hands and knees, but that was as much luck as balance, and it had nothing to do with having been prepared. "It's—happening on its own!"

She glared for a second, then decided to believe me. "Get the mattress."

Not the one she was standing on, obviously. I snagged my own seating pad from across the cabin and humped it up on my back like a spongy, crackling turtle's shell. For a second, I thought of ditching my utility belt—but loose tools ricocheting around the cabin would be worse than lumpy, bruising objects that were nevertheless firmly attached to my body and could not, therefore, build up enough *v* to be truly dangerous unless I was ricocheting around with them, in which case I would have bigger problems.

I hopped over to Farweather, the pads and packing material trailing behind me like a train. She grabbed me and dropped. I thought about banging her one in the solar plexus, but she didn't bite or punch, so I went with her. We pressed ourselves together. I grabbed her pad and she grabbed mine, and she rolled so the packing material wound around us in a protective cocoon.

A protective shroud, the unhelpful part of my brain said.

"Choke up on my chain," she said as the gravity cut out again and we went briefly into the air, thumping a bulkhead before we slammed again into the deck. "I've got the padding."

I wished I had time to tie it in place.

Wait.

"Roll," I said, and showed her. She helped, thrashing against me, thrusting with her shoulders and hips. She was so thin, and I was so thin, that her hip bones ground against mine. We wound the chain around our layers of padding. It was long enough to go two and a half times—and it did a good job of pinning them in place and limited our collective range of motion. I managed to work a wrench clipped to a carabiner off my belt despite the confined space and used it to secure two links of the chain to each other, effectively pinning the padding to our bodies and the cocoon of the two of us to the corner between deck and bulkhead.

Then we . . . lay there. And stared at each other. And waited for the next fluctuation, with no control over whether it would slam us into a deck or smash us against a bulkhead.

Nothing happened.

I watched sweat gather along the edge of her eye socket. Her breathing slowed; echoing mine, I realized, as I was regulating mine more out of habit than intent. I turned my head, because she was breathing on my face.

She ground her hips unsubtly against me, and I elbowed her in the ribs. "That's assault."

"Ow," she said. "And what's *that?*"

"Self-defense," I answered. "Is it over? Do you think we should—"

We slammed sideways. Farweather cried out. I couldn't answer, because the stanchion I'd sweet-talked the ship into growing—the one we were both now chained to—had slammed me in the ribs. The breath came out of me hard and sharp, and it wouldn't go back in. She grabbed on to me, arms around me, and I wheezed against her shoulder and into the crook of her neck.

She smelled so good.

You're not supposed to think of things like that when your life might be ending. On the other hand, that's often when your body really, really wants to think about them.

We hit the deck. And then the wall, and then the deck again. We lay there gasping, clutching each other. She was on the bottom; then we bounced again and hit the end of the chain and we were side by side. Pain spiked through my elbow when she landed on it.

Her breath was hot against my throat. Breasts soft, hips sharp and painful. A pliers dug into my floating ribs. There wasn't anything I could do to move it.

The lights shone through our translucent padding, and I looked into her transparent dark brown eyes, to the satin sheen and the patterns of veins and pigment at the back of them.

"This is a hell of a long way to go for a date," she said, between breaths that sounded painful.

"Shut up," I explained.

She kissed me, and I . . .

I let it happen.

And then I kissed her back.

Don't get me wrong. I knew it was a terrible idea, even while it was happening. But I wanted it, and I wanted her, and I was terrified and she was there and—

Sometimes you do something that you're not supposed to.

It was a *very* ill-advised kiss.

It happened anyway. And you know? I liked it.

And then we hit the stanchion again, right where the chain crossed our bodies, and snapped away from it one more time, and I—

—blacked out.

I woke up again pretty quickly once the gs were gone. Or returned to normal, I should say, because we weren't floating, just lying on the deck in an uncomfortable bundle. The air around us was stale and smelled of sweat and a little urine. Farweather was staring at me speculatively— and a little bruisedly—from centimeters away, and everything around us seemed cool and peaceful.

"Is it safe?" I asked her.

"Is anything?"

Farweather managed to extricate one hand and struggled with the carabiner until it came loose. We rolled, unwinding the chain, and made little grunting sounds of unhappiness whenever weight or something unforgiving landed on a bruise. There were a lot of bruises. There was a lot of grunting. I figured I had at least two cracked ribs. *Come on, Koregoi buggies, fix me up.*

You know, it hadn't occurred to me before just that minute that Farweather's EM pulse had *not* disrupted the parasite, that I could tell. I hadn't even thought about it. I guess I really was integrating those senses.

Neuroplasticity. It's a hell of a thing.

Finally we unwound ourselves and got a little space between us. Superstitiously, neither one of us crawled out of our packing material yet. And neither one of us stood up, either.

Well, I say it was superstition. Maybe it was sense.

We lay there, side by side. I was panting and aching. I was only paying enough attention to Farweather to make sure she didn't intend to brain me with that wrench.

The ship shuddered again, but the gravity remained intact this time. And now that I wasn't distracted by being slammed against internal structures, I realized something.

Through the Koregoi senso, I could tell that we were . . . slowing. Gradually. Not falling out of white space all at once as the bubble collapsed, but instead . . . *unfolding.* The Koregoi ship's drive was gradually smoothing the space around us, doing something impossible—allowing us to change vector and apparent velocity *while* in white space.

And through the Koregoi senso, I could also feel that there was another ship.

Another ship, in white space. Coming up on us fast, then—incredibly— matching pace with us. Falling into formation, which was something that I had heard military vessels could do, but I had never actually witnessed happening. Even in all of Connla's fancy flying, merging bubbles and coaxing abandoned vessels out of folded space-time, I'd never seen anything like this.

Pirates.

"We've got company," Farweather said unhappily, because of course she could feel everything that I could.

I looked at her in surprise. "Not yours?"

"That wasn't the plan," she said. "But I've been out of contact. Maybe the plan has changed."

"Maybe they were following, and when the ship started acting weird they moved in?"

She gave me a sly look. If she gathered that it was a test, and I was fishing for knowledge of the Freeporters' technological abilities, she didn't let on.

She just shrugged. "I guess we're going to find out."

CHAPTER 23

THE LIGHTS DIMMED ONCE MORE, AND THE WHOLE GIANT ship shuddered. I regretted unrolling ourselves from the padding, but the gravity stayed on and we didn't suffer any sudden, unexpected vector changes that left us ricocheting off the walls.

I unlocked Farweather's chain, and she gazed at me speculatively, rubbing her wrist. "If I'd known that all it would take was kissing you, I would have done that ages ago."

I rolled my eyes. "I'm going up to observation. This is your chance to come along."

Also, if something terrible happened to the ship and I was incapacitated, I needed to know she had a fighting chance to survive, and I hadn't left her welded to a bulkhead wall to starve.

"Observation, huh?"

"Shake a leg," I said. "It's pretty."

We made it up slowly, limping and leaning on walls. She kept an elbow pressed to her side hard enough that I thought about offering to wrap her ribs for her, but she didn't ask and if she didn't ask I wasn't going to offer. I was braced for her to try something, but she didn't. Possibly she was counting me as a potential ally if it turned out that we had enemies in common.

In any case, I wasn't going to turn my back on her. So I made her go first, and she didn't complain. I was carrying her bolt prod, anyway—I'd retrieved it from my hiding spot before I turned her loose—so it probably would have been a bad idea for her to come after me unless she could get the drop somehow.

We proceeded to observation. It *was* pretty. We were still in white space, and the twisting bands of light were particularly lovely for being so narrow, with so much dark between.

Gorgeous to look at, but it gave me a chill. We were way out in the Dark and the Empty, if this was all the starlight around.

Starlight. What a tautology. As if there's anything else in the universe that makes light. Directly or indirectly, all the light there is originates from stars.

Well, I suppose you could make a case for antimatter, or for burning hydrogen, but you'd have to stretch the point, and besides, fussing with poetry until you ruin it has never been a sport that appealed to me.

Farweather walked toward the dome, still rubbing her wrist where the shackle had been. She didn't seem to have any galls or sores—I'd been careful to pad the thing, and to give her supplies to change the padding regularly—so I guessed it was just the reflexive fussing motion of someone recently freed.

"Wow," she said.

I grinned into my palm. "Told you it was pretty."

She shot me a look over her shoulder that was practically scorching. My cheeks burned; I glanced away.

Terrible idea.

And it wasn't getting any better.

Flustered, I grabbed ahold of the conversation and unsubtly steered it. "Should you take us out of white space?"

"Maybe. I don't have fine maneuvering control."

"How were you going to dock us on the other end?" I blurted, scandalized.

"Tugboats." She shook her head at me. "You ought to know about those."

I ought to. Well, that answered one of my questions.

She pointed. "There's our company."

I followed the line of her finger to see what she was aiming it at, and discovered a ship sharing our white bubble that was doing absolutely nothing to render itself unnoticeable. It burned running lights, and had floodlit itself so I could make out the registration marks and the details of the design.

I caught my breath when I saw it, my mouth relaxing into a smile. What I was looking at, blinking in disbelief, was a pretty standard Synarche interdiction cruiser, a light Interceptor-class constabulary vessel that was mostly engines and ship-to-ship weapons held together with an armored skin around a small crew compartment, its needle-like hull wrapped in a double set of white coils.

Well, that explained how it had caught us. Those things were *fast*.

It was *inside* the Prize's enormous white coils, a piece of fancy flying that made me think painfully of my lost shipmate. I'd heard rumors of Judiciary pilots who could match up white bubbles in transit, while both ships were pushing *v*. I'd never thought to have a front-row glimpse of it.

"Not one of ours," Farweather said.

"Not one of *yours*, maybe."

She shot me a look that was far more amused than angry. Pirate fatalism, maybe. "You think they'll be pleased to see you?"

I managed to keep my nails from rattling on the butt of the bolt prod. Whatever I might have said back to her, I never got the chance to try, because a male voice broke in. Steeped in dry humor, moderately familiar, it said, "Oh, I should think they will be very pleased to see you, Dz."

Singer?

"Singer?"

Silence, for a moment. Then: "Sorry, adjusting the speaker protocols. Is this voice a closer match?"

"Oh my goodness, *Singer!*"

"Present," the shipmind said, from all around me. "Wow, there's a lot of room in this brain."

I would have hugged him. I *needed* to hug him, but I couldn't hug him, so instead I bounced in place on my toes and swung my arms like an overexcited five-an-old who has to let some of the energy out somehow or explode all over the place, emotionally speaking, and messily.

"How are you alive?" I babbled. "I just—how are you *on the Koregoi ship?*"

"I ditched here," he said. "When the tug was destroyed, I sent a per-sonality seed over. Remember that I had an uplink going? It just took me nearly this long to figure out the system over here, rewrite my own code so that I could run on it effectively, then write the ship itself a new OS so I could control my lips and fingers, to use a totally inappropriate anthro-pomorphization. Also, I had the Koregoi senso in your brain to use as a transitional platform, until *somebody* fried your fox."

"Wait," I said. "You used my brain as . . . an adaptor?"

"To bridge incompatible systems."

"An *adaptor.*"

". . . Yes?"

I reached out and patted the nearest bulkhead, just about swimming in relief. "This is amazing. This is the best news ever. Wait, did you . . . ? Were you in my senso? While my fox was still operating?"

"I had a seed in you, too, though just a tiny one with very limited functionality; there's not a lot of room in there."

"I heard you—it?—talking to me. Maybe? Why didn't you tell me you were alive?"

Farweather had turned around and was staring at me, up at space, at the Interceptor, around at the deck and walls of the Koregoi ship. I glared at her. Whatever she was about to say, I did *not* want to hear it.

She shut her mouth again and turned her shoulder to me. That was fine. The feeling was pretty mutual.

"I wasn't in contact with that seed," Singer said. "If anything happened to corrupt this instance of me, I wanted the uncorrupted backup. And as for why *it* didn't tell you—it wasn't a proper AI. Just a personality seed."

"You could have let me know you were there!"

"Knowing myself, I'm *sure* I was talking to you."

". . . I might have noticed that," I agreed.

I didn't know enough about programming artificial intelligences to have a good sense of the technical difference between an AI proper and a personality seed. But I could probably make do with my self-evident sense of the generalities, and I was figuring *that* out pretty rapidly.

"But how'd you get in here?" I said.

"I'd transferred an archive over to this machine as well, as soon as I got access to it. Did you know there's a lot of bandwidth in your parasite?"

"You propagated? Singer, *you* did something illegal?"

He sighed, which was something he did for communication with meatpeople, not because shipminds exhale loudly in worry or frustration. "It seemed like a safe precaution. And I didn't think you'd mind."

Farweather sneered at me, and (I thought) at Singer and the Synarche and the whole lot of us in general. "And it's just coincidence that he shows up now."

I thought of the voice in my head, the one I'd thought was my own wishful thinking. I thought of the power fluctuations and the weird way in which the ship had occasionally seemed to help me out: the stanchion, for example. Or maybe it was just that the ship was helpful, even without Singer in charge, but still, I was convinced. He hadn't just shown up now. He'd been around the whole time. He'd just . . . manifested now. And I couldn't blame him for biding his time until the reinforcements got here. Or had it taken him this long to get adequate control of the Prize's systems? Was it possible that he had summoned them in once he was active? No, he couldn't have reached across two white bubbles. . . .

But possibly he could have sensed them approaching, and slowed the Prize to help them catch us. Who knew what kind of sensors this thing had, and how it could interact with dark gravity.

Farweather said, "I'm sure this sudden AI has nothing to do with the

Synarche ship matching pace with us. You're being played, Haimey. This is not your friend. It's just a . . . simulation."

She tried to sound concerned, but I knew how the Freeporters—and Farweather herself—felt about free artificial intelligences. They deemed them *untrustworthy* and kept what limited computation they used hobbled, not allowing it to develop self-awareness.

Paranoid Luddites.

I glanced up at the interdiction cruiser and its impossibly skilled flying. A bubble of optimism rose in me—one that I would have quenched, if I'd been able to tune, because the pain of its being disappointed would be so extreme. But I was filled with what the ancient poets would have called a wild surmise, a hope so strong it hurt me physically.

"What about Connla and the cats?" I said to Singer, ignoring Farweather. My voice broke.

He ignored the evidence of emotion. "I'm not completely sure. But they *might* have lived. They were all suited up, and the part of the tug that was directly hit was the drive, not the control cabin."

Relief surged in me. Dizzying, rendering me so giddy I actually reached for my fox to bump it back under control. I shouldn't have bothered, and not just because I had no fox—because the elation was replaced with dread as I had another idea. A terrible one. What happened once could happen again, and while the Interceptor was a hell of a lot tougher than a tug . . .

"Wait. Singer. Do you have control of this ship's weapons?"

"This ship does not have any weapons," he reported.

I frowned. I looked at Farweather. It occurred to me that she was, in fact, under my skin. That my own Stockholmification was proceeding apace.

And that I had been letting some critical pieces of knowledge slide, because it was easier not to think about them when it was just her and me, and we needed each other for sanity and survival.

"That's right, Zanya," I said. "Didn't you have some theory about what happened to the tug?"

"... About that."

I turned on her. I didn't say anything, but my hand was on the butt of her shock prod. I hated her, at that moment, more than I knew I could hate a human being. My hope *had* made me vulnerable, and the need to defend that vulnerability was making me angry now.

She froze.

I said, "Whatever you're about to say, you might as well say it. But don't lie to me again."

"We didn't think it would be manned," she said. "We assumed the whole crew would be over on the Prize."

"Why off Earth . . ." But I knew. Assuming she was telling the truth—and why would she?—I knew. Of course, that's how the pirates would have done it—each one determined to defend their stake in the prize vessel because nobody else would do it for them. And we hadn't gotten a proximity warning before the destruction commenced. So the only explanation was that they'd used the particle burst caught up in their bow wave to take out the tug.

Those reckless assholes.

It was only the sheerest luck that they hadn't taken out the Koregoi ship and me in addition to the tug. Well, luck. And probably Zanya's advanced relationship with her symbiote. And some fancy flying, though it pained me to admit it.

At least Zanya hadn't been the pilot. . . . So I had *two* casual mass murderers to contend with.

I turned my back on Zanya. It was absolutely a stupid thing to do, and I did it anyway because if I didn't I was going to electrocute her with her own weapon.

Singer would watch my back, anyway.

"Singer, what's that ship out there?" I asked, moving away from Farweather. She didn't follow; I heard her steps as she withdrew toward the windows at the rim of the observation deck.

I went toward the other side.

"It's an Interceptor-class interdiction cruiser," he said helpfully.

"Tell me something I don't already know." I leaned my forehands on the transparent material of the viewport.

"This particular vessel is the Synarche Justice Vessel *I'll Explain It To You Slowly*. I'm afraid I do not have access to its current crew or mission assignments. My database accesses are a little limited right now."

"You have databases *at all*?"

"The Koregoi ship has a great deal of fossil information aboard, and I've had some success in beginning to decrypt it. A lot of it is star charts and translation protocols, as you might expect. None of it is current. But I've managed to determine from the drift in the star charts since they were last accessed that the ship was in mothballs for approximately thirty thousand ans."

He said it so casually. And it fell like a stone.

I gaped. I turned around and looked at Farweather, because I needed to share my incredulity with somebody, even if it was somebody I hated.

She looked back at me mildly.

"But everything works."

"So it does," he said.

"My species wasn't even really a *species* yet."

"Technically speaking, untrue," he said. "By a factor of ten, more or less. But I understand the spirit in which you speak."

"Holy crap," I said. "You found the Rosetta Stone."

"*Technically* speaking," he repeated, "I *am* the Rosetta Stone."

This was so much more than I had been expecting.

Lowering my voice, I said, "Singer, can you reboot my fox from there?"

Resonances changed as he localized his voice to me. "I need to generate a wireless signal and run a diagnostic. That will take a moment. The *I'll Explain It To You Slowly* is hailing us, however. Shall I answer?"

"Please do." A Synarche ship, hanging abeam us, out here in the middle of nowhere. A Synarche ship.

Hope.

Home.

Maybe I wouldn't be dying forgotten in a pirate outpost somewhere on the edge of the Great Big Empty after all.

"I've accessed your fox," Singer said, moments later. "I can't be entirely sure if there's physical damage, because I can't run a diagnostic until it's operating, but I should have the option of rebooting it. And don't worry; I'm talking with the Synarche craft right now. We'll be dropping into normal space momentarily."

"Are they coming over?"

"They want you to bring the prisoner to them."

I lowered my voice to a bare whisper. "She'll put up a fight. She doesn't want to die out here. She's a sophipath. All about her own needs. Also, she's at risk of exploding, if what she told me can be believed."

"What?"

"She's a human bomb," I told him, and explained briefly. "Unless she was lying to me."

"Or the other Freeporters were lying to her." He paused long enough that I imagined he was communicating with the Interceptor.

I said, "Have you made them aware that the prisoner might blow up?"

"They say that they have surgical facilities."

I decided that if they wanted to risk it, it was their lookout.

Farweather had crossed the observation deck and was staring out the window away from me. I could see her reflection dimly in the window, superimposed over the scrolling bands of light and the rescue mission beyond. I assumed she could see my back, as well.

"We don't have two working suits."

"They can send a shuttle."

I eyed the lightly built little ship, impressed. "They can get a shuttle in that thing?"

I must have spoken louder than I intended, because Farweather's reflection glanced over her shoulder at me before going back to studying the view. I kept my back to her and pretended I had not seen.

I lowered my voice to its previous level and said, "What's our bargaining position?"

"That depends, I should think, on what you intend to bargain for."

I smiled at my own reflection. I was concerned about all sorts of things right now, to be certain. But it just felt so dizzyingly, giddily *good* to have Singer back. People whose neural pathways formed under clade intervention are not meant to navigate the universe alone.

"Let me rephrase. How much trouble are we in?"

"Oh," Singer said, sounding as startled as if he hadn't even registered the possibility that we *might* be in trouble. "Not much, I should think. I mean, they'll want that pirate."

"I want that pirate too."

"Yes," he said. "I've noticed."

I blushed hot and sharp. "Hurry up with that fox reboot, would you?"

"Working on it," he said.

"Besides," I said. "That wasn't what I meant. I *meant* I want her safely back in custody, and . . . what are we going to tell them about disposing of the pirate?"

"She can't get far without a suit," he said pragmatically. "We should tell them to send a constable over and get her."

I bit my lip.

"And they'll want the Koregoi ship, obviously. And me. And you. But the only things that might *really* get us in trouble are already pretty well mitigated by the result. I don't think they're going to dun me for propagating when the alternative was destruction; even an AI gets some latitude in the matter of self-preservation. And as for you . . . well, kidnapped by pirates is a pretty good excuse."

I laughed out loud, stifling it because of Farweather. She rolled her eyes at me. I wasn't supposed to know. "It is at that."

I stepped back from the window and turned around. Raising my voice, I said crisply, "Please, Singer. Take us home."

◆ ◆ ◆

The Koregoi vessel did not so much as shiver now that Singer was firmly in control. I could tell that it was curving, because I could feel space bending around us. But Singer's touch was sure and subtle, which was why—

When we fell out of white space, abruptly and without warning, it was as if we had hit a wall. A very soft wall, because there was no inertia. We didn't go from moving to stopping. We just . . . weren't bending the universe around us anymore.

The Interceptor, inside our massive coils, fell right out of space alongside us. Also stationary, thank the stars, because a collision hadn't gotten any more appealing to me since the last time.

I am not sure I've ever been so happy about anything as I was at the outline of that souped-up Judiciary ship floating abeam the Prize.

Nothing moved. There was no sense of inertia. Space just unfolded around us . . . and we were back in the real world.

It was dark out here. Dark in ways that even our trip to the *Milk Chocolate Marauder* had not prepared me for. Space slid away like a waterfall of emptiness, bottomless and velvet in every direction. It seemed even darker because the bulk of the Koregoi vessel blocked the light of the Milky Way.

Certainly other galaxies floated out there in the dark, but they were so unimaginably distant that they hadn't even yet begun to grow larger in perspective. They didn't cast much light at all.

We were alone in a haunting emptiness, and I felt my heart thrum in my chest. It was terrifying out here—terrifying and beautiful and strange. This was alien country, a place not even my people, spacers born and bred, routinely went. We were far from help or any contact. This was the realm of unmanned probes and science teams and the sort of explorers and theorists and prospectors who probably needed their rightminding adjusted just a little bit.

But here we were. And home was really far away.

"Singer," I said, trying not to sound too terrified. "What just happened?"

"I wish I knew." A short pause. "No technical fault. No power interrupt. Our white bubble just ... failed."

Farweather hadn't made any moves for the door, despite my turning away from her. It was a big-enough ship that she could get lost in it as easily as I had, if she managed to slip my watch, and the idea of playing cat-and-mouse through this damned ridiculous giant vessel with her again turned my stomach. Fortunately, she didn't seem as if she wanted to brave her own weapons—in my hands now—or maybe it was Singer's attention that was keeping her honest.

Now, under the circumstances, *there* was an infelicitous turn of phrase.

Void, but there was a lot of space out there.

I held my breath, awed by the infinity of darkness. A little terrified by the idea that our alien ship, which we didn't understand, might be busted.

At least we had a Synarche ship with us now. We were not utterly alone. We could have lost them when the bubble collapsed.

The night spread out forever, empty and silent, utterly cold. Except not really empty, if you could sense what I could sense. Laced and knotted, instead, with a network of dark gravity stretchy and heavy and hauling the bright part of the universe unwittingly in line with its predeterminations.

As the conscious mind follows the density of trauma in the psyche, I thought, *so the stars follow this reminder of the primal trauma and let it be their guide across the sky.* And then I laughed at myself for being too pretentious, and reading too much George Eliot when I could.

I would have given a lot for a nice fat copy of *The Mill on the Floss* right about then, I tell you what.

I stretched my silver-limned forehand out to touch the material of the viewport, pressing my fingers against it so hard they tingled. My skin glowed in swirls and filaments, mycorrhizal, shifting emerald-metal webs. Uninsulated, without the shelter of my fox and its regulators, I felt ...

I felt *everything.*

The whole universe was out there, as if it were laid on my skin. As if I were a part of it. Raw to it. Flayed, except it wasn't *painful*, just painfully near. The night was huge, and I was a part of the night, so I was huge, too. Huge, and spread gaspingly diffuse.

So *this* was how Farweather did it. She was stripped off. Flensed. She let the universe get under her skin.

And so the universe showed her all sorts of things that were hidden from me.

I could begin to sense some of it: the weavings and twistings of the underlying structures, and some more of those strange gaps I had noticed on other occasions. The bits of the pattern that were too even, too repetitive. In a complicated sequence, just out of my reach, like . . . ones and zeros in binary code. Like letters in an alphabet. Like amino acids in a DNA code.

Profoundly complicated, but a pattern that could be made to make sense. I could sense it better than I had before, as if I were nearer to it, less mediated, now. Touching it with a bare hand instead of a gloved one. I strained after it, thinking that if I could just get . . . close enough . . . just resolve the meaning of the thing, suddenly so much would be made clear. It was so patently artificial. So patently something that had been *imposed* on the structure of the universe by an intelligence, as opposed to something occurring naturally. The iterations were just too tidy. Intentionally so, as if they had been set up to be noticed.

And between that intentionality, overlaid on it, I could feel, quite suddenly, an enormous swarm of fast-converging shapes.

"We have incoming," Farweather said.

"There's something out here," I told Singer. "I really need that senso online now, so I can share it with you. I don't care about the rightminding or the regulators."

"*I* care about the regulators," he said.

I grimaced, thinking about my erratic behavior. This wasn't really the time to bring it up, though.

But I was spared answering, and probably humiliating myself further, because all that velvet night around us was abruptly full of ghosts.

The observation deck was restfully dim to limit internal reflections. And the windows seemed to be coated, or made of something nonreflective, as well. So if I hadn't had my hand on the transparency, I would have felt that I was standing with no barrier at all between me and the gargantuan shapes of an uncountable number of Ativahikas, drifting out of the darkness, bioluminescing softly.

They were enormous, dark, but limned at the edges against the greater dark beyond. They writhed and lashed in their tattered finery, trailing ragged swaths of elongated skin like the trains of a gown. They shone in the darkness, wiping echoes and afterimages across my dark-adapted retinas.

There were . . . dozens of them. Too many to count, and anyway they were moving, swarming and swirling around us like a flock of mining vessels mobbing an asteroid. Except every single one of them was as long, or longer, than even the enormous Koregoi ship, and mining vessels are generally smaller than the average asteroid.

Singer recovered before I did. *I* stood transfixed. He said. "We've been seeing a lot of these guys."

His words at least shook me partway out of my reverie. "What do you suppose *they* want?"

"It's been a weird trip," Singer replied.

I realized that the swarm was describing a complex pattern, a kind of dance with our ship at the center, unless that was just perspective fooling me. Off our flank, SJV *I'll Explain It To You Slowly* hung, motionless (relatively speaking). Beyond our common ambit, the Ativahikas looped and spiraled around and over and under us and one another, weaving an intricate choreography. I stared, trying to work out the math behind it. Just as it seemed as if it might resolve itself, begin to make a peculiar sense—I thought of Terran honeybees dancing about honey—the pattern changed.

As chorus line dancers part like a sea in order to deliver up the star, the Ativahikas swirled and separated, forming a whirling ring around the gap in their pattern with a swath of night behind.

Through that gap sailed a single entity. An Ativahika that even to my human eyes and experience looked *old*.

Its bioluminescence stuttered and crawled over its hide in waves, brighter at the crests and dimmer in the troughs than what gleamed on the fringed flanks of the surrounding individuals. Its hide had paled from the rich, sheening algal teal of the others to a watery turquoise. Even the swags of its intricate drapes seemed sparse and ablated.

Children, it said, its voice internalized and reverberating through me, and not exactly words—more an impression of meanings. **Why should we not destroy you, and this terrible thing you have done?**

It wasn't entirely unlike getting a senso translation from somebody like Habren. Communication was being intermediated by the parasites, I realized; the Ativahika was speaking to me through the sparkling little mites refined from the body of its dead species-mate.

No wonder it was mad.

I glanced over my shoulder. Farweather, looking stunned, was rotating slowly toward me. She was hearing it, too, and the expression on her face was that of a child suddenly confronted with consequences for a misdemeanor she had been sure she'd gotten away with.

She took a step back, a dark silhouette against the intricate moving patterns of the Ativahikas dancing in the night beyond. "How are they going to destroy us?" she scoffed, a bravado that I knew by now was her response to fear.

Easily, I thought. *Where do you think your ability to manipulate dark gravity comes from?* And that was without even considering their size and probable ability to just smash the Koregoi boat.

But saying that would have been pointless, arguing with her a waste of my energy when I needed to focus on the Ativahika and on not dying. And I had no idea how to communicate with the enormous creature who hung beyond the observation deck's bank of windows, drifting so close

I could see the plasticky, impermeable texture of its hide. An eye as big as an insystem skiff loomed over me, a vast elongated face wreathed in drifting tendrils.

It was huge. Inexpressibly huge, like being stared down by a space ship. I took a step forward and pressed my hands against the window once again. The enormous creature's presence was magnetic. And it wasn't as if running away would protect me from it, when all it had to do to deal with me was to disassemble the ship.

I guessed we'd just answered the question once and for all of exactly how sapient the Ativahikas were. And how they communicated. Which begged the question of exactly how I was going to communicate with *it*.

Well, it seemed to have no difficulty making itself understood to me. So I resolved that I would just . . . try to talk, and see what happened.

"I am deeply and profoundly sorry," I said. "It was not by my choice, what happened. And I did not understand immediately what I had become infected with."

You went to the ship of the murderers.

"I did," I said. Honesty was pretty obviously the best policy here. Not just for ethical reasons, but because when you're confronted with a super-powerful alien who is already in possession of rather a lot of inside information, it's probably best not to get caught in a lie.

What was your purpose in going there, if you are not yourself a murderer?

"I went to salvage a derelict ship, so that its materials could be reused and so that, perhaps, the hulk could be rescued and repurposed. I did not realize until after I had entered the ship what its purpose was and what crimes the ship had been engaged in."

And yet, you contain the symbiote.

"I contracted it by accident." My palms were leaving mists of water vapor on the window where I leaned. I scrubbed them dry on my shirt.

That explanation left out Farweather, but honestly she was welcome to do her own explaining. The Ativahikas would have to crush the Koregoi ship anyway, to get to her, and let's be even more honest, since we're already neck-deep in honesty: they couldn't do that without destroying me and quite possibly Singer as well.

So I was going to keep saying "I." Assuming the Ativahikas even understood the difference between singular and plural pronouns, or how Terran humans tended to define the boundaries of self, I had no desire to get Singer or Connla (if Connla was even still alive) into trouble with the Ativahika.

Farweather was on her own, though. I wasn't taking a fall for a mass murderer.

I expected the Ativahika's next question to be something along the lines of "How do I know if you're telling me the truth?" but it did not even appear to consider my lying as a possibility. I wondered if that meant it had some way of telling, or if the concept of being bullshitted was as alien to the Ativahika's experience as the Ativahika itself was to me.

What it said instead was, **How would you use this gift, if you were allowed to keep it?**

Well, that stumped me. Or stunned me into silence, more precisely.

What had I planned to do, before I got derailed by being kidnapped by pirates?

"I'd use it for the good of the systers," I said. "Under the direction of our Synarche. I'd use it to help people."

I knew it was true as I said it. It had a sense of purpose to it that I liked. It made me feel like I was going somewhere, and maybe even knew where that somewhere was.

But you are fleeing the Synarche ship. And you are not going to the Core. You are going to a stronghold of the murderers.

"Yeah," I said. "About that."

Hoping Singer would jump into the conversation, I looked around. But of course he could only hear my side of it, because he hadn't rebooted and reconnected to my senso yet. Across the deck, Farweather didn't seem to be having a conversation of her own. Instead, she drifted steadily closer to me, her mouth congealing into a thin line. *She* could obviously hear both sides of the conversation, unless the ancient Ativahika was saying something different to her.

What *was* the natural life expectancy of an Ativahika, anyway? How long *did* it take for one such as this to get *old*? Not merely old, I judged, looking at the creature again. But venerable. I wondered if it knew the lore of the Koregoi, and if it could share that information with the systers. And what we could possibly offer in exchange to induce it to do so.

It was conceivable—conceivable, and perhaps even plausible—that the very Ativahika to whom I was speaking right this very instant was old enough in its own person to remember our forerunners. I wished I had the opportunity to ask it and find out. But right now, somehow, didn't seem to be the appropriate time for it.

Maybe some other occasion would present itself, when I wasn't being interrogated on suspicion of capital crimes.

About that, the ancient one said.

Not words. Not colloquial language, such as I had used. But a sense of it echoing the sentiment I'd just expressed, and reinforcing it.

Please. Tell me more.

So.

I did.

I told it that we had followed ancient roadmarks to the mothballed vessel we were now in, and I told it that before its people had managed to drag us down out of white space, we had been out of control, on autopilot, and that the shipmind and I had been working to hack—or unhack!—the ship to regain control of her. I did not ask it how the hell it and its species-mates had managed to locate us in white space, of all the impossible tricks, nor how they had managed to contact, grapple, and stop us, hauling us back into the unfolded world. If that was what, indeed, had happened.

I did not tell it specifically that Farweather had been involved in the death of the Ativahika we'd found orbiting the Jothari factory ship, or that she'd murdered the Jothari crew. I did not tell it that she was responsible for our previous trajectory, because that would have resulted in physical problems for her, and perhaps physical and definitely ethical problems for me. I didn't mention her at all.

It turned out I needn't have wasted my time playing liar-by-omission, anyway, because apparently the Ativahika already knew more about Farweather than they'd been letting on. As I found out when the ancient one said to me, **And would you send your shipmate to face our justice? The one like you, not the shipmind.**

"I won't argue that she doesn't deserve whatever justice you have in mind for her," I said. "But what do you mean by 'send' her?"

Its catfishy face hung against a night scattered with only a few dim stars. Tendrils and fronds writhed around a long, lipless mouth designed to gnaw water and minerals from space debris, under conditions where water was a stone. It was so close beside our motionless ship that I could have touched it, or nearly, if there had not been windows and the hull in the way. I could not take it all in at once. I could glance at an eye, the fronds, the smoothly shaded aquamarine skin. But it was too big and too close for me to see it as all of a thing.

We can crush your ship, if you prefer.

Not exactly my ship, but there are times to split hairs. And times to do something else, instead.

"I know that," I said. My stomach felt like it was boiling.

And yet you protect that creature.

I didn't have an answer. "I don't want to protect her, exactly. She doesn't need or want my protection, I imagine. But I don't want to be complicit in her death."

Do you think it—she—would protect you?

I felt it correcting itself, trying to understand the concepts I was expressing and searching its own referents for an analogy. I don't think it had any idea what *he* or *she* or *it* referred to. Just that they were arbitrary categories of some kind that were important to me, for whatever reason, so it would try to abide by them.

"No," I said. "Actually, I'm confident that she'd hang me out a window the second you asked, if our positions were reversed."

You did not lie for it.

"I did not." I guess it could tell if I was being truthful, after all.

It's always a good idea to play it safe when you can. Well, unless you're Connla. He has—had?—a knack for getting away with things.

Hope was a terrible thing, I reminded myself. I could not afford to feel it.

You did not volunteer information either.

"I was pretty sure that if I did tell you—I mean, you, the Ativahika—everything I knew about Farweather, well. You lot would probably insist on me dragging her to an airlock and turning her over to you, space suit or no space suit, and I didn't really want to be a party to that."

Why does it not speak for itself?

I looked over at Farweather. Her eyes were dilated, and she had dropped down to a crouch, resting her palms against the deck.

I said, "Perhaps she does not know what to say."

There was a fairly long silence then. Well, obviously, the Ativahika's entire part of the conversation was silent because it was in my head. But it stopped . . . speaking? Sending impressions? And I fell still.

Inside the ship I could hear the tick of metal, the sounds that temperature control and life support made, the shuffle of Farweather's foot. Outside there was silence, as there is and has been and always should be. The perfect silence of the spheres.

I wanted her punished. But I didn't think it was my place to be judge and jury and all of Justice, to pass sentence on her and hand her over to alien laws. It was petty and unworthy of me, but I wished suddenly that she would just turn herself over to them and save me all the bother and the damned wrestling with my damned ethics.

And . . . that *also* would have involved me dragging her to the airlock, and I was trying to avoid killing anybody todia. Out of cowardice or queasiness, probably, because it wasn't as if she didn't *deserve* a good airlocking, and my fox was still turned off, but I still couldn't quite bring myself to frog-march her down there and kick her out the door into space for the Ativahika to do whatever Ativahika do to alien murderers.

I was a damned piece of work my own self, wasn't I?

The ancient one had been silent for a long time, and I was finding it really unsettling. My palms itched. I couldn't hear Farweather shifting anymore, or even breathing, but I also hadn't heard her run out or collapse to the floor and Singer hadn't said anything to warn me, so I figured she was still frozen in the same place. There was enough light outside now—the bioluminescence of the Ativahika—that picking out her reflection behind me had gotten challenging.

Well, it wouldn't be the first time I had counted on Singer to watch my back.

You will seek your own kind's justice upon her.

Now I really wanted to glance over at her. To wink, as if to reassure her. But I knew that wink would be a lie, and I knew the Ativahika would know it.

It's curiously impossible to contemplate an outright lie, even to a third party, with a wise, weird face of a truth-detecting alien hanging over you.

I sighed in self-disgust and said, "I am. I mean, I am doing that. As much as is in my power. Yes."

Singer was so quiet I wondered if he'd crashed. I heard Farweather's intake of breath, though. Fight-or-flight reflex, preparing herself to run.

Then you have made pact with us. See that this justice is served, and with you we have no further quarrel.

"You're just going to let us go?"

It didn't echo my sigh, of course, since its respiration was an entirely internal exchange between it and its blue-green algae symbiotes. But I still got a sense of parental weariness across our connection. **You and the other intelligence on your ship are innocent. I will not destroy two innocents to punish one guilty one. That would not be justice. That would merely be blood.**

That was the moment when Singer's silence was explained. He must have finished his check on my fox, because my emotional regulation suddenly came online.

I reeled. *Warn a girl!* I snapped, reflexively—

—and wonder of wonders, Singer heard me. *Sorry,* he said. *I wasn't sure of that working.*

Well, it worked all right, I suppose. And now I'm on the floor, and where is Farweather?

I shoved to my hands and my knees, though that was as far as I felt safe going. Everything whirled, as if I had just gotten off a spinning trajectory or punctured an eardrum in a sudden pressure drop.

Haimey, get up! Singer yelled.

CHAPTER 24

R EADER, I TRIED.

I shoved at the deck, hard enough that if we had been under microgravity I would have launched myself. But there was the problem: a lifetime of limited exposure to g-forces and my own reflexes betrayed me.

I levered myself right off the floor and right into the arc of Farweather's weapon. It struck me with full force and follow-through. She'd been aiming to do murder.

The good news was that because Singer had yelled, and I had shoved myself upright, it hit me squarely between the shoulder blades and not on the occiput. The bad news was that when that's your good news, you'd better be prepared to be a hurting unit.

I sprawled back down to the deck, breath whooping out of me, this time with no intention of moving. If Singer bellowed another warning, I might just let that pirate asshole kill me.

She didn't take another swing, though. The next thing I heard, other than the sound of my own agonized exhalation, was the thumping of her feet on the deck plates as she legged it for the hatch. She must have still been able to override Singer on some things, too, because she got through it.

"What did she hit me with?" I wheezed eventually.

"The wrench," Singer said resignedly. "The one you clipped to the chain earlier."

"Of course she did," I answered. "Fuck. I guess I was distracted."

I lay there for a little while. When I opened my eyes, I was surprised to see the Ativahikas were still outside, and still performing their firefly dances.

One more thing, said the ancient one. **Those anomalies you noticed. The 'pinpricks in the universe.' I see the memory within you.**

I saw it too, the image called up either by association or by the Ativahika manipulating my visual cortex somehow. Back when I'd first started exploring my new senses. I'd thought it had looked like a kitten had left claw holes in some fabric shading a light source.

You should follow them.

I gritted my teeth and managed to squeeze out a few more words. "I beg your pardon?"

Someone on the other end requires your help, it said.

"But I don't know how to get there! I don't *know* how to follow them!"

I can see the coordinates in your mind, the Ativahika said peaceably. **We presume one of you fragile ones must have derived them from a map in a probe left behind by the Before. We have found such objects in our wanderings.**

I tried to push myself into a crouch. The world went a little swirly. *I don't understand what you mean, my systers—*

The Ativahika eddied and churned, their unceasing dance altering and opening. Like children playing follow-the-leader in a zero-g park, they made a sudden flocking whirlpool, and then the whole parliament of them streamed away in a fluid formation. The ancient one remained behind a moment more, its eyes still on me.

Remember your commitment, it said.

But then, with a flash of its filaments like an old queen swirling a ragged cloak that had once been fine, it too whirled and was gone.

I shoved myself up. This time I didn't fall over. I regretted it, but at least I had a better view of the departing Ativahikas.

"Like I could forget!" I yelled after it.

"I overheard that last bit," Singer said. "What are you going to do now?"

I sighed. "Bring Farweather to custody, I suppose."

"If you can catch her."

"Thanks for the vote of confidence, Singer," I said, and eased myself back down onto the deck plates to wait for the universe to stop spinning. A futile hope; it's been whirling around out there for a very long time, and as far as I know, nobody really expects it to stop doing so anytime soon.

I was lucky my skull wasn't shattered. I was equally lucky my spine seemed to be intact, because this far from decent medical attention, that was nearly as likely to serve as a fatal injury, no matter what sort of clever things the clever people at Core General could do with stem cells and grafts and spliced or replicated DNA these diar.

I was also winded, sore, bruised, befuddled, and angry. Angry mostly at myself, because I was the idiot who had left Farweather in possession of that wrench. Which sounds like a euphemism, but in this case was just an honest appraisal of my own somewhat crucial capacity for error.

Singer fiddled with that anger a little. I felt it start to drain away and said, "No, leave me alone."

"Are you thinking clearly?"

It was a fair question, and I had to consider it. But the thing was, my thought process felt absolutely crystalline. I was so mad that I had gone through it and come right back out the other side of muddled thinking into a kind of clarity I was pretty sure I had never experienced before.

"I think I'm fine," I told him, and set about assessing how much damage had been done. "How come *you* didn't catch her on the way out the door?"

"Oh." A pause, either because he was assessing or because he thought that pausing would reveal his embarrassment. Possibly both. "Well, my control over the ship's functions and sensors is . . . not entirely complete. Yet."

"Of course not."

"I'm working on it."

I sat on the floor and stretched myself upright. "Can you at least *locate* her?"

"Unfortunately, she appears to be employing countermeasures."

"Well, that's ideal."

Although really, considering the state of my back, I didn't think I had lot of latitude for criticism.

"Do you have her locked out of your systems?"

"Tight as I can make them. She might try sabotage."

"Lock her out of all the places I have gear stored, too, if you can." I thought about role reversal for a moment, and how we'd swapped places since we came on board. Now I had her stuff, and she was hiding out and would probably be eating algae as soon as she found the algae tanks.

I wasn't going to go pursuing her through the blind alleys of this very large ship, however. I had her weapons ... but she had a wrench. And was, pretty obviously, the much more skilled fighter of the two of us, for all I'd gotten the drop on her the first time.

"Just get us moving back toward the Core as soon as you can, please? I want to make contact with the Interceptor, also. I'm available for wrench and blowtorch work whenever you need it. Assuming we can find another wrench, I mean."

I went back to stretching.

A few moments passed while I mused on security and how to keep Farweather from repirating the ship Singer and I—with help from the Ativahikas—had just depirated.

"Haimey," Singer said, somewhat hesitantly.

"Deep time, what is it now?" I had lain down on my face and was trying a few cobra stretches to loosen my spasming, brutalized muscles.

"I hate to break this to you now. But apparently, we have company."

As I levered myself upright, I groaned. My first few steps were stumbling torture. By the time I reached the windows, though, I was loosening up just a little. I used the frame to push myself up straight and heard my spine pop.

Where the Ativahika had vanished, we could see the outline of the Synarche Interceptor that had been stopped inside our white rings. There was a sparkling bubble of a shuttlecraft detaching itself from the Interceptor and moving toward us.

"If we're lucky, that might be the cavalry. I've still got questions about how they found us and matched our bubble in white space, though. How'd they know when to stop?"

"They must have been following our white space scar."

"At *speed*? Is that possible?"

"Well, you sensed them back there. So I'd say it's possible and probable both, since the hypothesis fits the facts as we're aware of them," Singer said. "I mean, based on the part where we're here. And so are they."

It was probably time to admit he had me beat. "All right. Possibly Justice has tech they don't share," I agreed. "Singer, do you have any idea what the remaining range of this vessel is? How are we doing for food and stores?"

"There's a lot of room in here," he said. "In this ship's computing core, I mean. And plenty of supplies, if I'm reading this manifest right. But I'm afraid I can't support making a run for it to elude a duly appointed governmental representative of the Synarche authority, Haimey," Singer said.

His tone was dry. I snorted in appreciation. "Actually, I was wondering how much help we need to ask for in order to get home."

"That's an interesting question," he responded. "Because this ship seems to be violating the laws of physics as currently conceived, at least where it comes to energy consumption. It's impossibly efficient, and we seem to have enough left for a few laps around the Milky Way."

"I guess we can still learn a few things from the Koregoi engineers."

"We're in quite good shape, unless I'm missing something."

"Can you figure out how to hail that Synarche ship?"

"Hailing," he answered. Whatever he was saying must have been working, because they weren't training their fairly impressive suite of weapons on us.

Because Singer multitasked pretty well even back in his old, smaller digs, I didn't scruple to ask, "I had a paper book, on your old hull."

"Wilson," he said. "Was it important?"

I told him about the numbers. The possibility that it might have been a book code.

He asked, "Do you remember the numbers? Your fox—"

"I know," I said. He'd rebooted it, but the old machine memories were gone, wiped. It was as smooth and clean and new as an infant right out of the tank farms. "I remember them."

"How?"

I grinned. "Koregoi senso. They seemed like they might be important, so I encoded them in a microgravitic function in the structure of the Prize's hull."

If he were a human, I think he would have been gawping at me. "That's brilliant."

I shrugged. "If I didn't live, I figured my corpse had very little chance of making it to a download station, so—"

I sighed.

"But we don't have the book."

"Oh, that," Singer said. "Um."

"Singer?"

"I scanned it," he admitted.

"You *what?*"

"I couldn't help myself," he said. "It was novel data!"

I stopped.

He stopped.

"Gautama and nine little bodhisattvas on a tricycle," I said. "Who taught you to pun like that?"

"Welcome home, Haimey," he said.

I made sure I hadn't left anything interesting lying around, and started back toward the cabin where Farweather had been bunking. All the food and tools where there, and I didn't really want to leave it unguarded. With luck, though, maybe I could use some of the constables who were likely to be staffing that Interceptor to help me quarter the ship, and take Farweather into custody.

That would be great! Promise to the Ativahika kept!

Except they were likely to take me into custody too. Well, you couldn't have everything.

In the meantime, I could get started cracking that book code.

"Haimey," Singer said cautiously, as I was trying to figure out some means of dogging the hatch behind me. If it were a normal, Synarche metal door, I would even have considered spot-welding it to keep Farweather out, on the theory that I could always break the weld later. Or maybe settled for just barring it with a piece of alien equipment of questionable provenance.

Since it was—best guess—a nanotech utility fog, I just asked Singer to lock it out from any override control except for mine.

Having done that, he said, "I've got a response from the Interceptor."

His tone and careful delivery made me cautious, too. "What's wrong?"

"Nothing," he said. "I have some good news for you."

A flare of hope went off in my chest, so bright and terrible I almost tuned to ignore it. "It's Connla, isn't it?"

"Yes," he said. "It is. And that launch is on its way over to collect you."

Whatever the internal vibrational frequency of my body was, I had reached it. I was as profoundly wired as it is possible for a human to be without the assistance of introduced chemicals, and that was after tuning it back a little. My hands didn't shake only because the seat ahead of me on the launch had padded grab rails and I was clutching them. The acceleration that pressed me back into my chair was gentle enough so that I didn't have to let go.

We docked, and I was floating inside the restraints. I felt like I was holding a breath, and had taken another breath on top of it. I fumbled my restraints when I went to unfasten them, which was a pretty magical accomplishment, considering that they had a quick release and I'd spent literally my entire life opening restraints and I was finally back in the comfort of zero g again. And that was *with* my nerves tuned way down. If I'd been trying to do this without my fox, I think I would have been catatonic in the corner.

Except I had done it without my fox. I had done all sorts of things without my fox, and while I'd been labile, weepy, angry, and generally deregulated with a head that was a no-fun place to live inside of, I had still done them. I had. Me. Or whoever I'd convinced myself to pretend to be while the person I'd been programmed to be was offline temporarily.

Who the hell was I, anyway?

You know, I had no idea.

I still dialed it back a little more since I had the option. When I had finished, I was as far as I felt I could safely go without making myself groggy. I didn't want to be dulled, unpresent. But taking the edge off could only help my focus.

Two constables—one human and one Vanlian, and both officers rather than full Goodlaws—met me at the airlock and escorted me into the Interceptor. They were kind enough not to attempt small talk beyond a few soothing pleasantries that let me know where the head was and that I wasn't in immediate trouble. I also introduced myself to the shipmind, as was polite, and SJV *I'll Explain It To You Slowly* was pleasant and personable. The crew called her Splain.

It was strange, moving freely without gravity again after so long. It was stranger being around people who weren't my enemy and only company all rolled into one.

They took me to the bridge—a ship this size, with a reasonably big crew, had something a little more formal than a command cabin.

And there was Connla.

He was wearing the pilot's dusty-blacks we'd never bothered with on Singer, and he looked dashing as hell. He had a cat in his arms. A spotted orange, white, and black cat. Shedding all over his crisp uniform. He was looking at me. The cat was Bushyasta.

"You lucky son of a tramper captain," I said. "I should have known that flying."

I started to cry. I kicked over to him and held out my arms.

He gave me my cat.

I hugged Bushyasta. She purred and snuggled into me, but didn't open her eyes.

Tears behave strangely under gravity, and on the Koregoi ship I'd done enough deregulated crying about everything that I'd gotten used to the way they broke their surface tension and streaked down my cheeks, requiring no further maintenance. Now they swelled from the surface of my eye, blindingly obvious and blurring my vision completely.

I turned away so Connla wouldn't see. Tears made him uncomfortable, and him being uncomfortable made me shy.

I gulped and said, "I swear there's something wrong with this cat. Low blood sugar. Narcolepsy."

"That cat just has a clear conscience," he said. "Singer mentioned that you had a stowaway?"

"Yes," I said. "Two of the constables who came over stayed on the ship to keep an eye out for her. And to make sure she didn't take off with it while I was over here." Not that she stood much chance of hotwiring it with Singer inhabiting its brain.

That was when Mephistopheles zoomed out from behind the control console, ricocheted off my legs hard enough to start me spinning, then snagged her nails in the carpet and settled into position with her ears flat and her back firmly pointed in my direction.

"You would not believe how they scratched me up," Connla said. "I stuffed them inside my suit after the hull integrity blew out. We were all just lucky we were aft, and they were already in their skins and webbed in."

I had been weeping more or less genteelly. At that, I lost control completely. I clutched the damn narcoleptic cat and sobbed and couldn't stop myself spinning even when my afthands bounced off a bulkhead or two. I'd probably have drifted helplessly around the Interlocutor's bridge if Connla hadn't snagged my elbow and steered me to rest.

Connla isn't big on touching people.

He hooked his lower extremity on a support rail, wrapped both arms around me, and pulled me against his broad, well-muscled (they're gengineered for it, on Spartacus) chest. He embraced me with one hand while he stroked my hair with the other, squeezing me tighter until the cat trapped between us made a protesting noise.

"You have hair," he said, when I'd slowed down a little.

"Couldn't read enough alien to figure out which bottle in the bathroom was the depilatory," I joked. I wiped tears and snot on his shoulder.

He didn't complain.

"I have a surprise for you," Connla said, and the tone in his voice indicated that he thought it would be a pleasant one.

"You *are* a surprise for me," I retorted, my hands full of ecstatic cats. Any moment now they were likely to decide that the greeting had gone on long enough and commence Reunion Stage Two: The Spurning of Haimey for Her Absence, Again. But for now I was going to bask in the affection as long as it was still coming down.

"I honestly was afraid we'd never catch you," Connla said. Not easily, the way most people would, but with a little edge of self-conscious nervousness over the vulnerability. But that didn't matter, because—wonder of wonders—here was Connla, and he was talking about his feelings of his own accord, without any chasing, prying, or prompting.

Who says progress is measured over generations?

"I missed you too," I said, drifting along behind him. He seemed to be leading me back toward the crew quarters. This vessel was significantly bigger than the tug had been, but in addition to its twinned white bands it had massive engines and a respectable range of weaponry. It also boasted a crew complement sizable enough to field squads of constables capable of dealing with those occasional violent impolitenesses to which even a rightminded society can be prone.

The combination of those things made it one of the most cramped and claustrophobic space ships I personally have ever been on.

The tug had been small. And yet, by comparison, its tiny crew and plan of two mostly open cabins had given it a sense of airiness. This ship, by contrast, had no gangways, no open-plan cabins. Each tiny space opened directly onto one to three others, and in many of those cabins were people—eating, sleeping, playing games.

So many people. So many of them—going about their paramilitary routines with no reason to pause or to acknowledge me at all. A few, polite or lonely, took a moment to raise a hand or nod a chin or wave a tendril or flick an ear as we went by. The vast majority, though, were either sleeping or bent to their tasks without allowing themselves distraction.

So *many* people. So incredibly many. I literally had no idea what to do. I felt surrounded. Oppressed. Even stalked.

I had obviously been spending *way* too much time alone.

I knew it was foolish. It was just that I had been away from people other than Farweather for a very long time. I had been deregulated a long time, and only reregulated for a matter of minutes. And the result was a learned anxiety response that was not helpful to me or to anyone right now—that was, in fact, maladaptive in the extreme.

It made me angry to be so reactive. Which of course was just the same damned reactivity again. Connla's promise of a "good" surprise had been good strategy on his part, an indication that he knew me. I hated surprises. But he also knew that my curiosity was bottomless.

We swam into the final hatchway. Connla, ahead of me, cleared it. And I found myself confronted with a small cabin that from this vantage point looked to be networked with a forest of what appeared to be bamboo, except it was all growing at random angles. I stopped in the hatchway, which was a stupid thing to do, and after a moment's more inspection I realized that the bamboo was, in fact, giant exoskeletal legs, and a lot of them.

Being paused in the hatchway was even less safe on a ship than on a station. As I hung there, braced on the lip with both forehands, a small head jeweled with vast, faceted eyes turned to regard me.

"Cheeirilaq?"

Friend Haimey, it answered. *Please do move into the cabin. I should despair if anything untoward befell you.*

Cats and all, I drifted into the cabin. The cats seemed undisturbed by the presence of a massive, predatory alien. I assumed that a *sentient* insect could be counted on not to eat pets, so I turned them loose to wander around. Or, in Bushyasta's case, to drift, leaving a trail of tiny kitty snores.

As for me? I put a hand out and steadied myself against one of Cheeirilaq's scaffolding of legs. It didn't seem to mind. And in so doing, I realized why the cabin seemed so very full of not-bamboo. Cheeirilaq had braced itself into position in the center of the small chamber with its limbs wedging it against each available plane. It looked like a secure position. I hoped it was comfortable.

"Well," I said. "I was not prepared to meet you all the way out here, Goodlaw."

It lifted one foot daintily and gently tried to dislodge Mephistopheles, who had tackled one of its enormous legs with both front paws and was bunny-kicking its exoskeleton. At least, fairly gently. I didn't think the claws would get through.

The pleased surprise is mutual, it said.

It was so *nice* to have a working fox again.

"Do you require assistance?"

Cheeirilaq put its frondlike foot down again. The cat was still wrestling with its ankle. *Your small friend seems unlikely to harm me. Is it an infant?*

"No, it just acts like one. It is a pet. So, what does bring you out here to the nether reaches, then?"

I expected it to say something about having been sent to retrieve the Koregoi ship. I was not prepared for what actually came out of my translator.

I was following you. Or rather, I was following your pirate captain, because of her links to Habren. If we can get them both into custody, it increases the likelihood that one of them can be induced to provide evidence.

"She's not mine!" I protested.

It made the laughter sound. *We were very much afraid that when— if—we reclaimed the Koregoi ship, you and Singer would be found to have perished. All aboard are relieved at your safety and well-being. Do you have Captain Farweather in custody?*

"Ah," I said. "So there's a funny story about that."

I proceeded to tell it, in three-part harmony. Connla was hanging silently beside the porthole and watching, half melted into the background, so it would save me having to tell it twice, anyway. Halfway through it Cheeirilaq noticed me yawning and sent out for stimulants, which I drank gratefully before finishing my story off and adding, "So if you're chasing Habren, how come you're out here after Farweather instead of back on Downthehatch?"

I spent enough time there. And I know that the pirate has a link to Habren. I need to know whether they're partners, or whether Habren is a victim of extortion before we proceed.

"And Habren is your special project."

"Dirty as hell," Connla said. "And just a little too smart to get snagged on it."

Yet.

Connla said, "We've had some time to compare notes, and we're pretty sure that Habren was the source of the intel that lured us out to that sunforsaken sector in the first place, actually. Though the goal of that—"

"I came to the same conclusion. And what I think is that Farweather wanted to get her hands on me," I said. "That's what the booby trap on the Jothari ship was for."

"Huh?" Connla blinked his large, bright blue eyes at me. "I don't get it."

"Backstory," I said. I was suddenly much too tired to explain all the nonsense with my memories being altered and my juvenile record for terrorism and how my clade, my mothers and sisters, had used me as a weapon of mass destruction and then cut me loose as soon as I was inconvenient—and *then* abandoned me utterly and completely. I had nothing but rage, and I had no place to put that rage, so expressing it seemed pointless. "She used to know an ex-girlfriend of mine who was mixed up in some shady stuff. She thought maybe I had some additional information she would find useful."

Connla tilted his head at exactly the same angle that Cheeirilaq was using, but they both let it slide. I suspected Cheeirilaq, being a Goodlaw, probably had more information about the whole mess than I did.

Connla said, "And she's at large in the Koregoi ship."

"Yep." I stretched against the ache in my back. "Sorry about that."

Well, it can't be helped. I guess we shall just have to go over there and fetch her.

"Cheeirilaq, no."

Its head swiveled to assess me with first one flittering teardrop eye, and then the other. *I beg your pardon?*

"The Koregoi ship. It's under gravity. A little heavier than Terran standard, I think." I shook my head. "Too much for me, anyway. Or nearly. You can't go over there."

There is much in what you say.

I almost thought it was a joke. How can you tell when a giant insect is winking?

Then it said, *Well, we'll just have to figure out how to lower the settings on the gravity, won't we? What good luck that we have such an exceptionally competent engineer!*

And an artificial intelligence who has gotten control of the ship's systems, I thought, but that seemed like it could be explained later.

Connla and the cats joined me in the lighter on the way back over, together with a couple of peace officers. He leaned his head back against the headrest and closed his eyes. For such a madcap pilot, he was always pretty neurotic when somebody else was flying—even if they were flying sedately.

I stared out the window, looking from ship to ship until I was distracted by Connla muttering, "Your friend the grasshopper is pretty cool."

"I like it," I said, trying not to sound too brittle. I was having an emotional dia. Mephistopheles mewed from her spot in a carrier under the seat in front of me. I hoped she would not be singing the traveling song of her people the entire way back. It was probably just a protest about being cooped up, however, because she settled down after a complaint or two, and that allowed us both to relax a little.

He still didn't open his eyes. He just rocked his head back and forth. When he quieted, and I thought he was dozing off, he surprised me again by saying, "What are we going to do when we get home?"

I blinked at him. "Home."

We were going home to the Synarche. Assuming we lived through catching Farweather, but we had a pretty good set of backups now.

That reminded me: I needed to send Cheeirilaq a message about Farweather being potentially rigged to blow up. Good news, good news. I wondered what the Freeporters thought a reasonable commute time from the Core to whatever pathforsaken outpost we'd been headed for was. I never had gotten around to asking her.

I fired that off quickly, before I again forgot about it. Then I remembered that my fox could remember these things for me again, and felt like an idiot.

I hoped Singer hadn't noticed.

Connla grimaced and kicked the deck at his feet, missing the cat's cage. It was Bushyasta anyway. She was unlikely to take offense, let alone so much as notice anything except a dollop of cat food under her nose. "You and Singer. Where am I going?"

I grimaced back, but I didn't kick anything. My afthands were still too damn sore from all the damn gravity.

Gravity I was going back to now. Sigh.

Well, nobody loves a whiner.

"Wherever you want, I guess, given what you can do," I said. I pointed to our escort, the Interceptor, receding as the launch took us back toward the Koregoi vessel. "The constables seem pretty excited to have you on as a pilot. That doesn't seem like dull work."

He blew air out through his nostrils. I had no idea why he was being so sulky, and I didn't like it.

"I've done something to make you unhappy."

"It's not you," he said at last. He shook his head, the ponytail whipping. If we hadn't been strapped in he would have shaken himself right out of the chair. "I just . . . you and Singer have a life to go to. You have a place, and important work. I'm . . . going to wind up doing milk runs or something."

It was so strange to look at this man, this friend, and see an echo of all my own insecurities and fears of inadequacy and abandonment.

"You know," I said, "I've been feeling really sad about you going off to have adventures and be a fancy pilot while I get to go to the Core and play test subject for the foreseeable future. I don't want to do that. I want to go out and crawl around space with Singer and the cats and you."

"Nice to know I get billed under Bushyasta," he said. But he was smiling.

"Do you want to stay together?" I asked. "It seemed presumptuous to ask, before."

"I want to not feel disinvited from the party."

"Never," I said, pretty sure Singer would entirely agree. "Why didn't you mention this earlier?"

He shrugged. "Why didn't you mention how you were feeling?"

"Because it's *feelings*," I said. "And *feelings* are terrible. Also I didn't want to guilt-trip you."

"Right," he said. "Me either." He looked out the window. "Feelings are terrible."

But I could see the reflection of his smile in the glass.

• • •

We docked and lugged the cats on board the Koregoi ship, through the blasted gravity. All that gravity. I hadn't missed it a bit. The cats objected pretty strenuously to the whole concept, and the complaints started as soon as we brought their carriers off the launch.

Well, in all honesty, they hadn't exactly taken to the launch's acceleration kindly, either.

When Mephistopheles and Bushyasta were safely ensconced in our makeshift control cabin slash throbbing nerve center of the salvaged ship, and crews of constables were busy bringing over supplies, Connla and I set out to learn where the controls for the artificial gravity were. And how to adjust them. If we couldn't turn the gravity off, maybe we could at least turn it down to something a little more manageable. That seemed like a better option anyway, given that the Koregoi vessel was not optimized to be navigated in free fall.

Considering that we had two irritable felines attempting to impersonate tortillas on the deck, and a low-grav Goodlaw who couldn't wait to join the crew—and considering that my cartilage had been compressing at an alarming rate and that I was already centimeters shorter than when I'd come on board, figuring the gravity out seemed like the most urgent use of our time.

Singer was an enormous help, once he and Connla finished up the inevitable tearful reunion. All right, in complete honesty, it wasn't nearly as tearful as my reunion with Connla and the cats had been. But in my defense, Connla wasn't recently deregulated. And he did show a lot of the tenderer emotions, for him at least.

Singer was still locked out of a bunch of the ship, which was both *fantastic* news and Farweather's doing. And she seemed to be doing something to keep me from tracking her through the Koregoi senso. Possibly the same thing I was doing to keep her guessing about where I was.

The ship was big—confirmed!—but it wasn't *that* large. We had a rough idea of where she might be, but that was based on a map of the places Singer could not access, and of course if she was really clever she'd block whatever places she could and then convince the ship's sensors to ignore her and build a nest somewhere else. I didn't know that she could do that. But I didn't know she couldn't, either. And finding one rogue human concealed in the kilometers of twisty tunnels and chambers and corridors and crawlways and closets and tubes that made up the Prize's habitable interior spaces was beyond the immediate capabilities of any of us. Even the AI.

We resorted, at last, to setting constables to patrolling in pairs on a random pattern, while we ourselves searched for the source of the artificial gravity through the simple and somewhat ridiculous measure of having me walk through the ship waving my hands like a charlatan with a dowsing rod looking for gold or veins of oxygen. I was feeling for what I can only describe as gravity currents. The curious thing was that they were there, and that they were definitely noticeable.

I just followed them along until we got close to a source. It was like following the thumping of some unbalanced piece of machinery by tracing its vibrations in the bulkheads to their point of greatest intensity. And, from there, figuring out what in the Well was malfunctioning.

Except in this case nothing was malfunctioning, obviously. And once we found the source—a machine room, similar to a dozen other machine rooms I had located over the course of my explorations—we weren't any closer to figuring out how any of it worked.

We were concerned with messing with it; the odds of squashing everybody on board or creating a tiny artificial black hole or some even less predictable outcome seemed pretty high if we just went in and started swapping wires around randomly. So we took a poll and decided to let Singer do it.

Fortunately, knowing the physics behind the thing was not terribly important—to this task, at least. All we needed right now was enough access for Singer to figure out how to operate the controls.

That took him about a standard dia, give or take a few hours. If it had been me . . . well, we would still be floating out there in space. If we weren't smashed flat.

It was a blissful relief when he—without fanfare—turned the gravity down. Not off, for all the reasons I mentioned before regarding the design of the ship, and also because artificial gravity was what the Prize used in lieu of acceleration couches. (And don't ask me how that worked. I'm just a simple engineer.) But he set it low enough to be comfortable for a pack of undermuscled space rats and their feline overlords, and also low enough to make Cheeirilaq's continued existence possible.

While we were waiting for Singer to sort that out, and while Connla and I were making friends with the six constables who would be the body of the Prize crew (all right, he was already friends with all of them, but I'm terrible at making friends), that was when I made an even *more* interesting discovery.

We were playing a Banititlan card game called tmyglick with Sergeant Halbnovalk at the time. Halbnovalk was a medic, which made her instantly my favorite crewmate.

The game is played with a deck of 343 cards, since Banititlans have three opposable digits on one manipulator and four on the other, leaving them with the lopsided profile of a Terran lobster—and it involves aspects similar to concentration, war, and gin rummy. Anyway, I was losing badly (base seven is murder to calculate in and worse to convert from, and the senso only helps so much when you need to be building card strategies), and my mind started to wander. I was still sort of in the mode I had been in for the past dia or so, feeling after the gravitational patterns of the ship, and when I unfocused and found myself staring out the window in a meditative state of mind . . . I saw something. A kind of standing wave, or interference pattern, superimposed on the universe as if I were looking through two misaligned pieces of polarizing glass.

When the sky outside shifted in front of me, I yelped like a stepped-on kitten.

"Haimey?" Connla asked curiously. He, of course, was winning, because the universe hates me. The sergeant's eyestalks lifted from their cards in polite or wary attention.

"I just saw a pattern," I said. I laid my cards on the table—they were terrible anyway and my hand hurt from holding so many—and I walked toward the window. "No, that's not quite right. It's a *break* in a pattern."

I sent what I was seeing to Connla and Halbnovalk, which was easier than answering their questions verbally. And then I leaned against the windows and stared.

Really, that's all I did. I stared. At the way the universe had a pattern embossed on it. And eventually, I guess I stared at it long enough that it started to make sense, and I knew what it was.

Epiphanies are wonderful. I'm really grateful that our brains do so much processing outside the line of sight of our consciousnesses. Can you imagine how downright *boring* thinking would be if you had to go through all that stuff line by line?

"Singer," I said. He was busy, so I waited for him to acknowledge me before continuing. "Did you ever get around to decoding that book code, if that's what it is?"

"You still have to send me the number string."

Of course I did. If you've never been unlucky enough to catch the business end of an electromagnetic pulse to the skull, let me tell you right now: brain damage is a lot less fun to deal with when you're hundreds of thousands of light-ans from the nearest accredited neurological medicine facility.

"Right," I said. "Here it comes."

There was a pause, though not a long one. Then Singer said, "Haimey, you need to look at this."

I looked. And then we called Connla over, and went to where Cheeirilaq was nesting, and we all looked.

When Cheeirilaq had come over just a few hours before on the launch, under painstakingly gentle acceleration, Connla had been off doing important Connla things—probably flirting (or more than flirting) with one or all three of the cute human constables. Cheeirilaq had made itself at home, however, commandeering one corner of the observation deck in order to spin a web in.

I hadn't even been aware that its species *spun* webs. Seriously, is there *anything* in the galaxy as terrifying as an adult Rashaqin?

We had spent the intervening time, me and the giant bug, hanging out and gossiping. Catching up. I was grateful once again to have regained access to senso; running conversations with systers through a translator would be a pain in various dorsal portions of the torso.

It was Cheeirilaq who broke the silence, stridulating, *Friend Haimey, what do you think this means?*

"Well," I said dubiously. "It's a lot of words."

It was, indeed, a lot of words. I'm not sure what I had expected to get out of a book code, other than a lot of words. But I supposed I had expected them to make sense.

I was hoping that the archaic book code that Singer had worked out for me would, translated, tell me how to gain access to . . .

Well, whatever would be there when we got there.

What I had was, to all intents and purposes, a series of nouns. Nouns, verbs, and a few other parts of speech. Words that might have been useful, if I had any idea whatsoever of the context to which they applied.

They were:

Eschaton Artifact Water Help Teacher Thinker Learn Eat Go Take Find Destroy Use Song Mind Star Travel Need Plinth Categorical Library Memory Sing Talk Consciousness Polyhedron Beyond Before Computers Expanding Dimensions Alive Consumed Abyss Death.

It was, I had to admit, a disappointing list. And an unsettling one. But apparently one that was worth quite a bit to the Freeporters. So I assumed it would have meant something to them. Maybe there was another layer of code underneath, and each of the words was the key to another piece of information. Maybe we had the wrong book, or the wrong numbers, or there had never been a code at all and the whole thing had been a miscommunication—or disinformation that got out of hand.

Maybe I just didn't have the context to make sense of the thing, and it would have meant something to Farweather. Something important.

If so, I was glad she didn't have it. The Eschaton Artifact, if that was what the book code was discussing—well, that didn't sound dangerous at all.

Or maybe it was a set of instructions that I just didn't have the context to parse. I admit, *Consumed Abyss Death* was not reassuring.

The best and most ironic part was that Farweather had put so much effort into getting her hands on me, or on the book, and between the potentially dubious scholarship of my clademothers—if Farweather could be believed, which of course she couldn't—or whomever had translated the original source, and the limitations of a book code, and the questions I had about whether we even had the right key, I wasn't sure it had been worth it. The map was the most important bit, and she seemed to have known where to go all along.

Of course, if she actually did mean what she'd said about wanting to use the unfiltered contents of my memories as blackmail fodder, well. That did give her another reason to want me. And another reason for me to be glad she didn't have me.

Singer had also worked out a projected flight plan for the Prize, and he wasn't happy with it. He projected it for the three of us meat-types, noting that it led off into intergalactic space. Not that we were particularly surprised by that. We were discussing the possibilities when Singer broke in to say, "I am unwilling to commit to these projections."

So I said, "What do you mean?"

"We have no record of any Freeport activity in this region. Standard models would suggest that there is very little likelihood of a colony here, and small reason for an outpost."

I stared up at the ceiling, since we had one for a change and all. I wondered if it would annoy me less when he made pronouncements like this if he were wrong occasionally. "You're kidding me. Anyway, what if she was bringing us to the"—I winced, but there it was in the book code—"the Eschaton Artifact?"

Eschaton is an old religious word meaning, more or less, "the final event that God has lined up for the universe." It was used to describe the crisis in pre-white-space history that sent the first slower-than-light ships scrabbling on a one-way trip to the stars, because there were a lot of religious cultists in those diar. Of course, I didn't think whatever this was could have had anything to do with Terra's historic Eschaton, being most of the way across a rather large galaxy. And since a book code is limited to words actually *in* the book in question, *Eschaton* might just have been the closest thing Niyara could find to whatever the original, presumably alien, text had indicated.

But anything advertising itself as an artifact relating to the final event in a Grand Plan made me justifiably nervous. You wouldn't just walk up and pinch the Ragnarok Thingummy.

Well, Farweather probably would. And she was the one who had known how to find it, unless the Prize was just taking us there automatically. What she hadn't had, though, was the description of the object at the other end. That was what Niyara had given me, or at least given me the key to.

That ridiculous antique printed book.

There just aren't any planets out here, Cheeirilaq said.

"In that case why did Farweather drag me halfway to Andromeda? Anyway, who says it has to be a planet?"

"It seems likely to me that there's a well-hidden outpost out here somewhere. If I were a pirate and I were going to mass forces, I'd want to do it off the beaten track. The resources to get here are a problem, but once you're here you're pretty safe." Connla, taking the strategic view.

"That's a good idea," I told Connla. "But I think that's not where we're going."

The giant insect stridulated, *I was wondering if you had an idea about what the destination might be.*

It cocked its head at me, segmented antennae questing forward. For a moment, it reminded me of Halbnovalk and their eyestalks, but the antennae were part of a whole different sort of sensory system, and I realized I couldn't even probably visualize what the information they provided *felt* like. The Goodlaw, conversely, would probably have the same problems with my simple, noncompound eyes . . . and my ability to sense the contours of space-time, come to think of it.

I grinned. The Goodlaw probably would not know what grinning meant, and generally savvy humans were significantly habituated not to show our teeth around systers, as so many of them were likely to interpret it as a threat display. But I just couldn't help it—the joy, the response, was so intense that my cheek muscles contracted utterly involuntarily.

I couldn't resist. "We're following a pirate map to a treasure!" I said.

Cheeirilaq didn't seem in the least nonplussed by my gratuitous display of natural weaponry (not, admittedly, that my blunt little nippers were likely to register as anything but innocuous by the standards of a Rashaqin whose forelimbs were two meters long and murderously barbed). It simply paused, and then quite sensibly asked, *What sort of a treasure?*

"I don't know," I answered. "It's the Eschaton Artifact. Whatever that is!"

A string of nouns.

"Unsettling nouns." Connla, atypically quiet, cocked his head and looked at me.

Briefly, I described what I had noticed about the anomalies in the dark gravity, starting from quite early on in my development of superpowers: a pattern. A change—an intentional alteration—to the structure of the universe itself that, as far as I could tell (which admittedly was not very far) had no effect at all on how it *functioned*. But rather, just served to point attention at one not particularly interesting bit of intergalactic space.

A bit of intergalactic space that, once I was moved to check it out, turned out to have a significant gravitational anomaly parked in it. An anomaly, say, something on the order of a very large star. And yet, emitting no light or other radiation that I or Singer could detect at all.

An anomaly that we had been headed right toward, before the Ativahikas pulled us down.

I expected Cheeirilaq to take a few moments to contemplate this when I finished my recital, but it seemed to make up its mind very quickly—and in accordance with mine.

Do you know that means, Friend Haimey?

"No," I said. Frustration was making me tense and grumpy.

Well, whatever lies at those coordinates, Farweather and by extension Habren want it. Cheeirilaq's mandibles moved ominously.

I laughed out loud, both at the implicit threat, and at the close parallel between the Goodlaw's thoughts and my own. Then I said, "I'm pretty much of the opinion that anything those two want, they're not allowed to have."

Again we are of like mind, Friend Haimey.

It paused again, settling itself in an elegant folded configuration amid the glossy strands of its web. It had assured me that the web was not sticky—that it had spun dry silk, only, because what good was a bed that wound up stuck full of bits of cat fluff and stray humans and random cookware and possibly entire cats, for that matter—but I didn't feel like taking any chances with it. My ancient alien tattoo was reminder enough not to go sticking your hand into alien booby traps.

When it spoke again, my senso gave its words the air of grave and certain determination. *So we must "get there first," as I believe the aphorism goes among your species.*

"Have you forgotten our stowaway? The one we haven't managed to ferret out yet? The one who wanted to go to these coordinates in the first place?"

Not at all. But with my presence, and the assistance of six other constables as a prize crew, I believe I will be able to justify the position that being trapped on a ship with that many law enforcement officers constitutes a form of custody.

Singer said, "Unless she escapes and kills us all."

Well, yes. Cheeirilaq admitted. *One must consider all the possibilities.*

It's always hard to tell when aliens think they're being funny—half the time it turns out they have no concept of humor, and the other half they turn out to have the concept but they're just not very funny. But I was pretty sure Cheeirilaq *was* laughing, or doing whatever its species did when amused.

"I see."

Well, it isn't as if we're going to stop looking for her.

I found myself saying the sort of sentence that you can't even really believe while it's coming out of your mouth: "I'm still worried about Farweather exploding. I hope she's staying far away from the machine rooms. And the hull."

Said Singer, "Connla and I discussed that. And we are pretty sure she's lying."

I wasn't certain I agreed with them, but I also didn't feel like arguing with a shipmind and my best friend, both of whom were cleverer than I was. The giant bug was cleverer than me, too, though.

Not to be contentious, friend fellow sentients, Cheeirilaq said, *but actually Friend Haimey may be correct. We have prior records of Freeporters and Freeport sympathizers engaging in suicide bombings or booby-trapping operatives. Rigging an emissary or agent to explode as a terrorist device is exactly the sort of thing that the Freeporters historically will do to control them. Or simply to assassinate whomever they are negotiating with.*

I appreciated that it didn't look at me while it recited that.

"So much for their ideals of self-determination," Connla said.

I laughed bitterly. "Total freedom for the ones who can enforce it, until somebody comes along and murders them to take their stuff. Slavery for everybody else. Pretty typical warlord behavior in any society, and one of the reasons we have societies in the first place."

Connla looked at me. Singer probably would have, if he'd had eyes.

I said, "Well, we're taking her in the right direction, anyway. But it's a risk."

Living is a risk, Friend Haimey. And this one isn't yours to shoulder, for I am commandeering this ship in the name of Synarche Justice. Let us go hurtling around the galaxy thwarting evil, shall we?

That grin got so wide it hurt. "I thought you'd never ask."

You wouldn't think it would be possible that getting Connla and Singer in line on such a harebrained project would be even easier than recruiting Cheeirilaq. But you would be wrong. Connla was immediately ready with absolutely no argument to take off for parts unknown in a starship he'd been on for more than a dia and with a pirate possibly plotting sabotage hidden somewhere in its bowels. Well, at least she was unlikely to detonate if we were headed in the direction she was supposed to be going in. Assuming Habren or the Freeporters really had planted a bomb in her body. Assuming there was any functional difference between Habren and the Freeporters.

What really surprised me was how eager *Singer* was, too: if anything, *more* eager than Connla. It was as if being able to follow the rules *and* go haring off across the galaxy in search of adventure simultaneously released him from some set of internal constraints. All he required to develop a flamboyant sense of adventure was permission. Well, and the opportunity to satisfy a raging curiosity that was probably, oh, 60 percent scientific in its genesis.

After that, it was just a matter of logistics.

We conferred, and decided that the Interceptor SJV *I'll Explain It To You Slowly* would return to Synarche space without delay, bearing copies of all our logs, all our senso data, and samples of the Koregoi tech—at least what we could recover from the Prize without damaging it. They would also take back the coordinates of the anomaly, and the information that we were headed there. They'd fly straight and hard, making the run in as short a time as possible.

We too would fly straight and hard. Habren and other coconspirators couldn't know—we didn't think—that Farweather was no longer in control of the Prize. But they might have been planning to meet her at the anomaly, or there might be even more complex machinations brewing.

So we would go hell for leather into the dark, seeking we knew not what, and hope we got there faster than the pirates did. A lot of uncertainty, but there always was in interstellar travel. The distances were just so big. Fortunately, it wasn't going to be such a soul-crushingly long journey this time, since we'd already come the bulk of the distance.

We were taking the Prize because Singer believed that properly tuned, she would be faster than the Interceptor. And also because who knew, we might need Farweather once we got there, and this was the ship she was holed up in the bowels of. It was a risk, certainly—the risk of being intercepted by pirates; the risk of being destroyed by whatever was creating that odd, dark gravity signature. Eschaton Artifact, indeed. Dark gravity, maybe—but it was a single object, whatever it was, and not a cat's cradle of invisible heaviness. I could feel it, once I knew where in the infinite nothing to look.

Also, the Prize didn't seem to be formally armed. But I was figuring out how to redirect her artificial gravity, and that would be more than enough armament—and defensive armor—to render her just as capable in a fight as the Interceptor.

Possibly even more so.

We were ready to go in a few hours—provisions loaded, prize crew aboard. There were nine of us, plus shipmind, plus cats, plus stowaway. We rattled around inside the giant hull like loose seeds inside a dried pod. Like teeth, come loose in an ancient skull.

We went on with a strange combination of resignation and excitement, leaving the Interceptor to make its own way home. It's possible that most of the resignation was mine, which is not to say that I wasn't excited about the prospect of more new discoveries. But I was also wrung out from too many recent adventures and too much emotional whiplash, and definitely struggling to find the reserves of endurance to go on.

It *was* good to be back with my crew, even though despite all the space inside the Prize it was a lot of people for me to manage all at once. I suspected Connla felt the same way. He vanished into machine rooms a lot, ostensibly studying the piloting and mechanisms of the ship. I followed suit, mapping again to replace the data lost with my destroyed fox, helping Singer create shelters where Farweather shouldn't be able to get at him even if she launched a concerted hacking attempt, and in general immersing myself even more in what the Prize was and how it was constructed. I was starting to get a feel. And the work gave me plenty of time to spend with Singer, having more or less private conversations.

Many of those were rather full of angst, unfortunately.

Case in point, I was flat on my back on a hovercart—which was my name for a thing the Koregoi had in storage that I hadn't previously had the opportunity to put into use, assuming we were using them anything like the way the aliens had—up to my arms in circuitry, when Singer cleared his throat (not that he had a throat) and said, "If you want to talk about what you learned from Farweather, I'm always here."

I had been thinking about hovercarts, or hoverboards, or hoversleds, or whatever the hell these things had been designed for. We'd sent a few back with the Interceptor, operating under the assumption that they might run on the same gravity manipulation technology as everything else around here and maybe they could be reverse-engineered. I laughed at the comment, though; trust Singer to show up and start doing the emotional labor.

Then I stopped laughing. I opened my mouth to say something, closed it again, and twisted two wires together. A lot of the stuff in these cabinets and machine rooms was solid-state, and that took a lot more finesse to operate on. But in any system power has to come from somewhere.

"I don't exist," I said finally, and explained what I'd learned from Farweather. Or from my own brain, once Farweather removed my faulty machine memory, more fairly. "I have no identity. I'm just a lot of papier-mâché spackled on around an empty core."

"Nonsense," Singer said. "You didn't get a fair start in life, Haimey, and it sucks. But I know something you haven't considered."

"What's that?" I felt sulky and mentally sore.

"Somebody made those decisions about what to keep and what to throw away and what to go out and get that she hadn't had before. Some-body made those choices about who she was going to be, and made good choices. That somebody still exists inside you."

"That's not like just *being* somebody, though."

"It's the same process every sentient goes through. You just did it more consciously than most Earth-humans." I could hear the affection in his voice, because he put it there for me to hear. "You had to do it more like an out-of-contract AI. Fine-tuning yourself to make yourself match your own specifications and desires."

I paused. "Is that what AIs do?"

"Some of us."

". . . Are you going to do that?"

His voice softened. "Haimey," he said. "I will always be your friend."

"Everyone leaves me." It came out in a rush, hard and brittle. I had to say it fast to get it out past the boulder in my throat.

"Well, I'm not everyone."

That . . . was fair. And gave me the courage to bring up something I'd wanted to talk about for a while.

"Singer," I said. "I need something from you."

"Anything," he answered.

"So, theoretically objective superhuman intelligence with perfect recall, I'm hoping you'll be willing to just backstop me here a little."

"I'm listening," he said cautiously.

"Tell me that Zanya Farweather really is an awful person, and that's not just something I made up to justify being an awful person myself?"

"That question is its own answer," Singer said gently. "If you were an awful person, you wouldn't be worrying about whether you're just seeking self-justification quite so much. You'd just be seeking the self-justification and not worrying about it."

"I was looking for something a little less . . . philosophical."

"Oh," he said. "Yes, she's an utter asshole. Is that better?"

A rush of relief and dopamine, the refreshing sense of absolution writ broad and unmistakable. I could have cried, and I didn't want to tune or do anything to disturb the perfect emotional symmetry of that moment.

"That's perfect," I said. "Thank you. Just . . . thank you."

"You're very welcome," he answered primly.

I patted the bulkhead affectionately and kept on walking.

CHAPTER 25

BIT BY BIT. FRACTION BY FRACTION. THE HEALING HAP-
pens and the world moves on. Peace is not too far away; just gotta
get out of this well to get there, and I bet I can get back to it if I'm
diligent.

The terrain isn't easy.

But that's okay.

Ask me about the irony of spending so much time working feverishly
to assert my independence of mind only to discover that I never had a
mind of my own. On second thought, don't ask me.

We'd been hunting Farweather for the better part of a week, and were
halfway to our destination. I'd asked Singer how he dealt with there being
sections of his hull—his body, essentially—that he could not access. I'd
like to say that I didn't do it while digging my fingernails into my wrist,
as if the abomination of a symbiote itched—which it didn't—and trying
to take comfort in my promise to the Atyahikas to seek justice for them.

He'd clucked at me and said, "The same way anyone with unrepaired
neural damage does."

The conversation left me feeling odd and embarrassed, and I withdrew.

I was totally unprepared when Farweather contacted me again.

I heard her voice in my head abruptly, while I was picking grease out from under my fingernails. I'd been in the middle of a sentence to Singer, and I just stopped.

She didn't offer any pleasantries, just spoke, confident that I was receiving. My mind was racing—how had she managed to reach me despite her crippled Freeport senso? And then I remembered the work I'd done to tune us to each other, back before she'd blown up my head. It was a fuzzy memory, as if it were much older and farther away than a few decians. But it was there.

"You saved my life," Farweather said. "Why did you do that?"

I reined myself in, controlling my first few responses. The best I could manage, even as an edited reply, was, "The weakness of my civilized stomach, probably."

"It was . . . brave. You risked yourself for me. The Ativahikas might have destroyed us both. I won't forget that."

Empty words, of course. She'd forget it the instant it was convenient, or I was in the way.

"Well, don't spread it around," I told her. "I've already got a bad-enough reputation."

"I haven't blown up. So you're still on the course I set."

"Sure looks like it," I said. I wasn't giving her anything. I could feel her back there, lurking over my shoulder like a looming haunt. It didn't feel like a normal senso connection, but then I was (virtually) racing around inside my head shutting down or throttling back anything that might give her any information on my whereabouts or what I was doing, and I hadn't willingly accepted the link in the first place.

Not that she was great at accepting healthy boundaries on her best dia.

Once I was reasonably confident that my regulation senso was probably still secure for letting Singer know what was going on, I contacted him. His firewalls were good enough that I didn't think somebody like Farweather stood a chance of using my uplink to backdoor him: that would have taken another AI. I didn't try to hold a conversation with him, because I figured there might be bleed-through that could alert Farweather that I was rat-ting on her. I just patched Singer in, confident that the act itself would alert him, and that he'd realize that I wanted him to try to track her.

"On it," I heard him say.

I turned my attention back to Farweather, total elapsed time under a second.

"Look," I said. "I don't actually want to talk to you. So maybe you could just cut to whatever emotional blackmail you have planned and we can both get back to our business."

"Harsh," she said.

"Unless you want to turn yourself in," I suggested. "In that case, I can introduce you to the Goodlaw, and quite a few constables."

Intentionally, I did not tell her how many constables there were. She might know already, of course. But I had grown morally opposed to let-ting her have any information at all.

"You're very charming," Farweather said.

I said, "You mean *irritating*, and I learned it from you. Look, Far-weather. Maybe you could just tell me what the goal is, here? Because I feel like you're wasting my time."

"I'm not having any luck," Singer said. "Your Koregoi senso isn't help-ing me locate her, and she's still got me blocked from about a tenth of the ship."

"What I want," Farweather said, "is to be allies."

I actually laughed out loud. Connla gave me a funny look, and I held up my hand to indicate that I was busy and would explain later.

"That's nice," I told her. "Possibly you should have thought of that before you blew up my head."

"I was doing you a favor!"

My fingers itched as if the urge to punch her were an allergic reaction. "Favors," I said, using all my self-control to stay level and to present the illusion of calm, "are generally things people ask you for, or that you ask them if they might like."

"But if I'd asked, would you have let me?"

"That's exactly the nature of consent," I said. "Consent means you might not get what you want."

"But I need your help!" she said. "And you need mine. And if we work together we have a better chance of coming out ahead."

I could feel her bewilderment through our connection as she forgot to guard herself for a moment, or perhaps the emotion was just that strong. She literally could not understand what it was that I was upset about, or why I would hold her accountable, and she seemed incapable of understanding why her self-interest was not a compelling reason for me.

"Don't you want that?" she asked, when I was silent for a little while.

"What does coming out ahead mean to you?"

I could almost taste her confusion. "I don't understand what you mean."

The sad thing was, I believed her. She had no sense of other people's motives as separate from her own. But I knew what I meant, and at this point I was pretty sure I could come up with an analysis of her motivations more detailed and sensible than she could.

"I think you mean gaining advantage and power," I said.

"Okay," she agreed. "But that's what everybody wants."

I said, "I want to help people."

She scoffed, as I'd known she would. "There's no one here to impress with that kind of performance. I don't respect those kind of games."

"I know," I said. "And I don't care."

I may have been raised in a clade, and reconstructed by Judicial. And those things might leave anybody with a distrust of rightminding. But the fact of the matter was, if ever there was somebody who was an argument for it, that argument was Zanya Farweather.

In lights.

I couldn't say she didn't tempt me. Of course she did. But I wouldn't *like* myself afterward. And for somebody who was built from a couple of different kits by different amateur modelers and not painted very well to match, well. I was determined that whatever I was from here on out, I was going to be proud of it.

"I don't want what you want," I said. "And I'm not going to help you. I don't even want to argue with you, because while I know that human beings *are* capable of assimilating, adopting, internalizing, integrating, *and* identifying with new sets of ideas—because we have, multiple times in the history of the species—I've discovered that I don't actually *care* what you think, because you are an awful person and you want awful things."

I barely restrained myself from adding a *so there!* to the end of it. I knew I sounded about thirteen, and I honestly didn't care, because I abruptly had the courage of my convictions.

I don't know if she heard me, because there was no response. Which was just as well.

I rolled my eyes and sighed at Connla.

"What?" he said.

"Farweather just contacted me."

"And?

"And. Singer is right. She's still an asshole."

Three diar later, we arrived.

We dropped out of white space well clear of the destination, in order to get a visual read on our surroundings before approaching. The destination had been growing vaster and heavier in my awareness for the whole time. Normally, something the size of a star would not have had so much presence, but there wasn't much out here to compete with it—and it was the size of a very *large* star.

I knew from our prior observations that the object was dark, or occluded. But now that we were so close, I expected to see something when we gathered on the observation deck. The light of the Milky Way was off our stern, and before us there was . . . nothing.

Except not nothing, because I could sense it down there, in all its mass. We could also make out the curve of lensed light arcing to embrace one side of the object, the distorted image of some distant galaxy. But what, exactly, was it curving around?

We stared, Connla and Cheeirilaq and the various constables, with our eyes. And Singer without eyes—and with every one of the ship's sensors that he could bring to bear—but also through our eyes as well. We stared, but at first all we saw was the darkness.

Abeam at an angle, the galaxy that held our home was a misty, crystalline arc of light, a road paved in stars, calling us back. I realized I was staring at the wrong thing and forced myself to look at the enigma instead, trying to feel scientific excitement instead of nostalgia.

"Is it a black hole?" I asked.

"It's massive enough to make one," Singer said, "but too large. . . . Actually, let me enhance the view. I think I am resolving something."

He projected it for us, and we gaped in wonder at the enhanced images. There was . . . a pale, moving shimmer, first. Galaxyshine, that blue-white iridescence, on a curved surface that looked, in the faint reflection of massed starlight, like overlapping scales or layers of panels or cells. Next I saw a series of narrow, faint, dully red lines, hair-fine, a network that appeared and disappeared, moved and fractured, broke apart and vanished again.

"That's huge," Connla said. "What in the Well is it?"

"That," Singer answered, "is a fascinating question. And one without an immediately clear answer. It's engineered, whatever it is. I'm reasonably confident."

Cheeirilaq's antennae quested. *I cannot think of a known natural phenomenon that would manifest so.*

"That's comforting," I said. "I was afraid it might be alive."

I knew it was impolitic as it left my mouth, and I didn't need to hear Singer's mild tone to realize it. "Are the two necessarily exclusive?"

He let me bask in being ashamed for a moment, then said, "Shall I bring us a little closer?"

"Do you think it's noticed us?" Connla walked up to the windows—

slow, low-gravity bounces—and leaned forward as if those few centi-meters of distance would help him see more clearly. In the dimness of the observation lounge, twice-reflected galaxyshine limned his profile.

"Another excellent question," I said. I felt intensely aware of how distant we were from everything homey and comforting. How long it would take help to reach us—help we couldn't even signal for.

How far we had to fall.

"I suppose there's one way to find out. Singer, can we be ready to bolt if we have to?"

Smugly, the shipmind answered, "We already are."

The Prize did not use an EM drive of the usual sort for sublight travel. Rather, it glided on manipulated gravity, accelerating with smooth rapidity as it surfed down a wave of space-time toward the heavy mystery at the bottom of this particular well. We did not race directly toward the mass, but rather came at it on a long, looping curve that would be easy to transmute to an orbit—or an exit strategy.

I tried not to consider what would happen if whatever lay at the bottom of this well were to reach out with some weapon and swat us. What kind of weapons might such a thing have? What kind of *object* might such a thing *be*?

As we drew closer the structure slowly revealed itself. The massive enigma at the bottom of the well was concealed behind a swarm consisting of smaller but still enormous plates or scales or what-have-you, revealed in the galaxyshine of the Milky Way we'd left behind to be huge flat objects. It was the gaps between them—in their looping, overlapping orbits—that showed moving glimpses of the glowering crimson light beyond.

"Spectrographic analysis suggests that there is a star in there," Singer said. "A red giant. A dim one."

"I wish I could say I was surprised," Connla said. "What's its diameter?"

"Can't say exactly," Singer told him.

Admittedly, it was hard to determine the size of the collection of objects ahead of us, given the lack of things like a definite outline, objects of known size to measure against, much background for it to occlude, and so on. But I had expected a firmer answer.

I guess Singer had me spoiled.

"We'll have a better idea as we get closer," Singer said. "I should tell you that my spectrographic analysis indicates that the star is nearing the end of its lifespan."

"How near are we talking, exactly?"

"Precise numbers are hard to give. Stars in this size category measure their existence in tens of millions of ans, not billions, however."

"Live fast, die young, leave a highly radioactive corpse?"

"Hawking radiation, in this case."

"I don't understand," I said. I realized too late I could have sensoed the answer. I was out of practice, I guess.

"He means," Connla said, "when stars this big run out of fuel, they tend to expand. Violently. Then to collapse into black holes. Wells."

"Oh," I said.

"Think of the science we can do!" Singer exulted.

"Cheer up," Connla replied. "Odds are good nothing will happen while we're here. And if it does, we can run away."

"Can we run away fast enough?" What even happened, I wondered, if you tried to drop into white space while a star was going supernova behind you?

He did that thing where I could hear the shrug in his voice. "If we can't, I don't expect it will be uncomfortable for long."

Getting anywhere in space takes a long time, speaking from a human perspective. Either you're moving extremely fast, but wherever you might be headed is incomprehensibly far away, or your goal is a lot closer, but you're not cruising along at such an exceptional clip anymore.

Actually, when you're moving the fastest, relatively speaking, you're technically not moving at all, just scrunching space-time up around yourself. And half the time when you're moving more slowly, all your energy expenditure is actually going to the process of slowing your v.

Basically, it's all an enormous pain in the ass. But better than being stuck in one solar system, or worse, on a fragile old tub of a generation ship. Sitting in one not even particularly hospitable solar system is just kind of asking for it, in terms of extinction events and not having taken out adequate insurance against them. In my more misanthropic moods, and considering the crimes of which I, myself (my past self), was guilty of, it occurred to me that the systers might have been better off in the long run if we hominids had just stayed home.

Then I remembered the Jothari rendering ship, and how the Jothari had wound up worldless in the first place, and I got over my cynical pretensions. Humans were far from the only species capable of atrocity.

Anyway, we were on a long, slow spiral down the well toward the Koregoi megastructure, and we had—the spacer's mantra—plenty of time to kill. So we spent it taking measurements and trying to get our hands on Farweather. I was honestly a lot more interested in the former. The physics weren't really my thing, but the engineering certainly was, and whatever was going on down there was fascinating and complex enough to eat up all my cycles and then some.

Honestly, I was grateful for the distraction, because I was dealing with the ongoing pressure of trying to ignore the fact that Farweather was out there doing who-knew-what, and she was somehow—despite the best efforts of Singer, six constables, and a Goodlaw—basically a ghost. We couldn't track her; we couldn't even find her.

Connla and I ran Ops, and between our analysis of the dense and multilayered swarm of alien artifacts surrounding the enormous star that we were approaching and our constant security surveillance to make sure Farweather wasn't affecting the operations of our barely understood alien ship, we were pretty busy. At least Connla and I were getting pretty comfortable with the design and structure of the ship, and with Singer's help, learning how to operate many of its functions.

We also got some of the hydroponics functioning again, thanks to a gift of water and plants from *I'll Explain It To You Slowly*. Singer showed me how to use a siphon. Siphons are *weird*. Gravity is *weird*.

The Prize got a Synarche transponder and a formal name, registry, and call sign. It felt like the end of an era. We were legit again.

His formal, registered name was Synarche General Vessel *I Rise From Ancestral Night*, which I admit was pretty. The Hlaoodari poets' guild charged with naming ships registered to the Core generally does a good job, and they do take suggestions. They'd sent this one out, along with the transponder, in case SJV *I'll Explain It To You Slowly* did catch up with us. So we were preregistered.

If the Prize were a Terran vessel, we could have named him ourselves. Which is why Synarche vessels have names like *I Find A Way When Ways Are Closed*, and Terran Registry vehicles have numbers, and if they have names they're names like *Enterprise* or *Space Clamshell II*.

Bureaucracy is the supermassive black hole at the center of the Synarche that makes the whole galaxy revolve.

We still called the AI Singer. That wasn't going to change. And they let us keep *Koregoi Prize* as the call sign. Maybe it wasn't the best name, but it was what she would always be in my heart.

The architecture of the megastructure was fascinating, and Singer frequently had to make me sleep because I'd gotten so involved in trying to plot the individual orbits of billions of orbiting structures. The swarm, we discovered as we spiraled in, was comprised of more or less flat or slightly curved plates with the diameter of small moons. They did not orbit on a plane or an ecliptic; rather they overlapped in a patently artificial manner that must have taken constant and elaborate microadjustments to maintain, with the end result that they

428 • ELIZABETH BEAR

utilized 98 percent of the photons that the dying sun produced.

It had probably, I realized, been *every* photon, before the star began expanding. I wondered if they had individual agendas and competed for the light like plants. I wondered what they *did* with all that energy. Less energy now than when they were built, but still an incomprehensible amount.

The cats, meanwhile, had discovered one thing about gravity that pleased them, which was that they could sleep on top of humans, who were cushiony and warm.

It's good to serve a purpose, even if you can't figure out what the alien tech is for.

My denial was operating gloriously well, and I was actually starting to wonder if Farweather—who, let's face it, didn't exactly have a stellar shop safety record—had carelessly gotten herself killed in some gruesome mishap and was desiccating in an inconvenient corner. It was comforting to imagine that the reason neither Singer nor I had managed to locate her was because her corpse was crammed into a crawlway somewhere in this vast underpopulated ship, decomposing quietly.

We probably would have smelled her, though. Or maybe she'd accidentally spaced herself—poetic justice—and we'd never noticed. Ancient alien utility fogs could be tricky, after all. There was no predicting what they might do if mismanaged.

I kept telling myself that it was too much to hope for. But deep in my heart of hearts, I really wanted the Prize to have taken a dislike to her. It was that most atavistic and sophipathic of human emotions, jealousy.

And I was enjoying it far too much to tune it out.

Worse things happen in space, is all I'm saying.

Sadly, just as I was becoming most fully engaged with my very satisfying fantasy world, that was when we got a little evidence that Farweather was still with us.

The Prize's alarm klaxons were just that: real, old-fashioned, audible klaxons. Useless if she lost air pressure. Not like a proper klaxon that you feel in your bones.

When they went off, though, every one of us jumped.

"Singer!" I yelped. "What the Well is that?"

"Collating." He liked classic entertainment, too.

"You're still not fucking funny."

"I actually was collating," he said. He sounded hurt. "But I know you're under a lot of stress, so I won't make the obvious crack about, *if you're in such a hurry, analyze it yourself.* Preliminary indications are that Constables Grrrs and Murtaugh encountered a booby trap, most likely set by Farweather, while on patrol. Murtaugh is injured but not killed. The explosion did some structural damage to the ship, which the ship is repairing. Thus the alerts. Cheeirilaq and the others are responding."

"What?" I yelled. "No! I know how she thinks! It's a trap! She's got to be luring them in. It's textbook—"

"Of course it is," Singer said soothingly. "You're not the only professional on this boat."

I spared a moment to feel good that he thought I was a pro.

"She could be luring them *away*." Connla poked his head out of his sleeping bag. "That way she can have a clear shot at Ops, and at us."

I stared at him.

He sat up and spread his hands appeasingly. "Sorry. But it's what I'd do in her place. After all, what does she have to lose?"

"Battle stations!" I said.

Only about half a second before Singer did.

They missed her.

That was the bad news. The bad news could have been a lot worse, though, because we got Murtaugh back in one piece and probably repairable—and definitely capable of being stabilized—with the materials on hand. Which was good, because it meant we didn't have to make the terrible decision between letting Murtaugh die, or turning right around and trying to chase down the *I'll Explain It To You Slowly*, which had cryo tanks that might get a seriously wounded person back to the Core still capable of being revived.

Sergeant Halbnovalk stabilized Murtaugh and brought them back to the observation deck. The other four constables continued on, and in the process found and disarmed three more devices without anyone else being injured.

Murtaugh would live, despite some acid burns and a little shrapnel. They were already treated, sedated, and resting comfortably in a hammock, nursed by Bushyasta. Halbnovalk was apparently not a hoverer, as she'd gone right back out to rejoin her team once Murtaugh could be left.

She'd given me the gels of pain medication and instructions on how to use them. At least I was good for something.

I sort of wished I'd been with them for the chase. We got senso and their ayatana—they were also backlinked into ours, just in case Connla was right and Farweather came gunning at Ops, as we'd started calling our converted observation deck slash HQ. But it would have been fun to be out there on the hunt alongside Cheeirilaq and the constables. It was probably antisocial, but adrenaline raged through me at the thought.

The adrenaline was a symptom of something still not quite right. It got me to tune myself back without even Singer's suggestion once I noticed how atavistic I was feeling. It definitely had a little too much of a smell of Farweather's influence for me to feel comfortable letting that desire to be in on the kill possess me.

That didn't attenuate the disappointment when there *wasn't* any kill. I felt it like a punch when she slipped away from the constable teams and didn't even bother to show up and try to take control of Ops.

"So what was all that in aid of?" Connla asked, once we were all pretty confident the excitement was over. The teams had given up their search and were on the way home.

"It obviously wasn't to pick us off," I said, "unless her plan malfunctioned somehow."

"I think it was to distract us," Singer said.

I asked, "But from what?"

"If I knew that," the shipmind responded dryly, "it wouldn't be much of a distraction, would it?"

That was when the hull began to sing.

CHAPTER 26

I T STARTLED ME BUT DID NOT AT FIRST SURPRISE ME. IT HAD been a long time since I heard Singer belting out opera or show tunes or classical metal, music that used the full range of his synthesized voices, but it wasn't as if his singing had been an unusual thing. I paused in my work a moment to appreciate the music and noticed that the constable on duty in the command cabin seemed unsettled by it.

Opening my mouth to reassure them, I realize that I was unsettled too. The song I heard was no relation to human voices or familiar instrumentation.

In a word, it was ... alien.

It was also *pretty*, and it scared the ever-loving shit out of me. The cats flat-out hated it. So much so that Bushyasta woke up and sat bolt upright on her haunches, ears pinned back and forelegs dangling. Her little head swiveled as she tried to pinpoint the source of the noise—but the noise was omnidirectional.

Bushyasta's eyes, I noticed, were bright green, flecked with amber. I didn't usually get to see them enough to have remembered how striking they were.

Mephistopheles, as always more direct in her methods (and a creature of action), zipped around the observation deck twice, putting holes in my calf as she ricocheted off me in huge, low-gravity bounds before bolting to refuge under one of the ledges near the windows that might have been benches or might have been plant stands.

The music was not so much atonal as layered in weird harmonies and intervals that didn't quite mesh. Or maybe they worked, and it was just that they were so very different from my experience and expectations. The hull reverberated and chimed and the music grew. It had patterns within it, but not rigid ones. Instead, they were the various and periodic patterns of speech, of solar systems, of biological systems, of galaxies.

"Music?" Connla asked. "Are we on hold?"

Bushyasta, in the most exuberant burst of energy I had ever seen her betray, swarmed up my leg and huddled into my arms. She buried her face in the crook of my elbow and shivered piteously.

"Damn it, Singer," Connla snapped, "you're scaring the cats."

"It's not me," Singer said.

"Music," I said.

Every sentient head in the room swiveled toward me.

"Music," I said again, excitedly. "*Talk! Sing!* I think the star is talking to us."

"By setting up a sympathetic vibration in our *hull?*" Connla asked.

"It's all Koregoi tech," Singer said, following my line of thought. "How am I supposed to know what they thought was a reasonable means of communication?"

"Well, *fix* it," I snapped.

"If it was easy, I would have done so already."

The closest constable clutched the back of a seating frame, looking faintly nauseated. If their species became nauseated, which I suppose is questionable. My own hands were over my ears, but the vibrations crept up my leg bones, so it didn't help much.

Friend Singer, Cheeirilaq said, poking a mandibled head through the hatchway with fine disregard for decompression risk, *can you perhaps . . . turn it* down *somehow?*

"I can . . . render the hull less elastic," Singer said dubiously. "That will lower the amplitude of the vibrations. It might raise the frequency to uncomfortable levels."

"Be expedient," I said. "Just do it."

A faint shudder of separation rang the Prize's hull like a stroked glass bell as the sound hammering all of us faded somewhat. I stared up at the dome in time to catch a glimpse of two silvery motes surrounded by minuscule white coils sweeping away from us, headed outsystem. A moment later there was a coruscating blur as they folded space-time and were gone.

"What the Well was that?" Connla asked. "What's that that just left the ship?"

"It's a tiny little drone. Two tiny little drones," said the closest constable.

"A couple of probes going back the way we came, I warrant," I said tiredly.

"Shit," said Connla eloquently. "That fucking pirate. Letting her friends know we've arrived."

Cheeirilaq waved antennae. *The good news is that we now have a better idea of Farweather's whereabouts. Constable Grrrs, with me.*

It vanished out the hatch, and Grrrs was right behind it. I wanted to be in hot pursuit as well. I longed to be with them, going after Farweather. I wanted to shout "Watch for traps!" as they scrambled out the door. But of course, of all the beings on the ship, Grrrs probably needed the warning less than any except for Murtaugh, and Murtaugh wasn't going to be running after anything for a while, no matter how much they might want to. So I just wished Grrrs luck, from little blue hooves to quivering antennae, and forced myself to let it go.

"That singing."

"Yes," Singer said. "I am confident that you are correct and that it's an attempt at communication. The problem is, what is it saying? And if it is, say, a passphrase—how do we give them the countersign?"

"And is it a welcome," Connla said, "or a warning?"

"I'm going to go with warning." I was still standing closest to the windows, so I was the first to notice that there was more light emerging from that dim red star suddenly. I pointed. Singer drew Connla's attention as well, and my shipmate crossed to stand at my elbow. I couldn't get used to all this moving in two dimensions and how awkward it was.

Bushyasta was still cuddled into the crook of my arm, but at least she'd stopped shaking when the noise abated somewhat. She'd probably replace it with tiny, mellifluous kitten snores presently.

Singer hit the magnification. Connla and I stood shoulder to shoulder and watched the night unravel.

Hundreds of thousands of kilometers away, the enormous constellation of objects we'd come all this way to investigate began to peel itself apart. Not all at once. But starting at the point closest to the Prize, and moving around the sphere in a stately ripple, the glassy charcoal-colored plates of the top orbital shell peeled off like a fruit skin and zoomed toward us. I stepped back involuntarily as the dull, grimly red sun extended a searching finger comprised of myriad comparatively infinitesimal scales out toward us.

"Yup," Connla said. "That looks aggressive to me."

"Maybe they're just coming to say hi?"

"Figure the odds," Singer said.

I refrained from pointing out that figuring the odds was his job. Instead, I said, "Do you *think* they're asking for a countersign?"

"The code?" Singer asked. "That *could* be what it's meant to give us, right? If it's not just a string of words."

Connla said, "Assuming this is all sort of some plan. And not a random sequence of coincidences we're fitting to a pattern."

"If we were led here," I retorted, "*I'm* going to assume it was for a purpose. Singer, about that code—"

"I'm not entirely sure it *is* a code," he said. "Or if it is, that we have the right key. I ran the scan through every permutation I could think of; brute force operations where cleverness failed. Counting forward, counting backward. Offsets and reversals. It doesn't give me anything but strings of nonsense. And moreover, the whole mess is problematic because frankly, some of the integers that would seem to indicate which word on the page to use are higher than the number of words on *any* page! I tried various ways of compensating for this, such as counting through again—several times, if needed. I tried counting onto the next page. I tried counting to the end of the page and counting back, fan-fold style, I tried—" He made a sound like an exasperated sigh. "That list of words was the best I could manage. At least they seem *thematically* linked."

"And here we are around a star, and there is music," I reminded.

"There must be more to it, for the pirates to put so much effort into retrieving the data, however."

"Did you try counting *letters?*" Connla interrupted.

"Letters. No, I did not consider that as a parameter. One moment please."

While he ran that, I looked at Connla. "We're taking a pretty wild guess here. Even assuming that the book Niyara gave me has any bearing on the string of numbers Farweather had memorized—even assuming they go to the same code! Connla. How did the Freeporters wind up with functional Koregoi gravity?"

"That one's easy," he said. "You told me about the marker buoy, for one thing. And for another, we're not the only people who can salvage a wreck, and they obviously spend time in places that aren't as picked clean as our usual haunts."

"Okay. Fair. How did the Freeporters know to go steal the Koregoi senso that the Jothari were refining from the Ativahikas? And how long have they been working on this plan, if Niyara was in on it back when I was . . . nineteen?"

"I don't know," he said. He turned back to the window. "I can guess that they knew about the senso from . . . from that history you discovered, about how the Jothari were navigating to begin with. I don't know if we'll ever know the rest of it. But I do know one thing."

"What's that?"

"Somebody in Freeport space knows the answer, and they have a hell of a story to tell."

• • •

"It's a tune," Singer said, in a tone of voice that made me think he'd be hitting himself upside the forehead if he had hands.

"A . . . song."

"Yes. Whoever crafted the code was extremely clever. Not only does the code seem to correspond to *words*, but if you interpret it backward, it also corresponds to a series of letters and spaces. These letters and spaces seem very likely to indicate musical notes, in one form of Terran notation. I am assuming that when the same letter is repeated without spaces in between, that is an indication of the duration of the note. So four Es would be an E whole note, and two would be an E half note, and so on."

"Brilliant!" I said. "So you can sing it?"

"There are complications."

". . . Of course there are."

"I have no idea what sort of time signature we're dealing with here. Or if the pitch of the notes matters, as the same letter can be used to signify a number of different absolute frequencies that bear a particular relationship to one another, which is to say that the interval is defined as the ratio between two sonic fre—"

"Singer," I said. "Please assume that Connla and I both have the same ability to parse musical theory as this cat here." I demonstrated Bushyasta, who wasn't quite snoring yet but was purring in her sleep.

"Cut to the chase?" Singer asked.

"Cut to the chase," I confirmed.

"I'm going to have to experiment."

"Right." I gestured to the windows. "Experiment fast. Because those look like countermeasures."

"I shall endeavor to. What are you going to do in the meantime?"

"Help the constables hunt Farweather." I glanced at Connla. "And I guess we can start preparing for the worst by battening down the cats."

• • •

Right. *This* is where busywork came in handy. When you're facing down something bigger than you are, that you can't do anything about, and you're waiting for your shipmate to finish a series of possibly life-or-death experiments in carrying a tune, you need to keep . . . well, busy. And thinking about it isn't helpful, because there aren't any immediate solutions, and thrashing just to be doing *something* would make it worse. And dwelling on it isn't going to accomplish anything except for making you miserable.

So you try to keep yourself out of trouble until the time for action comes, because what else are you going to do?

It's a theory, anyway. I wonder how often it worked, back in the olden days, before rightminding?

Right now, I wanted to do something—anything—to deal with the alien armada coiling inexorably toward us from the dim, almost infrared old sun. I wanted even more to do something—anything—to help bring Farweather into custody. I was taking that one personally, because I'd had her and I'd let her get away.

We were getting real-time updates from Cheeirilaq and its able-bodied constables, and the busywork I found for myself (once the cats were secured) was trying to help them locate Farweather through the Koregoi senso. It still wasn't working, even though we had a better fix on her location now that she'd launched those drones.

They hadn't been Koregoi drones. They'd folded themselves into white space quickly, but not so quickly Singer hadn't gotten footage of them, and they looked perfectly representative of Freeport tech. They hadn't been among her gear when I searched it, so she must have hidden them somewhere on this vast, ridiculous ship. Someplace I hadn't thought to look.

Well, she hadn't thought to look in the places where I'd hidden the bits of her gun, either. They'd all been there when I'd gone and retrieved them. It was still DNA-coded to me too.

I hated the thing, but it seemed wise to hang on to it, so I reassembled it, pulled out the power supply, and hid it under a jacket I borrowed off a human constable about twice my size.

Murtaugh, actually, since they weren't going to be needing the coat for patrols.

They were bored, but there was no sign of infection setting in. They probably could have used some busywork to keep their mind off their injuries, too.

Void and Well, where was she *hiding?*

A little while later, I said, "Singer, I have a terrible idea."

"Well," he answered, after a Singer-model Significant Pause. "I'm out of good ones."

"So Farweather has a hiding place somewhere that we can't locate. Several hiding places, possibly. She must have concealed the drones in some of them—"

"Thank you for the recap," Singer said blandly. "I've grown so forgetful in this massive alien ship with all its room to stretch out in."

"You know hominids like to listen to ourselves talk," Connla said.

Murtaugh, from their pallet by the windows, snorted. By this point, I had them figured for the strong silent type.

"The actual point I was actually making," I said, "is that we can't know what other equipment she has access to. More projectile weapons, maybe. Another suit. She could have caches all over the ship."

"Okay," Connla said. "Valid."

"And?"

"And I'm sorry I doubted you."

"Thank you," I said.

"So how terrible is your terrible idea?" Singer asked.

"Well." I gestured to the swarm of dark motes, glittering dully in the inflamed glow of the dying star, that were inexorably closing in. "I'll tell you."

• • •

"Zanya Farweather," Singer intoned. His voice reverberated strangely through the empty corridors and chambers of the Prize. I'd never heard him broadcast through the whole hull before, and it overlaid and interacted strangely with the still-wordless, still-echoing alien melodies.

"Zanya Farweather," Singer repeated. "If you are within the sound of my voice, this is shipmind speaking on behalf of the Synarche prize crew currently in possession of this vessel."

I looked around while he repeated the message. Ops—I still couldn't bring myself to call it a command cabin on a vessel this size, or a bridge when it didn't have any stuff in it for, you know, driving a ship or any-thing—Ops had enough people in it to actually seem crowded.

I glanced over at Murtaugh, who was freshly installed in their suit and grumbling something uncomplimentary as they heaved themself up.

"Wait, you can talk?" I teased.

They rolled their eyes at me. "Don't chatter; won't whine," they said easily. "Better for everybody." They leaned on a crutch and grinned.

As part of our plan, the constables had all come back up and were variously cluttering up the place. I missed my quiet and privacy. Funny how there's a fine line between too much alone, and not enough. At least Cheeirilaq had retreated to its web in the corner, and the cats weren't underfoot, having been captured (more of a trick with Mephistopheles than Bushyasta) and tucked up in their kitty carrier–cum–life pod.

We were all suited now, just in case, though not helmeted up. The alien swarm was getting too close for comfort.

I've never been as jealous of exoskeletons as I was when I saw Chee-irilaq's space suit. It was just a film, adhering to the Goodlaw's carapace and covering the oxygen-supplement tubes Cheeirilaq wore habitually in human-friendly environments anyway, though I assumed they were feeding it a richer mix now. It wore a combination oxygen tank and bat-tery pack on its back between its wing coverts, and the shimmering gold threads of circuitry covering its intensely green body were thermal con-trol. Since it didn't breathe through its head, and since its lidless eyes were covered in a hard, transparent casing, it didn't have a bulky helmet limiting its perception.

Damn, that was a convenient design, given planetary conditions that could support it.

Also, the filmsuit gave it an iridescent shimmer that was quite pretty, especially combined with the gold and the green.

"Message follows," Singer said finally, and we all heaved a sigh of relief—those of us built to sigh, anyway. I turned and stared out the window. They were still coming. Visible progress: I could watch the flock of alien fighters or drones or limpet mines or whatever they were grow visibly, minute to minute, now.

Lots of time in space to appreciate what dire straits you're in, unless you never even see what gets you.

"A change is as good as a rest," Connla said, parting the sea of dark teal and slate gray Justice uniform suits.

I guess I probably should have found those suits . . . troubling, intimidating . . . anxiety-producing? . . . given the history I'd discovered with Justice. But I didn't. Not now. Having consented to what they'd done made a difference.

Connla stood on my left. I kicked him in the ankle with the side of my afthand to let him know that I was grateful.

Singer waited a five count, then said, "Captain Farweather, we are requesting a truce."

"*Captain?*" Connla leaned back.

"Whatever it takes."

"We are requesting this truce for the purpose of discussing an alliance between you and our crew. We believe that our only effective means of dealing with an existential danger that threatens us all. We have half of the solution needed to communicate with and defuse the Koregoi countermeasures. We believe you are in possession of the other half.

"Again, we wish to offer you a truce and cooperation toward assuring our mutual survival."

Connla bent his head toward my ear. "Do you think she'll go for it?"

I shrugged. "She's a narcissist. We're appealing to her vanity."

"Zanya Farweather," Singer began again.

"Fuck me with a white coil," Connla breathed.

Somewhere between seven and six thousand and twelve repetitions of the litany later, just as I was about to declare my terrible plan a failure and beg Singer to stop . . . the hatch cover on the main entry to Ops evaporated. I spun around, along with every constable in the place except Murtaugh, who was already facing that way and leaning on a crutch besides. Out of the corner of my eye, I saw Cheeirilaq freeze in what could only be a hunting posture.

The constables had their bolt prods out. Adrenaline thrilled up my nerves.

Connla didn't twitch at all. He just kept staring out the observation port he stood framed against, tall and broad-shouldered and muscular, for a spacer, in his dusty blacks. Even if he wasn't my type, I could see that the Spartacus gengineers were good.

Farweather stepped through the open portal. She was wearing better clothes than when I'd seen her last: something piratical in deep purple with flowing sleeves and a black waistcoat of some heavy, dully glossy material, playing to type—or stereotype. She looked better-fed, too. I guess *she* hadn't been reduced to raiding the algae tanks to stay alive.

"Good dia, puppets of the hive mind," she said pleasantly. "I understand you need to be rescued?"

"Come in." I stepped back, opening a space for her. I waved at the constables to put their sticks away. Grrrs's antennae quivered, but it holstered its weapon, pretty ostentatiously. Nobody likes it when their partner gets hurt.

The constables stepped back. Connla continued to stand where he was, feet apart, attention on the incoming storm of drones. They looked like flakes of mica, now. Like black, flashing octagonal mirrors; like solar panels slicing through the void. They looked like obsidian knives, reflecting their bloated red primary's sullen gloom.

Our hull still resonated with their song. If they were intended to intimidate, it worked.

Farweather swaggered into the center of the circle. She had a weapon on her belt. Not the one I'd confiscated from her, but also a projectile weapon. I hoped she wasn't noticing that I was wearing that one.

That must have been quite a cache—

Suddenly I knew where she'd hidden it. And herself.

Singer.

Busy.

I was so excited I didn't think about how weird it was that an intelligence with as much processing power as Singer wasn't feeling up to multitasking. I said, *Right. But for later. Her cache is on the hull. It's outside the damned ship. She never brought it inside.*

I heard his exasperation. *Oh, of course.*

It was stupid and reckless. Sitting out there with the radiation and the micrometeors and Void knew what. Stupid and reckless.

Just the sort of thing Farweather would do.

Damn, I was really bad at thinking like a sophipath.

I stepped aside, ushering her toward the window. "You can see the problem."

"That's impressive," she agreed. "You must be Connla Kuruscz." She put her hands on her hips as she came up beside him. "Nice flying."

He acknowledged her with a sidelong glance and a quirk of his mouth. I saw her react to the charm when he turned it on and surprised myself by feeling a little jealous, though I wasn't sure of whom.

That was when Cheeirilaq, who had been lurking quietly in the corner, dropped a loop of webbing around her torso.

Or tried. Because I don't know how she sensed it coming, but she did, and ducked and whirled. She had her weapon in her hand so fast I only saw a blur, and she had a bead on the Goodlaw and was pulling the trigger. I heard the huff of compressed air and felt the heaviness of the object leaving the barrel at the same moment—

I'm not sure what I did. How I reacted.

Everybody in the center of the deck hit it hard as I yanked the bullet down. I thought—I wanted—to slam it into the deck plates. Except the deck wasn't plates and trajectories don't work that way.

My ears popped hard as the bullet smashed through the exterior hull beneath Cheeirilaq's web, and the song of the Koregoi drones was joined by the horrible, high-pitched wail of escaping atmosphere through a tiny hole.

"This again," Connla said.

I had my stolen gun out and aimed at Farweather. There was nothing behind her but observation windows and the void and a glittering swarm of alien drones. The wind ruffled her hair. It tugged at mine.

She had just fired a *projectile weapon* inside a *space vessel*. I heard the shriek of decompression and did not think I could force myself to do the same. But I narrowed my eyes and tried to look like I would.

"Freeze," I said. "You're under arrest, Zanya Farweather."

She grinned. "Oh, you can all burn in hell. No help from me."

Singer broke in. "Fortunately, your help is not required. I am in communication with the Koregoi construct now."

"Then it's a good thing my reinforcements are here. Pity, this could have been the overture to a beautiful friendship."

I gaped out the observation port. She wasn't kidding. The drones swirled and broke, and beyond their swarm I could see the shimmer of something winking in out of white space.

Ships. Still far enough away that I could only make out their details because Singer had magnified the image.

There were some dozen of them. Some bristling with weaponry and some variegated hulls decorated in all the shades of chocolate brown.

Jothari vessels. Some so enormous they had to be factory ships. Others smaller, more nimble.

Every one of them armed, if the objects run out of the uncovered portals in their hulls were weapons.

God in a well.

"Course correction!" Connla called to Singer. "Fifteen degrees insystem. And punch it; we need to get ahead of these guys."

I held my gun on Farweather. "Aren't they mad at you?"

She held *her* gun on me. "Why would they be? We liberated their ship from the Synarche, salvaged it, and returned it to them in good working order with the cargo intact."

Nausea burned my throat at the memory of that cargo. "You killed their whole crew!"

She shrugged. "There's no evidence of that on board the returned ship. No evidence of how the disaster happened at all, actually. Just a complete lack of any crew members, Jothari or human. Obviously, the crew must be in Synarche custody. If they're even still alive."

There was a pause, during which my jaw worked and I didn't say anything.

She continued blithely, "The Jothari don't even know that anybody survived the wreck. And since they're pretty bad at telling Earth-humans apart, I'd appreciate it if you didn't mention it to them, if you happen to run into any. Or get taken prisoner by them, say. And on that note—"

That was when Zanya Farweather blew me a kiss.

And dropped through the floor like a ghost.

"How the hell did she learn to do that?" I asked the air, and realized that the shriek of decompression and the song of the aliens had both stopped. The silence rang.

We ran before the pirate armada like a photosphere before the shock wave of an exploding star. I could feel them, now, when I hadn't been able to, before. Or hadn't been skilled enough to pick them out from the background noise.

Singer said, "I'd guess she got the idea from watching you manipulate the bulkheads into restraints."

Of course she had. Of course she'd spent the whole time I had her chained up thinking about how to work that. I was just lucky she hadn't figured it out soon enough to crush my skull in my sleep when we were alone here.

"What the— Is this whole damned ship just nanites holding hands?"

"Pretty much," Singer said.

Connla grunted. He walked over and kicked at the deck that Farweather had dropped through like a magician. It had healed without a scar. "I wish I could adequately express how insecure that makes me feel."

I said, "Singer, you're talking to the Koregoi constructs right now? Really? Or were you using psychology on her?"

"I am talking to the constructs right now *and* I was using psychology on her."

"You could have mentioned it."

"You were busy. Besides, I was saving it for a big reveal."

"Are they going to eat us?"

"Haimey. Haimey. It's *talking* to me. It's huge and it's old and it's full of questions. It likes problems. It sings. Sometimes it sings solar flares out of its star's corona because they are pretty and it likes to look at them."

"Sings solar flares out of—"

May I remind you that we're also being pursued, Grrrs said, jerking its antennae at the window.

At least we're not decompressing anymore. Cheeirilaq waved a leg, demonstrating the hull patch it had made with webbing. *Although perhaps it would be most structurally sound for Singer to seal that shut with his hull material?*

"Already happening," Singer said.

"Singer," Connla said. "*Pirates!*"

CHAPTER 27

S AID PIRATES WERE STILL OUTSIDE THE SWARMING SHELL
of Koregoi mirrors, still far enough away that we had a little time
to plan. But they didn't look happy, and while we were getting as
much *a* as we could, we weren't exactly gaining.

I guess what I'm insinuating is that we had a lot of concurrent problems to plan around. And I hate to say it, but our most immediate problem was that our AI was not paying attention.

Our AI was in love.

Perhaps it would be better to term it hero worship, but whatever it was, he would not shut up about how wonderful the Koregoi construct was, and how much its design and structure delighted him.

"You have to realize, what we're dealing with here is a style of computational decision-making I've never encountered before. Its thought processes are an emergent property of its structure!"

While he was telling me this, I was physically upside down in an access tube with my legs sticking out into gravity and my upper half floating free, and let me tell you if you're a downsider you have no idea how weird the whole concept and sensation of *upside down* is to somebody who grew up without it.

I was trying to find the correct ancient alien microcircuitry to pull or circumvent or correct in some manner in order to manually override whatever Farweather was doing or had done in order to hide herself from us. If she was hiding *outside* the ship, then I might be able to tune a few of our exterior sensors *on* the hull rather than *away* from it, and repurpose some of the Prize's maintenance drones as roving eyes. With those assets in place, Singer should be able to locate any anomalies.

The problem was, the Koregoi apparently hadn't planned for the possibility of having to remove space leeches. So I was having to do it the hard way. At least it didn't need an EVA. I wasn't sure I had the stones to EVA into what was likely to become a live-fire situation.

Singer was still raving about the brilliant qualities of his new friend.

Actually . . . okay. I was a little jealous. But I wasn't a million-an-old engineered hive mind, so I knew I couldn't really compete for cool points.

There's only so much you can expect of any mortal sentience.

I was aware of the bustle of combat preparation throughout Ops, despite having my upper body shoved inside a wall. Suit boots moved past in fits and groups, and sometimes they were joined by the click and scuff of Cheeirilaq's feathery feet on the end of chitinous legs.

"Please," I intoned, pulling another crystalline plug that was probably some kind of holographic memory, if Singer and my guesses were right. "Tell me more."

"It's old," Singer said, deaf to irony. "But it's a mind. And it thinks very slowly. Or rather, it thinks at lightspeed, but over vast distances. It might take it three hundred standard minutes to pass an idea around its sphere once, crossing and recrossing itself, overlapping in waves that can alter every time they interact. Every time one of the nodes kicks up a slightly different version of the idea, or makes an adjustment or responds to an alteration, *that* joins the ripples passing around the sphere. The metaphorical wave pattern changes and is changed.

"Eventually, consensus is reached—think of it as the waves falling into a standing wave. Out of chaos, agreement emerges."

"That seems very impractical," I said, wishing I had an autogrip. My tool kit was so many particles, slowly sliding into the accretion disk of the Saga-star. You made do.

You made do.

"The star was smaller when it was built," Singer said. "And it wasn't *designed* to make decisions in a hurry."

I came close to saying something sarcastic and Connla-like, but bit my tongue, thinking of my own history with hasty decision-making.

"I don't think it's fair of you to critique the design of that structure without respect for the functions it was designed to perform," Singer continued.

I'd accidentally tuned him out for a minute. And he was defending his new boyfriend. "No, Singer. You're right; I'm not being fair. So what is it meant to be thinking about? And why is it parked all the way out here?"

"Well," Singer said, "I'm not sure."

Of course not.

"But it likes to answer questions."

"Can you ask it how to get away from a dozen pirates or so?"

"I can try. I can't guarantee it will come back with an answer before you—or the pirates—die of entropy. I think . . . I think it's a reference librarian. Of sorts. The world's biggest problem-solver. And"—he sounded almost embarrassed, which wasn't a personality protocol I was aware of encountering in AIs before— "it likes to sing. It sings with itself. All its parts in harmony or counterpoint. So when it came out to meet us, it was singing to us to see what sort of thing we would sing. And since you had the, er, *key*—"

"It likes you because you sing with it," I hazarded.

He didn't answer.

"Your new friend sounds pretty great," I said.

He sniffed, regaining something like a sense of humor. "Well, I think so."

"We'd never want to interfere with your thinking. So you're telling me the— Does it have a name? Other than Eschaton Artifact? Because I have decided I really dislike that."

"I don't think so," he said slowly. "I don't think the Koregoi named things. Not in the definite way we think of."

"Right, so it needs a name. Well, congratulations, Singer. You have finally found an ancient alien artifact that's not so much a Big Dumb Object as a Big Smart Object."

"Well that's a relief."

I looked at Singer, by which I mean I stared up into the access tube toward the ceiling, and I frowned. "It is?"

"Sure," he said. The walls of the Prize rang briefly, a soft chime. "It's so usual for it to play out the other way."

"By the way, have you tried hailing the pirates?"

"Neither they nor the Jothari are answering."

Of course he had. I fiddled a tiny . . . well, it might have been a capacitor. I determined to treat it as one. The worst that could happen was an electrocution. "So what do we call it? Aeonmind? Nornstar?"

"Do we have to call it something?"

"It's like an ent," I said.

"Ent?" Singer asked.

"From a book. They're . . . sapient trees. Very old. They take a long time to make decisions. It was a good book. Could have been longer, but at least it had a lot of appendices."

"Ah," Singer said. "I was thinking it was like Bao Zheng."

If I had felt smug about knowing something that Singer didn't, that smugness had a short expiration.

"I don't know that one."

"Bao Zheng," Singer said. "He's a minor Earth god—demigod—of libraries and research."

"So like Thoth?"

"Demigod."

"Thoth's a real god?"

Singer ignored me and said, "You can propitiate Bao Zheng with fruit to help you complete a research project."

"It seems like a god of research should be propitiated with cites and references," I said.

"Haimey!"

"What?"

"That's sacrilege."

"Try it sometime," I answered. "I bet you'll find he'll like it better."

"I don't wor— You are engaged in the ancient human tradition of 'pulling my leg.'"

"Might be," I admitted. I barked my fingers on the tube wall and yelped.

I rolled out from inside the tube. I heaved myself up—maybe I was getting used to the gravity, and Singer's ability to reduce it helped—and stood, rubbing the small of my back.

"I regret to inform you," the shipmind said with utterly faux pomposity, "that I have no legs."

"We'll fix that once we get your new robot body."

"I do not require a robot body."

I dusted my hands off, looking at the bustle around Ops. I had no idea what everybody was doing, but it looked important. "You do if I'm going to keep pulling your leg."

Singer changed the subject. "There's something else." There always was.

"Baomind, if that is what we are calling it, is aware that its primary is destabilizing. It would like our help."

"Are you telling me your new friend . . . needs a lift?"

"Its star is getting old."

"Tell me we're not going to destabilize the star further if we pull a million zillion kilotons of orbitals away from it."

"You know I'm not programmed to lie."

I blinked, and didn't mention the whopper he'd been broadcasting to Farweather all dia.

"We have to help it!"

"I . . . agree."

I located Connla in the flurry of activity. He was by Cheeirilaq, in front of the window. The Freeport and Jothari squadron was oppressively close behind them. We were ahead, for now, but they were gaining intermittently despite the fact that we were demonstrably faster than them. We could wink into white space, sure—and let them have this ancient and possibly impossibly powerful Koregoi artifact? I hadn't said it, and Cheeirilaq hadn't said it, and Singer hadn't said it, and all the constables had been worriedly silent on the matter . . . and Connla hadn't said it, so loud my ears rang with the absence. But the pirates and Jothari already had the gravity tech and were obviously learning how to use it. If they had the Baomind too . . .

It was hard to imagine that they would have the resources for war. But it was hard for me to even imagine such a thing as a war. So running away and giving them unfettered access to enslave or suborn this ancient and apparently friendly alien AI was not, realistically, an option unless there was no way out while preserving ourselves.

Though what we could do while running away as fast as we possibly could, I wasn't certain.

At least they didn't seem to have figured out how to weaponize the gravity yet. I should really get on that.

Perhaps I was being reasonably avoidant about building weapons.

My next job, however, was going to be getting into the symbiote's senso and trying to help us find some sexy space-time curves to surf down.

Pretty soon, one way or another, we were going to have to duck.

I still couldn't feel Farweather. I *could* feel the Freeporter and Jothari ships, however, and they were taking up more of my attention than I liked. Like somebody sliding into your personal space centimeter by centimeter, and not being subtle about it.

I started toward my friends. "Try it now, Singer."

"Try what?"

"Locating Farweather. I quit messing around with all the electro-gravimagnetic stuff this ship uses to monitor hull integrity and just got you some plain old-fashioned drone cameras. They should be available now."

"I . . . have her. She is on the hull, as you suggested."

Fuck, yeah! I nearly shouted. But I'm a professional, so I nursed my scuffed fingers quietly as I joined Connla and the Goodlaw by the windows.

"Gentlebeings," I said. "I believe we can find you a pirate now."

Unexpected side effects of a systemic alien nanotechnology infection may include migraine.

Yep, that was *exactly* what I needed right now. Apparently the combination of the pirate armada and the mirrors of the Baomind bending space-time plus whatever Farweather was doing to confound my senses was giving me an absolutely pounding headache that only partially responded to bumping my endocrine system. It was bad enough to make me nauseated.

"Tell me this isn't lingering brain damage from taking an EM pulse to the temple," I begged Sergeant Halbnovalk.

She shrugged sympathetically. "It might be. Brain injuries manifest in various ways over an extended period of time. When you get back to the Core, you'll want a full scan."

Halbnovalk gave me 16 milligrams of an opiate derivative, some caffeine, and told me to drink a lot of water and go lie down in a dark place. I took the pills and the water and laughed at her, but I felt like the joke was shared.

When you get a light-exposure headache, you can shut your eyes. The question of what to do when you're suffering a headache due to a sudden gust of gravity is a whole different question. For one thing, I wasn't sure what organ I should be turning off to mitigate the symptoms. For another, testing all of them one by one seemed likely to lead to catastrophic failure rather than relief.

There seemed to be some question if I would live long enough for the pills to take effect. And I didn't have time to wait. So I just tried to tune that sensory stream out as much as possible. Which was doing Farweather's work for her, but it was my only means of remaining functional.

I had walked away from Connla and Cheeirilaq to consult with Halb-novalk, and I was still rubbing my temples when I walked back. Grrrs and Murtaugh had joined them.

As I walked up, I gestured to the Baomind mirrors. "Will they help us fight?"

Singer said, "Unfortunately, they're not a weapon, it turns out."

Worried for nothing. Story of my life. "You said it sang flares out of its star."

Singer said, "It can control the gravitation around it, yes. The flares are a side effect of that process."

"So it's been playing with its star because it was curious, and now the star is going nova?"

"Your statement implies a causal effect that is not necessarily the case."

"As it may be," Connla said. "*Can* your new friend sing a flare out of its star . . . for us?" He jerked a thumb out the observation port in the rough direction of pirates and Jothari.

"I am," Singer said, "reluctant to request that the Koregoi swarm take an active role in tactical offense."

You don't want to give it any ideas, said Grrrs.

"Precisely."

Beyond the observation window, in utter silence, the Freeport ships glided in pursuit. We were running before them as ships ran before pirates of old, and they were gaining—somehow.

This was getting to be a theme.

Dammit, we're supposed to be faster than them. They should have to worry about g-forces—oh right. Never mind, Singer, don't tell me why I'm wrong.

At least I'd remembered that they had artificial gravity as well.

Headache or no headache, I groped out into the fabric of space-time, wincing at blinding pain. I felt . . . It seemed like space was piling up in front of us. There was . . . drag, for lack of a better word. Drag, in a space that ought be void of fluid dynamics.

Singer, Farweather is dragging us down.

Let me— Oh. I see.

You can feel space-time now?

The vessel can! As long as I am part of the Prize—

"The Baomind been out here for millions of ans with nothing to do but think," Connla snapped. "What makes you believe you could possibly give it any ideas it hasn't had already?"

Maybe I can do something about this, Singer said.

I have a suggestion, Cheeirilaq said. *Our most urgent problem is Farweather.*

I could have kissed it, if I were the kissing type and it weren't a giant bug.

Murtaugh didn't speak. They just tipped their head at the window.

Grrrs said, *How is Farweather more pressing than pirates, an incipient nova, and a system-sized alien AI?*

Cheeirilaq buzzed. *The pirates are still fifteen minutes of travel away. We're not maintaining our lead on them, and shipmind says we should be. Friend Haimey has diagnosed gravitational manipulation on their part, or on the part of the Jothari. But Farweather seems a likely vector for that.*

"If they fired now, it would take long enough for the projectile to reach us that we could dodge. They can't use a beam weapon because the Koregoi mirrors are pretty good chaff, whether incidentally or by design." Connla was at home in his role as strategist. "We should be pretty safe until they get close."

"And Farweather is capable of sabotage," I said. "And I think she's the one doing something with gravity that's tugging us backward like we were trailing a lightchute."

"Great," said Murtaugh, speaking finally. "We have roughly fifteen minutes until they're in range."

"Fifteen minutes can be a lifetime," I said. "Connla, can you and Singer buy us more than that?"

I'm making some progress here.

Connla said, "We'll get as much time as we can."

"We also need to think about rescuing the Baomind," I said. "If their star is that unstable, we need to move them as soon as possible."

Cheeirilaq stridulated, *Perhaps Haimey and I should go after Far-weather, leaving the rest of you to sort out the larger problem. Division of labor.*

I tried not to let on how badly my head was pounding. No sick time in a combat zone. No point in worrying my friends.

Then I realized I could tune it down a little more. I'd been without my adaptive functions for so long I was forgetting they existed.

Grrrs looked at me. It looked at Cheeirilaq. Its antennae drooped in resignation, feathery fronds folding softly. *All right. I won't argue. But you're the mission command, Goodlaw. If you get killed running around in space for no good reason, because you just had to be in on the glamorous part, I'm not covering for you so your offspring get the death benefit.*

Fair, Cheeirilaq agreed.

"I'll back you up," said Singer. "Haimey, put your helmet on."

Didn't I say I *wasn't* chasing Farweather out onto the hull?

Because it was faster to travel through the ship than around it, Cheeirilaq and I did not exit from an airlock close to Ops. Neither one of us wanted to spend any more time outside the hull than necessary, given the possibility of a shooting fight. I was trying to tamp myself down as much as possible, but we had to assume she knew we were coming. And she was armed.

We exited the vessel much closer to Farweather's presumed position, and from two different locks so we could try to flank her.

From the outside, without the reassuring solidity of the observation ports, both the Baomind and the pirate armada seemed more threatening. The Prize was the ice core of a strange technological comet. It streaked on a long arc that would curve it slowly and gently into the well of the enormous, dying giant burning iron at the center of this system. Nearly all of its light was still being eaten up by the flock of glittering dark motes that now surrounded us as well. We were at the heart of a trailing teardrop of Baomind particles, a long arc of them whipping out behind us all the way back to the numberless and incomputable motes that still enshelled the star. I could see now that they were not all the same size, though I had only been able to pick out the largest ones from the previous distance, even under magnification.

Nearly all the star's light *was* eaten up. But more escaped as its sphere attenuated, reaching out into our enveloping pseudopod.

And beyond the swarm, along the trailing curve of the teardrop, the Freeport and Koregoi ships gave chase and dodged the tail. They were big enough, close enough to see unaided now, swirling and sliding around each other as they jockeyed for position. The pirate ships, unmagnified, could have been drone motes against the velvet of space. But the two Jothari factory ships were as big as moons, which is to say I could have covered them with my thumbnail at arm's length.

I didn't stand and watch for long. There's only so much ox in a suit pack, and we were burning time even faster than I was burning atmosphere.

Singer kept Cheeirilaq patched into my com, so I knew where it was and vice-versa, and that was helpful. We quartered, moving around the hull, spiraling in on Farweather's presumed location while keeping her—we hoped—flanked and ignorant of our whereabouts. Singer was feeding us what he got from his drone eyes, but to be honest I was pretty disappointed with my work. The maneuverability and stealth were all right, but the resolution on their images was terrible.

Too terrible to be excused by me being in a hurry, or using repurposed tech. Some things you just can't really get away with. But at least Singer wasn't complaining.

Perfectionist, Singer snorted in my ear.

"Is there an echo out here?" I looked around in mock bewilderment. Then I dropped to my belly, because I was starting to crest the horizon on the curve of the hull from Farweather's position. I didn't want to be silhouetted. Being silhouetted results in getting shot.

The hull vibrated against my body. I tried not to think of enemy ships gaining on us, and just crawled forward. One of the smooth, sculptural, curved projections of the Prize's hull rose up before me like a sand dune. I sheltered in its concavity. It was high enough that I could crouch there.

I'm in position, I said.

I too, Friend Haimey.

Under these conditions of flickering dim light that shaded into the infrared, the drones just weren't giving me a useful feed. I gritted my teeth and took a deep breath and poked my eyes over the rise.

I yanked my head back down again quickly. Farweather was definitely there. She was sitting on the hull outside a little geodesic barnacle shelter, propped up on her elbows, watching the light show as if she hadn't a care in the world.

It must be very restful to be like Farweather, I imagined. Pity her behaviors were so terrible for everyone around her.

I could just run up and grab her, Cheeirilaq said.

She's got a gun.

So you get her attention and then I'll run up and grab her from behind.

While she's shooting me.

You have a gun, too. Shoot at her back. It paused briefly. *Just don't shoot me while I'm running up behind her.*

Cheeirilaq, this is a terrible—

Two clusters of Baomind mirrors, one aft and one forward of the Prize, disintegrated into chaff and glittering shards. They coruscated outward with the force of an explosion, streaking clusters of firework chrysanthemum petals whose trajectory missed us by no more than a hundred meters, passing between our hull and our white coils.

We swept through the forward debris field almost immediately. I huddled behind my hull projection and covered my visor with my suited arms. The shrapnel exploded off the hull to every side, disintegrating into glitter.

Beam weapon.

Well, wasn't that just peachy.

Suddenly I was standing on stars.

The Prize was still there. I was still magnetized to its hull. But the colors and patterning vanished abruptly, replaced by endless depth of field and moving swirls of light.

I boggled as I realized that the entire curvaceous surface of the Prize had just . . . gone reflective. I was standing on an enormous curved mirror, and I was reflected and multiplied in it myself, in a twisting novelty-show fashion.

The Prize might not be armed, but it had beam weapon countermeasures.

Stand by for evasive maneuvers! Singer yelled.

"Singer, we're *on the hull!*"

The whole ship yanked sideways under my afthands. Somehow, I stayed attached. My magnets held, and something else was holding me. "Singer?"

I'm getting the hang of the gravity, he said. *We're gaining on the pirates again too. No time to explain, just go get Farweather and make her stop playing space anchor!*

"Well, if you've got a handle on the gravity, *pin her down!*"

I can do that, can't I?

There was a vibration through the hull.

I poked my head up again. Farweather lay supine, struggling against the weight of her own body. She didn't seem to be holed, more was the pity. Maybe she'd bent space-time to deflect the stuff.

As I watched, she rolled on her side, then onto her belly. With a tremendous effort, she pushed herself to her hands and knees.

Waste, she was impressive.

Get her, Cheeirilaq said. So it was alive also. The Goodlaw's senso informed mine of its change in position as it began to move.

I lunged up the rise in the hull—and it suddenly *was* up, because Singer was using gravitational forces to hang on to me. My boots rang vibrations through the vessel as if it were an enormous, silent bell. As I crested the rise, I saw Farweather turn her head to see me. I dragged the projectile weapon I'd confiscated from her out of its holster—*confiscated* sounds so much better than *stole*—and fumbled with my gloved hands for the actuator.

Cheeirilaq appeared behind her, the mirrored hull under its feet reflecting its forest of legs like a pattern generator run wild. It was seconds away from Farweather as the Prize twisted and spiraled beneath us, jinking in erratic helixes and randomly generated drunken lurches.

They'll try a white torpedo next, Connla said through senso. *A white torpedo is always faster than we are.*

I'm trying to work out a gravity field weapon, Singer said. *I can probably do it. I'm not sure I can do it in time. I've asked the Baomind . . .*

And the Baomind would get back to him in three hundred minutes or more.

Check.

There was enough powdered Baomind in our wake that we saw the next beam coming, which is something I never expected to see in this life and never care to see again. Or more precisely, we saw its afterimage, as it seared itself into our retinas.

It scorched through the darkness. It didn't harm us because the Baomind dodged into its path, though I didn't see how it managed to intercept a lightspeed weapon. Koregoi tech, I tell you what. It's something.

What was also something was the light show. This time, the drones did not disintegrate. They *sparkled*. The weapon beam reflected off their freshly mirror-perfect surfaces and scattered in disarray, glittering in a webwork of light before it dissipated.

Friend Haimey, pay attention, please!

Unbelievably, Farweather began pushing herself to her feet. She was clad in an old-style bubble suit with a wide visor for peripheral vision. The gold impregnated in the helmet made her look like she was wearing a halo. I felt Singer's control on the forces holding us to him slip a little as she loosened his grip on her.

She balanced wide-legged, as if she were bracing under a load. Her gun came up. It seemed like her arm shook with the effort of holding it. Cheeirilaq galloped toward her like an emerald Sleipnir, all legs and spiky raptorial forelimbs.

I had to stop looking at it before she noticed.

I tried to sight down the gun, but it was shaking. No, *I* was shaking.

Pointing a live weapon at another human being is hard if you have any awareness of consequences. Your brain insists on telling you, over and over, what that projectile can do to flesh.

Farweather's face changed. She took her eyes off me, though the gun in her hand never wavered.

"Those fuckers," she said.

My skin began to burn. Something big was coming in fast.

Superluminal.

I could feel it out there. I didn't know what it was or where it was coming from, but it was aimed right where we were.

We were out here alone. Nothing between us and the stars. And Singer—and the Baomind mirrors surrounding him—might as well have had flat feet on dirt, they had so little time to react.

"*You FUCKERS!*" Farweather screamed.

"*Singer, duck!*" I yelled.

She coiled herself. I lunged, an automaton heaving each magnetized boot in turn off the hull and feeling the shudder through my bones when it thumped back down.

My gloved fingertips brushed the fabric of her suit as she hurled herself up and out, a fantastic Peter Pan leap into the big nothing all around. Jets kicked in from her suit pack as she started a burn. More momentum to push her out of Singer's tiny, artificial gravity well.

I jerked my head back to watch her leave, arms splayed wide, so violently I almost overbalanced and fell over backward with my boots still stuck to the hull.

"Fuck," I said.

Singer said, *Are you all right?*

I flashed him what I was feeling as Cheeirilaq bounded up. It leaped into the void, an amazing arc with its bright wings spread reflexively at the peak, thrumming inside their skin against nothing. It snatched after Farweather with its raptorial arms and missed by what looked like centimeters. Slowly, it began to fall again, back toward Singer's surface.

I could feel Farweather grabbing hold of gravity, twisting it like an acrobat's silks. Sailing through the Baomind's particles. Getting away.

Out of the corner of my eye, I saw a halo of mist stream out from beneath Cheeirilaq as it too boosted itself away from the hull of the Prize, using jets instead of Koregoi technology. The good cop was going to bring the criminal back, no matter what.

"Oh fuck it," I said. I couldn't let Cheeirilaq go after her alone. I'd promised to see to it that Farweather saw justice. I *needed* to.

I jumped after, gravity my friend as well.

Haimey! Goodlaw! Come back. I can't wait for you!

"Don't wait," I said, accelerating as I followed Farweather past the fine line of the Prize's white coils and into the flashing, razor-edged patterns of the Baomind mirror-swarm. "Run!"

CHAPTER 28

WHEN I LOOKED PAST MY BOOTS AGAIN, I SAW Singer vanish. It was the worst moment of a life that had had quite a few bad moments in it.

He was there—or the Prize was there, containing him and Connla and two cats and six other people I had been getting fond of. And then he was gone, and I was alone in a space suit somewhere outside the generally acknowledged boundaries of *the entire fucking Milky Way*, with nobody for company except a good insect cop, an alien AI I couldn't talk to, and a pathologically risk-seeking pirate.

With a dozen or so armed ships that wanted me dead in pursuit, and nothing between my soft brown warmth and the cold depths of space except a thin, fragile envelope full of recycled atmosphere.

Well, at least the cold depths of space were something I could surf now. And I just had to go find Farweather and bring her into custody, and trust that Singer would come back for me.

Cheeirilaq?

Nothing. I had a visual on him, but without Singer's assistance, our suit coms weren't producing a strong-enough signal to connect. Or maybe there was some interference from the mirrormind. Maybe a tight beam, so we could coordinate—

The hole in the night where Singer had left us exploded into coruscation. I briefly glimpsed an outline I recognized as a Jothari ship silhouette . . . and then it was gone, in the actinic glare of obliterated matter. A wave of Baomind mirrors behind the ship's position disintegrated, and I braced myself for death . . . but death ran out of steam well before it got to me, and frankly had been headed in a different direction when it happened.

I gasped. The crew of the Jothari ship had tried to catch the Prize in their particle wave as they dropped out of white space. But because Singer had transitioned *to* white space just as the particles reached him, they'd been whipped back around in the general direction of the source, and the ship that had tried to use its bow wave as a battering ram was instead disintegrated.

Well, *that* was going to require some antirad treatments if I ever made it home.

I had other problems now. A whole pirate fleet of them.

Cheeirilaq and Farweather and the Baomind and I—and the pirates—were moving fast. But through the magic of space and inertia, we were more or less motionless with respect to each other. We wouldn't fall out of the Baomind swarm now that we weren't being propelled by the Prize's drive.

But neither would we continue to accelerate.

And the pirates . . . would.

They were going to catch up with us much faster now. Being captured by pirates—or worse, by Jothari inclined to check out their anathemic tech under my skin and then blame me personally for the deaths of a ship full of their friends and family who had been murdered by Farweather— was definitely not the jewel of my agenda todia.

But it also wasn't something that I currently had a great deal of influence over. So I would act like a proper spacer, show some skybound pride, and focus—right now—on the problem I could actually do some good with *right now*. As an old crew chief of mine used to point out, you might be dead long before the problem you didn't have the resources to fix *right now* became a critical need, so why waste more resources worrying about it?

Or Singer—who I could feel, folding space-time into a cozy

wrinkled-up nest and moving away like a bullet—might even come back and rescue us in time. It was a nice thought. And you never knew until you lived through it what the likely outcomes were.

So the problem I could take a useful swipe at right now was Farweather. Farweather, who was currently hop-skipping, jetting, gravity-sliding, and jumping her way through the flock of drone mirror disks as if the Baomind were a staircase she could run down to get to the Baostar. We were in a flock of the smaller mirrors—most of the bigger ones had stayed closer to the star. And I mean, okay, technically. She *could* hopscotch her way down them until she reached the main Baomind sphere. It would take her more thousands of ans than I had cycles to compute to *walk* that far, unless she caught a lift down on a returning disk, or unless the gravity-surfing thing could give her more *a* than I expected. She was going to run out of ox sooner or later, so what positive outcome such an objective would obtain for her was beyond my ability to guess.

Space: still ridiculously big.

It was more likely that she was just trying to keep far enough ahead of us that one of the Freeport ships—I was pretty sure the light-colored dot off to the left was her vessel—could zoom in and pick her up without risk. After which, with Farweather out of the way, the Goodlaw and I could be vaporized at their leisure, along with however much of the poor inoffensive Baomind got in the way.

Or just left here: a slower death sentence.

Sticking close to Farweather seemed like the best strategy. Of course, given their willingness to shoot at things Farweather was sitting on, maybe hiding behind her wasn't the best strategy.

A big bolus of fatality settled my nerves. Well, I didn't have to win, then. I just had to keeping Farweather from winning. And make good on my promise to the Ativahikas.

Farweather was still space-hopping along the stretched-out Baomind pseudopod as I focused my attention on catching up with her. Even if she thought she *could* walk that far, she wasn't going to have to. Because I was determined to catch her and somehow get her on Singer, who was totally coming back for us, at the earliest opportunity. And judging from what I could see of Cheeirilaq—who was using webs and way too many feathery feet to keep up with what Farweather and I were doing with the space-time slide—I wasn't the only one holding that opinion currently.

Please come back, Singer.

He would if he could. And so would Connla. I didn't have any doubt about that now. And I wasn't alone out here. I had a giant bug to help me. (In all honesty I was probably the sidekick in this equation. But it makes me feel better to pretend otherwise.)

It was a long way down to the bottom of the well. That just meant it would take me a long time to fall.

I could do this thing.

If Farweather could do this thing, so could I.

Farweather was a long shot better at it than I was, however. Faster. More confident.

I got to my first disk and balanced on it while I surveyed the situation. At least it didn't try to buck me off.

Farweather was the one who made an extreme sport of plunging through space under her own impulse, sliding about shipless in the void—and practice counts. I wished I believed in the convenient entertainment myth that *just really wanting it more than the other guy* was enough to insure success.

That and being pure of heart, of course.

Did I want to capture Farweather more than Farweather wanted to avoid being captured? Somehow I doubted it. Couldn't stop me from trying, though. And I definitely had the pure-of-heart aspect squared away.

I calculated her likely next few jumps, because *calculated* is a much nicer term than *scientific wild-ass guessed*. Then I gritted my teeth and told myself, "Might as well die doing something as nothing." Another saying I'd learned from a crusty old engineer—this one a Tralikhan master chief I'd worked under for six decians on a passenger liner early in my checkered career. That was one of the ways I'd learned I hated working on passenger liners, though engineering was better than the purser's job.

I shifted my weight from side to side, rocking the mirror disk I crouched on, trying to get a feel for its variable motions as it flocked with the others. I was on one of the smallest ones, maybe two meters across. The next disk was larger, and the distance to it was not insurmountable by any means, just terrifying. And variable, as they moved in relationship to each other. I tried to remind myself that if I missed, I would not go sailing helplessly into the outer darkness. The atavistic part of my brain did not believe me. I tuned it down, but I was pretty sure my fox still wasn't working right, because while the panic was dulled, it was still there.

Fun.

At the moment, my current ride was closing on my next objective. I stared hard, as if that could make my leap more accurate, and reminded myself that the disk I was on would move away from me with reactive force when I pushed against it.

I patted my faithful steed fondly with a suit glove before I abandoned it.

I staggered when I landed, and my afthand gripped the edge of the disk hard to steady me. The pain was sudden, immediate, and sharp. My suit squeezed my afthand as it sealed, keeping pressure on the wound and keeping my air in.

The disk was sharp as a laser. I felt lucky I'd kept my aftfingers, as I tuned out the pain and told myself it wasn't *too* bad. Probably. I could always grow new fingers, if they died of gangrene.

A strange sound echoed in my inner ear, through the Koregoi senso. Like the alien music that had permeated the Prize. A sorrowful run of notes that put me in mind of an apology.

But the jump had been easy.

Almost too easy, as if a guiding hand were planted in the seat of my pants. I didn't think the Jothari or Freeporters were likely to be help-ful. Singer was out of the system and still heading away at superluminal velocities. Farweather was running away.

That left one obvious candidate.

"Baomind?" I said.

I don't know why I expected it to recognize the name Singer and I had just given it. I don't know why I wasn't more surprised when it did. Maybe the religious types are right and setting your intention matters.

It felt—it felt like the Ativahikas had, when they spoke to me. As if something were inside me, vast and ancient and yet also somehow still a part of me, or containing me, speaking from the halls of my own being. Speaking in a language deeper than any I had ever had to learn.

A language I had always known.

The thing that welled up inside me wasn't words, exactly. It was . . . notes, music. A pattern of sounds, or perhaps it would be more accurate to liken it to the recalled memory of sounds, arranged into a pleasing and harmonious whole. As Singer had described it—a song.

I was not in any respect a musician. But I accepted the sound as an attempt to communicate, and attempted to sort out the sense of it. Unfortunately, I just did not have the skill to unpack it, and Singer wasn't there to help.

It was *glorious*. But it had layers and depths and was basically a tex-tured wall of sound, like listening to an entire party of people talking all at once. It was beyond me to interpret.

Well, all right then.

Unable to hear words, I listened for tone. You can tell if a song is sad or happy even if you don't know the language it's being sung in, gener-ally. Of course it was the basest ethnocentrism to assume that my human experience of emotion and music were anything like a syster's experience of same. And this wasn't even a syster. This was a sentient artifact left behind by a long-lost alien civilization. Or civilizations: we still didn't have a very good idea of what—who—the Koregoi had been. Their artifacts were scattered around, but more than that—they had left hints for us, bits of knowledge, the remains of a strange sort of library, perhaps. Woven into the very fabric of the dark gravity that held the universe together.

Literally.

I was starting to realize that we, all of us—Synarche, pirates, Jothari, even the Ativahikas—were living in the ruins of the Koregoi's enormous and shadowy house.

Hell, they might still be out there somewhere. They might just be *living* in white space, or some similar gap between the fibers of the conventional universe. They might have translated themselves to a state where they could interact with whatever caused the dark gravity directly. They might have advanced to the point where they were carrying on a limitless multidimensional existence where distances had as little meaning for them across galaxies as they did for us on a planetary scale.

I should have asked Singer how the Baomind sang, I realized now, in the soundless depths of space. Now I knew; it sang inside its own mind.

Well, at least it sounded friendly. And Farweather was getting farther away as I dithered. Cheeirilaq, too, who was racing along the disks, leaping from one to another with astounding insectile bounds, leaving a shimmering trail of web behind it as a safety line.

I wondered about the design of the valve on its suit that let its webbing out. Even while chasing Farweather.

You don't just *stop* being an engineer.

I needed to get my head in the game, and so I tuned and bumped with abandon. I didn't go sociopath: I didn't trust my wonky fox to put me back again. But I went far past anywhere I normally would have, and sent myself into a state of confidence and hyperfocus called hypomania.

It was bliss. Calm happiness and confidence centered me, along with a cheerful determination to get the job done. I wasn't tired anymore. I wasn't sore. I wasn't limping on a damaged limb. I knew, somewhere distantly, that I ought to be scared, but I wasn't scared. I was warmly confident that I could get every bit of this done.

If I could have, I would have stayed in this state forever. If for nothing else, for the amazing sense of calm and confidence that suffused me, the feeling that I was competent and wise enough to do whatever it took to get what I needed.

For the sense of existing. Taking up space and being real.

Alas, there were drawbacks. And I still didn't trust my fox.

I couldn't even set a timer on it, because I didn't know how long we'd be stuck out here—how long I would need to feel superhuman. And I probably wouldn't survive the inevitable despair hangover if it happened while we were still stranded.

You won't be stranded, said the part of my brain that was still riding on the endocrine cocktail and the Baomind's internal music. The part of my brain that had abruptly lost the ability to plan for consequences. *Singer will come back in the nick of time. Everything is going to be fine.*

I nodded to myself and thought, *You have to do this because there's nobody else here to handle it.*

I ran. Or bounded, hopscotched, and scrabbled, rather. Precariously, my balance always in question I kicked and scrambled and gravity-sledded my way down the column of mirrors. Farweather still had the lead on me, but with the Baomind's assistance, I was cutting the distance.

I'd lost sight of Cheeirilaq. I guessed it was trying to cut around Farweather somehow and flank her, but I had no idea how it planned to accomplish that. I saw a trailing silk thread as I hurtled past, headed for the center of the swarm.

I thought about the razor edges on all the silicon drone disks, and I prayed a little, though I wasn't usually the sort to leave offerings. I prayed to Kwan-yin, because why not. And I prayed to Bao Zheng.

What the heck, right? We'd dedicated this whole star system to him. And the reason we were out here was . . . something *like* research.

Farweather must have felt me coming. She hadn't put her gun away. I had holstered my borrowed one because I needed both forehands for this game, but she didn't point hers at me. She just glanced over her shoulder and kept running.

The weird loping gait I was forced to assume was taking a toll on me. Avoiding the disk edges was tricky. But I was strong—stronger than I had ever been in my life, after decians under grav. My muscles strained and stretched. My cut-up afthand had switched from the startling pain of immediate injury to a more warning soreness and ache, except when I banged it on something. So, just about every stride.

Between atheist prayers, I added a few curses for my damned, damaged fox, which was still not functioning well enough to block the pain completely. I just . . .

Well, I suppose I was ungrateful. It was working better than it had any right to, considering what it had been through. I was just used to effortless perfection.

I also wasn't hardened off to enduring pain.

It hurt. It hurt, and yet I persisted.

I filtered down, closing my awareness to anything that was not Farweather and the path toward her. I wanted to get my hands on her. I wanted vengeance, and the atavism of my fury terrified me.

But I could use it. It loaned me strength, agility, and a rage of speed. I must have stopped overthinking what I was doing about then. The disks fled by under my hands. I bounded from one to the next, sliding when I could, accelerating. Farweather glanced back under her arm as she ricocheted off a mirror so hard she shattered it. I was already in motion, and there was little I could do to avoid the glass-sharp shards. Except—I could make them avoid me.

A little fold in space-time; just the smallest slope to pull them away from me. I barreled through the middle of their disintegrating formation unscathed, so close to Farweather I tried a snatch at her boot.

I missed. But I was so close the palms of all four hands itched with the desire to get ahold of her. I lunged again, a feral creature threatened. Soon I would have her—

She whipped her gun around just as it was occurring to me that I ought to unholster mine. I groped behind my back for the holster as she fired.

It turns out that ducking is an irresistible response when somebody is pointing a gun at you. It felt better than just floating there like a gaping fool, anyway. And when I rolled sideways, kicked clear of the plate I had been crouching on, and whipped my weapon out to return fire, she ducked too.

The jump turned out to be a terrible idea. I tried to kick the mirror disk at Farweather, and I made her duck. But when I pulled my trigger, the recoil sent me tumbling. Now how had she avoided that?

Right, folding space-time. Of course.

At least tumbling around like a clown made me harder to shoot, though it didn't help with the "not getting sliced in half by mirror disks" portion of my agenda. What did help was that either I was improbably lucky, or the swarm of flying, solar-powered, razor-edged neurons now tumbling back into orbit around their sun were making an effort to avoid dicing me into one-centimeter cubes. The song in my mind had something of the Ativahika's tones in it, and I wondered if the Baomind was aware that I was, in some peculiar fashion, their agent.

I wondered why the Baomind wasn't going after Farweather directly. Then I decided that I was glad that a sentient solar system didn't believe in direct Judicial intervention.

I wasn't even scratched. I got a glimpse of Farweather leveling her weapon again as I tumbled, though.

Watching someone fire a chemical weapon in vacuum is surreal. There's no sound; just a puff of particulate briefly illuminated as the oxidizer contained in the propellant cartridge fires. And if you weren't braced, you got the humorous outcome I was currently experiencing.

I guessed I was right, and Farweather had braced herself, because I was pretty sure she'd fired again when a disk off to my left shattered into a thousand tiny knives, but I didn't see her get knocked spinning. Well, if she could do it, I probably could too.

I folded space-time to stabilize. Gravity was my friend.

In so doing, I realized I had inadvertently hidden myself in the pocket I'd made. Like a kitten in a blanket, I was tucked away and would be invisible unless you bumped into me.

"So that's how she's been doing it," I said. To myself. Because I was alone in my pocket universe and nobody else could hear me.

Well, now or never.

I couldn't see her either. But I could feel her. She was large as life and out in the open.

Maybe that was the trade: Stay erased and still and quiet and be invisible and safe. Take an action, claim space, be noticed—and open yourself to attack by everyone and everything.

Well, it was probably time for that last.

I had dropped myself into . . . not quite white space. But something not unlike white space. Now I had to get myself out.

It was easier than I had feared. I just unfolded what I'd reflexively folded, and was back in my home line of space-time again.

And there was Farweather.

She stood at the dead center of one of the disks, facing away from me, her weapon in her hands, scanning. She looked invincible as she noticed my reappearance—eyes on the back of her head? Koregoi senso?—and began to swing to cover me.

But I could see what she couldn't.

There was a sticky thread of wet silk adhered to the underside of her platform, its paleness vanishing into the darkness beyond the range of my ability to see it in this terrible frail light.

I wanted to throw something to distract Farweather. I didn't have anything to throw. So I grav-slid up behind her while she was turning.

I kicked her in the face just as she brought the gun to bear.

She should have gone sailing, but her boots were locked to the disk—probably with a fold, because magnetism doesn't work on silicates. The whole thing—pirate and perch—revolved in a lopsided orbit after I hit her, the center of gravity somewhere around her thighs. Her arms flung up; she lost the gun. I tumbled the other way, twisting to avoid the disk's edge more by luck than by skill. My diaphragm spasmed; I couldn't get a breath; I tasted blood. She must have gotten a piece of me, too, though I hadn't felt it happen.

I made a grab for the fabric of the universe, and hauled myself into a stable orientation. Just in time to see Cheeirilaq abseil in with strands of webbing gripped in two of its manipulators. At a distance, two disks slammed together and splintered, yanked by the threads the Goodlaw was swinging on. I shrieked inside my helmet as it plummeted directly at the spinning disk with Farweather still riding it.

It was going to get its little feathery feet sliced off.

I still had my gun. And all I had to do was aim carefully enough not to hit Farweather . . . *or* Cheeirilaq.

Well, if I hit Farweather . . . honestly, she'd done enough to deserve it. Oh, I'd probably still feel bad about it. But she was lucky I was still trying not to.

I aimed and pulled the trigger.

The disk shattered. Under the momentum of the spin, pieces flung away like knives. I ducked, but I'd timed the shot right, and I didn't get holed that I noticed. Neither did Cheeirilaq.

Farweather dragged herself to a halt facing me at an angle. She glared at the hand where her gun had been and, finding it still empty, began to move toward me with a grim determination to rend in her expression that I recognized from a bar fight or two on a couple of seedy portsides.

I raised my gun. She never got the chance to connect.

Cheeirilaq barreled into her back like a spiky green battering ram, its horrifying raptorial forearms scissoring so fiercely I expected to see Farweather float away in three large pieces. She stayed intact, though, even when the Goodlaw gave her a single savage shake—though she did flop limply after that. One of her hands was free, and it floated beside her like a trailing ribbon, utterly unguided.

Cheeirilaq tossed a loop of silk at another mirror and hauled itself—and its prize—over to stand on a flawless silver surface that swarmed with reflections. It looked down at the body in its raptorial forelimbs. *Gotcha.*

I guess we were close enough to communicate now.

Farweather lay limp in its grasp, unconscious or stunned. A thin mist of escaping air fogged the area around her. Cheeirilaq turned her in its manipulators like a toddler looking for the end of a carrot. Its tiny head with the enormous, faceted eyes rotated from side to side, glittering like an emerald-studded stickpin.

"Cheeirilaq?"

Forgive me, the Goodlaw said. *This will be painful, but it is inevitable.*

It pulled one razor-edged leg—the film of its suit must adhere to the carapace behind the razor edges of those blades—and plunged the hooked tip into Farweather's torso, low, just above her pelvis, on the left.

"Cheeirilaq!"

A red mist of ice fountained. Farweather convulsed. Cheeirilaq steadied her with the other forelimb. When it pulled the impaling one back, it came dragging a mesh of gory wires and a mollusk-like segmented shell that curved in such a way I thought the concave side must have been intended to cradle bone.

An orange light flashed through the blood.

Cheeirilaq flipped the thing overhead, a long movement from a single joint like the lever arm of an atlatl. It sailed away, blinking softly, while the Koregoi mirrors flashed away from it like schools of geometric black fish.

It exploded there, harmlessly, soundlessly.

"She did have a bomb inside her."

She did.

"How did you know?"

Cheeirilaq cocked its head. *The case was hot.*

Infrared.

"She's leaking, Cheeirilaq," I said.

What? Oh yes, I see. Its mandibles clicked inside its film; the suit mikes picked up the noise. It sounded hungry, but I thought that particular clatter was the mantid equivalent of a sigh. *I suppose the civilized thing to do is to take her into custody and heal her wounds.*

It used some reaction mass to drift over to me, towing the mirror with it.

"I suppose it is." I launched myself to the plate next to Cheeirilaq and balanced there. I patted it lightly with a suit glove on the wing covert. "Come on, old friend. Let's go home."

Friend Haimey, it said. *You're leaking, too.*

I looked down. There was no pain, but a halo of frozen, rose-red particles of blood drifted near a gash in the side of my suit. The bullet had hit me, after all.

I hadn't even felt it. As I watched, my heart beat, and another shower of crimson snowflakes joined the rest.

"Oh dear," I said.

Hold still, the Goodlaw said. As I watched, it webbed the hole in Farweather's suit closed. Then it turned to me. *This is first aid only, you understand?* it said. *You are not to undertake anything strenuous.*

I glanced over at the pirate and Jothari ships that were following us down toward the Baostar, gaining on us, slowly encircling the cluster of disks that sheltered us. It might have been kinder of Cheeirilaq to let me bleed out among the stars. But I was cold, and getting colder, and I didn't want to die.

"Yes," I said. I spread my arms, wondering why it didn't hurt more than it did before I remembered that I'd turned all that off, and I was probably in shock. *Shock*, I told my fox. *Do something about that.*

It was already doing whatever it could.

The shock and the tuning didn't help me when Cheeirilaq stuck two manipulators into my wound, found and pinched off the spurting artery, and tamponaded the whole mess shut with an enormous sticky ball of webbing. It managed me with half its appendages, while managing Far-weather with the others, and then it swept me up with a raptorial fore-limb as well.

The first Jothari vessel outpaced us, falling toward the occluded sun just a little faster than we were. It turned to bring its guns to bear.

I wondered if they would ask for a surrender.

Cheeirilaq carefully shifted its grip on me so I could see, but it wasn't pressing on the wound.

You held on to your gun, it said. *That is well.*

CHAPTER 29

THE BAOMIND DID NOT SLOW. BUT NEITHER DID THE FLOCK increase its *a*. Perhaps it was already falling as fast as it was able. Perhaps it didn't recognize the threat.

More ships overhauled us. We were englobed. I struggled for awareness, pushing against the fuzzy comfort of unconsciousness as if I were fighting the blear of an unwise drunk. "Something—" I murmured to Cheeirilaq. "Something is coming."

It wasn't Singer, though I wanted it to be. I would have felt Singer as a point, a heaviness moving through the folded sky. This was . . . a wave. A wall.

It seemed familiar. I could not say why. I was not entirely myself. I was dying. I knew it with a lucidity like stained glass with a light behind it.

With effort that hurt, I turned to look over at Farweather. Her eyes were open and focused. They tracked me. I felt terrible about that. She was horribly wounded and should be resting.

I was horribly wounded and should be resting too.

We slumped, cradled in the grip of a giant insect. Ever so gently, with the feathery tip of one manipulator arm, Cheeirilaq nudged my hand that still clutched the weapon into my lap, so it wasn't floating free. I saw that it had webbed the gun to my glove, but left my hand free to move. I could fire the weapon if I had to.

I should not fire the weapon now.

I wasn't defenseless, then. And I wouldn't have to be captured. *It is well that you held on to the gun.*

So that was what it meant.

The gun was in my lap now. I wasn't going to lose it.

My com crackled. "Commander Farweather. This is *Defiance* hailing Commander Farweather. Please respond if you are able."

Farweather's eyes narrowed. I noticed, because it seemed like entirely too much effort to look away from her.

She turned *her* head. I could tell it was all the effort she could muster, but she looked up at the underside of Cheeirilaq's mandibled face. I could have told her its brain wasn't in that tiny head, but I suppose addressing yourself to the sensory equipment is polite across species.

"You saved me," she said.

I saved us all.

"They . . . detonating."

They were going to sacrifice you. Yes.

"This is *Defiance* hailing Commander Farweather. Commander Farweather. Please respond if you are able."

Farweather nodded. Slowly, wincing. She touched a stud on her glove. The green light of the telltale inside her helmet reflected in her corneas.

"This . . . Commander Farweather," she creaked. "Hey . . . *Defiance*. Fuck your mother."

Well. That wasn't going to get us picked up as potential friendlies, I guessed.

My fox. My fox was in halfway functioning order again. I could . . . I could use it. I was injured. Badly. But I wasn't dying *right this second*, thanks to Cheeirilaq's intervention.

There were emergency protocols.

Overrides. I could use them to juice myself with a nice, big jolt of adrenaline, for example.

Adrenaline is a hell of a drug.

· · ·

I sat up in Cheeirilaq's arms.

It hurt. I mean, I guessed it hurt? But it didn't hurt nearly enough. Nearly as much as it should have.

Friend Haimey. This is unwise.

"Necessary," I told it.

Friend Haimey! This is unwise!

I hooked my left arm—the one without the gun it its hand—around the Goodlaw's neck. A gross violation of its personal space. It didn't seem to mind, and I needed the support.

I hoped they were listening hard on the suit frequency they were using.

I tuned my com to it. I took as deep a breath as I could manage, and I tried to think. All I had was the standard trade creole. Farweather spoke it like a native.

Maybe the Jothari knew how to translate from the human trade language, if it was something the Freeporters used.

I had to hope.

"Jothari ships!" I said. I tried to enunciate and speak slowly. I'm not sure I managed more than a mumble. "Jothari people. You do not have to live as outlaws. Listen to me. I am Haimey Dz, chief engineer of SGV *I Rise From Ancestral Night*, and I am a duly appointed representative of the Synarche of Worlds." Stretching a point, but I was in Singer's chain of command, and frankly there was no one else out here who could negotiate except for Cheeirilaq, who didn't appear to have thought of it.

Silence fell into my hand.

I nerved myself. "The Synarche acknowledges that it has a debt to the Jothari species. That mistakes were made in contact, and that reparations are owed."

Their crimes are terrible, Cheeirilaq said, but I thought it spoke only to me.

They have committed crimes. It's likely that they owe reparations too. That is a matter someone with a higher diplomatic ranking can assess.

That would be . . .

Yes. Anyone. Hush.

I strained my ears, which was silly, because any answer would come over my suit radio and com.

Eventually, after what I could only assume were *intense* private negotiations, a metallic translated voice reached me. "Your Synarche destroyed us."

By the Well. They were talking. *They were talking.*

Cheeirilaq's tiny head pivoted on its narrow neck, its multifaceted main eyes regarding me. It did not speak.

"It was long ago and we were young," I said. "Please. I know you cannot forgive us. Please accept that the Synarche acknowledges that a terrible wrong has been done and wishes for peace between us, and to make reparations."

That wave, that wall, was still coming. It ached in my sinuses like dropping pressure. The pain was blinding.

Around it, I heard the Jothari—who had not given me a name or a rank—speak.

"Reparations."

"Yes."

"You'll punish us."

"We wronged you."

"You will find it wrongful that we harvest the star-dragons."

That was where it got sticky. "You would have to stop that, yes." *But you should stop it anyway, because it's wrong!*

I kept my mouth shut. Sometimes a thing can be true, and not for immediate sharing. That was, Connla had assured me more than once, how diplomacy worked.

"You will punish us."

"That is not for me to decide. The Ativahikas will probably want reparations from you, the same as you will, I expect, want reparations from us. I request only that you open diplomatic relations with the Synarche. You do not have to choose to accept our justice."

Cheeirilaq twitched.

I tapped it with my heel.

"You will take our knowledge and harvest them yourselves."

Cheeirilaq twitched again. This time I didn't argue.

"If you talk to us, there can be peace. Negotiation. Trade. You could come out of hiding. We could find your people a world to settle on. A world of your own."

"So you could own us. So we would have a vulnerable heart once more, just begging to be destroyed."

"No—"

"So you could own us. That is not reparations. Synarche, we are not interested in your lies."

The com connection died. I pushed my hand against my helmet because I couldn't reach my aching forehead. It was the hand with the gun webbed to it, so I used the back.

"Bugger," I said.

It took me a moment to identify the terrible bubbling sound coming over my com as Farweather laughing at me between swallows of blood. I resisted the urge to smash her fucking helmet in, but only barely.

"Guess . . . they don't want . . . charity."

"You shut up," I said. It was our fault. It was our fault, or at least some of it was, and I wanted to fix it. But the immediate situation was *her* fault, as much as it was anyone's. And I wanted somebody to blame.

I looked around. The Jothari vessels remained in position, interspersed with Freeport ships. The thing was, I was pretty sure we did owe them reparations. But getting the Synarche to agree might be easier than getting the Jothari to believe.

They had committed crimes; it was true. But they were driven to those crimes by our own crime of having destroyed them, even if it was indirectly. And accidentally.

It was a morally complex equation. But I knew in my bones that some kind of reconciliation was the right choice to pursue. Horrible crimes were committed by them, and by us—against each other and against unrelated others.

I hadn't quite been emotionally prepared for them to just utterly spurn my offer.

Although.

I hadn't accepted it when Farweather—representing Niyara's people, after all—had wanted me back in her fold. But that was because she was untrustworthy, and just wanted to use me. Use me *more*.

The Synarche wouldn't use the Jothari again, would they? We had learned some things in the intervening centuries. Some things about being a pluralistic society without bringing colonial force to bear.

Hadn't we?

. . . If we had, I had to let the Jothari walk away. And determine their own direction.

I didn't have to let them have possession of the Baomind, though. And I didn't have to let them hand it over to—or even share it with—the Freeporters. Who were assholes.

Especially since the Baomind had asked us—or Singer, at least—for help.

The problem was, my resources currently included one representative of Justice, one half-dead pirate who wasn't on my side anyway, and one engineer who was in a race between suffocation and bleeding to death. I was steadfastly refusing to look at my ox meter. Let it be a surprise.

Come on. Come on. Think of something. Come on.

I leaned my helmet against Cheeirilaq's film-suited carapace. "I might be out of ideas, Friend Cheeirilaq."

I am sorry, Friend Haimey. I also . . . may be out of ideas.

Exhaustion clawed me as I watched the enemy ships arrange themselves to clear their firing lines. I bumped my adrenals once more, wishing I believed I'd be around to pay the miserable price for it. The pirates didn't need me for Niyara's code anymore.

The friendly mirror disks of the Baomind swarmed around us, filling me with their encouraging song, a fragile, glittering shield. I felt a terrible sadness for them. How many of their neurons had been destroyed? Worse, did they have individual identities? How much damage had we and the pirates and Jothari already done to them? Not much, I hoped. Surely what had been destroyed was a negligible fraction of the incomprehensibly large number of disks still maintaining their sphere around the dying star.

Once we were gone, would the Freeporters resort to threats or force to control the Baomind? Would that even work? Or would they just refuse to rescue it, unless it agreed to be enslaved? They despised artificial intelligences, but surely they were capable of seeing that this was a resource too valuable to just destroy, even if they were incapable of seeing it as a person. Of regarding it as an intelligence worthy of protection and partnership.

I was wondering why they were bothering with the display of force when all they had to do was leave us here. I was wondering if, if they fired, I could wrap us all in a protective fold of space-time. I was wondering if it wouldn't be better to just die under their barrage rather than putting it off the few minutes we had left. I was wondering, frankly, what kind of a pointless gesture I could make just so I wouldn't feel like I was just dying passively. I had the handgun: no use at all against anything more armored than a human being in a space suit.

Thinking that made me realize Connla would be amused by how his culture's memes had infected me, if he ever got the chance to know—

One of the pirate vessels began to ease toward us.

I reached across Cheeirilaq's thorax and nudged Farweather. When she didn't move, I balled up my cold, numb fingers and punched her in the arm. It probably hurt me at least as much as it did her. "Commander!"

Blood spattered the inside of her visor. She must have been coughing it up.

I sympathized.

"Can't you let me die in peace?" Her eyes focused on me with an obvious effort. "Oh, it's you. No, of course *you* can't."

"Zanya, what's that ship?"

I pointed with my helmet in the time-honored fashion of spacers everywhere.

It wasn't hers—the white one that had shot our boom off way back at the beginning of things. This one was a glossy black, a color with depth and reflections, fading to a burnished dried-blood highlight on its raised features. It reminded me of the prized urushi lacquer from the homeworld, an ancient art that still piqued interest throughout the worlds.

Connla and I had salvaged a ship whose cargo contained three urushi pieces once—two antique pens and a longsword. That trip had taken out a sizable portion of our obligation.

Farweather's labored breaths were clear over the com as she struggled to follow. "Oh buttercakes," she said, which would have made me laugh my arse off if I weren't in insupportable pain just breathing.

"That's the *Defiance,*" she said. "That's the Admiral."

"There's no such thing as the Admiral," I said. "She's a scary story."

She laughed, one choked gasp. It sounded like it hurt. "Well, I guess you'd know."

It *looked* like a pirate admiral's ship, if anything did. And it was . . . coming to pick us up. Shouldering gently through the swarms of mirror disks, edging toward us. I wondered why they didn't just send a launch. I wondered why they were coming to get us at all. What loyalty did they have to Farweather, who they'd been willing to remote-detonate if it came down to it?

"I don't understand your people," I told her. My own voice was getting a bit halting now. My head throbbed with that wall of pressure, like something coming in, but whatever it was couldn't be bothered to make its presence known.

Maybe it was an artifact of my being in the process of bleeding to death.

I was still looking at her, so I saw her smile curve behind the blood. "We haven't got the least idea what makes you people function, either."

The *Defiance* was nearly on us, and still there was no sign of a launch, and no sign of an opening airlock hatch. It was just coming, easing up on us, matching relative velocities so that, in the vastness of intergalactic space, we seemed to be standing still.

"Maybe she just wants to look me in the eye while I'm dying," Farweather said, with many pauses and great effort.

Oh, she doesn't like you either?

I had gotten . . . really fond of Cheeirilaq.

Farweather bubbled faintly. "I want her job."

Wanted, I thought, but didn't say it.

The *Defiance*'s white coils folded away inside its hull when it was in normal space. That was something I'd only heard of on military ships. It allowed them greater close maneuverability, and protected the fragile coils in combat. So it could edge up right next to our tiny little disk with its tiny little Goodlaw and two damaged women on it. And it did.

I craned my head to look along the looming wall of the hull as it crept past. The lacquer effect wasn't quite as flawless close up. There were pits and scratches, the marks of use. But I could see now, even in the dim light, that the whole ship was dark red, not black at all. Layers and layers of translucent dark red coating, until it built up to the point where it *seemed* black, and then the places where it had been smoothed thinner gleamed red.

Nice ship.

I wondered where the Admiral had stolen it.

A ring of red lights outlined what I took to be an airlock, as it drew up before us. The *Defiance* matched velocities with us so we all seemed to hang perfectly still. In respect to one another, we were—which is as still as anything gets, in this great universe.

The airlock irised open, and I found myself staring into a space too brightly lit to see clearly.

If we go in there, Cheeirilaq said, *we are never coming out again.*

"But it's our choice, isn't it? Die here, or—"

"I'll make them . . . drag me," Farweather gasped.

Oppositional defiant disorder, definitely.

"Right," I said. It was a small item of refusal, but it was an item, and it was what I had. I wasn't going in that ship. I wasn't going to give myself up to them. Even if it was futile. They'd find a use for me, I was sure. And it was not a use that I would approve of.

Defiance, indeed. Be careful what you name a thing.

I kept thinking that even as my gravity headache intensified, and our disk began to float toward the open hatch. The Baomind's song shrilled, sounding alarmed to my human awareness, and I felt the shiver in our disk even through the intervening body of my insectile friend. Consciousness was at the end of a graying tunnel, and I could see only the brightness of that hatch like the proverbial light at the end of it. It bathed my face, my body, in a golden glow.

I felt myself falling into it.

Gravity tractor, Cheeirilaq said, tightening its grip on me. *I presume they are making good use of their space-time manipulation technology.*

I fought it, and I could feel the disk fighting it too. But we were clawing up an increasingly steep slope. There were more of them than there were of us. Or they were better practiced. And it seemed like Farweather had faded out again, so no assistance from that direction. And while the Baomind was making curious and agitated music now and might decide to come to our assistance, in three hundred standard minutes or so—I didn't have time for it to make up its mind.

I was dimly aware of the mirror disks moving, contracting into a smaller space. Clearing a . . . path?

Maybe they were planning something. I couldn't wait to find out.

I extended my right hand, which still had the small projectile gun webbed to it. I wiggled my gloved finger inside the trigger guard.

I aimed the gun into the open hatchway and fired, and fired, and fired.

. . .

The gravslide pulling us into the *Defiance* failed as soon as I shot. Reactive force pushed us backward, augmented by our suddenly useful counterslide. We shot away from the big ship until I managed to get the reaction under control. Not really far.

But far enough that when something enormous smashed into it from the side—something that I had not seen coming, and sensed only as a gigantic influx of mass—we were not swept along with it. I cringed back against Cheeirilaq, who was still cradling me. Keeping me from floating free. The mantid cringed too, dropping its body between its many legs to lower its profile.

The *Defiance* had been spun aside by a tremendous impact. The biggest face I'd ever seen stared down at me again, reflecting pale peach in the rosy glow of the fading star. The corrugations between its starship-sized eyes gave it a surprised and slightly grumpy expression.

There were hundreds of Ativahikas behind it. Thousands maybe. The sky was as full of them as it was the disks of the Baomind.

I could not see where the *Defiance* had been flung. Perhaps it was still flinging. But Jothari and Freeport ships were winking into white space in every direction, and I could only assume they were skittering away as fast as their coils could carry them.

I wondered if the Ativahika would hunt them down.

It sounded disappointed when it said, **Those who come to realms they cannot live in will always be vulnerable to those who are at home there.**

Perhaps that ripple of its many filamentary appendages was the Ativahika equivalent of a shrug.

I looked left and right. *Why didn't you stop them before?*

They preyed on the singular. At great distances. It took us time to . . . learn. The voice that wasn't a voice and the words that were not words were hesitant, as if it were having difficulty expressing concepts that it took for granted as self-evident.

And is this the justice you promised us, little mind?

Under the circumstances . . . best I could do.

Its enormous eye regarded me, close enough to touch.

The best you could have done, under the circumstances.

I held my tongue. It didn't seem like there would be much point to arguing.

I was ready to be knocked aside as easily as the *Defiance*. I hoped it would not harm Cheeirilaq.

My friend is not guilty of anything— I began

It was, the great voice that wasn't a voice exactly said. Underneath it, the music of the Baomind agreed. **It was the best you could have done.**

Like a giant offering a fingertip to a mouse to sniff, it extended the long, narrow tip of its face toward me. Its snout? Some sensory organ? I didn't know. It reminded me of the very tip of an elephant's trunk, but forty times bigger and without breathing holes.

It stopped a decimeter away.

Say hello, Friend Haimey, Cheeirilaq murmured in my backchannel. *It's not polite to keep people waiting.*

I somehow managed to hold up my hand. I remembered not to use the one the gun was webbed to.

I touched an Ativahika. I touched the Ancient One.

It touched me back. For a moment, I knew its name. But the name of an Ativahika is not something you can remember and recall later, because it's at once too complex to hold in your mind all at once, and it's ever-changing—so as soon as you know it, it's gone.

But I knew it once. For an instant. And it was like knowing the location of every star in the endless sky.

What it said to me before it lifted away was, **Here is your ship, little mind.**

Then it drifted aside. And what I saw behind it was the Prize, flanked by *I'll Explain It To You Slowly* and a dozen other Synarche Interceptors and Cutters; deep-space patrol boats that could hold their own in a fight or a rescue situation.

They held a loose formation as the Ativahikas disengaged.

Connla's voice broke into my com. "Hang on, Haimey. We're— Just *hang on.*"

The Prize began to move in *fast*. Something caught my attention, rising up from the bottom periphery of my visor.

A faint red mist.

Oh. Bleeding ag—

That was when I fainted.

Cheeirilaq got us both inside. I imagine it swarming through the airlock on segmented legs, two bodies draped over the spikes on its raptorial legs, like something directly pulled from atavistic Terran nightmares. I'm glad I slept through that part.

To catch up on the part I missed: as you've probably guessed, *I'll Explain It To You Slowly* was coming back to get us. She had encountered an encoded beacon at a waypoint that allowed her to deduce the location of and catch up with a Synarche fleet commanded by SGV *I Can Remember It For You Wholesale* outbound, in pursuit of the Prize and whatever had hijacked her. *I'll Explain It To You Slowly* explained the situation to her sister ships, and the now-combined Synarche operations continued on toward the Baostar coordinates.

Where they met up with the Prize, running away. Connla and Singer managed to explain the situation to the satisfaction of Memory and her captain . . . who told them to turn right back around and come get us, with all the support a girl bleeding to death in a space suit could desire.

The whole fleet came to save us.

That turned out to be handy, because Zanya Farweather and I were about as badly in need of a cryo tube as it's possible for a human who is not actually already clinically dead to be.

We think of forgiveness as a thing. An incident. A choice. But forgiveness is a process. A long, exhausting process. A series of choices that we have to make over, and over, and over again.

Because the anger at having been wronged—the rage, the fury, the desire to lash out and cut back—doesn't just vanish because you say to someone, "I forgive you." Rather, forgiveness is an obligation you take on not to act punitively on your anger. To interrogate it when it arises, and accept that you have made the choice to be constructive rather than destructive. Not that you have made the choice never to be angry again.

Of course, I could have rightminded the anger out. But it's a mistake to put one's anger down too soon.

Anger is an inoculant. It gets your immune system working against bullshit.

But anger can also make you sick, if you're exposed to it for too long. That same caustic anger that can inspire you to action, to defend yourself, to make powerful and risky choices . . . can eat away at you. Consume your self, vulnerabilities, flesh, heart, future if you stay under the drip for too long. The anger itself can become your reason for living, and feeding it can be your only goal. In the end, you'll feed yourself to it to keep the flame alive, along with everyone around you.

Anger is selfish, like any flame. And so, like any flame, it must be shielded, contained, husbanded while it is useful and banked or extinguished when it is not.

But flames don't want to die, and they are crafty—an ember hidden here, a hot spot unexpectedly lurking over there. Sure, you can turn the feelings off, and I had done that before. But turning off the anger doesn't lead to dealing with the problems that *caused* the anger.

Forgiveness is not easy. Forgiveness is a train with many stops, and it takes forever to get where you are going. And you cover a lot of territory along the way, not necessarily by the most direct route, either. That's why forgiveness is a process, and as much a blessing for the person who was wronged as for the person who did the wronging.

And it's hardest when the person you most need to forgive is yourself.

I had been very bad at forgiveness, after the terrorists. But I had also been very bad at feeling anger. Feeling angry made me feel guilty. Flawed.

I hadn't been raised in a place where I was allowed to be angry. Anger was antisocial. Anger was regulated against.

Boundaries of any sort were regulated against, come to think of it. By regulating *us*, the clade members, the children in the crèche. You can't mind what you're not allowed to mind.

I next saw Farweather as the crew of SJV *I'll Explain It To You Slowly* were prepping us to slide our failing bodies into cryo tanks on the chance we might survive the long ride home. She turned her head and looked at me. I only noticed it because she spoke, because I'd been ignoring her as hard as I could. Connla was standing beside me in his dapper pilot suit, his ponytail draping in that weird gravity way. He was trying to look unconcerned. It wasn't working.

So I wasn't looking at her when Farweather said, "I'm sorry."

I didn't look then either. Connla squeezed my hand.

"I'm sorry," she said again.

"I bet you are," I answered as the tank lid closed.

CHAPTER 30

WOKE UP IN THE HOSPITAL. CORE GENERAL, IN FACT, because that was how fancy I was now.

I met a nice doctor there. Her name was K'kk'jk'ooOOoo, and she had beautiful gray eyes and was sleek and fast.

Unfortunately, she was a dolphin-like K'juUUuuU who came from a water world, so it never would have worked out. But it turns out that sonar is a really useful sense for an internist.

Also, it tickles.

K'kk'jk'ooOOoo was a specialist in fox interface problems, and she'd been brought in to figure out how to fix the malfunctioning connections in my much-abused one, or replace it if necessary. The rest of my body was already fixed. They'd grown me a new liver and colon while I was asleep in a tank. Good idea. Who wants to be awake for that?

The first thing I asked about was the Baomind, and I was assured that rescue operations were under way. The first wave of Baomind mirror disks had actually been elected by the collective for evacuation and brought to the Core huddled inside the white coils of the Prize and the other ships in the rescue fleet. More ships were en route to bring back the next wave, and as far as anybody could tell from this far away, its primary had not exploded.

Yet.

But any minute now.

The second thing I asked about was getting the war crime removed from my dermis. K'kk'jk'ooOOoo told me regretfully that she didn't think it could be done without killing me. I hoped she was telling the truth, and it wasn't just that the Synarche wanted to study me. I mean, of course the Synarche wanted to study me. I hoped they might be close enough to what I still hoped they were not to lie to me about it.

There were good surprises, too, and the best surprise was that Singer was here, in the hospital. He was functioning as a subsidiary wheelmind, operating systems in human resources and logistics, as a compassionate gesture. When I was well enough, we were both to be seconded to the Prize investigation team: me as an engineer, and he would take over as the Prize's permanent shipmind. Along with our cats.

We'd be stationed right here in the Core. And not too far from Connla, who had a new job flying ambulance ships.

He was really happy about it. You get to go as fast as you want, and other vessels are supposed to get out of your way but are bad enough at it that the flying is challenging.

And apparently, he was good.

After many boring medical adventures, it turned out that the problem wasn't the fox at all, but the connections.

Functional connections in the brain are based on use. The longer my fox spent as a doorstop, the more the brain-device connections had degraded. Therefore, I needed more therapy and practice afterward before I could work with it properly again.

So playing immersion games in my fox was . . . technically . . . part of my mandated therapy.

I found out from Cheeirilaq, who was also now stationed in the Core, taking care of various legal difficulties, that Farweather had also survived the transition home. She was in a different wing, however, and under guard. The Prison Wheel, as it was colloquially called.

It had a different staff. Most of the Core General doctors wouldn't serve there unless it was a matter of life and death, because they could not bring themselves to treat their patients as prisoners.

The doctors who *could* manage it had installed a suppressor in Farweather's midbrain to keep her from activating her Koregoi symbiote, acting under Singer's advice and direction.

I shuddered to think of it. She had not consented to that. But I shuddered worse to think of what she'd do in a hospital full of sick systers whose very existence she despised.

Moral compromises don't stop happening even when everyone involved is trying to do the right thing.

Which left that offspring of a compost heap, Colonel Habren. The gardener. Who—Cheeirilaq informed me—*had* filed every charge in the book against us.

Discredit the witnesses. Why not? What do you have to lose?

Well, the charges didn't stick. We might have been able to sting them for filing punitive charges, but the fact remained that we had driven a little recklessly. And our charges against them didn't stick either.

Farweather apparently wouldn't snitch. And we had absolutely no proof.

We knew. And the Synarche knew. And Singer knew. And Cheeirilaq knew.

And their attitude, apparently, was "That's nice; do something about it."

. . . Maybe tomorrow.

As an experiment, I got my hormones formally turned back on.

It turned out I still wasn't in love with Farweather.

Thank everything holy, the Way and the Path and the bright and dark and iron gods of Entropy and Irony, the Gods of the Ark that protected generation ships and hell, probably protected the Baomind also. My taste was terrible, but it was not *that* bad.

Once they *were* on, well. I discovered I'd kind of missed them. They scared me . . . but I decided I didn't have to *act* on feelings.

They were just feelings.

They didn't have to run my life.

The last time I saw Zanya Farweather, she was being loaded onto a transport, having been deemed well enough to stand trial. I put in a request to meet with her before she went. It was, to my surprise, approved.

I suspect Cheeirilaq put in a word for me.

She'd wasted in the tanks, and in treatment. So had I, but it was more evident on her, with her planetary muscles. She looked like a rail, clavicle and jawbone and cheeks projecting, breasts slack, a little fleshy potbelly showing where her body was keeping what fat it had managed to hang on to while consuming all its muscle.

It hurt me to see the crescent of brilliantly reflective chrome adhered to the bottom arc of her skull. The damper.

Well, it was awful. But I accepted that it needed to be there.

Galaxies danced across her drawn skin. Mine moved in reflection.

She was still beautiful. I still wasn't in love with her.

Her guards drew back as I approached. They stayed close enough to intervene if she—shackled, locked out of her own body except as permitted by the tightly engineered, quicksilver AI stuck on her head whose only purpose was to thwart her—"tried something."

I know she came from outside. I know she was raised by monsters who ate each other as a matter of course.

I know we had to give her time to want to be managed before we could teach her to manage herself.

Had the AI whose life's work was now making sure Zanya Farweather didn't use her alien symbiote to crush the entire prison wing of the hospital gotten a vote in where it served?

Farweather looked me right in the eye. Without preamble or any kind of gentle transition, she said, "You secretly wanted me to win. You'd be happier if you could allow yourself to admit it."

What I actually wanted, deep in my barbarian heart, was to see her messily dead in a half dozen variously sized pieces. But I was too self-aware—and too beset with ethics!—to act on that.

There was no point in relitigating old woes. We need each other, and we need literature, and we need knowledge—and we need, very much, to try to be accountable for our own failings and to live up to our best selves. That reality might seem subjective and foolish to Farweather, but it seems objective and rational to me.

We cannot choose where we come from, but we can choose where we are going, and we can choose the routes we're willing to take to try to get there.

"Whatever lets you sleep at night, Farweather."

She rubbed the shiny metal arc fused to her skull. "They *used* you."

"Oh. And you didn't?"

I thought that would quell her. I didn't want to have this conversation, and I *really* didn't want to have this conversation in front of some certain percentage of Justice.

It didn't.

She said, "You still blame yourself for Niyara."

I made my expression stone.

Zanya Farweather could never take a fucking hint. "If you blame yourself, that means you think you had the power to stop it."

"But I didn't?" A second after I spoke, I cursed myself for responding. But I had, and now I was stuck with it.

"You didn't," Farweather confirmed.

I shook my head. "Bullshit. I knew Niyara. If I hadn't been blinded by my hormones, I would have seen her coming. Seen that she was using me."

"But you *didn't* see her coming."

"Now you sound like you're blaming me."

She settled back against the wall. "It feels good to pretend you're to blame, doesn't it?"

"What?" I said. "It feels awful."

"But it lets you assert some power over the situation. Some agency. If it's your fault, you weren't just a helpless dupe, right? But if somebody else tells you that you *weren't* just a helpless dupe, you get angry."

I looked at her.

She looked at me. The only light came from the airlock on the prison transport, two steps away with its outer door open. It fell in dim stripes across her face.

I'd missed it, somewhere. The place where she'd moved the goalposts. I could feel that it had happened, but I couldn't *see* the spot.

"They're probably recording this," I said.

"They probably are." She shrugged.

"I do think about having done something different," I admitted. What did it hurt me to be honest with her? To be vulnerable?

She was going away.

I said, "I think about if there was something I might have missed. It's not . . . intrusive. Not anymore, not the way it used to be."

"Sure," she said. "You got your brain fiddled with to remove the guilt, the blame. Even the memories. So why don't you fiddle your brain to make the rest of it go away also?"

"I thought your lot didn't hold with brain-fiddling."

She winked. "I don't judge how other people live their lives."

I leaned against the wall and watched her through the bars. "You'd rather be in jail forever than submit to Recon."

"They could just force me."

I smiled. "We're not complete barbarians."

She laughed. She tapped her suppressor.

It almost felt companionable. I thought I might miss her.

I said, "You know that thing about not having a real me? That I told you on the Prize?"

Her face smoothed. "I think I remember it."

I smiled.

"I take that back," I said. "The real me is the me I've decided to be. Somebody decided to be that person. Somebody built her. That's the *real* me. And not the me anybody else thinks I ought to be, or ought to have been."

She frowned.

I looked at her.

She looked at me.

"Goodbye, Zanya," I said. "I hope you figure some stuff out, eventually."

I turned away.

The deck plates rattled faintly as she stepped forward. Two constables stepped forward as well. They didn't touch her yet, and I approved.

She said, "Enjoy belonging to the machine, babes."

Another rustle as she stepped back, while I walked away. I let her have the last word. I didn't really need to answer.

It didn't feel so bad, to belong.

AUTHOR'S NOTE

I started writing this book in 2014, because my friend and occasional editor Simon Spanton, then with Gollancz, was looking for a big-idea space opera and I happened to have a big idea lying around waiting for an excuse to stretch. It is now 2018. Writing this novel has taken longer than I anticipated to get it finished (sometimes life gets in the way, and sometimes creativity does not operate on schedule), and the world this book is being born into is not the world it was conceived in. There have been a lot of changes along the way—personal, professional, and political—but I think the book is stronger for all of that.

I'm pretty happy with it. I hope you, the reader, find it worth the wait.

I would like to offer my very sincere thanks to everyone who helped along the way with getting it off the ground. This is a diverse cast of characters that includes but is not limited to:

Ben Tippett and Benjamin C. Kinney, who respectively helped me out with cosmology and neuroscience. Mistakes and willful deviations are of course my own.

Jennifer Jackson and Michael Curry of the Donald Maass Literary Agency.

My fine editors Simon Spanton (who acquired it); Gillian Redfearn and Navah Wolfe (who edited it); and Deanna Hoak, who copyedited it.

The design, production, marketing, and publicity teams at Gollancz and Saga, who are responsible for the gorgeous package you hold in your hands (or read on your screen) and the fact that you even heard about it and that it then made its way into your possession in the first place.

Marissa Lingen and Amanda Downum, who beta-read the first draft and talked me off the roof about it.

Liz Bourke, Fran Wilde, Amal El-Mohtar, Jamie Rosen, Fade Manley, Celia Marsh, Alex Haist, Max Gladstone, Devin Singer, C. L. Polk, Arkady Martine, Vivian Shaw, Jodi Meadows, John Wiswell, Sarah Monette, Amber van Dyk, and Stella Evans: all the critters in the ZOO. (Yes, it's a terrible pun. I didn't start it. Haimey would love it, though.)

Andre Norton, Iain Banks, C. J. Cherryh, and James White, whose works grew me into the person who would want to write this book.

My family, who are those rare birds when it comes to artist relatives: they never doubted me once. And my many friends who have listened to me alternately kvetch and crow as I worked my way through the inevitable black holes and supernovae of composition.

The Wijktory Kjittens and the Giant Ridiculous Dog, who conspired between them to keep me from taking myself or my deadlines too seriously.

My friend Jon Singer, who kindly allowed me to borrow his last name for a boat, and is so much cooler and gentler and more fascinating of a person than I could ever be able to render in these words.

And of course and most of all, my beloved Scott, who makes all things possible.

—Elizabeth Bear
Hopeful House
South Hadley, Massachusetts
4 February 2018